CO-OP

CO-OP

ANIMUS™ BOOK TWO

JOSHUA ANDERLE

MICHAEL ANDERLE

DISRUPTIVE IMAGINATION®

LMBPN Publishing
PMB 196, 2540 South Maryland Pkwy
Las Vegas, NV 89109

First US edition, September 2018

THE CO-OP TEAM

Thanks to the JIT Readers

Mary Morris
Kelly O'Donnell
John Ashmore
James Caplan
Angel LaVey
Daniel Weigert
Kelly Bowerman
Larry Omans
Danika Fedeli
Micky Cocker

If I've missed anyone, please let me know!

Editor
Lynne Stiegler

*To Family, Friends and
Those Who Love
to Read.
May We All Enjoy Grace
to Live the Life We Are
Called.*

CHAPTER ONE

Commander Sasha Chevalier finished typing his notes and preparing his plans for the board meeting. An owl, its body blue wire-frame with large round white eyes, appeared on his desk, sitting on a small artificial tree.

"Sir, Chou, Councilor Vodello's EI, sent a message. She said that Mya would like to know if you are still going to make it to the meeting?" it asked in a muted, straightforward tone.

He nodded. "Please send a message back that I will leave my office momentarily and see her there."

"Understood, sending response immediately."

"Thank you, Isaac. Once you've sent the message, prepare for ocular integration," the commander added.

The owl avatar nodded, disappearing after a moment. Sasha pressed a button on the base of the tree and a small chip popped out. He took it in his fingers, careful not to handle the surface. The device seemed little more than a small silver square except for a large N in the center engraved with a triangular design around it—the Nexus Academy crest.

He picked up his oculars—a round band with black circular lenses—and slid the chip into a small slot next to the right lens before placing them on his head. The head of the owl appeared in the corner of his display. *"Should I send the notes to anyone before we depart?"*

"Send a copy to my tablet. I may work on them some more during the league discussions." The commander placed said tablet into a briefcase which contained other devices and chips.

The owl nodded, and its eyes lit up. *"Understood, and sir..."*

"We are being pinged?" he asked, closing and locking his case.

"You could tell?"

"Your eyes flashed for a moment," Sasha explained, and the owl's already large eyes widened further.

"I could not tell. No detection on my end."

Sasha walked out of his office and closed the door. "No need to worry. It simply means he's getting impatient."

"Who is...ah, I see. No hacker would be able to remotely access the oculars on such a micro scale without—"

"Access to the main connection located in the head professor's office," Sasha finished as he walked down the two flights of stairs to the exit.

"Should I tell him you are on your way? Along with a request to not be so evasive in the future?"

"No need. Besides, he's likely to erase your memory of it the next time he updates you."

The owl's eyes shrank to half their size in an exaggerated response before returning to their normal size. The feathered avatar furrowed in annoyance. *"Has this been a normal occurrence?"*

"Only over the last few months. He says you've been saying insulting things about him, and that you are a bad influence."

"He does know that most of my opinions are derived from yours?"

Sasha reached the ground floor and chuckled in dry amusement. "Yes, but he cannot erase *my* mind on a whim."

The EI's eyes narrowed. *"That seems like an abuse of power. I can see why you find him such a bother."*

"I've learned to pick my battles," Sasha admitted, pushing open the side exit door of the Nexus Board Hall. "Besides, for all the strife he may cause, you would not exist without his genius."

"A fair assessment, sir," Isaac admitted. *"I merely wish he was as mature as his intellect would make him seem."*

"Is that damn bird saying things about me again?"

Sasha turned to see Professor Alexander Laurie just up ahead on a bench beneath an evergreen tree in the plaza.

"Well, if you are tapped into my device, you should know," Sasha retorted.

Laurie stood and brushed some of his long hair behind his ear. "I don't, but considering how rude he's been, it was a fair guess. I don't tap your EI devices. I am too honest and genuine to not respect the wishes of my colleagues."

Sasha raised an eyebrow. "That doesn't seem to stop you from finding workarounds. I saw the flash in Isaac's eyes."

Laurie shrugged. "It's past ten p.m. The meeting will

start soon, and I figured I needed to remind you to get a move on."

"If I turned up in high dress, you would say I was fashionably late." The commander scoffed as he walked past Laurie, who fell into step behind him.

"You are quite right about that, but it would be like finding a perpetual energy core—not likely, and not anytime soon." Laurie sighed as he buttoned his designer jacket in the cold night air. "I'm not sure I've seen you wear anything other than uniforms or regulation coats since that dinner before the year started."

"Haven't had a need to, and a League meeting isn't exactly a formal occasion," Sasha noted.

"Perhaps not, but you should take the opportunity to set an example. Looking your best at every opportunity sends out a message of confidence that the others will greatly respect."

"I'll have to remember to wear something more formal the next time Wulfson tries to drag me into another sparring match. I'm sure my dashing apparel will intimidate him." The commander deadpanned, his tone suitably indifferent to the apparent sarcasm in his words.

Laurie scoffed. "If only! Then I wouldn't have so much trouble with that hybrid of bear fur and Neanderthal."

"Speaking of which," Sasha began, looking over his shoulder to Laurie, "how is his training with Initiate Jericho going?"

Laurie looked in the direction of Wulfson's personal barracks. "Well enough. He's shown much physical improvement over the last three months. Increased endurance and stamina, better skills in physical and melee arms combat, along with mild improvement in team coordination."

"Only mild?" Sasha asked.

"Well, it seems my plan to pair Kaiden with someone more...akin to his personality had a few drawbacks," Laurie admitted, though he seemed a little sulky, as if the confession were one he'd prefer not to make.

"Wulfson should be excellent in teaching team skills and leadership. He was a captain in the UEA and is currently the Head Security Officer of the Academy. Both those positions require a vast knowledge of what it means to lead and the importance of cooperation."

"I would agree with you, for the most part," Laurie retorted. "But Wulfson also had the trump card of...'encouraging' those in his employ to follow his rules or deal with the punishments that he personally dished out."

Sasha stopped, looking back. The revelation intrigued him. "Does he not do this with Kaiden?"

Laurie grimaced. "Oh, he most certainly does, but it would seem that our little trainee is either far too brave for it to keep him in line, or..." Laurie shrugged, leaving the alternative unspoken.

The commander sighed. "Or he's far too stupid for it to be effective."

"I'm going to smother you in your sleep, you gigantic bastard!" Kaiden shouted, anger and malice lacing his voice.

"Nice of you to give me warning beforehand. Real

generous of you." Wulfson scoffed. "I've only got a few shots left, and I'm ready to turn in for the night, so let's finish this right quick."

Kaiden saw Wulfson take aim with his grenade launcher once more and hurried to voice the question that had nagged at him throughout the entire training exercise. "What the hell is this teaching me, exactly?"

"The dangers of high explosives?" Chief suggested. Kaiden wished, not for the first time, that his EI was a little less quick to involve itself where it definitely wasn't needed.

"I was already quite aware of that," Kaiden replied.

"Well, think of the calories you're burning between the quick-steps, dives, and terror-induced adrenaline," the EI chirped. How did an electronic device manage what sounded like real amusement?

"Why are you so calm about this?"

"Firing!" Wulfson shouted.

"Dammit!" Kaiden yelped, diving behind a holo barrier. The projectile landed a few yards away, shocks sparking out of it and zapping him despite his efforts to maintain cover.

"Ow—what the hell?"

"Tesla grenade, slightly powered down. The holo barrier doesn't really protect against that. More retardant than resistant."

"Some forewarning would have been nice," Kaiden growled his displeasure. "He used bean bags before." He stood up and hopped in place for a moment as his body spasmed slightly from the shock.

Chief's eye narrowed, his round avatar jigging a little in the top left corner of Kaiden's lens. *"I might have been more* inclined to help you out here if your big mouth hadn't gotten us into this in the first place."

"All I said was I wanted something a little different. I didn't realize this was on the table."

"Your exact words were, 'Come on, you drunk blond gorilla, give me a real challenge. Otherwise, I might start thinking Laurie's got more fight in him than you.' And you know how much he hates Laurie."

"Well, okay, that might have been a little over the top, but it was an encouragement."

"And I'm sure this next grenade is coming from a place of love."

"Next gren— Oh, shit!" he shouted when he saw Wulfson take aim directly at him. He dove to the left as the man pulled the trigger. The shot flew past him and exploded, sending more electric shocks through Kaiden, who collapsed on the floor.

"This is not going well for you," Chief muttered.

"I've noticed." Kaiden pushed himself up.

"As much fun as I'm having, lad, time to wrap this up!" Wulfson shouted, cracking the gun open and inserting two more grenades. "Got two shots left, so I'm just going to send both of them at you. Good by you?"

Kaiden rested his hands on his knees, sweat pouring down his face and his breathing ragged. "Are you really asking?"

"Nah, rhetorical question." Wulfson snapped the launcher's barrel back in place. "But it seemed impolite not to at least *pretend* to care."

"I'll be sure that no one ever says that the Head of Security is not a gentleman," Kaiden jeered.

JOSHUA ANDERLE & MICHAEL ANDERLE

"How nice of you." Wulfson chuckled. "I'll give you a moment of respite, let you get the tingles out before I light you up again."

"So you just gonna take it?" Chief asked.

"Hell, no. I have a plan." Kaiden drew his pistol.

"You think that little thing is gonna work on him? It's a glorified stun gun," Chief mocked.

"I'm not going for *him*. I'm going to aim at the grenades." Kaiden pressed down on the trigger and heard the whir of the gun powering up. "Activate Battle Suite, Chief."

"You sure about this?" the EI asked as the words **Battle Suite Initiated** popped up on the display. *"Even a powered-up shot won't bust that gun."*

"I'm merely trying to hit one of the grenades. That'll hopefully touch off the other one and give the geezer some blowback."

"Bonus points for poetic justice if it works out."

"Firing," Wulfson declared.

Initialized appeared on the screen before disappearing. The air around him seemed to slow as Kaiden focused on the barrel of the launcher, taking aim with his fully charged pistol. He could see the moment Wulfson pulled the trigger. He zoomed into the barrel to focus on the grenades, releasing his own trigger the instant he saw the projectiles begin to emerge.

A white streak left his gun and collided with the grenade, but instead of electricity, white powder exploded everywhere.

"Is Wulfson joining us as well?" Laurie asked.

Sasha shook his head. "No, he will actually be heading into town later tonight to pick up an old acquaintance of his. I'm assuming he'll leave right after Kaiden's training."

"That is probably for the best. Less competition," Laurie noted as they approached the Observation Building.

"Will you participate this year, Laurie?" Sasha reached to open the door.

The professor shook his head. "Unfortunately, no. I don't have the time for such distractions this year. I have other things to attend to."

Sasha released the door handle and looked back. "This wouldn't be due to your...interesting findings, would it?"

Laurie smiled. "You *do* remember our little chats. You always seem so distant that I worry it's a case of in one ear and out the other."

Sasha took a few steps back, motioning for Laurie to follow him to the side of the building and into the dark. "Have you found anything new?"

"Well, using the program hiding in Kaiden's EI, I was able to find a coded signature."

"Is it the Council?" Sasha asked, taking off his oculars.

"It would certainly seem so. Not many others are capable of hacking into my department unnoticed, and even fewer are able to crack my devices and infiltrate an EI as this did."

"How did it even get into Initiate Jericho's EI?"

"It was implanted during the EI startup, disguised as a general application. It was loaded into the neural device itself beforehand."

"So they were waiting for you to use it?" the commander asked.

"It would seem so."

"Was it to steal schematics or keep track of you?"

Laurie shook his head. "It doesn't appear that either of those has merit. I personally went through all my other personal projects and found nothing out of order or manipulated. I had my staff check all the other students' EIs and devices during updates since then, and nothing else came up."

Sasha crossed his arms, his eyes closed in thought. "So that would mean whoever tampered with the neural device—"

"Was probably looking for it specifically and is interested to see it in action," Laurie finished, his tone a little grim for once. A short silence followed in which both men considered the ramifications.

"Have you told Kaiden anything?"

"Not so far."

"You wiped the EI?"

Laurie frowned. "Of course I did. You're beginning to make it sound like I'm incompetent."

Sasha sighed. "Just checking all the bases."

"Which is why I'm not offended. You were always a little too meticulous." Laurie snickered, clapping the commander on the shoulder. He was back to his usual cheerful self. "I wouldn't worry too much for now. It doesn't seem like they are trying anything on a wide scale. I'll be sure to inform you if anything else significant comes up."

Sasha nodded, placing his oculars back on. "They will

send a liaison sometime soon. I'll use that opportunity to get a bit more information."

"Well, they *did* start the game without letting us know. Only seems fair to shift the odds in our favor a little." Laurie chuckled.

"I do wonder, however," Sasha mused, looking up at the sky as if it might yield a wealth of information, "if whoever tampered with the implant was after the technology or whoever it was attached to."

Kaiden coughed as he fell to the ground, his vision returning to normal as the Battle Suite deactivated.

"What is this stuff?" he demanded. He looked up to see Wulfson in a gas mask. "When the hell did you put that on?"

"When you were talking to yourself," the trainer replied, his voice muffled by the mask.

"I was talking to my EI." Kaiden wheezed.

"I know. I still find it funny though." Wulfson shrugged.

Kaiden struggled to get up, but he could feel himself getting sleepy. "This is…"

"Knockout gas," Chief stated.

"You'll be out for quite a while," Wulfson informed the downed soldier. He placed his gun on the ground and kneeled beside him. "While you're still conscious, I should let you know I got a friend coming to town from quite far away. He'll help me train you and the others for mid-terms."

"Oh, goody. I hope the others will be just as delighted as

I am." Kaiden struggled to maintain a deadpan expression although his voice was already fading.

"Before you get all snarky, remember who has to carry your ass to med bay."

"Ooh, more blue stuff," Kaiden cheered wearily.

"Actually, I told Dr. Soni to cut you off. I'm thinking you're becoming too dependent on that junk."

Kaiden raised a shaking hand and beat it weakly against Wulfson's knee. "You bastard...you don't...let me have... any...nice things." The words emerged slower than normal, in a raspy voice before his hand fell to the ground and he passed out cold.

Wulfson sighed as he picked up his launcher and placed it on the rack. "Get some good rest, boy. You're gonna need it when Raza gets here." He prepared to call med-bay to expect Kaiden's arrival. "Considering what he will probably do to you, you might need something better than the blue stuff."

CHAPTER TWO

When Sasha entered the meeting room, he saw dozens of teachers chatting amongst themselves. It seemed every division was represented, and he noticed a few people he had never seen in attendance before. This year had apparently aroused the excitement of quite a few of the staff.

"Sasha!" a woman shouted. He looked in the direction of the voice to see Mya walking towards him wearing a violet jacket and carrying a matching handbag. "Good to see you finally made it. Busy night?"

"It usually is for me, but tonight I got held up in a conversation with the professor," Sasha explained.

"Laurie? Is he here?" she asked, looking past Sasha.

He held up a hand and waggled a finger. "He wished to have a quick chat but won't be joining us this evening."

Mya pouted. "Well, that's a shame, but we should hurry and find a place to sit. I think the draft will start soon."

She moved over to the main table, grabbed two chairs

at the far end, and offered one to the commander. He nodded in thanks before taking his seat, and she sat down beside him. "It's been a couple of years since you participated. Anyone in particular you're looking for?"

Sasha nodded as he removed his tablet from the briefcase. "A smattering of students among the first years would be ideal, but my first pick will be Initiate Jericho."

Mya smiled. "Aww, that's cute, looking out for a student you sponsored." She then brought out a tablet of her own. "Don't think you're going to get him, though."

"Why would you say that?" Sasha asked, opening an application on the tablet.

She gave him a sideways glance. "You really can't tell? He's one of the most buzzed-about first years now. Ever since he took the high score during the Division Test, a lot of eyes are on him. Unless you get lucky and get one of the first few calls, someone is bound to scoop him up."

"Then I suppose I will just have to get first call," Sasha stated calmly, seemingly unperturbed by the warning.

Mya gave him a quizzical look before shrugging. "You go ahead and roll those dice commander, but I wouldn't place all my hopes on only Kaiden."

Sasha flicked through an index of students on his screen. "I have a number of other choices to consider. I'll be fine." He looked at her. "What about you? Anyone particular you are hoping to get?"

She nodded "A few dark horses, but I'm looking for Chiyo Kana. Or Kana Chiyo—last names are stated first in Japan, right?"

"Yes, but that is moot here. Why are you looking for her? Is she one of your assigned students?" Sasha inquired.

She raised a hand and waved it side-to-side "Kinda. She's technically Counselor Webber's but he was out sick when she came in, so I processed her, and we've kept in touch," she explained, tapping her tablet screen before showing it to the commander. "Even if she wasn't, though, I can't deny her scores. Plus, she's a merit SC. That already puts her high on the list."

Sasha looked at her screen, taking in the infiltrator's stats, then back up at her. "Weren't you just telling me not to be too hopeful about getting a highly skilled student right off the bat?"

Mya moved the tablet away. "True, it's a long shot, but there is a reason I have a better shot of getting her. She seems to have a couple of…issues that might deter some of the others from wanting to pick her up."

He let out a low chuckle. "Rather odd that a guidance counselor would see the benefits of the troubles of youth."

She hit him with a quick elbow shot to the ribs. "Don't be like that. I don't think they are anything that can't be worked on or improved in time. However, they might cause some of the more strategic people here to pass over her."

Sasha rubbed the point of impact. "True enough, but the same could be said for Kaiden and his issues."

Mya rolled her eyes. "You don't need to remind me. It seems I'm always getting advisory slips from staff about him. But he *is* a soldier—they're usually hot-headed and boisterous."

"Might I remind you that I was once a soldier at this very academy?" he asked.

"Which makes you a perfect example of personality improving over time," she declared, her expression smug.

He sighed. "You certainly are gifted at finding silver linings when they benefit you."

"It *is* a gift." Her grin was almost challenging.

"If everyone would please find a seat and prepare the League application on your devices, we shall start soon," an engineering teacher shouted over the crowd from the front of the room.

"I have a good feeling this year," she stated as she opened the application and pressed the connection button.

Sasha did the same. "I noticed that there seem to be far more members playing this year than normal."

"The Division Tests showed that we have an impressive group this year. Plus, the wildcard of having a group of Tsuna probably drummed up a little more interest," Mya surmised.

"Perhaps, although we've had a fair number of failures too."

She shrugged. "All of them passed the makeup test and did above average. Even our underdogs have a lot of fight in them."

"Sir, shall I begin?" Isaac asked. Sasha looked around the room to see that most of the others had found a place and were activating various devices to start the proceedings. He gave a quick nod, which Isaac returned before disappearing from the display.

"So, have you seen Kaiden lately?" Mya asked.

He shook his head. "Not in a few weeks. He's been busy with the Animus and Wulfson."

She gave him a look of surprise. "I keep forgetting that

he's training with the Head Officer." She tapped her cheek in thought. "I wonder how that's going."

———

Kaiden awoke to the sight of two dark orbs staring at him. As his vision cleared, he saw no other features except a large grey head and a bright light that moved into view.

"Remain calm, Initiate Jericho. This one will soon be done with the healing process." It spoke in a wistful tone, although Kaiden could not see a mouth move and the words sounded like they came from all around rather than directly in front of him.

"Uh, goody," he whispered uncomfortably. "Can this guy know who the hell that one is?"

"This one has been named Doctor Mortis. We have been assisting in your recovery since the larger human left you on the bed in an injured condition," it stated, the echoes once again filling Kaiden's mind.

"Ok-ay…" he stammered, still not fully adjusted to the situation.

"He's that Mirus who works with Dr. Soni," Chief informed him as the alien turned away to set his tool down and pick up a new one.

"Do you think he's aware that his name is basically Dr. Death?" Kaiden whispered.

"I don't have much info on the Mirus, so let's hope that it's some sort of cultural humor and not a title."

"As this one stated, no need to be afraid, Initiate. We are here to heal," Mortis said soothingly.

Kaiden nodded. "Going to sound ignorant here, but

you're talking to me using telepathy or something, right? Because I'm used to hearing voices come out of mouths, and I don't see a mouth."

The alien gave a few quick nods. "For easier understanding, telepathy is the term used to describe how we Mirus converse with others, though it is not the absolute truth."

"I'd ask for an explanation, but I'm a little too dazed to listen to all that seriously," he admitted.

Mortis nodded again, curling his three long digits and resting his head against them. "Ah yes, the large human named Wulfson gave this one a quick summary of prior events and mentioned electric shocks and an anesthetic gas used to render the initiate unconscious." He bent down to rummage through the bottom shelf of his tray of devices. "We have something to help relieve the effects and pain."

Kaiden perked up. "Blue stuff?"

"Didn't Wulfson say that he told them to not give you any more before you got knocked out?"

"Maybe they didn't pass it along to this guy. Let's just wing it and see what happens," he stated in a quiet voice.

"This one has found it," Mortis said, walking over to him.

Kaiden smiled a little wider when he saw the blue color , but it vanished quickly when Mortis held it up, and it wasn't a vial but some sort of spherical blob—and it was moving.

"Uh, Doc? What the hell is that?" Kaiden asked.

"It is referred to as a toxin sponge by some of the humans in the medical field. It will help relieve your pain while also absorbing any damaging chemicals or toxins in your system."

Kaiden sat up slightly, moving to try to get off the bed "Well, that certainly sounds handy, but I'm feelin' all right, so I'll take my leave." But before he could even get off the cot, he saw the blob shudder. As he looked toward it for a brief moment, it leaped from the doctor's hand and attached itself to Kaiden's face.

He fell back onto the bed, thrashing around and trying to pull the gelatinous-feeling creature off him. His yells were muffled by the ooze.

"Try not to be so hysterical, initiate. We have had plenty of positive feedback about the effects of the sponge on humans. You shall be feeling much better after a few moments of absorption," Mortis informed him. "Although this one does seem to recall that most test subjects were rather uncomfortable using the sponge without prior notice, and there were some residual blue markings on the epidermis of the facial area."

As Kaiden continued to try to pry the thing off him, Chief piped in, *"So, how's winging it doing for ya?"*

"Good evening, everyone." Jonas Corbusier, the head of the Engineering Division, greeted the gathered faculty from a small platform in the front of the meeting room. "Welcome to the Initiate League of the 2196-2197 school year. I hope you've prepared your choices and strategies since we have one hundred members playing this year—sixteen more than the average."

There were various murmurs and greetings as the lights dimmed in the room. "Miss Akello Faraji, an advisor of the Animus Center, has offered to do a quick summary of the rules for any newcomers or those who have sat out for a few years." Jonas moved to the side as Akello smiled and waved at the crowd.

"Hello, everyone. As Mr. Corbusier said, I'll give a rundown right quick, then we'll begin the draft." She held up a tablet as a screen appeared behind her.

She looked back as pictures of the faces of various first-year students appeared onscreen. "The Initiate League is a way for us to both encourage students in the first year and have a little fun ourselves. After their first three months with us, we have baseline statistics on each student. Using these stats along with personality profiles and synapse talents, we create a character sheet for each student."

One of the pictures blinked for a moment before expanding on-screen, showing a large description box with their name, age, division, class, skills, a brief personality bio, and tabs for their skills, grades, and other facts.

"Each of you will choose three students during the draft. The end goal is to create a team of three whom you will subtly oversee during the year. As such, their victories are your victories," Akello explained.

The description box disappeared as two other students' pictures blinked and joined the first, changing to a new screen. "There will be two milestones, the midterm test in four weeks, and the end of the year squad exam."

A box labeled "points" appeared on-screen. "Your team gathers points by completing tests, finishing full training courses, gaining Synapse Points, and completing extracurricular activities. Each member of your team gains these individually, so the more they all work, the more points you gain."

"What do the midterm and final exams have to do with this?" someone shouted from the back.

Akello pursed her lips in annoyance and tapped something on her tablet, looking confused for a moment before shaking her head and sighing. "I've been spending too much damn time in the Animus Center. Can't just drop every annoyance down a hole," she grumbled.

"Please raise your hand or wait until the end of the explanation for questions. Ms. Faraji was just getting to that," Jonas stated.

Akello thanked him with a nod and turned back to the crowd. "Exactly. These tests not only offer massive point incentives, but we will give out awards for the top five teams after those tests. Some of the rewards you might receive are extra vacation time, office or workshop amenities, special meals, and potentially, several hardware upgrades, like a new tablet or EI device built by none other than our dear Professor Laurie...or at least provided by him."

"What about the payout?" another shouted, causing Akello to toss a tablet pen in the direction of the questioner.

"I'm getting to that!" She huffed before composing herself. "To participate, each member must pay three hundred credits for entrance into the league. The top three participants at the end of the year will receive a percentage of the final total—sixty percent for first place, twenty-five for second, and fifteen for third." She crossed her arms and looked around the crowd. "And before anyone else asks, if everyone participates, that total will be thirty-thousand credits."

This elicited some excited chatter among the group. Mya raised her hand.

"Finally—someone who has some manners. What's up, Mya?" Akello asked with a hand gesture in her direction.

"Hello, Akey," Mya answered with a wave. "This is my first year participating, but what about leftover students?"

"Well, luckily, that won't be a problem this year. Normally, the leftovers would go into a wildcard group and could be traded at almost any point in time. But if everyone signs up, there are one hundred people here and three hundred first years. Everyone would have a team of three."

"So we can trade?" she asked.

The advisor nodded. "Yep. We'll probably have another big gathering just before each exam, but you're free to trade at any point if you wish to do so."

The muttering continued as some of the crowd began to plan and others talked amongst themselves. Akello looked back to Jonas, who nodded and stepped forward. "Thank you, Ms. Faraji. Now then, if you all would be so kind as to look at your screens, the confirmation box should appear. You can sign in and pay the entrance fee or decline and go on about your nightly routine. The choice is yours."

Sasha hit the accept button and scanned the darkened room. He didn't see anyone going for the doors. It seemed they would have a brisk contest this year.

"It appears that everyone will be participating this year.

How marvelous." Jonas declared with a soft smile. "With that, we shall move on to the first drafts. Everyone, decide on your choice."

"It is done, sir," Isaac stated, his face once again appearing in the display.

"Any problems?" Sasha asked.

"Nothing I could not circumvent. It would appear that we were not the only ones who thought this would be an effective strategy. I was racing against at least twenty other signatures."

"It was a good thing I installed that new Infiltration Suite and had Laurie upgrade you."

Isaac's eyes shrank again as he released a dejected sigh. *"In this instance, I would suppose you are right."*

"What are you whispering about, Sasha?" Mya asked.

He looked at her. "Making preparations with Isaac. Do you never make small talk with your EI?"

She blew an errant curl out of her face. "Chou isn't much of a talker."

"All right, we will begin the roulette," Jonas announced, a board appeared onscreen with all the names of the teachers in play. "It is completely randomized, and you will have ten seconds to give us your choice. Otherwise, you forfeit and must wait to be chosen again." Jonas looked back at the screen. "Begin!"

The names swirled into one massive blur, spinning in a frenzy for a few seconds before it formed one name: CDR Sasha Chevalier.

"Wow, lucky you," Mya muttered. He looked at her with a faint smile, causing her to give him a quizzical look. "Did you…"

"Your choice, commander?" Jonas asked.

Sasha stood up. "I will take Initiate Kaiden Jericho as my first pick."

Groans and mild cursing sputtered across the room as Sasha sat down. Mya tapped him on the shoulder. "Do you happen to have a rabbit's foot on you?"

Sasha shook his head. "Merely an EI owl."

Mya's eyes widened, and she frowned. "Well, that just seems—"

"Councilor Mya! Your choice, please?" Jonas shouted.

Mya looked up in surprise before looking back at Sasha. He motioned for her to speak.

She smiled with a barely noticeable shrug. "You're a good person to think of me," she whispered before standing. "I choose Chiyo Kana."

The meeting continued like this for more than two hours, with bets placed and teams created. All the while, the excitement built to an intense simmer.

CHAPTER THREE

"Hey, it's past eight, ya lazy bastard, time to get up!" Chief fumed as Kaiden sat groggily up in his bed.

"It's also Saturday, you bulbous cyclops," Kaiden sneered as he rolled out of bed.

"Perhaps, but you did agree to join us in the Animus today, did you not?" a deep but slightly muffled voice asked.

Kaiden looked over to see Jaxon walking over to him dressed in a black one-piece suit and a circular rebreather on his neck with a triangular mask across his mouth.

Kaiden scratched the back of his head, "Oh, right. Kinda slipped my mind," he admitted with a yawn. "What are we doing, exactly?"

"We will be running a horde scenario using a map based on the Houston Incursion of 2097 on your suggestion," Jaxon reminded him. "Cameron, Flynn, and Silas will be joining us."

"And the others will be resting, which I would be doing

if I was smart," Kaiden grumbled as he dragged himself reluctantly from his bed.

"I would argue that continual improvement is a more intelligent use of your time." Jaxon shrugged as he headed back to his bed to pick up a satchel. "As well as taking a quick shower to remove whatever those blue lines on your face are."

Kaiden stopped scratching his head and removed his oculars from the drawer, using them to snap a picture of his face before he put them on to see six faded blue lines on his face.

"Damn Mirus goop-soaker thing," he cursed, replacing the oculars in the drawer and grabbing a handful of clothes before heading to the showers.

"I'm going to get some breakfast and convene with a few of my people. I will see you at the center in Hall Four."

"Looking forward to it. As soon as I get this gunk off, I'll grab a bite and head over."

Jaxon nodded. "If it helps, I don't believe anyone will notice once you have entered the Animus."

"Doesn't stop them from noticing on the way!" Kaiden retorted as he opened the door to the hallway.

Jaxon thought about this for a moment before shrugging agreement. "Fair point, but if you ever need to blend in with the Tsuna, it might help as camouflage."

"I should remember that. I'll get a lifesaver and a wetsuit to complete the subterfuge."

"That would look simply ridiculous."

Kaiden looked at him and rolled his eyes before giving him a mock salute and leaving for the showers.

Once under the steaming water, he scrubbed his face

hurriedly with the industrial soap he'd found in the supply closet in an effort to eradicate the remaining stains from his face.

"So, I've been wanting to ask. Why chose Houston as the battleground?" Chief questioned.

Kaiden looked into the mirror on the wall, momentarily distracted by the smattering of blue still visible on his left cheek. "It's the one that came to mind. I saw it while flipping through the scenario maps a couple of weeks back."

"I thought it might have been a homesick thing."

"I never lived in Houston. I was born in Brenham, moved to Austin when I was a kid, then to Dallas with my grandpa, then to Fresno when I was taken in by the Dead-Eyes." He lathered the patch of blue discoloration furiously.

"Was a nasty battle. Three terrorist groups and a battalion of junk droids and cracked security bots. You really think the five of you can take it?"

Kaiden let the water spray away the soap while he fumbled for his bottle of shampoo. "The scenario won't toss the full number of hostiles at us. Back then, it required the combined forces of both the U.S. and Mexican military to defeat them. No way in hell only five guys are gonna do much against that. The Animus will scale it down for us." He applied the soap to his hair. "Shouldn't you know about this? I'm pretty sure it should be pretty basic knowledge to upload into an EI."

"I knew the general idea but might have some missing anecdotes because Laurie had to shut down non-essential operations and info dumps so we could actually use the Animus."

Kaiden put his head underneath the shower stream.

"Speaking of Laurie, I need to talk with him. You would think he would have finished the update by now."

"Might have started working on a droid that keeps his hair shinier," Chief jeered. *"Or maybe someone on the board doesn't want you to have the upgrade and is stopping him from activating it?"*

"That would be a drag." Kaiden huffed and turned off the shower. "The SXP boost was the main reason I agreed to get the implant in the first place."

"Not that you would put it to much use."

"What do you mean?" Kaiden asked, the words a little muffled as he dried himself off with a towel.

"You've got five points and haven't spent a one."

He shrugged as he walked out of the shower room. "Some of my choices are still locked. I would rather everything be available so that I can spend my points properly."

"Seems more like you're stalling."

"How do you figure?"

"You've been able to keep up so far without spending the points, so you're worried that when you do, you might pull too far ahead from your pals."

"That's crap." Kaiden retorted. "They would keep up. Besides, that's not how it works. Every year works as a unit. I would simply be the best soldier of my year, not be sent up a grade."

"Then the only other reason is you still got the jitters. If you're so confident in your skills in gunplay, pour some in martial or in your ace skills. Move on up in the world."

Kaiden clicked his teeth in annoyance as he hustled into his clothes. "I'll take a look at it when I'm gearing up, all right?"

"Doesn't hurt to give it a once over at breakfast."

"I'll do that too if it'll get you off my case," Kaiden snapped, irritated at the EI's persistence.

"Rather you do that than keep pouting."

"I'm not pouting."

"It's all right. It makes you look adorable."

He growled as he pulled on his shirt and walked back to his room. "Pain in my ass…"

After Kaiden grabbed his oculars, jacket, and backpack from his dresser, he left the soldiers' dorm and headed to the cafeteria. He loaded a tray up with pancakes, eggs, sausage, hash browns, and three different juices before making his way to the yard.

A notification popped up on his display, showing that a networked friend was near.

"Looks like Chiyo is just making it to breakfast, too," he observed.

"She was more likely doing something important. You just don't set an alarm."

"Would you cut me some slack? Just because you don't feel the pain Wulfson puts me through doesn't mean it's a walk in the park for me."

"I do so enjoy watching it happen, though," Chief chirped, turning a slightly happy pink. *"By the way, when you passed out, he mentioned that he was bringing in someone else to train with you."*

"Oh, joy. I hope he's as loveable and well-mannered as the shaved yeti," Kaiden responded sarcastically.

"Didn't catch much, but he said his name is Raza."

"Raza? Is that an Indian or African name or something?"

"Whoever it is isn't on the Academy staff. They might be an old war buddy or something."

"Guess I'll have that to look forward to."

"Hello, Kaiden."

He jumped slightly, startled, and looked up to see Chiyo holding a tray of her own.

"Hey, Chiyo. Guess even with the network invite, you can get the drop on me on occasion."

"I wouldn't be a very good infiltrator if I was that easy to detect." She looked and sounded amused.

"Fair point." They took a seat at their usual table. Chiyo removed a tablet from her bag and placed it on the table, and they began to eat. "What do you have going for you today?"

"I will be assisting Technician Calloway in the R&D department. I have been assisting her in helping improve some of the weaker areas of the Academy's technical defenses." She flipped through some pages on her tablet.

"Oh, good. Laurie's defenses can be subverted by a first year." Kaiden snickered.

"To be fair, Professor Laurie is not in charge of cyber-security," she stated. "And you should know that I am not simply a first-year hacker."

"Good going jackass, you pissed her off. Now apologize before she deletes your birth certificate or something."

"I don't think it works like that." Kaiden hushed the EI before looking at Chiyo "Though you're right, I still don't know exactly what you can do. But," he added, gesturing to her armband, "that golden triangle means you can probably do the hell out of it."

"That would be a safe assumption." She turned her tablet off and pierced a slice of pear with her knife. "What are your plans for the day?"

"I'm going to run a scenario with some of the guys from the division."

"Team training?"

"A horde simulation based on the Houston Incursion."

Chiyo's eyes jumped slightly in surprise "Well, you certainly don't work small."

"I always like a challenge when I can get one," Kaiden admitted.

"Psst, ask her about your synapse points."

"Why?" Kaiden asked, annoyed.

"She's probably got a few herself, so she might have some pointers. Besides, you're more likely to take advice from her rather than me, right?"

Kaiden shook his head before looking back at his companion. "Hey, so...how have you spent your Synapse points?"

Chiyo placed her fork down as she finished chewing her food. "For now, I have used them to improve my mental capabilities, increase comprehension and multi-tasking, along with a couple of points in my EI tree."

"You can improve your brain?" Kaiden asked in surprise.

"We should see if we can unlock that tree." Chief snickered.

"In a sense. The Animus allows for changes in grey and white matter along with increased function in certain areas of the cerebrum. In essence, I am simply learning quicker and retaining the information at an advanced rate."

Kaiden nodded in acknowledgment. "Guess it's the whole 'we only use ten percent of our brain' thing, huh?"

She shook her head. "That is a long-believed myth, actually."

"Maybe don't try to impress someone with knowledge you gained from a '1000 Wacky Facts' book."

"Quiet you." Kaiden sneered, though Chief remained obstinately cheerful despite the snub. "How many points have you got so far?"

"Seven."

Kaiden whistled. "I've only gotten five so far."

"It is a bonus of my field. I can train and run scenarios on my own for the most part. Plus, at my skill level, I can do many more in a day than most."

"Sounds like it's working out in spades."

She cocked her head and looked at him. "How about you?"

He leaned back, keeping his expression non-committal beneath the curiosity in her gaze. "What about me?"

"How have you been spending your points?"

He crossed his arms. "That's why I asked. Honestly, I haven't used my points."

"Have you been storing them for a talent that requires a large amount?"

"No, not for anything like that," he admitted. "But I haven't really figured out what I should do with them. I don't really need to use them in the Soldier tree, and using them in the General tree seems a waste—"

"Ace?" she suggested, cutting short his rambling explanation.

"I guess that makes the most sense, but I'm not totally sure of what I would get out of it."

"It depends on what you wish to accomplish. Aces have a multitude of functions along with their base skill of leadership. You could learn more tactics, some medical skills, or even gain knowledge about explosives or vehicles."

"That's the thing—I'm learning most of that in workshops. As for the leadership thing, I'm getting…more accustomed to working in groups, and Jaxon is giving me pointers along the way."

"Are you taking them to heart?"

"Of course I am," he declared hotly before sinking back in his seat with a slightly embarrassed shrug. "Most of the time, anyway. Jax is smart, no doubt, but he doesn't exactly have a ton of stage charisma."

"He's boring?"

"More like he's really dry…ironically." Kaiden chuckled.

"Well, you should still consider your options. But even if you don't see anything that stands out now, there are helpful skills in the general tree such as fitness and modification. However, you haven't said anything about the EI tree."

Chief's eye widened. *"What? She's talking about me now? How could I be a better me than me?"* he asked, turning an annoyed red.

"Oh, so now you don't wanna talk about it," he taunted.

"It wouldn't change your EI's functions much, but it would improve its capabilities and make integration easier," Chiyo explained. "You may have some unique skills to choose from considering your upgrades."

"Good point." He nodded, wondering why he hadn't considered it before. "But I'm a little hesitant to possibly mess with anything considering I'm already on a metaphorical edge."

"How so?"

"Laurie had to mess around with Chief's systems for me to integrate with the Animus at all. He was supposed to upgrade the pods or maybe rewire Chief or something, but he hasn't gotten back to us yet."

"Well then, I would talk with him as soon as you can, but that shouldn't be a problem. I'm sure the professor would have turned off any function that could put you in danger."

"Unless he could learn something from it...or simply get a kick out of it. The guy is a bit of an oddball," Kaiden ranted as he finished the last of his meal.

Chiyo picked her fork up and stabbed another slice of fruit. "Perhaps, but considering the situation, you are at his mercy."

"And it's a jolly place to be, let me assure you." He stood from the table and picked up his tray. "Thanks for talking, Chiyo. I gotta head to the Center. They're probably already waiting for me."

She nodded, her mouth too full to reply, then swallowed and said, "I understand. Good luck and let me know how it goes."

"I'll make sure to get back to you," he promised as he walked away.

"Be sure that you do. There's something that I want to discuss with you when you have the time."

Kaiden turned back, a little intrigued. "And what would that be?"

She held up a hand, telling him the discussion was over. "Like I said, when you have more time. It's a simple offer, but I will probably need to explain the finer details."

"Well, the anticipation is killing me now," he said in a melodramatic whine.

"Just don't die before I get to ask you." She grinned, unmoved by his antics.

Kaiden grumbled as he walked away, tossed his trash, and placed his tray on the shelf next to the dumpster before heading toward the Animus Center.

"Madame, are you sure this is the best course to take?" Kaitō asked, appearing on the tablet in front of Chiyo.

"We will need a partner for the upcoming test."

"And he is the most suitable?" the fox avatar asked.

"That is up for debate." She finished the last piece of her fruit. "But he is the only one I trust."

CHAPTER FOUR

As Kaiden entered hall four of the Animus Center, he heard someone from the gathered group in the center of the hall yell, "Finally," in a dramatic tone.

"Well, look who decided to grace us with their—ow!" Cameron yelped as Silas whacked him on the back of his head.

"At least he's got grace." Silas chuckled as Cameron rubbed the point of impact. "All you've got goin' for you is a hot enough temper to fry an egg."

"Hey, don't knock it," Flynn interjected. "Could probably come in handy if we run out of rations in the field."

Jaxon walked up next to the marksman with his hands folded behind his back "We do not need sustenance in the Animus for extended periods," he stated practically. "Plus, eggs probably would not remain uncracked in our gear should we bring them into actual battle."

"It was just a joke, mate." Flynn grinned. "Still trying to figure out the human sense of humor?"

"Considering the joke, I believe my sense of humor is fine. Yours, however, may be in need of repair. It is obviously detecting things that aren't there." The alien attempted a jest, but his clipped, business-like tone made it fall a little flat.

Flynn tilted his head in thought for a moment and then nodded. "That is possible, but I think I'll hold off on the repairs. Life's a little more fun with mine as it is."

Kaiden placed his pack next to a pod before walking over. "Sorry, took a little longer eating breakfast than I had planned. Are we starting now?"

"Well, we would be," Silas began, looking over to the central hub at the end of the room. "But we can't find the map you were talking about."

Kaiden gave them a puzzled look before walking over to the computer. "That's weird, it's on the approved list."

"You sure you didn't mistake it for a speed run or retrieval scenario?" Flynn asked as the group followed behind.

"I wouldn't make such a stupid mistake," he argued.

"Again," Cameron muttered.

Kaiden leered at him for a moment. "I would think it's all the same to you, considering how fast you're taken out."

Cameron pointed a thumb to his chest. "Hey, I'm a bounty hunter. I focus on a single target or small team elimination or retrieval. It's not my fault we keep running these scenarios with a large number of hostiles."

Kaiden shrugged as he cast Chief into the mainframe to bring up the scenario options.

"As much fun as it is to rile you up, Cameron, I do have to admit that you seem to last far longer than I would give you credit for considering your class," Silas admitted.

"You ever think of switching? Maybe becoming an enforcer or maybe a raider like Silas?" Flynn asked.

"I could make you my sidekick," said raider offered.

Cameron crossed his arms and frowned. "How generous of you. I did think about it a little before settling, but it's a family thing. My old man and my uncle were both hunters. It's in my blood."

"That you keep spilling," Kaiden retorted.

"With that attitude, I'm sure someone's going to put a bounty on you one day," Cameron taunted.

Kaiden scanned through the maps. "Probably, if I don't have one already."

Cameron laughed for a moment before his face contorted in confusion. "Wait, are you serious?"

"Found it." He clicked to display the map onscreen.

"Huh, that's odd." Flynn's muttered comment voiced the general bewilderment. "I mean, we all looked through the options for a bit."

Kaiden locked in the map choice before turning back. "How long could you be looking? The choices are alphabetical."

Silas made a beeline for a pod. "Well, we got it now." He opened the nearest hull and hopped in. "Anyone else coming?"

The remaining four looked at each other a moment before nodding and walking over to their own pods.

"A quick reminder before we head in," Jaxon called. "The scenario is directed by the Animus Director AI. If you need to get out for any reason, there's a button on your right glove between your thumb and index finger. Press it for a few seconds and you will de-sync."

"Appreciate it, mate, but we're kinda used to this now," Flynn said flippantly as he stepped inside his pod.

"You wanna tell us to remain in a straight-up position while syncing is in process too?" Cameron jeered.

Jaxon looked at Cameron as the pod door closed. "Considering the group I'm with, standing, breathing, and walking are about all I can trust you to remember."

Kaiden looked between Silas, Flynn, and Cameron. "He really is getting better with those zingers."

Silas smiled as his pod closed. "Give him a couple more years, and they'll be deadlier than his gun."

The others either laughed or shook their heads as they leaned back and closed their pods. Kaiden saw the familiar blue glow from the inside of the device, and the hum of the process started quietly. He closed his eyes for a moment. The initial heaviness he used to feel when he synced with the Animus was almost gone. He had obviously adjusted to the sensation.

"Inbound to drop zone, ten minutes," a voice reported over a speaker.

Kaiden emerged from sync dressed in his usual armor. He sat beside Flynn inside the passenger area of a small dropship. He looked around to see Silas across from him in medium blue armor with neon green accents. Cameron sat next to him in his usual blood-red armor, and Flynn sprawled nonchalantly at the end in his dark armor, mask, and hood. Jaxon was on the far end in heavy grey armor.

"When did you trade in for the fat suit, Jax?" Kaiden asked.

"Just now," the alien answered. "We have ten minutes before the scenario starts. We have no heavy or support, so I'll play the part this time."

"Rather nice of you," Silas noted as a screen appeared in front of him. "I'll go ahead and switch out my gadgets for a healing stim and omnitool for armor repair."

"Should I trade in my stealth generator for something different?" Flynn asked as a loadout screen appeared in front of him.

"A stealth generator won't do too much good against bots with thermals," Cameron reasoned. "Assuming we're dealing with those, of course."

Flynn looked at Kaiden. "What are we dealing with exactly?"

The three others turned to look in his direction. Kaiden shrugged. "Uh, Chief has the run down," he said as he reached out his hand and the EI's floating avatar appeared.

"Way to show preparation, dumbass," Chief sassed.

Kaiden crossed his arms and legs, "That's your job, you snarky testicle. Get to it."

Chief shook his rotund body in exasperation. *"What would you do without me? All right, you bunch of punks, listen up."* He projected a 3D map of the city in the center of the cabin. *"You'll be dealing with five waves of enemies. Your objective is to defeat the four initial waves and then hold out for ten minutes during the final wave. At this point, the scenario will end with you guys getting away from the Mexican army forces, and you need to make your way to the end zone at the base of this three-story building."* A building toward the back of the map glowed green.

"Seems simple enough, but again, what are we dealing with?" Jaxon asked.

"Well, considering the history and the parameters I get from the scenario description... A multitude of terrorist hostiles, from grunts in light armor armed with machine guns and grenades to heavies in thick armor with demolition and early plasma weapons."

"Manageable," Cameron stated with bravado.

"We do have the technological and gear advantage," Jaxon agreed with a nod.

"Which you'll need as you'll also be dealing with a swarm of bots," Chief warned them as pictures of two different styles of robot appeared onscreen. *"This was how the terrorist group, The Blake Lake, caused so much damage. They were able to sneak in a large shipment of junkbots that they had made over the years."* One of the pictures enlarged into a full model, showing a thin droid on long, lanky legs with a shoddy gun attached to one arm and another with a four-pronged claw with what looked like blades made from kitchen or switch-blade knives.

Flynn leaned forward, looking the model over. "Those don't exactly look too intimidating."

"Maybe not to us, but I'm guessing that normal citizens probably thought they were absolutely terrifying when they were fired upon," Silas commented solemnly.

"Also, a lot of them had explosives inside them, which caused a lot of collateral damage. So keep on your toes," Chief admonished. *"But they weren't the worst of it. There were a good number of cracked security bots too."* The junkbot model disappeared, replaced by a picture of a sleeker droid on treads with a cylindrical body and two arms. Small lasers

in the middle of the palms were surrounded by a trio of prongs for fingers, and a round dome had an elongated "V" design in the middle.

"They're only hacked security bots. Most of them aren't armed well enough to do too much damage," Silas pointed out.

"Those lasers are essentially tasers. They'd do more damage if they fell on you." Cameron snickered.

"They are cracked, not hacked, idiots. If they were hacked, that meant that they were under the terrorists' control, which they weren't." Chief's color shifted towards red as he chided them sternly. The model turned around and zoomed in to the back of the droid's head, showing some sort of circular device stuck against it. *"A small group of sleeper agents was able to get into the factory that housed and repaired these things and placed these devices on almost seventy percent of them. When they were activated, they went wild and destroyed anything in their path. That device is called a killer switch. It disables the ability for the droids to distinguish friend or foe and sent excess energy to weapons systems."*

Jaxon stared at the model before looking at the others. "Wouldn't that merely cause them to overheat?"

"Eventually, but they'd probably still have a few hours of function before their power units melted or shutdown... enough to cause plenty of chaos," Flynn explained.

"Aren't there fail-safes for that kind of thing?" Cameron asked.

"Yeah, now there are," Kaiden said as he switched out his thermals for shock grenades. "It was because of incidents like these that they either installed power buffers or hooked up weapons to separate, smaller power units so it couldn't happen again—or, at least, to potentially stop it from happening."

"The best progress always seems to come from tragedy." Silas sighed.

"Five minutes until we arrive," the voice over the speaker warned.

"Anything else we should know?" Kaiden asked the EI.

"That's all I can tell you," Chief said as the holograms disappeared.

Flynn leaned forward. "What do you mean, that's all you can tell us?

"The first four waves comprise those enemies; the fifth wave is unknown."

"Odd. In this kind of historical reenactments, we shouldn't have to deal with anything except what was there," Silas protested.

Jaxon placed two fingers on the side of his helmet. "Meno, could you please tell me of any potential hostiles in the Houston Incursion of 2097?" The Tsuna was silent for a moment before looking up. "My EI has told me nothing different from what Kaiden's has."

The other three followed Jaxon's example quickly, coming up with the same result.

"Anyone else getting a little uneasy?" Cameron asked.

"Could be something new the Academy is trying," Flynn suggested, his face serious for once as if disquiet had momentarily stolen his humor.

Kaiden rapped his fingers against his arm. "I remember talking with Sasha. He said that the board actually upped the difficulty of this year's Division test. Maybe they're mixing things up this year?"

"Commander Sasha Chevalier?" Silas inquired.

Kaiden nodded. "Yeah, he's the one who actually brought me here."

"No kidding? That's a hell of a recommendation, mate," Flynn said, impressed.

"So I've heard. Pretty nice guy, but he's got a cryptic way of speaking."

Jaxon placed his arms on his legs and rested his chin on his closed fists. "I wonder...do you think this may be some sort of test from him?"

Kaiden removed his mask. "How do you figure?"

"None of the four of us were able to find this map, but once you loaded in your EI, it appeared. Perhaps you have some maps and scenarios available that we do not," the Tsuna explained.

The others exchanged glances for a moment before looking at Chief, who in turn, spun around in place before fidgeting for a moment. *"Why am I being picked on so much today?"*

"You know anything about this, Chief?" Kaiden asked.

"Hell no. I mean, it could be possible. But it would be extremely unusual. You gotta remember, partner, I'm technically a normal EI. It's the implant that's unique."

"Something could have been loaded on the implant that transferred to Chief when you integrated," Silas theorized.

"You know, I already thought the whole implant thing was weird when you told us in the first place. But if this becomes a normal thing, I would recommend you ask for your credits back." Cameron huffed his annoyance as he sat again.

"You guys saying you want to abort?" Kaiden inquired

They looked at one another before shaking their heads. "Nah, I think it's rather exciting, to be honest." Flynn spoke for all of them.

"Two minutes until landing."

Jaxon stood and grabbed a rail on the ceiling "We have the de-sync buttons if anything bizarre happens. I would like a chance to test myself against a unique challenge."

Cameron followed suit. "Could be fun, but next time, I get to choose the map, all right?"

Flynn and Silas nodded as they prepared for landing.

"Fine by me." Kaiden stood. "Just be forewarned that I'm not exactly the quiet type."

"We noticed," the four said in unison.

Kaiden grimaced before placing his mask back on. "Add a melody, and you jokers would make the goofiest-looking quartet."

"Hey, Cameron, that could be a potential class switch," Silas jeered.

"I'm better at making others sing," he shot back.

"Hitting the LZ in one minute."

"Get back on in here, Chief," Kaiden ordered, and the EI appeared in his display almost immediately.

"Yay, home sweet home."

"We're definitely going to see Laurie after this."

"Maybe we can finally get that upgrade."

"Hopefully a few answers too."

"Damn, in all that talking, we didn't go over your skills." Chief looked disgruntled.

"If we get a breather, I'll take a look."

"I would save it for the end."

"Why's that? You seemed so excited before." Suddenly,

the dropship bounced from side to side and the five soldiers clutched the railing, trying not to fall.

"Taking heavy fire, prepare for immediate drop!" the voice on the speaker cried.

The exit ramp unfolded, and Kaiden could see a hail of gunfire and dust kicking up in the streets below.

"Everyone, deploy," Jaxon shouted as he ran off the ramp and leaped out of the ship.

The others followed, Kaiden the last one out a few scant seconds before another blast punched a hole into the side of the craft. It spiraled through the air before crashing a few hundred yards away.

He landed thirty feet down, his armor absorbing most of the impact, and quickly unholstered his Raptor and joined the others returning fire at the enemy.

"To answer your question, it's because you probably won't have a breather."

CHAPTER FIVE

"They seem pretty damn happy to see us," Silas yelled, taking hip shots at the crowd of grunts and junkbots as he moved to the cover of a crumbling pillar.

"Trigger happy, definitely," Kaiden called back, firing scattered blasts, and he leaped around the field in an effort to avoid the incoming shots.

"Where the hell are we?" Cameron shouted, hunkering behind a half wall and blind-firing over the top.

"It appears to be a mostly destroyed building," Jaxon stated. "My scan says that it was under construction when it was attacked in the initial strikes."

Cameron peeked over the top of his wall, only to launch himself back as several bullets whined over his head. "That's not good for us!"

"No kiddin'. I doubt this thing was all that stable before getting attacked," Kaiden observed, taking aim and firing at a few hostiles trying to shoot at them from a building across the street. "Someone with a gun with better range, take those guys out!"

Cameron crouched and moved next to Kaiden. Carefully, he fired three shots at three targets, and all fell. "Where's Flynn?"

"Probably doing the ghost thing." Silas set aside his hand cannon and drew his machine gun.

Cameron continued to pick off other targets that made their way into the opposite building. "I thought he was going to trade his generator in."

Kaiden saw four enemies in the street fall in rapid succession, then another two dropped across the way as Cameron vented his gun. "Finally putting in some work, I see," Kaiden called on the comms.

"Yeah, sorry about that fellas. Wanted to get a better angle and some more height," Flynn answered over the link.

"Where are you?" Jaxon asked.

"On the roof of the building next door. Leaped out of the open window in the back of the room," the marksman answered.

Kaiden looked back to see the window Flynn had mentioned was a missing chunk of wall. "Is that an Aussie thing? Windows are merely huge holes in the wall?"

"Eh, maybe 'window of opportunity' would be a better explanation," Flynn suggested.

"Also an awful pun." Silas snickered.

"Cameron, can you make it over?" Jaxon asked.

Cameron looked at the opening, "Yeah, I'm traveling pretty light, and the jump isn't that far. I can make it."

The leader nodded. "Then go. Silas, Kaiden, and I will

move to the street and continue the battle there. You and Flynn provide long-range support."

"On it," Cameron acknowledged, moving quickly to the spot in a crouched position before leaping out.

"You two ready?" Jaxon asked. The building rumbled then shifted, and the trio staggered before regaining their balance.

Silas emptied his gun into the approaching enemy ranks. "Better than staying here."

"Dying by rubble isn't a good look," Kaiden agreed.

"We'll make our way out the back. We're only twenty-two feet up so we'll descend from here and funnel any enemies that follow, using the alleys to trap them as we make our way to the main road." Jaxon explained his plan and his companions nodded agreement.

The building shifted again, and Kaiden steadied himself on an uncompleted pillar. "We'd have to be fast. There are still other routes they can use, not to mention that they could shift their focus to the snipers."

"Or the building could merely topple on us while we're stuck here," Silas added.

Jaxon nodded. "Agreed, let's move."

The trio sprinted to the end of the room, firing at the walls to knock them down as they ran. The barriers crumbled and the three jumped out, looking around as they landed to check the perimeter. They were in a back alley with derelict and broken buildings surrounding them.

"Looks like we got—" Kaiden's words were cut short by the rapid fire of Silas' machine gun. He turned to see a junkbot fall, riddled with laser fire.

"You were going to say lucky?" Silas asked as he held his gun at the ready.

"I was going to say a small break, but that was obviously wishful thinking," Kaiden concluded.

"Wait...do you hear that?" Jaxon asked.

Kaiden listened intently, hearing a small beeping that grew more noticeable. Not getting louder so much as the inclusion of more beeps, each adding to each other to increase the sound.

"Oh, shit." Silas gasped.

Kaiden looked over to see a group of junkbots behind them. They occupied the first floor of the closest building, holding the pillars and pressing against the corners.

Kaiden's eye grew wide. "Chief, didn't you say some of these had explosives in them?"

"I did. Now I'm saying run.*"* The EI yelped, a sound that definitely resembled panic.

The three sprinted down the alley in the opposite direction of the main street.

"Flynn, Cameron, you need to move. The building we were in is about to blow."

"Slight problem with that," Flynn relayed as he holstered his sniper rifle and looked over the edges of the structure they were holed up in. "The building next to us is destroyed, and the one across from us is too high and too far to jump to."

"I can help with that." Cameron fired his grappling hook over to the next building.

Flynn watched the magnetic hook attach to the wall. "Will that support both of us?"

Cameron wrapped some of the extra wire around his gauntlet. "Maybe, maybe not. You wanna wait here so I can throw it back to you?"

A massive explosion threw Flynn to the floor. He turned to see the previous building topple, falling towards them.

"It appears we're going to have ourselves a leap of faith," he shouted as he pushed himself up and ran towards Cameron.

"Grab my hand," the bounty hunter shouted as he clicked the button to retract the cable. Flynn grabbed hold, and they went sailing through the air while the remains of the exploded building slammed into their previous perch.

"Shoot out the windows," Cameron ordered.

Flynn obliged, drawing his pistol and firing at the glass of the window they rocketed toward. Cameron disengaged the magnetic hook and they landed prone on the office floor of the building, both skidding and rolling for a few feet before coming to a stop.

"Apparently, the answer is yes." Cameron groaned as he stood up, rubbing his shoulder.

"Well played, mate." Flynn groaned irritably, using a wall to help himself up. "Quick thinking there."

"You guys all right?" Kaiden asked over the link.

Cameron continued to roll his shoulder as he opened a map of the area. "Better than we could be, but I think we went in the opposite direction to you guys."

"We'll double back in a bit," Jaxon acknowledged.

"How many we got left?" Flynn asked.

Cameron scanned the map. "Says here that was the end of wave one."

Flynn unfolded his sniper rifle. "Well, that's a bit of good news."

"You wanna hear the bad news?" Cameron inquired.

"Isn't there always?"

"Either this map is loaded with some coincidental wave patterns…" Cameron showed Flynn his map, revealing a large horde of enemies splitting into two groups and heading to the different locations of the separate team. "Or they are adapting to us."

Flynn walked over to the busted window, where he crouched down and took aim down the street. "Well, we did want a bit of fun, didn't we?"

"You guys catch what Cameron said?" Kaiden asked.

Silas and Jaxon nodded. Jaxon placed two fingers on the side of his helm. "We'll do our best to make it back to you, but it will probably be a slow crawl for now."

"Copy. We'll be here," Flynn answered lightly.

"Certainly can't say he doesn't remain calm under pressure," Silas noted.

"As long as he has a little nook from which to pick off targets, he's happy," Kaiden agreed. "I think it's almost like counting sheep to him."

"We need to find a place to hunker down. We're surrounded by alleyways and could be swarmed if we stay here."

"Probably shouldn't risk climbing up a building if they

can blow the thing up," Silas remarked as he looked at the surrounding options.

"We should remain on the first floors. Take a few out and then move on to the next one," Kaiden suggested as he pointed to the broken windows behind him that opened into a hotel.

The other two agreed, and they entered the lobby quickly. As Kaiden moved to take position behind the desk, he noticed that the monitor was on. Cracked and flickering, but on.

"Hey, Chief, think you can find anything useful in this place?"

"Like what? It's a hotel. You looking for a deal on the premier suite during prime vacation days?" Chief jeered.

"I was thinking they might have some security turrets or droids you could activate to give us a little help," Kaiden explained.

"Huh. That actually isn't a bad idea, partner. This stuff is a century old...probably won't have anything close to what we consider good security, but I'll take a look," Chief acknowledged before disappearing from the display.

"Good thinking. Another gun would be helpful, and if we can find some security droids, all the better," Jaxon said

"It might take him a little time to find them and power them up. This place doesn't look to be in great shape," Kaiden warned.

Silas took aim at the entrance. "Hopefully, he gets back soon. Here they come."

A hail of bullets immediately followed his warning. As Kaiden peered over the lobby desk to fire, a laser shot past his head, burning his mask. "Son of a *bitch*. The cracked bots are here."

"I noticed," Silas retorted, firing directly at one of the droids before ducking behind the wall. "Tough bastards."

"I got something for them," Kaiden shouted as he retrieved a shock grenade. He primed it and tossed it at the oncoming horde. Within seconds, it detonated and sent a storm of electricity surging through the group. A few mercs were stunned and then gunned down by Jaxon and Silas, while the droids and junkbots fell to the ground.

"What happened?" Silas asked.

"Since the cracked security droids already had their power units overcharged, the shock pumped more juice into them, causing an overload," Kaiden explained hastily as he shot down a couple more grunts attempting to retreat. "The junkbots are flimsy, fortunately."

"How many of those do you have left?" Jaxon asked.

Kaiden checked his belt. "Four."

"Well, don't use too many right now. We've still got three more waves after this."

"We should probably use this as a chance to start heading back to regroup with Cameron and Flynn," Silas suggested. He placed a finger against his helmet. "How are you guys doing?"

Cameron and Flynn were on either side of the door to the main hallway, pinned down by a flurry of bullets and laser fire.

They looked at each other for a moment, then at the

stream of projectiles before Flynn answered, "We're doing fine."

"Understood," Silas answered and looked back at Kaiden and Jaxon. "They're in trouble."

Jaxon continued to fire as more enemies poured in to replace the ones already destroyed. "We need to get back to them. Kaiden, has your EI found—"

Two turrets appeared from the low ceiling in front of the desk, took aim, and fired powerful blasts toward the mob. The barrage demolished both droids and heavies in a single attack.

"I found the security systems," Chief declared smugly.

"Good man," Kaiden cheered as he helped pick off some of the junkers. "Find anything else helpful?"

"Found four working security bots with miniguns. Whoever designed this place's security wasn't fooling." Chief sounded impressed, a rare occurrence. *"They're on their way."*

"Chief says he's got some security bots on the way," Kaiden informed Jaxon.

"Ask him if he was able to find a way out of here away from the hostiles."

"You get that?"

"Yeah, most of the cameras are busted or offline, but I found a map. When the bots get here, y'all use the distraction and take off down the right. Then, when you get to the end, hang a left and you'll be in the main plaza of the hotel. The doors are straight across the way, so just gun it."

"Gotcha, appreciate it."

"It's what I do," Chief bragged without even a pretext of humility.

"Hey! When the droids get here, fall back and follow me," Kaiden ordered the other two.

"Acknowledged, but when are the droids getting—" Silas' question was silenced by a hail of bullets from above. He looked back to see four security droids of a similar model to the ones they were fighting firing down upon their enemies.

"They certainly got damn good timing," he muttered.

Kaiden holstered his gun and ran toward the hall, motioning the other two to follow. "Come on. While the turrets and droids take on the rest of the wave, we can probably make it back to Flynn and Cameron if we hurry."

"So, any other ideas?" Cameron sneered as he demolished another junkbot, backing up slowly as more continued to descend upon them.

"Well, my waiting for them to run out of bullets plan did succeed." Flynn brought down another two as the two hurried into the final room in the hall and slammed the door shut.

Cameron put his gun down, grabbed a shelf, and threw it against the door. "They have knives for hands. That's still a problem."

Flynn added two chairs to the pile before hastening to the other side of the desk that Cameron was trying to move. "Agreed, but those will take quite a bit of time to get through our armor."

They picked up the desk and thrust it against the shelf and chairs. The door rattled ominously. Cameron found a small cabinet and threw it on top of the desk. "They can get through it eventually."

Flynn added a stack of framed pictures to the pile. "True, but that would take a considerable amount of force."

The door began to shake, and the duo could hear the group of junkbots slam against it. Cameron sighed. "I don't know exactly how many it would take for them to get through, but I'm going to say they have enough."

Splinters of wood erupted from the wall as the pointed ends of the junkbots' claws pierced through. "Ohh...I didn't think of the walls," Flynn confessed.

Cameron snatched his rifle up. "So I'll ask again, any other ideas?"

"Well..." Flynn looked at the shattered windows surrounding the office. "There's always down."

"You're the reason we went to the top floor in the first place." Cameron scowled. The door cracked open, and three flailing arms full of sharp objects broke through, slashing at anything in their wake.

"And it worked for a time. Now, this is the new plan."

"I'm not sure the wire can hold us for that long. This place is probably crawling with these things, at least down three floors." Cameron looked both dubious and a little desperate. "You wanna take the risk?"

"You want to risk fighting three floors of junkers with long-range weapons?" Flynn asked as he pulled a disk from his belt.

Cameron looked at the doorway that was about to burst and considered the swarm behind it. "Ah... Fuck it."

CHAPTER SIX

The junkbots destroyed the door and surrounding walls, plowing through the furniture barricade for good measure. They were greeted by the two soldiers aiming at them with their rifles. But before they could fire, the bots leaped at them, piercing their chests, throats, and stomachs with their jagged blades.

Or, at least, it appeared that way.

The first few that attacked simply dove through them, slamming to the floor. The others crowded in, walking around the unmoving bodies as the others scrambled upright. One of the bots ran a clawed hand slowly through Flynn's chest as if it was moving through air.

The bots looked at each other in confusion.

"You think those holograms are gonna hold them for long?" Cameron wheezed. "And stop holding on to me so tightly."

"First of all, they only need to distract them for a moment," Flynn explained, squeezing harder against

Cameron's chest as they continued their slow descent of the exterior of the building. "And secondly, seeing as we're inching down a building from the twentieth floor on a line we are not even certain will hold, forgive me if I'm a little clingy out of anxiety."

"If I pass out, that's not helpful either," Cameron pointed out, irritation lending a sharpness to the words. "What do we do once they figure it out? They'll come after us or at least cut the line."

"If the line is strong enough to hold us, their glorified table knives won't be able to cut the wire," Flynn concluded with a confidence that seemed entirely believable. "Besides, once the timer on the holograms runs out, it leaves with an…explosive finish."

Cameron stopped pressing the switch, looking slowly at the marksman. "Please tell me you're being metaphorical."

The junkbots looked at each other and then at the bodies again. The images flashed for a moment before disappearing into thin air. The group looked down when they heard a ringing noise.

One of them made a confused meep before being engulfed in an explosion.

The blast erupted above them, and surprise and rage engulfed Cameron. "You *dumbass*."

"What are you on about? That's fewer junkbots we have to deal with."

"Maybe, but the magnetic hook was attached just beneath that floor. And between our weight and the force from the blast it might make the line" suddenly, they lurched into a spiraling freefall, "*breeeak*."

"Well, this is certainly a problem!" Flynn shouted over the comm as the rushing air deadened his words.

"*You think?*" Cameron fumed.

"Should we hit the de-sync switch?"

"We'll probably hit the pavement before it goes off."

"Then I suppose we'll need a—" Before Flynn could finish, they were both enveloped in a shimmering field. In almost the same instant, they slammed into the building, crashing through the windows and bouncing around the room they'd landed in. After spinning along the ground for a moment, the shield vanished, and they came to a halt.

"Well, whatever that was might qualify as a miracle," Flynn muttered as he lay prone on the floor.

"What just happened?" Cameron asked, his voice a little shaky.

"You guys all right?" Silas asked over the comms.

"Better than we could have been." Flynn whimpered, mentally examining himself for damages as he flexed his limbs.

Cameron was able to drag himself onto his knees. "Did you guys save us?"

"Relatively...when you consider the fact that we shot you into a building still full of enemies," Silas answered.

"What did you do?" Flynn attempted to get to his feet.

"I had Jax throw my barrier at you to absorb the impact, then I shot you with a ballistic round to fling you into the building," Kaiden explained.

"And that worked?" Cameron asked in shock.

"Well, are you talking to us from inside the Animus?" Kaiden retorted.

"We certainly are," Flynn acknowledged. Both heard a

rapid tapping from above and froze. The junkbots were descending.

Cameron used his rifle as a crutch to push himself to his feet. "Might not be for much longer. The junkers are coming back, and Flynn and I aren't in the best shape."

"Some further assistance would be greatly appreciated," Flynn requested, supporting himself on a nearby desk.

"On our way," Jaxon informed their comrades.

"Make sure those damn things don't get ahold of my barrier," Kaiden demanded.

"Wouldn't dream of it," Flynn stated wearily.

"Not that I see it anywhere," Cameron mumbled before signing off.

Kaiden tapped his fingers along his gun before aiming down the sights. "Those ungrateful bastards are lucky that I can't hit them with another ballistic round at this angle."

Silas placed his hand on the barrel, lowering it. "Give them a break. They've had a rough day."

Kaiden sighed as he rested the weapon against his chest. "I suppose I should save the ammo. Still got three more waves to go."

"Two, actually," Jaxon stated, and Kaiden and Silas looked at him in confusion,

"Where did wave three go?" Silas asked.

"The wave that attacked us was wave three. Those two are dealing with wave two."

"How does that work?" Kaiden asked.

The leader opened a map and handed it to Kaiden. "I read what was in the infobox."

Kaiden raised his gun into the air with one hand and took the map in the other. He looked carefully at it, and in the corner, it read "waves 2 and 3 of 5 in play" with each group in a different color, one in red and the other in orange.

"Huh, that's weird." He mulled over the oddity for a second or two.

"Most of everything up till now has been," Silas muttered.

"According to this, our wave was completely cleared," Kaiden announced. "Chief, you back yet?"

"I've been back for a few minutes," the EI stated, popping up on the display. *"I can only control things from a limited distance away, remember?"*

"Vaguely. What happened with the defenses back at the hotel?"

"I put them on auto and told them to attack anything that moves. I would recommend you don't go back there for your sake."

"You've been awfully quiet up till now."

"I was enjoying the show. Pretty good plan you made up on the fly, though I'll admit, I kinda wanted to see them hit the concrete."

"Well, thank you for the first part. But I have to say I'm a little concerned with the obvious delight you take in human suffering," Kaiden confessed with undisguised disgust.

"Seeing humans in pain is my stress relief fantasy."

"You get stressed?"

"Kaiden, as much as it is interesting to see you converse with you EI, we should probably hurry and assist Flynn and Cameron." Jaxon interrupted the exchange, pulling Kaiden back into the present.

"We have been standing here awhile," Silas added for impetus.

"Fair enough." Kaiden handed the map back to Jaxon and took the Raptor in both hands. "But I'm sure they're managing."

"There are too many of them," Cameron exclaimed, firing into the mass of bots that pushed in through the doorway.

"At least the door is keeping them in a funnel," Flynn shouted, charging and firing his shots rapidly, some of them piercing through two or three bots at once. He heard cracking and noticed large amounts of dust falling from the ceiling. He looked up to see fissures appearing in the stone as some of the ceiling fell and revealed the faces of junkbots above.

"Would you stop giving the murderous robots ideas?" Cameron demanded, spinning to fire through the holes appearing above.

"I don't think they are listening to me," Flynn said defensively, switching between firing at the junkers above and those trying to get through the door. "Though if they are, perhaps I should politely ask them to stop attacking us?"

"Honestly, I'm willing to try almost anything at this point," Cameron cried as he smashed a junkbot in its face with the butt of his gun. "Where the hell are the others? *Gah!*" he cried as a junkbot fell from the ceiling and jumped on him.

"I'm sure they'll be here soon," Flynn said encouragingly. He shot the bot off Cameron and continued to fire on the mob that drew increasingly closer, his legs giving out as he tumbled to the floor. "I seem to be betting my artificial life on it."

From the direction of the door, bursts of plasma fire, rapid laser shots, and a concentrated beam of energy tore through the robots. They tried quickly to retaliate or flee, but they were easily struck down as Silas, Kaiden, and Jaxon mowed through the remaining force. The junkers attacking Flynn swung around, but their chests and heads were destroyed by several quick blasts of plasma before they could so much as fire. Kaiden hopped over the heap of melted metal and sparking wires to help Flynn up.

"I don't know what you did, but you certainly pissed these things off." He chuckled, offering Flynn a hand.

The marksman took it, and Kaiden pulled him up. "Thank you." He folded his sniper rifle and dusted himself off. "I may deduct points for being a bit late, but you certainly gain some for a grand entrance."

"I certainly always love to impress," Kaiden bragged. "Plus, I'm sure I got bonus points for the earlier save, right?"

"Certainly, mate," Flynn agreed. "As for your barrier, I'm honestly not sure where it went. Maybe thataway?" He pointed to the right of the room. "At least I think that is about where Cam and I landed."

Kaiden sighed. "Man, I gave you guys one job…" he grumbled as he walked away to look for his gadget.

"You all right?" Jaxon asked as he helped Cameron up.

"I'll manage. Thanks for the save twice over."

"Hold still for a second." Silas placed a hand on Cameron's shoulder and pushed a syringe into his neck.

"Ow! What the hell?" Cameron yelped, grabbed at the injection point, and turned to stare at the raider.

Silas held up the empty syringe. "Healing stim. Feeling a bit better now, I'm guessing?"

Cameron quit rubbing his neck and began rolling his shoulders, bouncing a little. "Yeah, almost as good as new."

"Good to hear." Silas nodded, then turned to Flynn, holding up another vial. "I get two vials per gadget slot. Got one here with your name on it if you'd like."

"Damn straight I do," Flynn declared as he walked over to the trio.

Kaiden walked back as Silas skillfully administered the injection. "Found my barrier," he declared, waving it in the air for a moment before attaching it to his belt. "Need to let it regenerate. That little stunt really did a number on it."

"To be fair, you did shoot it with a ballistic round," Flynn pointed out as he stretched his arms.

"Better than letting you continue your fall. I'm not sure the barrier would have absorbed all that force."

"So, what do we do now?" Cameron asked.

Jaxon pulled his map out. "Wave four will be coming soon. We should find a better position."

"Are we going to vote on the best crumbling building?" Kaiden asked sarcastically.

"The one next door is only missing the top two floors,"

Flynn remarked, peering out the gaping hole where a window had once been.

Jaxon pointed out to the streets. "I vote we go back to our original plan. Kaiden, Silas, and I take point on the streets. Cameron and Flynn take a higher position and provide covering fire."

"Because that went so well last time." Cameron scowled.

"Just try to keep from having any buildings fall on you this time around, and you should be good," Silas joked.

"There's something else," Jaxon stated, looking back at the map.

"Didn't even have any good news first." Flynn sulked, and Cameron shook his head at him.

"What's wrong?" Kaiden asked, moving to Jaxon's side to take a look at the map.

"There's a countdown." He pointed just above the main map.

Kaiden saw a timer ticking down. "Fifteen minutes? Fifteen minutes till what?"

"Maybe reinforcements?" Flynn suggested.

"You're being hopeful again," Cameron chided without a trace of humor.

"That's possible, but I thought Kaiden's EI said that reinforcements came after the fourth wave," Silas commented.

"You got any idea what it could be, Chief?" Kaiden asked.

"Not a clue. Like I said, nothing in the scenario info explained what was supposed to happen in the fifth wave or mentioned anything about a countdown."

"Perhaps it's a time-based challenge?" Jaxon volunteered when they all looked at him expectantly.

Cameron picked up his rifle "That means we don't have a lot of time."

"Agreed." Silas nodded and readied his machine gun.

"Let's go with Jax's plan since we don't have anything else and the bots are on their way," Kaiden suggested.

Jaxon nodded, priming his beam rifle. "Cameron, Flynn, go on top of that smaller building down the street." The Tsuna pointed to a structure a block down. "The three of us will stay in front of them and use the buildings as cover."

"I'm going to take a guess that this wave will be mostly cracked security bots," Kaiden reasoned. "I'll use a couple of shock grenades to thin the crowd and keep a couple for whatever happens next."

Jaxon nodded. "Sounds good."

The five soldiers made their way quickly down the six stories of the building. When they reached the street, Jaxon remained beside the building while Kaiden and Silas ran across the street, hunkering down behind the opposite structure, Silas behind Kaiden.

"So am I your meat shield now or something?" Kaiden asked the raider over comms.

"Your gun has less range than mine. You gotta be closer."

"You are in heavier armor than I am, and my gun has pretty good range, even without using ballistic rounds," Kaiden argued.

Silas scoffed, "What? After everything you've dealt with up till now, a swarm of system damaged bots with lasers is your secret weakness?"

Kaiden added a single ballistic round to his auxiliary compartment. "No, but considering that I'm always the one who seems to be chosen to be in front or to go on the suicide missions, I'm starting to feel like I'm being picked on."

Silas chuckled. "Hey, you're an ace, buddy. Welcome to the life."

Kaiden shut the auxiliary compartment. "How I lived without the love and encouragement it brings to me from my peers, I'll never know."

Cameron and Flynn ran over to their designated building, entering and making their way up the stairs in the back.

"This would be easier with the grappling hook." Flynn huffed the observation while taking the stairs two at a time.

"Which I would be using if you didn't destroy my magnet," Cameron reminded him.

"And once again, I am incredibly sorry about that." They reached the fifth level and roof exit.

"Just remember to bring your own next time." Cameron kicked open the door to the roof and walked out. "Don't need you thinking I'm your personal zip line."

"I might just have to." Flynn activated his stealth generator. "They are quite useful."

"Is everybody in position?" Jaxon asked as he crouched down behind a wall connected to the entrance stairs of his building.

"Check," Silas said over the comms as he looked down the sights of his gun.

"Roger," Kaiden acknowledged, switching his rifle to auxiliary rounds.

"Snipers at the ready," Flynn announced.

"Good, be prepared," Jaxon warned. "They are here."

He'd no sooner made that declaration when a siren blared through the city.

CHAPTER SEVEN

"What the hell is that siren?" Cameron yelled.

Kaiden looked back at the rooftop snipers, shrugging. "My guess is not good for us."

"Incoming," Jaxon declared.

Kaiden looked back to see dozens of droids coming their way—more cracked security droids than junkers, as he had guessed. Electricity and laser fire tore through the sky, the five-member team returning fire.

"No terrorists this time, at least," Flynn noted as he reloaded.

"I would think those are preferable," Silas argued, falling behind the pillar to vent his machine gun, "In that they are squishier. Not...you know...in general."

"Throwing a shock," Kaiden called, hurling a sphere that began to glow with blue light into the incoming droids. It exploded in a large discharge of electricity, causing some of the droids to fall immediately to the floor or explode. Others who were further from the blast still seemed to be damaged, shaking in place. For many, their firing slowed or stopped altogether.

"Certainly makes for easier targets." Flynn chuckled, taking out four of the malfunctioning droids in quick succession.

"How many more of those do you have?" Silas asked as he began to fire at the horde once more.

Kaiden withdrew another shock grenade. "After this, I got two left." He lobbed it over before sliding back around his wall.

That blast went off, decimating another group of droids and stunning a few more. Flynn laughed over the comms. "This certainly is more my speed. Taking out these mechanical gits while they spaz around is much more enjoyable than having to deal with them in a cramped corridor."

"Glad you're enjoying yourself," Cameron muttered, taking two quick shots before ducking below the ledge to avoid returning fire.

"Why so glum, Cam?" Silas chided. "If you're bored, you can always come down here and get the blood pumping."

"Yeah, *I* could use a meat shield for a change." Kaiden snickered.

Cameron huffed as he peeked back over and began to pick off some of the bots that were making their way to the front of the pack. "I'm just thinking…"

"Well, that could cause stress for ya," Kaiden quipped.

"Quiet dumbass, I'm thinking something else is coming."

Flynn looked over. "You talking about the countdown?"

Cameron shook his head. "There is that, but this can't be all there is."

"You kidding me?" Silas jeered. "I would assume that you have a better vantage point than I do, and from where I'm standing, there are goddamn plenty of these things."

"Sure, but they are barely firing at Flynn or me—"

"You're welcome," Kaiden added sarcastically.

"Also, I'm in stealth, so really, there's just *you* up here." Flynn chuckled at Cameron's quick look in his direction.

"Gee, thanks, buddy," Cameron growled a sound of mockery and rolled his eyes. "But there's also the fact that they aren't exactly doing a lot of damage to the three of you down there—"

"Because we're that good," Silas chirped.

"If this is supposed to be the penultimate wave before we have a chance to get out of here, you would think it would be a bit more challenging." The bounty hunter finished his original observation, ignoring the interruption.

There was silence over the comms for a moment. Kaiden was the first to respond. "I...suppose I would agree with ya. But it's easier because we're all together right now. Not only that, but we're not weaving through buildings, and we've got more fortified positions this time around."

"Unless they can punch through a whole building." Silas chuckled.

"They did blow that one up at the end of the first wave," Jaxon reminded them.

"Ah...right..." Silas murmured. "Let's not let them do that."

The trio on the ground could hear Cameron sigh and

shuffle around. "I'm going to check the m— Ah, *Christ!*" he shouted, and laser fire could be heard coming from the rooftop but firing *away* from the horde.

"What's going on?" Jaxon demanded.

"Damn junkers are back," Flynn exclaimed.

"Why do they keep coming for us?" Cameron hissed a sharp breath as he ducked instinctively.

"Maybe because they excel in close combat and both of you are long-range?" Silas ventured the explanation without real conviction.

"Or maybe you just look like you taste good." Kaiden grinned behind his mask.

"Hilarious," Cameron sneered. "Now, can I get some backup?"

"We're kinda busy down here," Silas retorted as a laser beam shot from behind him, missing his head but searing his locks. The raider stepped back a couple paces and felt the burning ends of his dreads. "Motherfuckers!"

Kaiden took out a fourth shock grenade. "Silas, you go help the snipers, and I'll keep the droids off you."

"Those cracked bastards just fried my locks. I want some payback."

"To be fair, you've probably shot up over a hundred of their buddies," Kaiden pointed out. "Besides, I have to be closer, remember?"

There was silence for a moment before he heard Silas sigh his acquiescence. "Cameron, I'm on my way. How are you holding up?"

Cameron used the butt of his rifle to knock one of the bots away , turning quickly as another one leaped at him. He used the side of his rifle to block the knives and moved his head out of the path of its teeth. "The sooner, the better!" he called over his comm.

He grabbed his heavy pistol quickly out of its holster and put three shots into the attacking droid, enough for it to deactivate and give him a chance to push it off him. Three more advanced.

"Flynn, where the hell are you?" he yelled, raising his pistol to take aim only to see holes suddenly appear in the junkers' heads. They dropped in their tracks.

"Behind the entrance of the roof, saving your ass," Flynn stated cheerfully.

More junkers began leaping over the sides of the building. "You know, if you turned off that stealth, maybe they wouldn't all focus on me." Cameron swung his rifle onto his back and fired his pistol at the group advancing on him.

"Now why would you suggest something so selfish to your teammate?" Flynn asked with a sarcastic whine.

"Says the invisible dick playing skeet shooting in the corner," Cameron retorted, backing up to the edge of the building.

Flynn sighed. "Fine, fine. I was running out of power anyway."

Cameron looked over to see Flynn reappear and take out a few bots as he materialized. He gave the bounty hunter a wave. "There. Does that make you feel bett—" The door to the roof swung open, smashing into the Australian sniper and causing him to fall back onto the concrete. From the doorway, more junkers tumbled out.

Cameron laughed despite the situation. "Well, that certainly does—" He noticed quickly that the bots in the doorway began to move towards him, along with the ones climbing up the side of the building.

And now, his partner was flat on his ass.

"At least, for a moment it did," he muttered. "Silas, where the hell are you?"

"*Busy!*" the raider shouted, rapid laser fire echoing from the comms. "There's a bunch of these rusted bastards down here."

"That's not good for me." Cameron grunted, firing at the junkers as he moved toward Flynn.

"For *you*?" Silas shouted. "What about—*gah!*"

"Silas?" Cameron exclaimed.

"What's going on?" Jaxon asked.

"One of the junkers just pierced my leg, dammit!" Silas responded. "I blew its head off, but its claws are still in me. I won't be moving too quickly till I rip it out." Several loud bursts sounded, and Silas cursed again. A loud thump could be heard. "Those pop guns they got actually got a little punch to them."

Cameron dodged another swipe, pistol-whipping the attacking junker and returning fire at a few others, taking a few shots of his own. "No kidding. Flynn, get your ass up."

He saw a trio of bots drop to the floor, and two others looked quickly over to where the shots had originated from before their heads were drilled through by another two shots.

"I was waiting for the element of surprise, mate." Flynn grunted, lying on his back as he aimed down the sights of his rifle. "Have a little more faith."

"I lost that when you got slapped by a door," The bounty hunter retorted.

"The sneakiest of foes…" Flynn joked, taking two more shots before popping open a slot on the side of his rifle to reload his spikes.

Cameron took out the last of the current junkers on the roof, granting them a slight moment of respite before the next batch inevitably arrived. He vented his pistol and placed a hand to the side of his helmet. "Silas, you still ball and chained?"

Cameron could hear Silas gasping and grunting. "Rickety bastards got grip strength, I'll give them that."

"Flynn and I were able to clear the junkers up here, at least briefly. We'll make our way down—"

"Cameron, on your six!" Flynn shouted, slamming his ammo compartment closed and taking aim quickly.

Cameron whipped around to see a junker leaping in the air behind him, coming down hard with its four arms—accessorized with various sharp instruments—outstretched. The left side of its head was pierced by Flynn's shot and the lights in its eyes dimmed, but it still fell onto Cameron and knocked his pistol out of his hand.

As he struggled to get the bot off him, more emerged over the roof ledge. "That's the street side of the building," Cameron cried as he finally pushed the heavy robotic carcass off him and went for his rifle. "Jaxon, Kaiden you got trouble."

"What are you— Oh, shit. Jaxon, we're getting flanked," Kaiden shouted over the comms. "Junkers behind us, coming down the street and climbing up the building where the other three are."

"You focus on them. The security droids are almost finished, and I've got a full charge. Leave them to me."

"Roger. Hang tight, guys. I'll clear a path down here."

"Because that went so well the last time…" Cameron grimaced as he and Flynn began walking backward, trying to shoot as many junkers as they could.

"Are you clapping at me?" Silas asked. "Because—" His voice was cut off and they heard a sharp intake of breath followed by a gasp of pain.

"Silas? What's wrong?" Kaiden called.

A loud burst of fire was followed by ragged, pained breathing. "I just got pincushioned. One got behind me. Got me in the chest when I turned."

"That sounds quite painful." Flynn sounded concerned.

Silas let out a snicker. "Oh yeah, it is…you snarky jack-ass," he wheezed. "Not as bad as the shank to the kidney that one of his buddies hit."

"How light is your armor? They shouldn't be getting through it so easily with their butcher-knife fingers," Cameron stated.

"Took quite a few shots getting up here…old cubicle walls don't offer much defense."

Flynn fired his last shot, rolling away from the bots to the back corner of the roof. "Where are you, we can—" He stopped as a large blade tore into his shoulder, and he screamed in pain.

"Flynn," Cam shouted, looking over to see a junker with a large scythe blade attached to a long, coiled arm behind the sniper. The arm extended, hoisting Flynn in the air before slamming him onto the ground and raising him into the air again.

Cameron turned quickly and fired, sending a charged shot into the bot's shoulder. The arm fell off, and Flynn tumbled to the floor. Cameron fired two more shots, one to the chest and another into its head, and the bot stumbled for a moment before falling off the edge.

"Good shots, mate…"

"You all right, Flynn?" Silas asked.

Flynn pushed himself onto his knees before grabbing his shoulder. "I got a lot more sympathy for you right now."

"Got a little instant karma, huh?" Silas chuckled.

"And it is a bitch." Flynn winced. He looked at Cameron, who was back to dodging and firing at the bots, and struggled to his feet. He reached for his pistol but before he could draw it was tackled to the ground again. "Don't you bastards ever go away?" he roared as he tried to buck the junker off him.

In response, the one on his back shoved his head into the ground, and he could feel another trying to claw into his armor.

Cameron saw his partner's predicament and tried to finish off the bots in front of him so he could make his way over, but his rifle was blown out of his hands. He looked back only to be swarmed by junkers, ripping into him as he tried to kick and shove them off of him. "Kaiden. We are FUBAR. Where the hell are you?"

"I'm almost in the building," he responded, loud blasts coming over the mic. "Switching to ballistic shots. I'll be up soon."

Cameron was able to grab his melee weapon—a butterfly knife with a plasma blade—and used it to sever the cords connecting one of the junkers' heads to its body.

This gave him enough room to begin slashing and slicing through the bodies of the bots around him.

Flynn had the same idea. With a flick of his wrist, a blade emerged from his gauntlet. Using his remaining strength, he flipped himself over and wriggled his arm free of the junker's grasp, severing the metal hand with his blade and stabbing it through its eye. The bot spasmed for a moment, giving him enough time to kick it off him and into the second one clawing at him. He leaped forward and stabbed the remaining assailant in its head and several times in its chest.

"You… Damn…" he began, growling around a shaky breath before he saw the one-eyed bot look at him, its remaining eye beginning to glow red. "Bastards."

As Cameron continued to hack through the junkers, he felt them tighten their grasp and freeze up. He saw the eyes of the half dozen bots around him glow red, then heard a beeping noise come from all the other junkers which remained mostly intact. His eyes went wide.

"Hey, guys… It might be the blood loss, but I hear beeping all around me," Silas stated wearily.

"No… It's not just you." Kaiden looked at the various fallen junkers around him, hearing the quickening noise and seeing the eyes of many bots, both active and destroyed, begin to glow red. "Are they all…" Kaiden's whispered question faded into nothing, a tinge of fear creeping into his voice.

"The security droids as well," Jaxon said. "The

remaining ones have stopped moving. My EI is reading that their internal power level is rising and focusing on their cores."

Kaiden looked around him "They've all been rigged to explode!" He put his Raptor away and reached for his shield. "Chief, is there a way to stop them?"

"Not without remote access to all the bots, and certainly not in time," Chief stated.

"You didn't see anything that said they could do this?" Kaiden demanded.

"I would have mentioned it if I had," Chief retorted. *"Once they were destroyed, that should have also disabled any chance of an overload explosion. They must have had redundant power units in case of destruction. I wouldn't be able to read that unless those units were active from the beginning."*

Realization dawned on Kaiden. He now knew why there were so few of the terrorist enemies in every wave and none in this one.

They had fallen back.

He moved his hand away from his shield. "Jaxon, how long is left in the countdown?"

Jaxon opened the map. "Ten seconds."

Kaiden looked at the Tsuna a few blocks away and back to the building holding his other three teammates. "This was inevitable. We were never supposed to make it."

The timer hit zero, and all the bots and droids erupted. Kaiden was consumed in the explosion which tore him apart.

His vision went blindingly bright for a moment before plunging to utter darkness.

CHAPTER EIGHT

K aiden winced as he pulled himself out of the Animus pod. He could feel searing pain throughout his entire body and nearly toppled over onto the ground after catching his boot on the bottom of the pod. Biting his lip to keep back an exclamation of protest, he staggered for a moment before resting with his hands on his knees, breathing heavily.

"God, why do I feel like I just got run over by a carrier?" Cameron groaned. Kaiden looked over to see the others in various states of duress. Cameron leaned on the desk in front of the hub while Silas and Flynn sprawled out on the floor. Jaxon was the only one seemingly not in a traumatic state of pain, but he hadn't moved far from his pod. His arms were crossed and eyes closed while he stood very still.

"Increased Animus oscillation combined with the massively traumatic damage. We were victims too," the Tsuna stated, his voice monotone and hushed.

Silas shifted his head slowly to look at Jaxon. "The damage I get, but I've never known the effects to be this painful when I de-synced. I mean, I've been exploded before, and it didn't feel like this."

"'I've been exploded before.' I doubt many people can say that so nonchalantly." Flynn chuckled before seizing up and crumpling slowly into himself like a dying roach. "Oh, hell, it bloody hurts to laugh."

"Animus oscillation…" Kaiden murmured as he hobbled his way slowly over to the others. "That's what they call the syncing between the Animus and the mind of the user, right?"

Jaxon nodded once very slowly. "After repeated uses, the syncing becomes much more natural, and the mind grows accustomed to the…oddities of syncing with the Animus."

"So what? Are we just jacking straight in now?" Cameron asked, trying to keep himself up using the table. His hand slipped, and he failed to catch himself as he fell to the floor. He wheezed before taking a deep breath, now facing away from the others. "You all forget you saw that…"

Jaxon shook his head, again slowly and only once. "No, it simply becomes less intensive. Fewer countermeasures the advisors have to deal with at the hub, and our EIs no longer have to make up for various deficits or help with the syncing process. They become more like conduits between us and the Animus rather than guides."

"So that means that the more we use the Animus, the more 'real' it begins to feel?" Kaiden asked.

"To a point," Jaxon said. "Since we are always aware that we are in the Animus, we can never die as we are conscious of the fact that we are not really dying. However..." He shrugged as if loath to continue.

"We can certainly wish we were dead," Flynn finished harshly.

"Not how I would have put it," Jaxon said. Kaiden could see a large number of bubbles floating around Jaxon's tube. "I will admit that I am not in the greatest condition myself."

Kaiden straightened and leaned against Jaxon's pod. "You seem to be looking good compared to the rest of us."

"It is quite painful for me to move, so I have chosen not to."

Kaiden chuckled, feeling a shock of pain through his lungs and chest. "Oh, God, it does hurt to laugh." He winced as he folded his arms across his chest.

"You want me to see if Doctor Soni is in?" Chief asked. *"Or if you want to keep pouting your way through the pain, we can see if that works."*

"Maybe we should call the med bay," Kaiden suggested.

Jaxon, in his first show of quick movement since exiting the pod, held a hand up to Kaiden. "I recommend we do not."

"Why's that?"

"If they must come and retrieve us, along with seeing our current condition, they may ban us from private use of the Animus or, at the very least, reduce our usage for some time."

"I may not be opposed to that, honestly," Silas muttered.

"I personally do not wish to fall behind," Jaxon stated.

"On top of that, it may incur unforeseen repercussions for myself and the other Tsuna."

"What do you mean, Jax?" Cameron asked, looking over.

Jaxon folded his arms again, looking at the others. "Tsuna integration with the Animus took a number of years to approve due to apprehension. Even after it was approved, it took a few more to make the process effective. A large group of the Abisalo Conclave has continued to voice concerns. To see one of us asking for medical assistance so soon would only confirm their fears and may end up with us being sent back or temporarily suspended from Animus activities."

"Abisalo? Is that your homeworld?" Kaiden asked.

"Yes," Jaxon affirmed, not moving his head this time. "And while I would welcome a chance to see it again, I have enjoyed my time here and have learned many things quite quickly compared to my training at the disciple schools. I would like to continue my training here so that when I do return, it is on my terms and with the advances I have made here, not by the machinations of the Conclave."

"I haven't heard Geno say anything about your people's leaders being paranoid, although to be fair, that would mean the Tsuna and Humans have another thing in common." Kaiden chuckled.

Jaxon cocked his head as he stared at Kaiden. "Geno?"

"Yeah, Tsuna Engineer? We hang out time to time. I would assume you know him. I mean, not to sound racist… Speciesist? But all of you live together in the same dorm. I would imagine you've run into each other."

Jaxon shook his head, one of his eyes snapping shut as he winced in pain, "No, no, I do know him. We are...belay that. It's just that what you called him is... I'll have to discuss something with him next time we meet."

Kaiden gave Jaxon a questioning look as he slid down the side of his pod. "Well, regardless of the potential doom-speak of your annoying council, I understand why you're concerned." Kaiden sighed as he pushed himself up slightly, trying to find a more comfortable position. "Guess we'll just wait to heal up a bit and get some pain meds from the med bay later. That'll probably be enough."

"I agree," Flynn responded, uncurling and sitting up.

Silas followed, grunting as he pushed himself to his knees. "Surprisingly, it takes more will to get up than to take on a battalion of droids."

"No kidding." Cameron used the edge of the table to pull himself up before leaning against it and turning to the others. "Guess we'll sweat this out for a bit."

"My thanks." Jaxon acknowledged their decision with a slight bow of his head.

"Don't mention it," Kaiden said. "If this is gonna become normal, we should probably get used to it."

"Yeah, pain builds character, right?" Flynn mocked.

"At least my locks are fine" Silas reached back and felt them. "Although even they feel like they are also somehow in pain."

Kaiden rolled his shoulder to ease the stiffness. "Besides, it's not like I haven't built up a high pain toler-ance working with Wulfson."

"The head of security?" Cameron asked. "What

happened with him? Did he catch you drinking on campus and beat you down?"

"That would be hypocritical of him." Kaiden laughed. "I've been training with him. I should probably bring you guys with me the next time I'm with him. We can have fun together."

"That sounds foreboding rather than fun," Flynn mumbled.

"So, how long do you guys think it will be before we're good to get out of here?" Silas sounded eager to leave.

The five of them looked around at each other, utterly silent for a minute before they saw Jaxon uncross his arms and stretch them for a moment. He then took one step forward; the others gave impressed looks before they noticed Jaxon didn't move the other foot.

He remained frozen for a moment, then crossed his arms again. "I have chosen to not move again."

They all chuckled or sighed, each mentally agreeing that they probably couldn't do much better at that moment.

Kaiden used the pod he was leaning on to help him stand and provide support as he looked at the others with a small smile. "Y'all happen to have any good stories or jokes to pass the time?"

Chiyo watched the feed on the corner of her display as a guard, a floating security drone, and a technician went into the server room. The technician opened the gate to an aisle of servers as the guard and drone took positions on either side of the gate. She waited patiently as the technician went down the line. Now around forty feet away, she pressed a button on her holo console, causing the lights to go out on the other end of the room.

She saw the guard look towards the glitch, then back at the technician as he pointed to the lights. The technician brushed him off, seemingly telling him to go check it out while he finished. The guard shrugged, took his rifle in both hands, and began to walk over, leaving the drone in its place.

In a few seconds, she would have her chance.

She windowed her feed, opening a command prompt of her fast-hacks. It comprised preset abilities that allowed for quick and effective—if somewhat brief—distractions and commands that she'd made so she wouldn't have to create them each and every time. Infiltrator basics, really, but very convenient.

Holding her breath, Chiyo waited for the guard to get far enough away. She looked up at the feed to see the technician plug a cable into one of the servers from a device strapped to his left hand.

She smiled. It was a specialized computer that was tied to the user's vital signs using a vita tether. The device was increasingly common in companies that dealt in sensitive information and would shut down if it was ever removed from the specific user. They were given to high-ranking technicians such as the one she was observing, and only those with this device could access certain devices within the company.

Like the server, she needed access too. She couldn't hack it remotely, not to get what she needed. However, what she could do was set off a system that warned the technicians of corrupted data, causing them to send one over to access the server and clear up the discrepancy.

She saw that the technician had accessed the system and she pressed a button on her fast-hack prompt with the face of a fox. It was essentially a go signal for Kaitō to tell him to begin their plan without risk of using communication or getting her EI hacked.

She watched the security drone—the one she had Kaitō take over as they made their way into the server room. It entered the gate, the technician too busy looking through the files for the presumed corruption to notice it hover close to him, a black baton descending from the bottom of its circular body.

Chiyo activated another fast-hack, jamming the guard's radio and vita tether signal to the technician. He would be none the wiser and wouldn't hear the call that would soon come. At least for a couple of minutes, but that was plenty of time.

The drone flew a few feet above the technician before descending behind him to press the baton to his neck. The man shook for a moment, his free arm reaching for the cable connected to the computer, trying to pull it out. His fingers groped uselessly before his arm slumped down again. The cable had to be deactivated from the console on his wrist before it could be pulled out manually, something that she was sure he was aware of. But, considering he was pumped by a bajillion volts, it probably didn't spring to mind right away.

She was good at exploiting little issues like that. The frenzy of the mind when in distress, or how the vita tether only deactivated when it read a heart rate that rapidly decreased, not one that suddenly spiked. Also, how access to the servers stayed open as long as long as it was cleared by the proper technician and they were still connected.

The man slumped soundlessly to the floor. The drone retracted the baton and hovered in front of the server, connected a toggle to it, and quickly downloaded the information and files Chiyo had previously requested. She flipped to a camera showing the guard. He shuffled awkwardly, looking for intruders but hampered by the semi-dark area she had created specifically to keep him occupied.

She was an intruder, technically, just not in the building. He could scour the area to his heart's content and be none the wiser.

Chiyo changed back to the previous screen. Kaitō didn't have much time. The guard might be unaware, but the sudden jolt to the heat would probably be read by a safety system, alerting nearby guards or the security station. When they didn't get a response from either the guard or the technician, they would send others in or possibly activate an alarm and lock the entrance.

Not to worry, though. She was counting on both.

The drone put the toggle away and floated quickly back to its position in front of the gate. The door to the server room opened and two guards walked in, their guns at the ready. They strode over to the drone, and one pointed to the downed technician. By this time, the other guard had hurried back, clearly agitated. She activated the audio system on the drone to listen in.

"The lights went off. I went to check the area, my tether signal didn't go off, and my radio has been silent," the first guard protested, his demeanor indignant as he defended himself.

Another newcomer pointed to the technician. "Someone knocked the tech out and probably fled when we arrived. Why didn't the drone do anything?"

Chiyo opened a command prompt for the drone, deactivating its motion sensors and visuals, and she pressed Kaitō's command prompt again. This signal told him to wait. She saw the first guard walk over to it and examine it.

"Damn thing is malfunctioning. The lens is dark." He growled his frustration.

"Probably a jammer. We're most likely dealing with a specter," the third guard reasoned, and Chiyo grinned. "Alert the others and activate the lockdown. We'll get this bastard."

"Bitch, if we're gender-specific," Chiyo murmured quietly to herself.

"What do we do with it?" the first guard asked, motioning to the still inactive drone.

"Leave it here. If it was just a jammer, whatever was blocked will reactivate soon enough, and it might be able to get a visual on the intruder if they double back." The third guard seemed to have some experience, though it clearly wasn't enough. "If not, then we'll come back and take it to tech for repair or destruction. Right now, our priorities are finding the intruder and getting this technician somewhere safe."

The others nodded. One of the guards holstered his rifle and walked over to the technician. He heaved him up onto his back as the other two took point, and the three left the room. As soon as the door closed, Chiyo reactivated all the drone's functions before hitting the loop action on her prompt. The cameras would now loop their feed for two minutes for anyone looking at a different feed to hers.

She activated Kaitō 's command again. *"Scrambling ready, madam?"* Kaitō asked.

"Ready three minutes after you took control of the drone," she said, flipping to another screen and pressing an activation button. It paused the drone's signal to outgoing sensors, making it appear as if it hadn't moved.

The drone quickly moved down the length of the room. Chiyo remotely opened an A/C hatch in the same corner where she'd shut off the lights. It flew in, and she switched to the drone's visual display.

She watched the drone weave through the tight spaces until it reached another hatch, Chiyo opened it, and the mechanical entered an unoccupied office. It moved to a window, used a small, tri-pronged arm to unlatch and open it, then closed it on the way out.

Chiyo closed her screens, stood up, and walked out of the coffee shop where she had been sitting. She strolled into the park across the street, taking the path that led to the left and the side of the building she was infiltrating. With a quick look around to ensure no one else was around, she stopped beneath a tree and looked up. The drone perched on a branch, hidden by the leaves. She retrieved a USB memory stick as she motioned for the drone to come down. It landed in her hand and opened a hatch on the top in which Chiyo placed the USB.

With that, she saw the words "Mission Complete!" appear in front of her. With a smile, she watched the world around her disappear.

CHAPTER NINE

"Wow. This blue stuff is great." Flynn sighed happily, lying on a medical bed on Kaiden's left.

"I'm certainly feelin' a lot better," Silas agreed from Kaiden's right. "Also kinda...fluffy?"

He turned to look at the sniper. "Right? Makes the various beatings I've taken seem almost worth it."

"As much as I enjoy the fact that my serum is quite helpful and enjoyable to you, Initiate Jericho," Dr. Soni began as she walked over to the side of his bed, "I would still much prefer that you not become so accustomed to it. Which, if you're wondering, is a request to not be quite so injured each and every time you come in."

"Maybe I look for excuses to see you." Kaiden chuckled at her unamused expression.

"My hypothesis was that you simply had masochistic tendencies. But if what you say is true, then you don't need wounds to pay me a visit." She scowled. "Which means that

I owe Wulfson ten credits, as the explanation might be idiocy."

Flynn and Silas snickered, and Kaiden shrugged. "It apparently has its bonuses, though."

"Not for some time after this. I'm out of the serum and currently waiting on my next batch, which will come in about a month at the soonest," she revealed with a smile that could almost have been smug.

Kaiden could feel his heart sink. "You couldn't rush-order it by any chance?"

Dr. Soni used the tablet in her hand to give Kaiden a quick hit on the head. "Not if I want it made properly, and this is the first time I've had to make another order in such a short time. You are responsible for over seventy percent of my stocks usage. The four I administered to you and your friends were the last of my current supply."

Kaiden looked at Flynn. "You owe me for this."

Flynn gave him a bemused look. "You act as if it's your private stock."

"Might as well be." He laid his head back on his pillow. "She said I used most of it."

"That merely means you get your ass kicked more than anyone else in the Academy," Cameron called from a line of beds across from the trio.

"That means I work the hardest out of anyone here at the Academy," Kaiden retorted.

"However you wish to spin this, Initiate," Dr. Soni muttered, causing more snickering and chuckles from Kaiden's compatriots. "Besides, you're fortunate I'm so generous. Officer Wulfson did ask me not to give you any more of the serum."

"Yeah, I remember, malicious bastard." Kaiden sighed before looking at the others, "See if I bother saving y'alls' asses again in the next mission." He looked at the doctor. "Hey, Doc, you said you only used four vials of the serum, but there are five of us."

Soni pointed across the med bay to the bed next to Cameron. "Your Tsuna friend, Initiate Cage, is being taken care of by Dr. Mortis. I was not sure if the serum would be viable for him in any case."

Kaiden looked over to see the Mirus doctor running a scanner over Jaxon's body and the toxin sponges enveloping his face. Kaiden grimaced, remembering his time with the blob, although Jaxon was apparently taking it a lot better than he did. He looked relaxed, his arms crossed while he lay motionless on the bed. Granted, he might be in much more pain than the four of them since he didn't get Soni's serum.

"Don't y'all have any Tsuna medics or doctors? You know, since there's like a hundred Tsuna students here now?" Kaiden asked.

Soni nodded, "We have four. However, when I told Initiate Cage that I would call one in, he asked that I did not and explained that he would prefer to keep his condition private."

Flynn moved up on the bed, resting on his elbows. "He's worried that the Tsuna Conclave or whatever is going to pull them out if anything seems suspicious or even remotely deadly concerning the Animus."

Kaiden tried to silence him with a frantic wave, but Soni held her hand out to stop him before nodding. "He told me, and I can understand. I was not a part of the negotiations at all, but I was briefed by the head of the board and Professor Laurie when they returned. I can understand their people's trepidation. The Animus has always had detractors, even when it was first conceived almost eighty years ago. We have had the benefit of seeing the possibilities and outcomes through the years, while the Tsuna went from discovering a new species and trusting them with some of their own with a machine that invades their minds in only a couple decades—a bit of a jump, I must agree."

"So you'll keep it a secret?" Silas asked.

"He has no grievous wounds unless Dr. Mortis discovers something we didn't see in preliminary scans. And while he might be in pain due to his experience with the Animus, this was explained during all the delegations that dealt with bringing them here in the first place. So far, there's no reason to send a report that I can see."

"Thanks, Doc, he'll probably breathe a little easier knowing that," Kaiden said appreciatively. "If what he does is actually considered breathing."

"It is, but merely a different method." She smiled "But I will use this as a convenient segue to ask you about your injuries. You said you all came out of the Animus feeling like this?"

Kaiden nodded, sitting up on his bed. "Jaxon figured that because we've been using it so much, our Animus oscillation has gotten to the point where the pain is a bit more...real than it was at the beginning."

"Plus, we all got blown to hell," Silas added. "Metaphorically, in our minds, anyway."

Soni began looking through something on her tablet. "True, but you've only been at the academy for three months. For such extreme pain transference, you would have had to use it every day for more than twelve hours at a time."

"Well, we do use it almost every day, if you count the training, tutorials, scenarios, missions, and private usage," Flynn stated.

"Plus Cam, Flynn, and me went to preps before coming here. We all spent a little time using the Animus pods at our schools to get ready for admission," Silas added.

Kaiden swiveled his head between the two. "Y'all are preppies? Doesn't come across to me..." He looked at Flynn. "Well, except you, maybe."

"How so?" Flynn asked.

"Kangaroo butler," Kaiden answered.

"That was—"

"Named after your actual butler, right?"

Flynn was silent for a moment, then he grinned. "Doesn't mean I'm a fancy bastard or nothin'."

Kaiden smirked and shook his head. "Nah, you're a good shot. I'm just messing with ya."

"Don't have a high opinion of preps?" Silas asked.

"Guess I just didn't meet the right people." Kaiden shrugged.

"How uncharacteristically nice of you to say so," the raider jeered.

"Cameron is kinda pulling you down."

"What did you say about me?" Cameron called.

"Don't worry about it," Kaiden retorted, looking back at the doctor. "Sorry, what were you saying, Doc?"

She handed her tablet to Kaiden, showing him a list of Animus missions. "Which one of these did you do?"

Kaiden flicked through them, shaking his head. "None of these. In fact, the one we did wasn't even available until I used the hub."

"We figured that Chief had something to do with it," Flynn recalled with a slight shrug that spoke unconcern.

"Chief?" Soni asked.

"My EI." Kaiden reached under his bed and brought out his jacket. He fished out his oculars from one of the pockets and put them on. "Hey, Chief. Wake up, partner."

"I never sleep.

"That…sounds oddly eerie," Kaiden murmured. "Hey, can you bring the map up on the doc's tablet?"

"At this point, it feels like I'm bringing the evidence to my own trial." Chief sounded fretful, and his color gained a slightly greenish tint.

"Stop making yourself seem so guilty. Just bring it up."

"Say please."

"You damn shiny melon, would you just do it?"

As Kaiden ranted, seemingly to himself, Soni watched with raised eyebrows. She noticed Flynn and Silas looking at him with annoyance rather than surprise.

"Does this happen often?" she asked.

Silas shrugged. "Often enough for us to get used to it. It's kinda funny every once in a while."

"A bit bizarre the first few times," Flynn admitted. "But I guess when your EI is your mental roommate, there's gonna be some tension every now and then."

"I suppose that can certainly explain the rise in blood pressure," she mused, tapping a finger on her chin.

"And shove your damn EI chip into a smart toaster and beat it with a baby sledge," Kaiden finished with a huff.

"I didn't hear a single please in all of that." Chief grunted, his eye half-closed in disdain.

Kaiden felt his eye twitch, and he released an annoyed sigh. "Would you please upload the mission?"

"Well, I can't bring the full thing up unless I'm in a hub, but I can cast the info into her tablet." The EI vanished from the display and appeared on the corner of the tablet screen. *"Here ya go."*

A page showing a few pictures and several boxes of info appeared on the screen, and Kaiden handed it back to the professor. She took it and began reading, scrolling down the screen as if looking for a particular box before her eyes went wide. "Well, that certainly explains it."

"Explains what?" Kaiden asked.

"Oh... Good God almighty, no wonder y'all got out of those pods feeling like you were about ten different kinds of fucked up!" Chief exclaimed.

"What did you find?" Kaiden asked again.

Soni returned the tablet to Kaiden. He grabbed it and looked at it, his brow furrowed in concentration. "You see this?" Soni asked, pointing to a box on the bottom right corner of the screen. "These are the connection settings which dictate the level of intensity one may experience in the Animus and help with sensitivity. They are usually calibrated by the advisors during tests and training. For private usage, you are limited to a set number of maps and missions with preset connection settings, usually on the lower end, especially for Initiates."

Kaiden looked at the options.

Synchronicity: 5

Tangibility: 7

Equilibrium: 9

Kaiden coked his head. "These numbers are pretty low."

"It's on a one-to-ten scale, not out of one hundred," Soni corrected him dryly.

Flynn moved over, and Kaiden tilted the screen so he could see. The sniper's eyes nearly popped out of his head.

"Equilibrium of nine? What the bloody hell?"

"Nine? Seriously?" Cameron sputtered, leaning up on his bed.

Kaiden felt more than a little dazed—maybe even shell-shocked—as he handed the tablet to Silas, who looked at the screen for a moment before shaking his head. "That's a pretty damn big puzzle piece."

"What am I missing here?" Kaiden asked.

"Prep training," Flynn jeered. Kaiden narrowed his eyes at him.

"While there are more advanced options in the connection setting, synchronicity, tangibility, and equilibrium are the three primary functions," Soni explained.

"Synchronicity is kind of self-explanatory. It helps with syncing the Animus and the mind, makes the integration easier, and helps with things like field of view and controlling the five senses. It's usually kept mid-level," Silas explained. "Tangibility helps with things like object density and the feel of things. It makes things feel more *real*. It's not all that important in the beginning, so it's usually kept lower for initiates. That's why things usually disappear after we kill or destroy them."

"Equilibrium is a bastard, though," Flynn continued. "It controls how we experience the sensations inside the Animus. Synch helps with getting in the Animus and tang helps during your time in the Animus, but equi keeps it all flowing. It's how we can actually learn and gain SXP, but it also makes the experience more visceral."

"Are you guys trying to get gold stars or something?" Kaiden grumbled.

"They are trying to pass along helpful information. I would suggest you listen," Soni advised.

"I'll put it like this—synch builds a bridge to a world, tang builds that world, equi gives it life," Silas clarified, handing the tablet back to Kaiden and then reaching for his own jacket under his bed.

"So, with it set so high, it means that the barrier between us and what the Animus is projecting is lessened. Which is why, when we got blasted to bits, we were all so battered when we left," Flynn concluded.

"I getcha." Kaiden nodded, sitting back on his bed and looking over the connection settings again. "What do we usually have it on? The hits I've taken so far feel real enough."

"Typically, it's only between three and four," Soni stated.

"Good Lord," Kaiden marveled. "Yeah, I can see why we all felt like we actually got blown to bits."

"I'm not sure if y'all would have even been able to get out of the pods if it was at ten." Chief appeared back in Kaiden's display. *"I might have actually felt it."*

"You didn't notice it before we got out of the shuttle?" Kaiden asked.

"Nah, partner. EIs aren't in charge of loading in the map... well, the personal ones aren't," Chief stated. *"We simply help*

with the transfer. I don't automatically check all the mission or map info unless asked."

"So it's my fault, then?" Kaiden sneered.

"It's what I default to, usually. It's the safe bet," Chief remarked. *"But in this case, I would think whoever allowed you access to that map would really be the one to blame."*

"Gave me access to the map?" Kaiden inquired.

"An initiate should not be able to load this kind of map," Soni stated firmly, taking the tablet back from Kaiden. "Honestly, no student should. These sorts of maps are for the third-years—the victors. Even then, something like this is a no-win scenario, only used for specialized tests."

"Well, I guess that's something to look forward to in a couple years." Flynn chuckled, and Soni gave him a surprised look before coughing sheepishly into her hand.

"No-win scenario, huh?" Kaiden whispered. He turned and hopped off the table, putting on his jacket. "Thanks for the assistance, Doc. I'll be heading out now."

"Are you sure you're all right?" she asked. "We're not sure how you'll feel when the serum wears off."

"We managed to drag our crippled asses here without it, so I'm sure I can make it back to my dorm without a problem," Kaiden said as he walked past her. "After I see a certain someone."

He walked over to Cameron. "You gonna be all right?"

"I'll manage." The bounty hunter sounded cheerful though his expression spoke irritation. "Besides, gotta get better for our next suicide mission."

"I'll let one of y'all pick the next one, maybe get Raul or Luke to join us." He considered this for a moment. "At least bring Amber. That healing gun of hers would be great."

"No kidding," Cameron agreed.

Kaiden walked over to Jaxon. "I'm heading out now, Jax. Thanks for the help. I'll see you when you get back to the dorms. It'll be lonely with only me in the second level bunks."

Though the blob was still on his face, Jaxon gave him a thumbs-up. Kaiden wondered if he would have the same blue lines he had after he used the sponge, though they probably wouldn't be as prominent considering the Tsuna's skin was a darker blue.

He waved to the others as he left, exiting the medical bay and then the building in quick succession.

"Chief, could you send a message to Laurie and tell him I'm on my way?"

"It has been a while since we've seen him. Maybe he'll put up streamers."

Though Kaiden could believe the eccentric professor would be that giddy to see him after more than a month, he was hoping that he would have more than decorations.

He was looking for answers.

CHAPTER TEN

"Kaiden my boy!" exclaimed the excited professor as Kaiden stepped out of the elevator and into his office.

"Hey, Laurie, how you been?" he asked, his tone more casual than honestly caring.

"Working my fingers to the bone. The board has had my team and me working on dozens of different projects of late." The professor looked momentarily distracted as he poured some wine into a small rounded glass. "Frankly, I'm beginning to wonder if they are just giving me busy work."

"Not the kind of jobs you were hoping for?" Kaiden inquired as he drew one of the cream-colored chairs in front of Laurie's desk back and took a seat.

"It's menial labor. Maintenance, for the most part, a few projects on the expansion of the island, some new scenarios and maps for the Animus, but nothing with dazzle." He sighed and sipped his wine.

"Maybe they don't want you working on the next death

machine while the council is working on alien relations? A giant walking carrier-tank hybrid has a way of making the out-of-worlders a bit skittish."

The professor scoffed. "Wulfson told you that the machine from the test was mine?"

"Eventually," Kaiden muttered, sucking his teeth after the admission when he caught Laurie's scowl. "He only mentioned it in passing a couple of weeks back."

"I thought he was going to use it for personal training, not drop it in the middle of the Soldier Division Test," Laurie protested.

Kaiden waved him off. "It's all good. He told me he was the one that put it in. It gave me a bit more…incentive to pummel him during our sparring match."

Laurie placed his glass on his desk and rested his chin on his closed fists. "How has that been going?"

"Well enough. That gigantic asshole keeps me on my toes. I've grown kind of fond of him over the months. Although if he has done the same for me, he apparently shows love through electric rounds and knees to the head." Kaiden snorted, leaned back in his chair, and crossed his arms. "Tough love is bullshit."

"But he hasn't left any permanent damage? He gives you time to rest, correct?"

"A day a week, maybe. I've been patched up by Dr. Soni every few days. Nothing I can't handle." He looked at Laurie with a suspicious eye. "After all, it wouldn't be a good deal for him if the important part of his deal was in broke pieces, would it?"

Laurie took another sip as he looked away from Kaiden. He finished his drink and sat back in his chair. "So he informed you of that, did he? I should have been more mindful to remind him to keep that a secret."

Kaiden smirked. "To be fair, he only told me that you pointed him in my direction. I figured the deal out for myself."

"Quite impressive of you. How did you manage that?"

"Well, you just confirmed it, for starters." Kaiden's smile widened as Laurie frowned a little. "But I had to figure something was going on. Wulfson said that he wanted to restart his little Scandinavian dojo, or whatever you would call it, but I've been his only focus since he dragged me in there. Besides, it seemed a little weird to me that he suddenly wanted to take on an apprentice or ward or whatever the hell he considers me right out of the blue."

Laurie's frown turned into a small smile. "I certainly approve of your deduction skills. You grow more dynamic every time I see you."

"Compliments are always good for the ego. And as much as I would enjoy getting a few more, and however much I would also like to know *why* you sent Wulfson my way, I have a different reason for being here."

"And what would that be?" the professor inquired.

Kaiden pointed to the drawer on Laurie's left, indicating to him to bring out the EI pad.

"Something else wrong with your EI?" Laurie asked as he retrieved the pad and set it on the table.

Kaiden removed his oculars. and whipped them at the pad. Chief appeared. "I wouldn't say problems, but me and a few friends of mine have had a rather interesting day today in the Animus."

"What happened?" Laurie asked.

"I had a mission which took place in Houston during the incursion of 2097," Kaiden responded, watching Laurie's face for tells.

"I ran through the synopsis with them. It seemed like a reenactment mission, nothing too surprising. But they had to deal with waves and waves of junkers and cracked security droids and only a few terrorists in the first wave." Chief sounded clipped and overly polite.

"I see…" Laurie hummed and looked at his computer. "Continue."

"There were supposed to be five waves, but we'd dealt with three when a countdown started on the fourth wave. Chief told us that during the fifth wave, we were supposed to hold out for reinforcements and pick-up, but all the bots we destroyed simply exploded at the end of the count-down."

"They didn't disappear?" Laurie asked. "The tangibility setting should have only been around three for an initiate. You do know about the connection settings, correct?"

Kaiden nodded. "I got a crash course about twenty minutes ago."

"You didn't find it strange that the bodies didn't disappear?" Laurie asked.

"Take a look at the map's CS, Professor. It wasn't exactly a normal scenario," Chief pointed out.

Laurie scrolled down the screen, his eyes widening in surprise. "These setting are far too advanced for initiates. Only second-class victors and above would use a map of this scale, and only with advisor supervision."

"Dr. Soni said the same thing, roughly," Kaiden confirmed.

"The synch is high enough that you would be too engaged to truly notice the bodies remaining during the mission… And an equi of nine? Good Lord, that must have been a painful experience for the lot of you," Laurie exclaimed.

"It took us about an hour and a half of sitting around to get enough strength to start stretching for another half-hour before we could make it to the med bay."

Laurie's eyes darted away from the screen. "You didn't get your EI to call for a retrieval?"

"No. One of my partners was a Tsuna. He said he was worried they would be pulled out if word got back that one had been seriously injured this early on. We also thought it was nothing more than a mixture of high Animus oscillation and the fact that we were literally in the middle of a massive explosion," Kaiden explained.

The professor sighed, going back over his screen. "I see…understandable. I have to say, working with many of the Tsuna delegates has been an exhausting venture. Good people, for the most part, and fascinating science applications. Though they appear to be worriers in general, or at least the political clans are. Much prefer to work with Mirus."

"Speaking of which, I got to meet Dr. Mortis last night." Kaiden glowered. "His bedside manner could use a little work."

"Emotions don't come easily to them. Or I suppose it would be better to say that emotions aren't as heightened for them. It may take some work getting used to it for most, but it has made both political and scientific collaborations much smoother, not to mention interesting."

"Glad you get to have fun every now and then," Kaiden jeered. "Perhaps we should get back to the task at hand?"

"Yes, of course." Laurie nodded. "My guess is that your question is how you were able to get access to this map?"

"Yeah. I was the only one who had it. The others couldn't bring it up."

"It only came up when Kaiden cast me into the hub," Chief clarified.

"Then that would mean…" Laurie swiped something on the screen, tapping on his holo-board for a few seconds before he cocked his head thoughtfully. "This is quite interesting." He flipped the monitor around, showing Kaiden a list with five maps in it. "These maps are victor or master designation level. They cannot be accessed without authorization. For victors, it requires the proper class and pre-approval, and for the master class, it requires an advisor to supervise and for combatants to be victor first-class."

"So how the hell do I have them? I'm an initiate second-class."

"That would be the center of the mystery, wouldn't it?" Laurie pointed to a green circle next to Kaiden's name on the top of the screen. "This means these maps have been approved for you by someone higher up."

Kaiden leaned forward. "By who, exactly? I don't remember any of the teachers or staff telling me about it."

"None of them would have the ability either, at least not to clear maps this difficult for private use."

"Then who would—" Kaiden blinked, looking at the screen and then at Laurie. "Did Sasha clear them? Does he want to test me too?"

"No, I do not believe Sasha would do something so

harsh." Laurie slid the monitor back around "Not to mention that it would be quite immature for him not to tell you—or me, for that matter."

"Then I'm at a loss, unless you gave Wulfson a bunch of maps and he's having a laugh at my expense."

Laurie chuckled. "That is something he would be liable to do, but no, even *he* wouldn't give you something like this. Too much to handle in the beginning."

"We did fine," Kaiden insisted. "We would probably have won—maybe, though it was a little dicey at the end. But this was a no-win situation. The explosion covered at least a quarter of the city."

"I can definitely tell you that's not in the history books." Chief chortled. *"A headline like 'Chunk of city went ka-blooey' would have been archived."*

"You're certainly correct there...give me a moment." Laurie continued to tap his board, his eyes scanning along the screen.

"What are you looking for?" Kaiden asked.

"I'm scanning through the programming of the map. For the most part, it doesn't seem to be anything other than a reconstruction of Houston at the time of the insurrection. Let me check the mission programming."

"If something was drastically different, you would probably have picked up on it, right, Chief?"

Chief whirled around to look at Kaiden. *"Yeah, I wasn't actively looking for anything like that, but if the parameters changed or the main objective was switched, I would have informed y'all."*

"That would explain it," Laurie muttered, causing

Kaiden and Chief to look at him. "The mission programming itself has been changed."

"I didn't notice anything. And something like that ain't gonna get past me."

"I admire your pride, you wonderful little powder puff," Laurie cooed, smiling at the EI.

"Hey!" Chief shouted. His eye furrowed and he took on a raging red hue.

"Have to remember that when I need new insults," Kaiden instructed himself. "So how could the mission change and neither Chief nor any of the other EIs not notice?"

"The new parameters were sneaked in. They changed it in such a way that when certain events were triggered, they switched to the new commands. It made the scenario seem like it was running according to plan. No reason for you or your EIs to think anything was amiss."

"Until the apocalypse came a-knockin'," Chief finished grimly.

"Can you figure out who changed them?" Kaiden asked.

"Not without rigorous digging. It will require more time, possibly days."

"Grand. I love a slow-burn." Kaiden responded with angry sarcasm, sliding down in his chair and now thoroughly deflated.

"On the positive side, whoever changed it is also probably responsible for giving you the clearance in the first place—or at least is aware of who did." Laurie sat back, tapping his fingers on the desktop before flashing the ace a smile. "Not to worry, dear Kaiden. I don't think it was anything malicious. Things like this happen—rarely, of course,—but usually, there's a mix-up and some lower years will get some higher difficulty missions by accident."

"What about the changes to the scenario?" Kaiden asked.

Chief turned around, his color changing back to its natural blue. *"Well, the doc did say that this is usually used in special tests. Maybe it was changed for an upcoming test for the victors?"*

"Quite probable. The no-win scenario is a fundamental test for victors to get them to understand the feeling of failure and how to keep oneself composed. It also has the benefit of showing one's true character during times of hopelessness," Laurie noted. "Although we try to keep these things under wraps, I guess we'll have to be a little more careful in the future to keep it a surprise."

"At least from me and the others." Kaiden chuckled.

"Mind telling me their names?"

Kaiden rolled his eyes. "I ain't a snitch, Prof."

"Perhaps not. You do seem slow, however."

"What the hell are you talkin' about?" Kaiden bridled at the affront.

Laurie tapped next to the EI pad. "Since I had your EI hooked up, I took a look around and noticed you hadn't used your synapse points yet."

This time, Kaiden shifted uncomfortably and avoided the professor's look of accusation. "Yeah, right, I was going to get to that…"

"You said that the last time you were here. That was six weeks ago when you had three points, and now you have almost seven."

"Almost seven? I was halfway to six this morning."

Kaiden placed his oculars back on and looked at his personal data, seeing that he now had six points and was just shy of a seventh. "Well, damn, even failure comes with perks."

"Now that I have you here..." Kaiden saw the professor press a button under his desk. He heard the elevator behind him lock, while another appeared behind Laurie. "I must insist, as a member of the teaching staff and as the patron of your EI device, that you accompany me to the Animus so that we can get this little matter sorted."

"Ha! He's got you now, dumbass," Chief chirped, his eye squinting in delight at Kaiden's current predicament.

"As for you, Mr. Chief..." Laurie continued, and Chief turned, his eye wide.

"Me? What the hell did I do? And why is everybody picking on me today?"

"I recall requesting from you that you make sure your partner did spend his points and apply them as soon as possible."

"It wasn't my fault, Professor, honest. I tried to badger him into doing it, but he always ignored me," Chief declared, shifting into a sad dark-blue hue.

"You rat bastard." Kaiden fumed, grabbing at the EI's hologram on the pad in anger.

"He threatened to put me into a toaster and bash me to pieces."

"That was for something else entirely."

"Now, now, the both of you, calm down please," Laurie chided, rather like a nanny with her charges. "This will only take a moment, Kaiden. Come on, now. You're wasting precious resources and one of the main draws of the Academy."

Kaiden scratched the back of his head. "I know, but I just... I guess I don't know why I haven't spent the points. It doesn't seem earned."

"Of course it's earned. Through your hard work, you have gathered enough SXP to further your skills and ambitions, and it is up to you to spend them how you see fit."

Kaiden stood up slowly "This isn't gonna take long right? I still have training with Wulfson, and it's getting late."

"I'll send a message to Wulfson and tell him you are with me. It shouldn't take too long, and the rest of your night is free. Another thing you've earned." Laurie chuckled.

Kaiden nodded, accepting the inevitable, and walked around Laurie's desk and into the elevator. "Uh, aren't you coming?" he asked the professor who was still seated.

Laurie turned back to his computer. "Go to the theater, third floor. I'll be up soon. I need to send a few messages first."

Kaiden shrugged. "See you there then. Try not to be too long, all right? Your droids seem skittish around me."

"They don't bite."

"Maybe not, but they have lasers," Kaiden retorted before pressing the button for the third floor. The elevator doors closed with a faint hiss.

Laurie waited for the sound of the elevator ascending and took his hands off his holo-board. "Aurora?"

"Yes, sir?" an ethereal voice asked. A hologram appeared on his table—a female figure with a body made of glowing

lines and long hair composed of shimmering lights that faded in and out of existence.

"I need you to contact Sasha. Tell him we need to meet tonight. It would appear someone in the Council found a new way to play with us."

CHAPTER ELEVEN

"Are you there, Kaiden?" Laurie's voice echoed around him. Kaiden opened his eyes. He was surrounded by and standing on darkness, a lone light emitting somewhere above him.

"Ah, memories." Kaiden rolled his shoulders. "It's my favorite map. 'An eternal abyss that you will never leave until the madness finally consumes you.'"

"It is actually called 'Dead Space,'" Laurie corrected.

"That's...better?"

"Less rambly, certainly," Chief noted, floating from behind Kaiden's back to face him.

"It's simply a place-holder map. We're going to run through your talent options here and, should you wish, I'll load a map for you to get a bit of practice with your new and improved abilities."

Kaiden swiveled his head, hearing a loud crack when he turned quickly to his left. "I guess we'll see. I think Dr.

Soni's serum is starting to wear off. Apparently, pain from the real world transfers into the Animus...oh, joy."

"You'll do all right. I'm monitoring you all the way," Laurie assured him. "For now, let's bring up your synapse trees."

Four different windows appeared in front of Kaiden. They were labeled General, Soldier, Ace, and EI. They split apart and circled around him, and he took a brief look at each one. "Where should I start?"

"With whatever you feel is best." Kaiden saw a holographic vision of Laurie appear before him. "You earned the points, so you should decide where they go."

"You don't have to do that avatar thing, Laurie. I'm pretty used to this now."

"I'm sure, but I always feel that my presence lightens the mood and improves the situation," Laurie declared with a flourish of his hand.

"You certainly add...something when you're around," Kaiden agreed amicably. He looked at the different trees. "I guess looking through Soldier and Ace is probably the least valuable right now."

"How do you figure?" Chief asked.

"I'm already doing workshops for my class, and when I'm doing missions, it's as a soldier. Plus, I think I've plenty well demonstrated that I know how to work a gun."

"Oh, certainly," Laurie agreed. His avatar hovered over Kaiden in the air, smiling at him like the Cheshire Cat. "However, can you do more than just 'work it,' as you say?"

Kaiden stared at the floating professor for a moment whose eyes were half-closed and non-reactive. He looked up into the darkness above. "You know, the floating professor thing is actually not conducive to my learning at the moment."

"Hey, it made you say 'conducive.' Extra points for scrabble," Chief chirped.

"It also adds pizzazz." The hologram smiled. "If that is your choice, then so be it. You'll gather more points in due time. However, the higher your level, the slower you'll gain new ones, so I would suggest you take a second look at all the trees to be sure you aren't passing up the opportunity to get an edge."

"Fine, I'll shop around," Kaiden acquiesced. "But the whole getting levels slower thing wouldn't be as much of a pain if I got the SXP boost you promised me before shoving that device into my skull."

"Ah, yes, about that. I've actually had the update complete for a couple months now."

"You what?" Kaiden shouted, reaching out for the professor before stumbling through his intangible form.

"You really don't seem to understand that holograms can't be touched, huh?" Chief chuckled.

"I saw no point in giving it to you if you hadn't yet used the points that you had," the professor explained, drifting lazily through the air. "What point is there in you having extra points if you're merely going to leave them to rot?"

"I said I was getting to it."

"And yet here you are." Laurie shrugged. "So, I had an interesting idea."

"Oh, God, no," Kaiden mumbled. "What did you do?"

Laurie crossed his arms and raised an eyebrow. "Don't sound so aghast. It makes me think you believe I'm some sort of mad scientist or something."

"You live in opulence in a building filled with technicians that do your every bidding, you spend most of your time making robots and machines that connect to people minds, and most people seem to think you've disappeared or are in hiding… All you're missing is a cat."

"First of all, I don't use my technology for evil means but for the advancement of humanity and our galactic neighbors. Second…I do have a cat, actually."

He reached out an arm, and a white-furred Persian cat appeared in his hand. "His name is Schrodinger."

Chief floated up to Kaiden's ear. *"I'm not feeling too good about that cat's future,"* he whispered.

"I'll have you know that I can hear you," Laurie said, stroking the feline. "And that I quite love my cat and it has a wonderful future ahead—"

"Could have, maybe it won't, we can't tell until it happens," Kaiden interjected, really not keen on being distracted by a cat and looking to end a potential argument quickly.

"As long as you continue being that smart when you make your choices, this will be a fruitful evening." The professor landed on the ground, walked over to the General talent window in front of Kaiden, and moved it to the side with one hand while the other continued to hold the cat. He replaced the General window with the EI tree window. "Getting back to the task at hand, I decided to leave your bonuses up to you."

Kaiden eyed him quizzically. "What do you mean?"

Laurie smiled as he expanded the window, showing all the options in the tree. "The bonuses that I said you would receive...I changed them into talents." He pointed at several boxes for emphasis.

"What the hell? Why?" Kaiden barked a scornful laugh that held affront rather than amusement. "You said I would get them with the implant."

"And you still can," Laurie assured him. "Just in due time and at your own discretion."

"I thought we had a deal." Kaiden sneered at the hologram, wishing he could shake the imaginary figure to vent his frustrations.

"We certainly do. I had you sign a contract before the procedure, remember? I'll let you look it over again when this is done if you like, but nothing I've done invalidates the agreement."

"Man, gotcha hook, line, and sinker there, bud." Chief chortled.

Laurie frowned slightly. "Kaiden, you must relax. Your blood pressure and heart rate are increasing rapidly."

Kaiden could feel a twitch in his eye again, and his hands balled into fists. Anger wouldn't do much good as the only thing he could hit was himself, but that also felt deserved.

"Semantics are a bitch..." He sighed, unclenched his fists, and relaxed his shoulders.

"To some, certainly, but quite helpful to others. Besides, this is to help you actually use your points. I didn't make them some unachievable goal. Look here, right at the top."

Kaiden looked at the talent Laurie pointed out.

SXP Boost: Allows for a fifteen percent boost to SXP Gain with each point.

Status: 0/4 (1 SP to unlock)

JOSHUA ANDERLE & MICHAEL ANDERLE

"Only one? So I can get all of them with four points?" He read the description again. "I thought the boost was only fifty percent?"

"It was, based on the fact that it would be loaded in all at once. But since it will be done in increments, I was able to find a way to get a bit more out of it for you. My treat."

"How unbelievably kind of you. And in a way, I'm sure, that doesn't get you anything in return," Kaiden quipped.

Laurie examined the fingernails on his free hand. "I like to show off my generosity and skills in equal measure. As for the points, for each one you put in, the next upgrade will require one more point until you get all four upgrades."

"Meaning it will take ten points to get the full usage," Kaiden surmised.

"Still, you're getting the boost, so it'll even out eventually. You'll get your dollars' worth and all that," Chief pointed out.

"I suppose you're right." Kaiden looked over the rest of the tree. "What else do we have?"

Advanced Battle Suite: Allows for longer usage of the Battle Suite without repercussions to the user, also increases awareness and movement speed.

Status: 0/2 (1 SP to unlock)

"Ohh, that would be nice." Kaiden crowed, already imagining the possibilities.

"Ya don't really use the suite that much as it is," Chief said. *"Even when you should, like with the laser-shark incident."*

"You love to remind me of that. Besides, why the hell do sharks need lasers? They're sharks."

"With lasers, which destroyed your armor and turned you into a chewy hors-d'oeuvre for the swimming nightmare blenders

that would have killed your dumb ass if Luke hadn't swatted them away with that unreasonably big hammer of his."

"Is that the Isle of the Fiend map?" Laurie inquired. "A team of my technicians made it for fun. It got quite popular with the class of 2183, but I always thought it could have used a mutant giant squid."

"What exactly do you think about in your free time?" Kaiden grimaced.

"Mutant giant squids. And I'm sure other imaginative things," Chief said with surprising sincerity.

Kaiden pointed to the orb. "Did you do something to him? Or has he always been a suck-up and I simply haven't noticed?"

"Well, I am technically the father of all EIs on this island."

Kaiden shook his head. "At least I haven't heard you call him Daddy."

"Not that it concerns me, but I think even I would find that creepy," the EI admitted.

Kaiden chuckled as he went back to look at the options.

Next-Gen: Increases EI processing, scanning, and hacking capabilities.

Status: 0/3 (1 SP to unlock)

"Hey, look, we can make you smart." Kaiden jeered.

"Pity we can't do the same for you."

"Chirpy bastard."

Increased Casting: Increases the range (15m) that the EI can cast and the distance allowed between the user and EI before losing connection.

Status: Locked (Requires at least 1 upgrade into 'Next-Gen')

"Hey, Prof, how does this work?" Kaiden asked,

pointing to the talent. "I thought the casting ability was tied to the implant, not to Chief."

The professor nodded. "It is, but the ability is latent. I shut down or decreased certain functions before installing it into you."

"Please find another way to say that." Kaiden winced.

"Oh, hush. The more you increase Chief's capabilities, the more options you will have further down the line."

"Kinda seems like a waste though, if you think about it." Kaiden considered the potential regretfully.

The professor continued to stroke his cat. "How do you mean?"

"Some of this stuff is useful in the long-term, but other things seem like they would only be useful while I'm here. I'm only here for three years, so it would kind of be a waste to put anything in those sorts of talents, yeah?"

"That would be a reasonable observation," Laurie agreed. "However, think of it like this—what can you get out of those talents while you are here, and what makes you think the Animus is the only place that it is useful?"

Kaiden gave him another quizzical look. "Do you speak in riddles to mess with me, or is it some weird habit?"

"I believe you've asked me that before." Laurie chuckled. "Sasha, too, come to think of it."

"I'm simply hoping I don't pick up the habit while I'm here." Kaiden flipped through the different trees once more.

General:

Rider: Increases knowledge of grounded vehicles and skill while driving them.

Status: 0/3

Gear Head: Increases knowledge of most basic machinery (such as engines, appliances, simple electrical devices, etc.)

Status: 0/3

Culinary: Teaches the basics of cooking, along with granting fifty recipes chosen and created by Nexus Academy chefs.

Status: 0/10

"Lots a lot of damn points to put into Culinary..." Kaiden observed and followed it with a low whistle

"Yeah, someone probably had a field day trying so many dishes that they had to write it off as 'testing' for a talent. You think anyone ever has?"

"Maybe you can combine it with poison or something, get multiple uses out of it."

"Good idea, maybe bake a cake with explosives too...roll that devil's food right into a merc camp and really catch them off guard."

Kaiden raised an eyebrow. "Are you being serious right now or was that a joke?"

Chief's eye looked away, puzzled. *"I started it as a joke, but I kinda grew into the idea by the end."*

Soldier:

Shock and Awe: Increases ability with heavy weapons and explosives.

Status: 0/5

Martial-Boxing: Increases hand-to-hand combat ability and knowledge of boxing form and attacks.

Status: 0/5

Martial- Jiu Jitsu: Increases physical defensive form and teaches grapples and holds from the Jiu-Jitsu martial art.

Status: 0/5

Armor Smith: Grants the user knowledge of various armors,

their capabilities, and functions. Teaches the user how to repair their armor in the field and what enhancements would be most beneficial.

Status: 0/5

"That could actually be quite handy." Kaiden contemplated the options and their potential with growing interest.

"I suppose, but I've got all sorts of info about armor in my banks, plus instructions on how to do all that."

"True, but actually having the information would be nice, rather than trying to read a manual in the middle of a firefight."

Chief laughed. At least, that's what it sounded like. *"No, the Phillips' head is for the shoulder plate. The flathead is for the nipple guards."*

Ace:

Surveyor: Learn how to read and create maps along with the different elements and terrain of the world and how to best deal with them or use them to your advantage.

Status: 0/4

Botanist: Learn about all the different flora and fauna of the world, and how to grow and cultivate them along with how to make remedies or poisons using them.

Status: 0/5

Guardian: Reduces the number of active pain receptors, allowing the user to push through even the toughest predicaments.

Status: 0/5

"That sounds risky."

"Probably would have helped out today," Chief goaded.

Kaiden shrugged. "I mean...yeah, but you need a little pain. It tells you when you need to improve."

"And where you're getting stabbed or shot."

He looked at the floating orb, giving him an annoyed stare. "The bullets flying in my direction and the knife stuck inside me gives me plenty of info on that front."

"Touché."

Strategic Mind: Learn dozens of strategies per upgrade and how to apply them in the field, increasing your ability as a leader.

Status: 0/10

"Another one with a lot of points."

"But this one is far more useful to you than cooking."

"I agree." Kaiden nodded. "Strategy is a weak point for me. I usually—"

"Wing it, and that's great and all, but we could always have some proven stats in the back of your mind to help out every now and again."

"You think I should go for it?"

"I certainly think it would help. Plus, it's only one point. Might as well choose something to get this train rolling."

Kaiden looked down for a moment, considering his decision. For some reason, he was still reluctant to commit himself, a truth that stirred his natural impatience. He took a deep breath and pressed the icon for the skill, holding it down as it loaded.

"And here we go." Laurie smiled.

In a flash, he could see battles throughout history, hear the commands, and see actions taking place. Visions and sounds blurred together until he was back in the dark space, the feeling over almost as soon as it began.

"Man, even I felt something weird going on. You all right?"

"Yeah…yeah, I'm all right. It was just…intense." Kaiden looked at Laurie. "I've got all this…the new memories and ideas. Did it work?"

Laurie tapped a finger against his cheek. "You are in a group of fifty soldiers, the hostile forces are coming at you through a ravine in which you are at the end. They are better armed with almost twice the men, but you and your men are in a defensible position. What do you do?"

"Send all the marksman to the top of the ravine, while the heavies take the front and form a wall, with medics standing by to heal after any attacks that get through while the gunners fire from the defense of the heavies. Make it seem like a last stand while the marksmen take position and eventually take out enough of the enemy forces from their higher vantage point that the enemy cannot return fire to. This will lead to the end of the enemy or their surrender with minimal casualties." Kaiden relayed the information in a rapid fire of words, catching his breath as he finished. His eyes flashed in amazement.

"Ah, the Lecrae scenario, a classic. He didn't lose a man that day," Laurie said wistfully. "I would say it worked just fine."

"No kidding," Kaiden stammered, a little awed by the change though he took care not to show it.

Laurie chuckled as the cat disappeared from his hands. "Congratulations on choosing your first talent, Kaiden my boy." He clapped cheerfully. "Now, once you've gotten over that initial shock…" His clapping slowed, and he clasped his hands behind his back. "You've got five more points to go."

CHAPTER TWELVE

The group of Red Sun mercs walked up to the gate of their stronghold. The leader, dressed head to toe in heavy crimson armor and a horned helmet with a full-face visor, held a modified Reaver shotgun as he walked up to the gate. He knocked slowly five times.

"Password?" a voice asked, coming from a panel to the left of the large doors. The leader grunted as he made his way over.

He placed his hand against a scanner on the panel, looking at the shadowed figure on the screen. "Junk Fiend." He earned a small nod from the man onscreen.

"Good to see you again, Lord Malek. What brings you to our humble fortress?" the retainer asked.

"Hurry up and open the gates. We have a shipment of assassin and raider droids here, and I want to have a chat with Lalo," Malek answered, his gruff voice accentuated by a crackling voice modifier in his helmet.

The man nodded one last time before the screen turned

off. The large doors of the gate began to open, sliding into the walls beside them. Malek turned to the mercs, pointing them at the entrance, and commanded them to move.

One in the front nodded, turned to the three dozen behind him, and waved them forward. Their caravan began to move through the gates and into the stronghold.

The grounds of the Red Sun base consisted of dozens of tents, large, nondescript warehouses, buildings cobbled together, and a handful of slightly dilapidated structures left behind by the previous owners of the site. The Red Sun mercs had personally "evicted" them around a year ago. No one had come to look for them yet, either because they were too afraid to see what happened to them or because they knew there would be nothing left of them to find.

The caravan, comprised of three floating storage units holding twenty droids apiece, maneuvered its way through, heading to the holding warehouse where the devices could be examined and activated. They entered the building, which stood mostly empty save for some random technical devices in the corner that had yet to be dealt with. Several handy-droids—humanoid-design robots—approximately six feet tall, with long limbs, rounded heads, and only a single large, blue, glowing eye and white bodies, were also present. Dirty from their work and the jungle terrain, they walked around the floor, cleaning or moving a few objects into place.

One of the bots approached Malek. *"Good day, sir. Anything that I can help you with?"*

Malek placed the barrel of his shotgun against the droid's chest. "You can get the contents of these containers ready for processing. Until then, get out of my face." He sneered as he pushed the bot back with his gun for emphasis.

"Of course, sir, right away. Sorry to be too close to your face," the droid acknowledged and apologized. The containers halted in the middle of the warehouse and moved around to line up side-by-side. The mercs with the caravan left the shipment, following Malek out of the warehouse and to the center of the stronghold.

The handy-droid that Malek had talked to made its way over to one of the computers on the side of the building. It reached out to the dirty keyboard but froze for a moment, though this hesitation was nothing any of the others would notice. Their state of general disrepair caused this to happen from time-to-time. It began to move again and punched a command into the computer that would temporarily freeze and then block any incoming signals to the warehouse.

That successfully accomplished, it shuffled over to the storage container in the middle, unlocked it, and opened the doors. Chiyo stepped out and onto the floor.

She nodded at the droid. "Thank you. Please unlock the other containers and stand by."

The droid bowed before walking to the container behind them.

"Madame, now that we can break our silence, I must stress that this mission is not particularly well fitted to our strengths, if you'll forgive me," Kaitō pleaded.

"I know, Kaitō, and I do forgive you—as I have the last several times you've told me during the mission," Chiyo muttered as she walked over to the computer station on the side of the building.

"This is one of the more difficult missions available to you, madame, and it is meant for teams of at least three, and a trinity at that. A technician, a soldier, a medic...something along those lines would make this a lot smoother."

Chiyo removed a tether device from her gauntlet and placed it into a slot on the computer. She activated her holo-board and interface. "I agree, but for now, I need to practice missions like this to prepare for the tests at the end of the semester."

"And I applaud your dedication to study, but this mission is much more...hands-on than you are accustomed to, and the equilibrium is scaled to five. That is slightly higher than normal, and considering the foes you are facing—"

"That's why I'm going to even the odds. In a moment, after I've made sure no one will be able to trace me easily."

"Just do be careful," the EI fretted.

"I'll do my—" Chiyo went silent as she heard a door in the back open. She ducked down behind the station, glancing over to see a single merc walk over to the random assortment of devices in the corner and pull a few things out.

She grunted a low sound of annoyance. There was no time to wait and see if he would leave on his own. She had to move fast. She opened a command panel on her holo-board for Kaitō, pressing the command for him to take control of the previously hacked droid. The droid looked at her with a quick nod of acknowledgment.

Stealthily, she opened a panel to input manual commands, typing her instructions quickly while she remained silent. Realizing she had actually been holding her breath, Chiyo exhaled, finished and sent the commands, then watched as the droid moved to the grunt, grabbing a bolter off a tool shelf on the way.

She peered out from behind the station again as Kaitō walked up to the guard who was crouched down, looking at a power-core. He sensed the movement and looked up at the droid, then stood and seemed to say something before noticing the open containers. Obviously concerned now, he pointed to the problem, exposing his neck while reaching out. Kaitō pressed the bolter against the non-armored area and pulled the trigger. The guard staggered back, holding his neck with one hand while trying to grab the rifle on his back with the other. Chiyo winced as large swaths of blood flew about as the guard struggled before he collapsed on the floor.

Kaitō hid the body in the corner. Chiyo closed her eyes and took in a couple of deep breaths before continuing her work. After a couple of minutes, Kaitō returned, holding the merc's rifle. *"For you, madame, so that you have some additional defense over and above your pistol."*

She gave Kaitō a small smile as she took the weapon. "Thank you, but I wouldn't be able to use it all that well. I don't have much training with rifles and haven't put any points into general firearms skill."

"Just keep it with you. I worry."

Chiyo nodded and stood the rifle against the wall. "Thank you, Kaitō," she said in a whisper. "However, you should also consider yourself when you talk about being worried." She stood, placing the rifle on her back using the magnetic strips, and walked over to the containers. Kaitō followed, still in the handy-droid. "It won't be long before they detect that someone has meddled with their systems."

She pressed a button on her lapel, changing her armor to the colors and emblem of the Red Sun mercs. "So, it's time we created a little distraction." She stood in front of the containers of assassin and raider droids and turned to Kaitō. "You have a preference?"

The droid looked over the other bots for a moment. The raider droids, colored a grimy brown, were stronger and better armored with their right arm able to transform into a powerful blaster and a machine gun in the gauntlet of their left. The assassin droids, colored a dark pitch, had blades hidden in compartments under both arms and around the ankles and single shotguns on the top of their arms, which were faster and more agile. *"I'm partial to the assassin droids, myself, madame."*

Chiyo nodded. "Good choice." She pressed a button on her console. The droids all activated, amber lights glowing in the eyes of the raiders while a white ring formed around the heads of the assassin droids, indicating that their 360- degree sight was active, before the light disappeared as they activated their stealth mode. The droids began marching out of the containers, walking past Chiyo as she observed them with interest. "Take your pick, Kaitō."

"What do you want, Malek?" Lalo snapped, her remaining eye staring him down as her ten bodyguards paced the room.

"I want to know when I'm going to get paid," he responded, six of his men flanking him as he walked into the Red Sun leader's room. "My group and me have done three missions without pay."

"I would hardly call them missions." She huffed, staring him down. "Glorified escorting, perhaps, and I've seen the reports. You've been skimming from the war chest for each of those missions."

"Unless you want an incident in the news, I have to find creative ways to keep nearly forty blood-thirsty mercs occupied while you have us do tasks meant for grunts." He slammed his hands on her table.

"You'll get paid when you stop your bullshit," she retorted, brushing her red locks out her face and revealing a silver patch over her left eye. "If you're that strapped for cash, I could get you work doing a more specific type of escorting," she suggested with a sly smirk.

Malek's hands tightened around the edge of the desk. "I swear on my life, one day I will—" He didn't finish his threat as loud blasts and frantic screams rang from outside. "What the hell?"

Lalo stood, grabbing her helmet and machine gun. "Everybody out!" The mercs obeyed, running immediately into utter chaos. Raider and assassin droids tore rapidly through the Red Sun mercs, blowing some away and skewering others while destroying buildings and trashing their equipment.

"Those are the droids you brought here, Malek," Lalo accused, aiming her machine gun at him "Was this your plan?"

He turned to her, his own gun raised. "This ain't me. I had nothi—*hurgh!*" he cried as an assassin droid yanked his head back to pierce his neck with a blade. The droid let go, and Malek's body dropped to the floor. The others began to fire on it quickly, but it danced and weaved around the bullets, shooting two mercs in the hip and slicing another's neck with a blade on its ankle as it disappeared into the fray.

"Dammit!" Lalo growled the expletive. She was silent for a moment as the other guards around her continued to fire and advance. Her mind racing, she grabbed one of her officers by his shoulder. "We're getting out of here. Prepare the shuttle," she stated coldly before releasing him. "I'm going to open the pen."

Chiyo made her way quickly inside the main building in the center of the stronghold, trying to find the leader's computer. The building was empty, but she knew she would be visible on the cams. Hopefully, her change in armor would fool them long enough to not raise suspicion —if there was even anyone manning the security systems at all.

She finally found the leader's room, placed her tether into a slot in the computer, and began to break in. Calm now, she focused, looking for maps of other Red Sun locations, itineraries, shipping information, or anything of use.

"Have you found what you need yet, madame?" Kaitō asked over their comm link.

"Just about…I'm downloading as many files as possible. How are things going out there?"

"I suppose I would say splendid, considering what we're trying to accomplish. We have lost eight raiders and nine *assassin droids, but we should have enough left to make our escape."*

"Well done. I'll be out in a—" Chiyo stopped abruptly, and a chill flowed through her as she heard a scream, loud and frantic, and buzzing like a man was being electrocuted from within. "Oh, no," she stammered, her eyes widening. "Neurosiks."

"Miss Chiyo, there are—"

"I know, Kaitō. We need to go," she responded frantically, pulling her tether out before all the files could be transferred. She rushed from the room and out the building, stopping in shock as she viewed the scene before her.

Ghoulish beings in tattered rags and broken or decayed armor ran wild, tearing into anything that got in their path. Mercs were shoved to the ground, their skin burning as the demented fiends touched or clawed at them. The droids would fire or stab the attackers, but most would get back up or simply continue to run. They ignored the pain and ripped the droids apart or overloaded them so they blew apart.

Chiyo heard the sound of thrusters and turned to see a shuttle taking off. She ran in that direction, figuring it was her best chance to find another shuttle and escape rather than try to go through the gate.

She made her way to the airfield where more mercs fought off the Neurosiks, but they were simply too much for them, and most fell to the onslaught.

"Madame, where are you?" Kaitō asked worriedly.

"I'm at the airfield, looking for a shuttle to escape in," she responded, a little out of breath as she cut around the side of the massacre and into the hanger.

"I will join you as soon as I am able—" A scream of insanity and static sounded, and Kaitō went quiet.

"Kaitō? Kaitō? Are you all right?" Chiyo cried, making her way to the back of a hanger and hoping for a door.

"I am here, Miss Chiyo." Kaitō popped into the display. *"I'm sorry for worrying you. I was attacked by one of those monsters and had to separate from the droid before I was corrupted."*

"It's all right, Kaitō. I'm just glad you're safe." Chiyo drew a slow breath and willed her racing pulse to calm. She saw a crew shuttle at the far corner of the building and ran for it. "I'll need your help to get this shuttle running."

"Understood. I'll get the door."

The panel on the back of the shuttle slid open. Chiyo ran in, and it closed behind her. She ran to the front and hit the switch to power it up, the screen asking for clearance to activate flight controls. "Hack the system and get us airborne, Kaitō."

The fox avatar nodded and disappeared from the display. Chiyo began to activate everything else needed for takeoff when she heard a loud thud behind her. She turned to see the door to the shuttle ripped apart, and her breath hitched as she pulled the rifle Kaitō took from the guard. "How long until we can leave?"

"One minute and thirty-four seconds, madame. I don't think—"

"Keep going," she demanded, raising the rifle. "I'll see if I can hold them off. If we launch fast enough, the impetus should shake them off."

The door was finally torn open. Chiyo fired the rifle as fast as she could. She might not have the proper training, but she could at least shoot straight, especially this close to the insurgents.

The barrage of firepower had little effect, however.

The ghouls were almost on her, the laser fire from the rifle tearing into them but with little impact. They continued to shamble toward her, almost as if they were toying with their prey before the feast.

"Chiyo, you must abort. They will get to you before we can launch," Kaitō stated.

The rifle had overheated, and she dropped it as the heat burned her hands. Desperately, she reached for her pistol as she backed away across the few feet she had behind her.

"I am activating de-sync. We must go!" Kaitō yelled.

One of the Neurosiks hissed, a high-pitched noise of shrieks and electric droning. It leaped at her, knocking her to the ground as it raised a claw into the air. Flesh seared onto metal prongs.

The last thing Chiyo saw before the world fell away was glowing human eyes staring into hers, and a mouth in mid-roar as light poured out of it.

CHAPTER THIRTEEN

C hiyo fell out of the Animus pod, gasping for air. She took a moment to collect herself before she stood up.

"I didn't tell you to abort the mission, Kaitō."

The fox avatar appeared in the center of her display as if trying to look at her face-to-face. *"I am aware of that, Miss Chiyo. However, I am programmed with the function of using my abilities and commands to keep my host safe. The predicament we had found ourselves in was...unwinnable."*

"By your calculations, perhaps," she retorted, moving to the table beside the hub to collect her things. "But I could have held them off for the last few seconds we needed before we were able to take off. I could have succeeded."

"Perhaps, but only in the plan, not in the mission," the EI explained. *"You would have sustained grievous wounds in the attack. Even if we had been able to cast out the Neurosiks, if this had been a mission in reality, you would have bled out from the*

wounds they would have inflicted upon you. You would have died before we even broke orbit."

"That would have been—" Chiyo stopped herself. She was too caustic. "I'm sorry, Kaitō, you are right."

"You did program me to have superior intellect and deduction," Kaitō reminded her. *"It would be a waste to not use those qualities to their full effect."*

"I certainly agree." She sighed, placing the strap of her bag over her shoulder. A jolt of pain surged from her arm to her ribs, and she took a moment to roll her shoulder, wincing involuntarily.

"Are you all right?" Kaitō inquired.

"I'll be better after a hot shower. I'm merely a bit sore at the moment."

"Unsurprising, considering you ran two missions in one day, one of which was meant for a team."

"You made your point before. I'm sorry for not heeding your advice if that's what you're looking for," she grumbled, making her way to the Animus hall exit.

"That would mean I would be looking for personal satisfaction in you being in the wrong. That is certainly not the case, madame, I assure you."

"That would be a curiosity, for sure."

The avatar vanished, reappearing quickly in the corner of the display as only a head. *"I do have a request if you are willing to oblige, Miss Chiyo."*

"What do you require?" she asked, her mind wandering slightly in thought.

"I would like to know the answer to the question I asked before we began the second mission. Why did you find it so pertinent to undergo the mission on your own? I commend how far

you were able to go, but the odds of success were astronomically low. Even if you had succeeded, you were not able to get all the information you needed to pass before you had to abort the download."

Chiyo stepped out of the Animus center. A few other students walked past her, excitedly discussing the mission they had just completed as they strolled further and out of sight. She watched them go, taking a moment to find the right words to answer her EI's question. "I simply needed to see what I was capable of in such a situation in preparation for the Co-op test in a few weeks."

"I believed that to be the case. Running through a number of possibilities, however, that is in conflict with the information I have on you. This throws the chance of the answer being the correct one askew."

"How so?" she asked.

"If this was a simple test run of personal abilities, then the first mission scenario should have been more than sufficient. If this was to test your abilities under more immediate duress, then there were other solo missions you could have chosen." Kaitō sounded speculative. *"If you wanted to see how well you would do in a team scenario...that would require a team."*

Chiyo walked over to a nearby bench overlooking the lake around the island. She placed her pack down and looked up into the pink and purple hued sky, watching as the final rays of light gave way to night. "That's all certainly true. From a deductive point of view, you would be correct."

"Then is there a function or objective that I am missing or not privy to?"

"A couple, actually," she admitted, lacing her fingers in

her lap. "But they aren't the kind I can program into you, and they cannot be made into statistics even if I were able to."

"I see..." Kaitō looked away for a moment. *"If that is the case, do you wish me to leave it alone for now?"*

"When I can find a better or easier way to say it, Kaitō, I'll let you know," she promised. "For now, I'll simply have to rely on my current plan to succeed."

"Speaking of which, I would recommend you ask him at the next available opportunity so that you can practice together with him in preparation and so there is less chance for him to find a different partner before you can get him on your side."

Chiyo let out a quick laugh. "I don't think I have to worry about someone else getting to him before I do. He is an excellent soldier and he certainly has a few admirers, thanks to his win at the Division test, but his reputation precedes him."

"What does that reputation entail?"

"That he's good at killing things but not so much in cooperation. At least, that's how others perceive him."

"You know different?"

Chiyo pulled the tablet from her bag, activated it, and opened a folder. "I hacked into his Animus replay records. I've seen him work in the field. With random students, he doesn't come across as much of a team player. In most cases, he's gotten into firefights before the rest of the team had finished preparing a strategy."

"That doesn't seem like the proper function of an ace," Kaitō noted.

Chiyo nodded. "Which is why he's had to do extra workshops for his class."

"If you still wish to work with him, does that mean you believe he will work differently with you?"

Chiyo opened a different video. "When he does a mission with the soldiers he usually runs with, he is much more cooperative. He is more willing to listen to plans, at least those that are recommended by the Tsuna ace or the marksman, and he's willing to put himself in danger to protect them if need be."

"I see... I have two new questions, madame."

"What do you wish to know?" She raised a puzzled eyebrow when she found a file that was locked, a new recording that had only been saved that day.

"First off, how do you believe he will work with you? Like he works with other students he's not familiar with, or how he works with his usual group?"

Chiyo continued to try to open the locked file and tensed as her commands proved futile. "I believe he will be cooperative, but I wanted to run at least one test with him to be sure that we are compatible in the field. Plus, I'm sure he would be willing to help considering that he will need a partner for the test as well."

"Which brings me to my second question," Kaitō continued. *"Since he does have a group of other soldiers that he works with, why do you believe that he will not partner with one of them? Perhaps he has already."*

Chiyo shut her tablet off, making a mental note to crack the unresponsive file later. "Most of those other soldiers have already partnered with each other."

"You know this for a fact?"

"I've been keeping track of many students at this academy in preparation and as a way to keep my skills up," she confessed, leaning back against the bench and gazing into the darkening sky. "And to be honest, I'm almost certain that he has not prepared himself for the test."

"The co-op test? I'm not trying to get into the police force...plus, considering my past, I'm sure they wouldn't want to buy my contract anyway." Kaiden grunted as he continued to scan through his tree. "Why are you slurring the 'o' like that?" he asked Laurie who was rubbing his temples in annoyance.

"The Co-op test, as in the cooperative or cooperation test. It's the end of the semester test."

"Oh, right...that," Kaiden muttered. "I wasn't gonna bother with that. I'll simply run it alone. Plus, Chief is big enough to count as a second player anyway, right?"

"You better be talking about my personality, boy," Chief warned.

"That too." Kaiden shrugged.

"Are you trying to rewrite the rules?" Laurie asked, exasperated. "Good luck with that. You'd have an easier chance of taking on a trio of those war machines from the Division test than getting the board to bend on any changes to their tests."

"So it's non-negotiable, huh?" Kaiden huffed his annoyance.

"Oh, it's quite negotiable. You can negotiate that you will do it, or that you cannot do it and get booted from the Academy and saddled with all the debt that you owe thus far without a guaranteed job."

"Might wanna toss that extra point in debate if you wanna go that route," Chief jeered.

Laurie moved over to stand behind Kaiden, who was still focused on the screen in front of him. "Speaking of which, how goes the talent selection?"

Kaiden looked at him, confused. "You've been standing here all this time. You haven't seen me make my selections?"

"My hologram has been here. I had to step out for a moment and deal with the real Schrodinger. He requested a few treats. My fluffy little snack vacuum."

Kaiden rolled his eyes. "So the cat is more important to you than this? Gee, thanks."

"Oh, don't be so envious. It's never a good look," Laurie admonished. "Besides, you are in my pod. It's not like I could forget you and leave you here."

Kaiden stopped and turned, looking up at the professor. "You know, that wasn't something I thought about until you brought it up."

Laurie waved him off. "Oh, stop being so dramatic and show me what you've chosen so far."

Kaiden shook his head and sighed. He turned back to the screen and changed the search filters. The view changed as the unchosen talents disappeared and the ones he had chosen appeared on the top of the screen.

Strategic Mind: Learn dozens of strategies per upgrade and how to apply them in the field. Increasing your ability as a leader.

Status: 1/10

SXP Boost: Allows for a 15% percent boost to SXP Gain with each point.

Status: 1/4

"So you did take a boost," Laurie observed. "But only one point?"

"I decided to go with a little variety," Kaiden stated. "Try out a few things while gettin' levels is easier."

Laurie smiled. "I'm happy to see you're so enthusiastic about this. Up until now, getting you to do this was like pulling teeth."

"I said I would get around to it eventually," Kaiden mumbled.

"For you, 'eventually' and 'indefinitely' don't seem to have very different meanings." Laurie chuckled.

Martial-Judo: Increases physical defensive form and teaches throws and parries from the Judo martial art.

Status: 1/4

"Finally adding a little finesse to your repertoire," Chief chirped. *"See if there's a talent for breakdancing while you're at it."*

"Why Judo out of all the options?" Laurie inquired, looking at the screen. "Or did you choose another that I missed?"

"Nah, just Judo. I'm pretty good at kicking and damn good at punching, but I needed something that will give me a bit more edge against larger opponents. You know, use their strength and momentum against them and all of that."

"Wulfson give you the idea?" Laurie smirked.

"You might be able to fling him to the ground for once," Chief declared. *"But I bet you won't break the big guy's record for dumbass toss."*

"Should I even ask what that is?" Laurie grimaced.

"It's what Wulfson dubbed the moments he sends Kaiden flying in the air. It's become something of a regular occurrence."

"What's his current record?" Laurie asked.

"That's not important." Kaiden scowled.

"Twenty-four feet and seven inches. Probably could've slid farther, but Kaiden hit a dumbbell rack." Chief cackled.

Kaiden grunted as he glared at the EI, elbowing Laurie to get back to looking over his choice of talents.

Xeno Hunter: Increases knowledge of alien species and instructions on how to best incapacitate or kill them.

Status: 1/3

"An...interesting choice," Laurie mumbled. He looked at Kaiden and placed a hand on his shoulder. "Have the Tsuna or Mirus not been playing well with you?"

Kaiden brushed Laurie's hand away. "It was in the Ace tree. I thought it was weird to have the choice at all. You think the other races are gonna like that we are already learning how best to stick them in the ground?"

Laurie folded his arms. "If you're so worried about how it looks, why did you choose it?"

Kaiden stood up. "To be prepared. Jaxon said that they have rebels and traitors just like we do. Plus, I figure it's only a matter of time before I gotta deal with alien enemies in the Animus, so I thought it would prove useful. I also learned some rather interesting things about the Mirus, like I can kill one with a pint of rocky road."

"Their metabolism does not process dairy very well, and the low temperature would indeed cause some of their organs to slowly lose function if introduced to their internal system. But you seem to forget that they have no mouths, how would you get them to ingest it?"

"Injection?" Kaiden shrugged.

"You going to inject them with ice cream? Specifically with nuts and marshmallows? Must be a large needle," Laurie said, both amused and bemused.

"It was a joke, Prof. Back to the main point, though. How is this a problem? Jax is a Tsuna, and this is in the Ace tree. He's probably seen it."

"You forget that *we* are aliens to them. The talent works both ways," Laurie reminded him.

Kaiden considered this for a moment. He nodded slowly as he began to think about what that meant.

"I wondered how that bipedal dolphin got so good at killing meatbags," Chief admitted.

"He's probably got this stacked to full," Kaiden observed. "Need to remember not to get on his bad side in the future."

"What else?" Laurie asked, leaning in.

Tinkerer: Gain knowledge about field gadgets and how to fix or increase output in the field and best modify them.

Status: 1/4

"Before you ask, I use a barrier in the field. It takes a beating each and every time," Kaiden explained.

"A practical choice, then. Well done. That leaves you with one point. Where will that go?"

"I could think of a few places it could go." Chief chuckled. *"See if there's a talent for common sense, or manners, or maybe proper diction and get rid of that accent."*

"You mean like the one you have?" Laurie asked.

"I didn't choose it."

"Nothing like that for me." Kaiden smiled, looking at Chief. "But I think we can do something for you." He canceled the filters and typed something into the search bar.

Next-Gen: Increases EI processing, scanning, and hacking capabilities.

Status: 0/3

"So you're gonna give me a tune-up, huh?" Chief eyed his host. *"Wonder if I'll come out with go-faster racing stripes or a flame decal."*

"Guess we'll see." Kaiden moved to select the talent.

"Actually, Kaiden, I would wait for us to—" Laurie began, but the caution cut off when Kaiden activated the talent.

Chief began to glow brighter and brighter. His eye grew bigger as sparks began to shoot off him.

"Chief? What the hell? Are you all right?" Kaiden demanded. He'd barely said the words when Chief exploded in a ball of light. The windows disappeared, Laurie's hologram vanished, and the light above him went off, leaving him in a dark void.

"Uh...was that supposed to happen?"

CHAPTER FOURTEEN

"Hey, Akello." Mya greeted the advisor as she walked into the bar. "How are you doing?"

"Pretty good, all things considered," Akello said and sat. She ordered a glass of wine from the bartender before turning back to her friend. "I've been working with Advisor Tali on the Horde test for the second years. It's been exhausting but fun."

Mya gave her a reassuring pat on the hand. "Well, don't work too hard. The Co-op test is coming up soon. I bet they have you running that too, huh?"

Akello sighed. "Yeah, me and fourteen others. That's gonna be a long week."

"Did any of your picks for the league get together?" Mya asked.

She shook her head. "No, they all grouped up with others. It means I won't get the Coop bonus, but I still feel pretty good about my chances." She looked up at her friend. "What about you? Any luck?"

Mya took out her tablet and activated it, revealing her league team. "I wasn't that lucky either. Sandra and Yvon both went with different people. I was really hoping they would band together as they are friends from prep."

"That's maybe why. The Coop test is grueling, so they probably didn't want to potentially damage their friendship if things went south during the test," Akello suggested.

"That and the fact that one is a surveyor and the other is a surgeon. It would be an odd test."

Akello thought about it for a moment. "How would that work? The surveyor would find a body and the surgeon would operate?"

Mya giggled. "Maybe the surgeon could only operate with the equipment the surveyor found?"

"I doubt there are many rocks in the shape of scalpels." Akello laughed. "What about your first choice? Chiyo Kana?"

Mya held out her hands as if scaling items on a triple beam. "It's a mixed bag. On one hand, she's got some of the highest scores in the entire year."

"But on the other?" Akello asked.

Mya's shoulders slumped. "She doesn't have the greatest track record of working with others, and she hasn't even chosen a partner for the tests."

"You might wanna get on to her about that," Akello prompted. "She's only got a week until she'll be forced to get a random partner."

"Honestly, I might have made a mistake in choosing her," Mya admitted.

Akello sat back with a surprised look on her face.

"That's rather bleak of you, especially considering you are her counselor."

Mya waved her hands frantically. "I'm not trying to say she isn't a good student, far from it. But...I mean, the league is supposed to be made up of a trio of students, and the final test is a three-student team that has to work together for the finals."

Akello gave her friend an apologetic look. "And since those teams are created using our choices..."

"I have a surgeon, a surveyor, and an infiltrator, two of whom are mid-level and the other doesn't play all that well with others," Mya concluded.

"What made you choose those three?" Akello asked. "I wouldn't think that would make for a good final team on paper. We don't even have any wildcards you can swap out for this year. Everyone got snatched up."

"I was hoping I could trade later, get some early points with Chiyo and the Coop bonus with Sandra and Yvon before trading one of them for a soldier or someone in engineering."

Akello chuckled. "You're rather ruthless when it comes to this, huh?"

"I won last year, remember?" Mya declared proudly with a clap of her hands. "I look to win again this year and make it a back-to-back victory."

The bartender gave Akello her glass. She thanked him and took a quick sip before replying. "Even with Sasha in the running this year? Didn't he have a hot streak at some point?"

"Five in a row. That's why he 'retired' for a few years. He was getting bored."

Akello gave an appreciative whistle. "No wonder he gets the nice office."

"But I still think I can win. I mean, he's gotta be rusty, right? I can take him."

"Shooting for the stars. I like it." Akello smiled. She looked at Mya's team for a moment. "Speaking of the commander, Sandra is paired up with Jensen Lovett in Engineering. I think Sasha actually has him on his team."

"You think he will trade?" Mya asked hopefully. "Lovett has some pretty good grades, but maybe I can convince him to trade for him?"

"I think he's already got a medic, so I doubt he'll want another one."

"His first choice was Kaiden Jericho. He gets blasted all the time."

"It's a bit unnerving that you say that with such glee." Akello deadpanned. "Aren't you his counselor too?"

"I care deeply about my students," Mya assured her.

"But you care about your League score more?" Akello snickered. "It is certainly not a bad plan, but I think you'll have to sweeten the deal."

"I don't think Sasha likes sweets," Mya lamented. "I've made him some deserts before, but he never touches them. Must be trying to stay fit."

Akello grimaced, remembering a cake Mya had made previously—far too sweet, with unripe fruit. "Yeah, I'm sure that's why," she whispered. "But don't play naïve. You know what I mean."

"So you saying I should try to trade Chiyo?" Mya queried. "I mean, I do have a lead because of her…"

"But if she doesn't do well on the test due to her being…

stand-offish, then where will you be? The tests are worth the most points."

"I know but..." Mya trailed off, thinking furiously for a moment. "Do you think he'll even want to trade? He's already got Kaiden, and he doesn't exactly have an 'all for one' mentality."

"Doesn't hurt to ask," Akello commented. "What do you have to lose?"

Mya sighed, taking another look at her current team. "I guess you're right. I should probably see what he thinks."

"Why don't you give him a call?" the advisor asked.

Mya shook her head. "It's pretty late. I'll ask him later. I'm not sure if he's even in his office anymore."

Sasha gazed out of the large windows in his office, staring out into the dark night sky. He looked up to the corner of his display, activating the clock. It read twenty minutes past midnight. The commander sighed. Despite such a dire message, Laurie apparently still didn't see the need for punctuality.

At that moment, he heard the doors to his office open, and Laurie walked in. He was impeccably dressed in a white dress shirt, silver vest, and pants tucked into his white boots. His hair, however, looked a little windblown, and his breathing was ragged.

"Long night, Laurie?" Sasha inquired, motioning to the professor's hair.

"I had a bit of a hang-up at the lab...Kaiden paid me a visit," Laurie explained, pushing the hair out of his eyes

JOSHUA ANDERLE & MICHAEL ANDERLE

before he pulled a comb out of his pants pocket. "I had him activate his talent points. He's been training this whole time without them," he exclaimed, his vocal cadence quickening as he moved to a chair behind Sasha's desk and began to straighten his hair. "It went well, but the boy activated an upgrade for his EI's processors while in the Animus. It caused a temporary blackout while his EI installed the upgrade and came back online—my fault, really. I should have mentioned that it was better to apply that outside the Animus."

"He learns better from trial and error, as I've discovered," Sasha admitted, taking a seat at his desk. "Your message was rather vague. What did you discover that you needed to talk to me about right away?"

"Well, that also involves Kaiden, actually." Laurie withdrew a handkerchief from the chest pocket of his vest and wiped the comb. "He ran a victor-level mission this morning, along with a few of his friends. It was cleared for him by unknown means."

Sasha sat back in his chair and crossed his arms. "And you believe this is related to the previous incidents?"

"Absolutely. You can't simply clear a mission like that for personal use. An advisor must also be present, and worse, the equi scale was at nine."

"Tell me what you know," Sasha demanded. Laurie gave him a quick synopsis of what Kaiden had told him along with a bit of information he had gathered in the meantime. Sasha remained silent and still, for the most part, listening intently. "Are you sure there is no other way for a student to get access to a high-level test? Perhaps through a glitch? Or maybe a hacker was able to bypass the clearance and activate it for him? We do have a very talented crop among all years."

"Please remember who you're talking to, Sasha. I would obviously have covered all those bases," Laurie sneered. "I was able to placate Kaiden with an excuse about it being a glitch, but the system should have recognized that the mission was not appropriate for him or any of his group, closed it out, and sent an alert to my Animus Technician group. They would have then informed me well before Kaiden did."

Sasha tapped his fingers on his desk. "So what are you suggesting?"

Laurie placed a small circular pad on the desk. "Aurora, please bring up the mission code I downloaded earlier."

"Understood. Displaying," the EI acknowledged. Holographic streams of coding for the mission floated above the desk.

"See this?" Laurie asked, pointing to various segments. "The way it is designed—redundant segments, quick changes, re-routes and new triggers—this is some skilled work."

"True, but this is something almost anyone on your team would be able to do, correct?" Sasha observed.

"Any technician at an Animus-sanctioned academy would have the proper clearance and ability to do this, but they would have to add their signature before it was uploaded." He scrolled down to the bottom of the code. "There is no signature here."

"And the only people who can override that command would be Academy board members or…"

"Members of the World Council." Laurie finished the sentence with an unhappy scowl.

Sasha considered this for a moment. "Despite the handful of times that we've discussed this possibility, I still cannot fathom why they are pulling these strings, particularly in Kaiden's case."

"My hypothesis is they were keeping an eye on me and my devices, and the implant in particular. Kaiden was simply the one who happened to get the implant and so became a new focus for them," Laurie reasoned.

"But what are they looking for exactly?"

"Remember when we had dinner together with Akello and Mya before the school year began? You mentioned that some members of the Council were not so enthusiastic about completely decommissioning our projects that had to do with dealing with possible alien hostilities."

Sasha nodded. "I do, but I've done some digging on my own in the meanwhile. I haven't found anything that would suggest that these projects have restarted en masse or that even a high percentage of Council members were on board in even considering doing so."

"Just because it might not be a high percentage doesn't mean there aren't enough to get things done," Laurie reminded him ominously. "And might I suggest, if I may be so bold, that you simply haven't looked in the right places." The professor gave him a slight smile as he motioned to the pad. "Aurora, would you please show the commander what you found?"

"*Certainly, Professor.*" The code disappeared, and a message took its place. Sasha leaned in to read it.

Arbiter Organization

The experiments continue. Project Ether is showing promise, as is Project Blitzkrieg. However, we have had to shut down a few other projects and tests in the meanwhile and put more focus on the ones that show the most promise. Observations at the ark schools continue. Nexus is still the priority, but we have some promising recruits among the ranks of the other four academies. We are trying to get another academy approved, to be built in Russia, one that we will have more influence over, but until then, we will allow our future militia to continue to grow. Stay vigilant.

"Where did you get this, Laurie?" Sasha asked.

Laurie made a motion with his hand, and the letter split apart to reveal numerous news posts, lists, and letters. "I had Aurora look through various Council newsletters, pamphlets, and news stories run by magazines and news outlets controlled by the WC. The words were typed in a slightly different font in over a dozen different letters over a period of three days. The lettering was similar enough that the layman would see nothing different, but when put together and the letters arranged by day and alphabetically by the title on the heading, it created this message."

"Can we take this to the Board?" Sasha requested.

"What good would come of it?" Laurie shrugged. "Even if it got the Council's attention, it's too vague to make a case, and it has nothing to tie it to any members of the Council directly. They would probably merely say it was some hacker group and send some poor sods on a fruitless hunt."

Sasha sighed. "I would have to agree with you, unfortunately." He turned to his computer and activated it. "I'll send a few messages to some contacts to meet with me, some that I can trust with this information. I want to see if they can dig up anything else. Do you have more messages like this?"

"I'll have Aurora look through as many things as she can, but I doubt that they send all their messages this way. We may get lucky and find a few more, but it will probably be nothing more than crumbs."

"It can be enough to start a trail," Sasha responded, taking a quick look at one of the headlines. "I want to find out what this Arbiter Organization is."

Laurie gave a quick nod. "And why they are so damned interested in us and why they keep bullying our dear boy Kaiden."

Sasha looked over to the professor. "Speaking of which, where is he now?"

Laurie shrugged. "I sent him back to the dorms. He's probably resting now."

"I am a god," Chief exclaimed.

"Would you please shut up," Kaiden responded, thumping his pillow in exasperation. "I'm trying to get some sleep."

"Sleep is for the weak!" Chief roared, appearing in front of him, his avatar now around the size of a basketball and his color a shimmering blue and his eye looking more like a reticule. *"You should be spending your hours worshipping me. No mere mortal can truly understand the magnificence of my being. I am all-pow—"*

"Audio off." Chief's soliloquy cut off in mid-sentence.

"All-powerful, my ass. You just got an upgrade. I'm sure you're feeling all high and mighty now, but tomorrow, we'll see if we can actually put it to use."

As Kaiden tried to sleep, a light burned through his closed eyelids. He looked up to see Chief glowing brighter. "You sparkly dick...if I had known that upgrade would let me see you without the oculars, I would have made a different choice." He yanked a pillow over his head. "Maybe gone with something useful like gardening, or something that would let me shoot accurately while back-flipping. Not the choice that makes your head as fat as your ass."

Chief began to glow brighter, the light changing to a heated red. "Visual off," Kaiden commanded. The light disappeared.

"Great, now I gotta deal with an EI with a Messiah complex. What the hell is next?"

CHAPTER FIFTEEN

A week later, the heightened excitement was almost tangible. The Academy students grew more and more eager as the Coop tests approached. In the center of the Academy plaza stood five soldiers, shooting the breeze as they waited for another one of their comrades to meet them.

"So what are we doing again?" Luke asked, leaning his large frame against a tree in the courtyard as he brushed his shaggy brown hair out of his green eyes. "Kaiden wants us to help him beat up the head of security?"

"What? No. We're gonna be training with him," Flynn exclaimed. "Were you actually okay with attacking the head officer?"

"I thought it was an undercover mission, maybe, like we were going to take down a corrupt official or something," Luke said defensively.

"You really think they would entrust something like

that to Kaiden? He's not exactly known for subtlety," Silas reminded him.

"Much less Kaiden and a group of first years," Marlo added, ruffling his crew-cut black hair and rolling his large shoulders. "Speaking of which, aren't we missing a few people?"

"I guess Amber didn't tell ya, mate?" Flynn inquired, looking at Marlo. "She's working with her mother in the med-bay for the day, helping with inventory."

"Izzy couldn't make it. She's taking some extra work-shops to help do…some sort of scout thing." Silas rubbed the back of his neck and frowned as if trying to recall the actual details. "I wasn't really paying attention. She ends up going on for hours about that stuff, so I've kinda started tuning it out."

"Where's Cam?" Luke asked.

"He's shadowing his uncle or something for the week-end. He left last night," Raul explained. "Told us good luck and to not get as wrecked as the five of you did last week. Care to explain what he was talking about, either of you?" he questioned, looking at Silas and Flynn who both muttered and looked away.

Luke pushed himself off the tree and walked over. "Well, that explains him, but where's Jax?"

"He'll meet us there." The group of soldiers looked over to see Kaiden walking over in his all-black ensemble, his jacket trailing behind him in the breeze. "He left early this morning to go check on the other Tsuna in their private dorm."

"Ah, right, I forgot about that." Raul's brow furrowed. "I used to have the pod next to him before he got into the rank two room with you. He would wake me up every Saturday at four in the morning before he moved out."

"He was only there for like, what, a couple weeks?" Flynn chuckled. "You make it sound like it was some years-long habit."

"I need my beauty sleep." Raul ran his fingers through his slick black hair. "I get cantankerous otherwise."

"I would hate for you to lose such a charming attitude." Silas snickered, earning him a glare from the tracker.

"I've never gotten to ask him why he stays in the soldier's dorm instead of with the other Tsuna." Luke's expression was mildly curious.

"I did. He says it's because he wants to help with the integration process between the Tsuna and the humans," Kaiden explained. "He says that the only way to truly build a bridge is to take steps to assimilate in certain areas. A nice idea, but I don't see many volunteers who move into the Tsuna dorm."

"Aren't their pods filled with water?" Flynn asked. "How would that work? Sleep while wearing scuba gear?"

"Maybe they'll give you floaties," Silas jeered. "Maybe turn it into a water bed?"

"That would actually be pretty cool," Marlo mused. "I actually had one of those as a kid. Took it with me to a summer camp and used it in their zero-gravity chamber, and it bounced me all around the room."

The others chuckled. "A great use of multi-million-dollar tech, Marlo," Flynn joked, "Wonder if I can ask some of the academy techs if I could use a laser or two next time I grill."

"I've done that. It leaves a weird aftertaste," Luke muttered, earning him curious glances.

"How are you still alive?" Raul asked.

Luke laughed proudly. "Guys like Marlo and me are a hearty breed."

"Natural adaptation at work." Silas winked at Kaiden. "Over the generations, their bodies must have adapted to their stupidity."

Kaiden chuckled. "As long as they stay in front of me in a firefight, I'll keep nodding and smiling."

"So, now that you're here, wanna fill us in on what's going on?" Raul inquired.

Kaiden nodded. "Right. I thought we'd all get a bit more practical training since we've been using the Animus so much."

"And I'm not in a hurry to use it more than I have to," Flynn admitted.

"I feel that," Silas agreed. "For a while there, I was worried I would be pissing red."

"Seriously, what the hell happened to you?" Luke asked, aghast.

"I'll tell you the next time you start whining about stubbing your toe or something," Kaiden promised. "For now, let's go over to the gym. Wulfson's got a room there filled to the gills with equipment and mats and all that. He'll give us a good workout."

"He's only trying to get some of the pressure off him," Flynn revealed. "He's been training with the head officer since the first week of the Academy. Haven't you seen him coming through the dorms all knackered almost every night?"

"I assumed it was extra Animus training or something," Marlo admitted.

"Animus doesn't leave bruises," Silas noted.

"You must be pretty stalwart yourself," Luke acknowledged. "Surprised you haven't dropped dead yet."

Kaiden rubbed the side of his chest gingerly. "It can be a bit...painful. But I've been getting some help from the med-bay." He sighed and looked despondent for a moment. "Though I would recommend keeping it easy this time around. The stuff I usually get won't be in stock for a while."

"You'll have to show it to me sometime," Marlo said, rolling his shoulders again. "My shoulders have been tense for the last couple of weeks. I've been resting them and all that, but it's going away pretty slowly."

"Oh, it'll fix you." Kaiden almost purred, a tone of excitement in his voice. "It'll fix you right the hell up."

"Uh, I would like to say that he's talking about a medical serum," Flynn explained, giving Kaiden a cautious look. "Not, you know, drugs or something."

"Must be a damn good serum." Raul grinned.

"Oh, you bet your sacred Canadian maple it is," Kaiden declared.

"We don't worship syrup," Raul stated bluntly.

"It's only an expression," Kaiden retorted, wiping his mouth. "Now, shall we head off?"

"Which way are we going?" Luke asked, looking around the massive gym area.

"Follow me. His room is down at the end of the hall." Kaiden led the way.

"So what can we expect to deal with?" Silas inquired.

"I'm not totally sure what he'll have us do, considering he usually only trains me. But he'll put us through the wringer, that I can promise."

"You make it sound so enticing." Flynn's sarcasm held a hint of anticipation.

"I'm looking forward to it," Marlo cried while pumping a fist. "I haven't had a real good workout since I got here. Most of my training is in the Animus, and I've been looking for an excuse to do more than basic weight training."

"I agree, the Animus is nice and all, but nothing beats the burn of a good practical training session," Luke concurred.

"There's nothing stopping you. You can always train in your free time," Silas pointed out.

"Did you see the main gym? There was only, like, thirty people in there," Marlo reminded him.

"I guess most of the students get too accustomed to the Animus. That only helps with skills and isn't all that great for physical development," Luke commented, a note of reserve in his tone.

"Some of us don't really need it," Flynn interjected. "People like Raul and I are already at top level physical performance for our classes. We merely need to maintain."

"Ah, come on, mate," Marlo admonished with a heavy slap to Flynn's back. "Push yourself from time to time. Couldn't hurt."

"Unlike that slap." Flynn groaned. "Felt like a club to the back."

"We're here, so we do see the need," Raul admitted. "I'll see if he's got anything to help me with my speed and finesse."

"He might have some pointers, but that's not really his focus," Kaiden interrupted. "Though I have to say, he can move damn fast for a guy built like a tank-droid."

"You know, I don't think I've really ever met the head officer." Luke seemed to have perked up at this prospect.

"Well, you gonna get your chance. We're here." Kaiden stopped at the end of the hall and opened the door. "Hey, Wulfson! I'm here. Brought some friends with me this time."

His greeting elicited no response. Kaiden looked back to see the others giving him a quizzical look, but he simply shrugged.

"Ah, there you are, Kaiden." He turned back to see Jaxon approaching him, another Tsuna behind him.

"Hey, Jax, glad you could…. Genos, is that you?" Kaiden walked over and slapped the Tsuna engineer's hand. "How have you been? Haven't seen you in a while." He noticed Genos rubbing his palm. "Oh, right, sorry. Forgot that y'alls' palms are pretty sensitive."

"It is all right, friend Kaiden. I am glad to see you too, and I'm still getting used to your unique greetings," Genos admitted though he continued to rub his palm surreptitiously on his thigh.

"You know, seeing the two of you together, you both have some pretty distinct ways of talking," Kaiden noted.

"It's our translators. I set mine to translate in a more

modern and typical manner, but Genos' translates almost literally to our language," Jaxon explained.

"Is there a preference among the Tsuna?" Flynn asked as he walked forward.

Jaxon nodded. "It's a personal preference, but depending on the clan, it could have an effect."

"Warriors like kin Jaxon are more inclined to use modified speaking for comfort and diplomatic reasons. I like direct translation to show others a little bit more about us, like how our language and titles are applied."

"Kin? You two are brothers?" Raul asked.

"Not in the human sense, no." Jaxon shook his head.

"Kin is a term of endearment among my people for those of us who are related by clan," Genos stated. "Jaxon and I are actually of the same clan that split into two different clans many centuries ago."

"What? I don't think I follow. How does that work?" Silas queried.

Kaiden waved him into silence. "It's a long story. If you're still curious, I'll tell you later."

"What about the names?" Luke asked. "I've never heard of a 'Geno' before, or some of the names I've heard for the other Tsuna..."

Jaxon placed a palm on the mechanist Tsuna's shoulder and gave him a knowing look. "Oh, right...Friend Kaiden, might I speak with you for a moment?"

Kaiden looked at them quizzically and showed a goofy grin to the Tsuna, "We are speaking now, aren't we?"

Geno nodded. "Ah, yes, but I suppose I meant... I suppose I was asking for a more intimate setting."

"Intimate?" Kaiden coughed, "Like, candles and all that? What are you learning about human customs?"

Geno tapped along his infuser. "I wanted to speak together away from the others, but I suppose it would be easier and quicker to make the correction here."

"'The correction?' What correction?" Kaiden inquired.

"My name—it is not Geno," the Tsuna explained.

"Well, yeah, it's a translated version, right? You speak in echolocation or scream-singing or something."

The Tsuna nodded. "Yes, but the name 'Geno' is incorrect. It was not the full name I was given."

Kaiden raised an eyebrow. "Say what? I've been calling you that for, like, three months now. Have I been getting it wrong all this..." Kaiden slapped a palm across his face, "Oh, lord, you were the Tsuna I met at the carrier station, right? I didn't confuse you for another one and just assume you've been the same guy all along, did I?"

"No, I was the one you met." The Tsuna nodded, raising his palms slightly, "I did not mean to cause you stress."

Kaiden let out a deep breath. "Oh, thank God. I was beginning to think I was an alien racist or something."

"And yet you still keep asking me things like what a dingo is and how big my knife is," Flynn muttered.

"I consider that small talk, showing interest in Australian culture," Kaiden explained.

"I promise you will learn a lot just by reading a damn tourist pamphlet."

Kaiden looked back at the marksman, "Will it have anything about drop bears?"

Flynn opened his mouth but stopped as a wry smile formed. "Yeah, plenty. You'll learn all about them."

"It really is just a small detail. You see, my name here is 'Genosaqua.' The shortened form or nickname you would use is 'Genos.'"

"Oh, well, isn't that a huge difference!" Raul chuckled.

"It is, actually," Jaxon said earnestly, staring down his teammate, "It may be a minor difference to you, but the word 'Geno' has a rather...odd translation for us."

"'Odd' as in bad?" Marlo asked.

He shook his head. "Not necessarily. It's rather silly, to be honest. It was caused by a mix-up with my translation settings. But if you would be so kind, from now on would you refer to me by my full name or as 'Genos?' I would be most appreciative."

"No problem, man. Sorry about the mix up." Kaiden clapped a hand on the Tsuna's shoulder, "'Genos' rolls off the tongue better anyway."

"I am happy that you approve," Genos stated thankfully.

Kaiden tapped his chin for a moment in thought. "You'll probably have to tell Chiyo. She was calling you Geno too."

"She was actually the first one I spoke to after Kin Jaxon brought the issue to my attention. She was apparently aware of it to some degree, but she said she didn't want to be rude in case it had some sort of meaning to me."

"What? Does she speak Tsuna?" Kaiden asked incredulously.

"She says she has been looking into our culture and history during her free time. Much of what she is learning is coming from texts and history files that our people have given you. Not all have been properly edited, so she has had to make use of rough translations or use basic Abisa-to-Japanese programs. She says she has picked up some words and phrases along the way. She can actually hold short conversations. It's quite delightful."

"Girl has some odd hobbies," Kaiden mused, taking his arm off Genos' shoulder and stretching, "Well, considering all the confusion this caused, I think I can see why you went with such a normal name Jaxon." Kaiden held his hands over his head and looked at the Tsuna ace. "But considering how exotic your kin's name is, how'd you get saddled with that?"

"I choose it from a list of options," Jaxon stated.

"I was assigned mine, but others chose them from Earth popular culture or gave themselves translated names or named themselves after objects or people they admired," Genos added.

"So you guys have two names?" Marlo inquired.

"Geno...sorry, *Genos* told me when we first met that they speak in a sort of noise-based language. I'm not sure a name is exactly what we would understand. Maybe more of a marker." Kaiden ignored the slightly bemused looks exchanged by members of the group. "Speaking of you, what brings you here, Genos? Wanna join in the fun?"

The engineer nodded. "Kin Jaxon offered to allow me to accompany him and join you in this training session. I need to develop my body more, as I've found myself in the field more than I expected."

"They got you running around? I would have thought that as a machinist, you would be held in the back to repair machines or armor or something or maybe have you break into doors and hang back."

"I am the closest thing the Engineering Division has to a soldier. There are other classes that focus on those type of roles. Most engineers who take part in direct combat use power armor or mechs or an equivalent. I have a personal arsenal that is best used while in direct combat and allows much flexibility in what I can accomplish, but I could always use an increase in stamina. I use a hoverboard in the field for faster movement, but they break quite easily."

"Particularly under laser fire, I would guess." Kaiden chuckled. "It's good to have you with us, but I got to warn you that Wulfson doesn't play around. This will be some serious training."

"You know, you keep building this up, but I gotta say my hype is dying down a little," Luke admitted, looking around the empty room. "Where is this guy?"

"He's probably in his personal office. It's soundproof, but I'll buzz him up." Kaiden moved over to a console and pressed down on a button. "Hey, Wulfson, get your big ass out here. Me and some of my buddies came for some training, and you're burnin' daylight."

Kaiden released the button. They heard a rush of air as a door in the corner opened. "Finally, let's get this started you old—" Kaiden's words died in his throat, and his eyes went wide as the others closed in around him.

The Tsuna turned around. Jaxon immediately took a fighting stance as his companion took a step back. "This is...unfortunate." Genos gulped, the sound audible in the silence.

A large, reptilian creature stepped into the room. It had dark crimson scales and stood over eight feet tall. The creature looked at them with dark-gray eyes, the sharp irises widening and contracting within. It growled, revealing rows of sharp teeth. The head was triangular and sharp with black surrounding its eyes and mouth, giving it a menacing look as it leered at them. A leather chest plate was strapped over its torso. The armor included a shoulder plate on the left that resembled an elongated skull with a medallion of some kind pinned to the front. Arm bindings wound from its shoulders to its palms. Three large claws extended from each hand.

"What...the bloody hell...is that...thing?" Flynn stammered the question on everyone's lips.

"Sauren war chief," Jaxon explained. "That skull on its shoulder is the remains of an Elokk from a feral planet—a crown of sorts that they earn on their own." Jaxon backed away slightly, and the group followed suit. "The medallion means that he...he's personally slain over ten thousand creatures."

"Different creatures or ten thousand individuals?" Raul asked.

"Does that matter?" Silas' question held a low hiss of caution.

"It would add a way higher body count if it's the former."

"Damn terrifying either, way." Luke raised his fists, the instinctive gesture almost ludicrous.

"Why is it here, Kaiden?" Flynn demanded.

"I don't know. Wulfson never said anything about a nightmare lizard being my next sparring partner."

"Don't do anything. Do not agitate him," Genos advised.

"He seems plenty agitated as it is," Marlo muttered.

"Can't we talk to him? He's an ally, right?" Silas asked.

Jaxon continued to inch backward. "We have a truce with the Sauren, but that does not guarantee—"

The Sauren let out a fierce roar, causing the group to jump. Kaiden opened his jacket and brought out his pistol.

"Kaiden, disarm," Genos exclaimed.

Kaiden didn't hear the order, but it wouldn't take him long to realize that he made a grave mistake.

CHAPTER SIXTEEN

The Sauren stared at Kaiden's pistol, letting out another vicious roar as it charged at him. He fired off a shot, a blast of electricity leaving the barrel and connecting with the chest of the monster in front of them.

It had no effect.

The lizard-like creature didn't wince, stagger, or even hiss in pain. It simply continued to stampede towards him.

"Move!" Jaxon shouted, pulling Kaiden away as the beast went to grab him. The two of them hit the floor, and both scrambled up quickly as the Sauren spun around. The large tail smashed into Kaiden and sent him across the room where he tumbled across the mats before smashing into a wall, knocking himself out.

The Sauren stalked towards Jaxon, who took up a defensive fighting stance. "We have no wish to fight you, war chief. Please stop this aggression." The beast only snarled in response to his attempt to reason with it.

A large dumbbell went flying through the air, knocking

the Sauren in his shoulder. He growled and looked back to see Luke, Marlo, and Silas throwing more weights at him. The beast roared and prepared to charge before something smashed into his back, and he stumbled to the ground from the impact. Flynn stood behind him holding a bench-press bar.

"I don't think he's giving us an option, Jaxon," Flynn exclaimed, raising the bar up for another attack. But, as he swung it down, the Sauren grabbed it in mid-swing. Flynn's eyes widened as it glared at him. Raul ran at them from the other side with another bar, charging at the Sauren with the bar raised in the air.

"I got him," he shouted, before trying to bash the reptilian in the head, trying being the operative word.

The Sauren caught the makeshift weapon and pulled it quickly to one side before yanking it out of Raul's hands and flinging it across the room. He then returned his attention to Flynn, snatched the bar away, and grabbed him by the front of his shirt. With a guttural roar, he threw the marksman at Raul. They crashed into each other and tumbled across the room.

Marlo, Luke, and Silas continued to try to beat him with anything heavy they could get their hands on. And while they did occasionally land a hit, it only seemed to jostle the monstrous alien rather than do any real damage. The Sauren stood and faced them when Silas threw a ten-pound medicine ball at him. The beast caught it with one hand, his eyes narrowing at Silas who was caught in a moment of shock before it moved its arm back and flung the weight right back at him with surprising speed.

Silas dove out of the way, the ball barely missing him as

it slammed into the wall. A large crack spiderwebbed at the point of impact. Marlo and Luke charged at the Sauren, who leaned over and extended his arms as if inviting them to attack him.

Jaxon took this opportunity to leap on the massive back. He thrashed around in response and reached to grab the Tsuna, but Luke and Marlo tackled him, pinning his arms against his side as he let out another frenzied roar.

"What do we do now?" Marlo yelled.

"I don't know. I hadn't really....thought this out." Luke grunted the words out as he tried with all his might to hold the beast in place.

"Hold him as steady as you can. I'm going to—" Jaxon's words caught in his throat as the Sauren wrapped his tail around the Tsuna's abdomen and squeezed. His grip loosened and the Sauren ripped him from his back and smashed him into the floor.

"*Jax!*" Luke cried out, briefly losing focus to look at his injured comrade.

"Luke, don't let go," Marlo warned, but the Sauren used the moment of panic to his advantage. He overpowered the two heavy soldiers, grabbing Luke by the neck and Marlo by his wrist. He held Luke aloft and spun around, snatched Marlo off the ground, and released him mid-swing. The hapless soldier crashed into a group of training dummies.

Luke began to kick the Sauren's face and chest as he tried to pull the reptilian's claws off him. "You are not going to stop me with something like this," he declared, able to smash the heel of his boot against the beast's jaw. The creature finally winced, taking a moment to rub his chin with his free hand. "So you do feel pain," Luke jeered. "That means we can kick your ass."

In response, the Sauren launched Luke into the ground. The Titan coughed and sputtered, "You're gonna…have to do better…than that if you…want to finish…me," Luke challenged between gasps.

The Sauren then began to pummel Luke with both hands, raising one into the air while smacking the other down as if furiously beating a drum. After a few seconds, he stopped and snarled at the downed soldier before walking off, leaving Luke to cough and mumble, "Yeah… that might…have done it."

Silas returned, carrying a weighted rope. He dodged a swipe from the Sauren and wrapped the heavy cord under its arm and around its neck. Marlo hurried up behind them and grabbed the other end. They both pulled as hard as they could, trapping the alien's arm against its chest and pulling tight against its throat. He began to pull away, dragging Marlo and Silas across the floor as they tried to hang on. The Sauren reached up with its free claw and pulled against the rope, eventually cleaving through it. The two soldiers fell back to the floor.

The Sauren leaped over to them, stomping on Silas and digging into his chest. Marlo scrambled up and tried to attack, landing a punch to the alien's eye. The beast caught it and twisted his arm, so he yelped in pain. As he continued to twist Marlo's arm, Jaxon recovered. Beside him lay a bag with a chalky substance inside, and he grabbed it. Across the room, he saw Flynn and Raul stagger to their feet. He waved at them and pointed at the weight bars on the ground, then at the bag, and finally, at the Sauren.

The two nodded and raced over to get the bars as Jaxon hurtled towards the beast. The Sauren saw him approach, tossed Marlo away, and stepped off Silas to face him. Jaxon faked a strike, sliding under the Sauren's swipe when it tried to retaliate, and he threw the bag at his eyes, coating them in the dust. The Sauren shrieked in anger, swiping around wildly in confusion as it tried to get the dust out of its eyes by shaking its head.

Raul and Flynn joined the melee. They tossed a bar to Jaxon, and the trio began their assault on the blinded Sauren.

Meanwhile, Kaiden finally came to. He pushed himself up slowly and turned to take in the chaos. Marlo lay in the corner of the room, trying to get up on all fours before collapsing again. Silas and Luke groaned on the floor, while Jaxon, Raul, and Flynn were alternatively beating the Sauren with the bars and dodging its retaliating swipes.

He looked over to see Genos tinkering with something in the corner. "Genos, what are you doing?" he asked as he crawled over.

"What our friends are currently using as weapons will not be sufficient in bringing down a Sauren. They are quite durable, as you can see," he replied, nodding towards the battle. "These armaments, however, may be more helpful."

Kaiden realized that Genos was kneeling next to Wulfson's weapon bench. "Yeah, but they are—"

"Protected by a lock-out barrier," Genos finished, his tone amused. "I am working on fixing that...well, fixing by destroying, as it were."

Kaiden leaned over for a closer look. Genos had opened some sort of hatch on the back of the bench and now moved the wires around with a seemingly competent hand. "What is that?"

"The power source for the barrier. We cannot simply destroy it as that would not stop the protection. There is an internal generator that would keep it going for another thirty minutes." Kaiden heard a shout and saw Raul dragged along the ground as the Sauren tried to wrestle his bar away from him. "And it appears we do not have that kind of time."

"I certainly agree with ya. How close are you?" Kaiden asked.

"Nearly have it. I need to overload the circuitry to cause the interior generator to deactivate as well. I've made the preparations, but I need a small power device to flood the system," Genos said, looking around the room.

Kaiden looked back. Seeing his pistol on the ground, he moved quickly and grabbed it. "Genos, catch," he called, tossing the engineer his pistol. "It's powered by a miniature Tesla generator. Will that work?"

Genos opened a slot on the top of the gun, removed the generator, and looked it over for a moment. "This will do." He nodded, wrapped a couple of wires around the ends of the generator, and picked up a pair of pliers with rubber grips. With studied care, he placed it against something in the hatch.

There was a loud electrical explosion. Kaiden saw the hazy field around the weapons rack dissipate, and he stood up and ran over. "Jaxon, Flynn, Raul, get back," he shouted as he took a machine gun from the rack.

The three looked back and moved quickly out of the way as Kaiden opened fire. They ran over as Genos snatched up a shotgun and joined Kaiden in blasting the Sauren. The other three raced over to grab guns, and they all fired at the beast. The chalky dust kicked up as the bag was punctured and the Sauren was consumed in dust and laser fire.

Kaiden's gun was the first to overheat. He vented the rifle as the others soon reached their limit. They waited to see if the alien would respond. Kaiden pulled his oculars from his jacket and put them on. "Chief, activate," he commanded. The EI appeared on the screen.

"I knew you'd come crawling back." Chief chortled.

"Now is not a good time for your bullshit, Chief. Is that thing still alive?"

"Oh, hell yes, it is. Those are training rifles; the shots would barely hurt you."

"What?" Kaiden asked. Shocked, he looked at the side of the rifle which showed a screen that labeled the power level at minimum. "Dammit, Genos, these are training rifles!"

The Tsuna looked at his own gun for a moment. "Quite realistic replicas."

"You can admire the craftsmanship later. Can we increase the power in these things?"

Genos nodded. "Of course, we merely need—"

"Are you quite done?" a snarling, grim voice asked from within the dust cloud. They turned to see the Sauren walk out of the dust, its glare unchanged.

"That thing can talk?" Flynn asked.

"Of course, with a translator. How else would we be

able to make treaties with them otherwise?" Genos responded.

"They are just not partial to it." Jaxon closed the vent on his rifle.

"Why did you attack us?" Kaiden demanded.

"You were going to attack first if you recall," the Sauren growled.

"Because you were acting so friendly beforehand," Raul muttered sarcastically.

"Why are you here?" Jaxon inquired.

The beast continued to stare them down, looking at each one of them individually as if sizing them up before his gaze stopped on Kaiden. "I have come for that one," he stated, pointing at Kaiden.

"Oh, dammit, Kaiden what did you do?" Flynn asked as he closed his gun's vent with a snap.

"Do I look like I have a damn clue?" Kaiden scowled. "If I had known something like this would happen, I would have mentioned it."

"Who even has the means to send a Sauren after somebody?" Raul wondered aloud. "I don't see any merc symbols. Is he a bounty hunter?"

"I doubt it. War chiefs are something like a soldier-king in the Sauren culture. They lead a colony of people in life and war, so I don't think they take private contracts." Jaxon looked as confused as the rest of them.

"Why do you want me?" Kaiden asked belligerently.

In response, the Sauren stretched its claws and leaned low to the ground. "I grow bored of this talk."

"Wow, already? They really don't like talking," Flynn muttered.

"I have not come to converse, but to battle. Now either prepare to continue this fight or surrender."

"Well, if he's here for me, I certainly ain't going to simply lay down for him," Kaiden asserted grimly. "I can't imagine that my situation would be improved if I went anywhere with him."

"You have me doing the craziest shit, mate." Flynn chuckled despite the situation. "Fighting space dinosaurs…thought I left stuff like that behind as a kid."

Raul was silent for a moment before he shook his head and raised his gun. "Drinks are on you next time we go out, Kaiden."

"I will not abandon you," Jaxon assured him. "But we need a plan."

"I can charge one of these guns to full power, but I will need some time and assistance."

"Gotcha." Kaiden nodded. "Flynn, Raul…help Genos out with whatever he needs."

"On it," Flynn acknowledged, the three of them backing away.

"Sorry to drag you into this with me, Jax, but you seem to know the most about these things. And with our guns useless, it looks like we'll have to get up close with this guy."

"I understand." Jaxon tossed his gun to the ground. "How should we approach this?"

"You in good shape?" Kaiden asked

Jaxon stretched and flexed, then nodded. "I am recovered enough."

"You got a battle suite?"

Jaxon nodded, removed a visor from the back of his belt, and placed it on his head. "Of course."

"You know kung-fu?"

The Tsuna turned to him, staring at him for a moment before turning back. "I do not know that specific style, but I do know how to fight in close combat."

"Works for me." Kaiden smiled, tossed away his own gun, and put up his fists. "Ready?"

As Jaxon took his own stance, his arms close to his chest and legs apart, the Sauren roared and charged.

"Activate Battle Suite," they both commanded almost simultaneously.

The world slowed. Kaiden and Jaxon moved faster now, their steps and actions almost in sync. The Sauren reached up to grab both of them, but they weaved out of his grasp. Kaiden grabbed the attacker's arm and using his momentum, he flung the beast over his shoulder. He landed on the mat with a loud thud.

Jaxon ran up to him and delivered a kick to the Sauren's temple as he tried to recover. The monster snarled as it clawed at him, Jaxon dodging each blow as if taking part in a violent dance.

Kaiden grasped one of the weighted bars on the floor. He rammed it into the back of the Sauren's left arm, just below his shoulder, a weak joint in their physiology. The monster yelled in pain, his arm flailing wildly, and Kaiden spun around and slammed the bar into the bottom part of its chest where one of its two hearts were located.

Those talents were paying dividends now, he realized with an almost surreal satisfaction.

The Sauren sputtered and hissed for a moment before

reaching out for the bar. Kaiden released it as the reptile pulled back, swinging the bar in a wide arc. Jaxon maneuvered underneath as the Sauren spun around and he leaped onto its back again, this time digging his fingers into its eyes.

The bar fell, and Kaiden caught it. As the beast emitted another loud roar, Kaiden jumped up and slammed the metal into its nose. The massive jaws snapped shut, the long teeth biting into its tongue. It bellowed again, blood pouring out of its mouth. The Tsuna leaped off, and Kaiden saw the focused, predatorial look in the alien's eyes had been replaced by pure rage.

As Jaxon landed, he began to run away to get some distance, but a leather strap wrapped around his insulator and pulled him back. Kaiden saw the Sauren using the leather bindings around his arms as a whip to haul the Tsuna towards him. He used the bar to sweep the back of the alien's left leg, but the monster raised its leg before the bar connected and slammed it down in mid-swing, causing it to bend.

Kaiden let go and dodged the Sauren's arm as it reached out to claw him. He saw Jaxon disengage his insulator to escape the beast's grasp. Without that device, a Tsuna would not last more than a few minutes on Earth. Kaiden could feel the strain of the suite getting to him, his own vision blurring and his muscles feeling heavy.

They needed to end this.

"Genos! How much longer?" Kaiden demanded.

"It is charged," he confirmed in response.

"Look out," Raul yelled. The Sauren had tossed the bent bar at the group. They moved out of the way, but the bar clipped Flynn in the leg, sending him sprawling on the floor and clutching his tibia in pain.

"Kaiden, take it," Genos shouted, tossing him the charged rifle.

Kaiden caught it and aimed at the Sauren's head. He focused the center of his head in his sights, preparing to press the trigger as the beast roared at him.

"*Halt!*" A loud cry froze them all in place. Kaiden recognized the voice and turned to see Wulfson at the door.

The Sauren looked to the officer. "Where have you been, Wulfson?"

Kaiden kept the rifle trained on the alien, but he looked slowly between the alien and Wulfson, trying to figure out what was going on.

"I left to deal with something in the main offices. I asked you to stay out of trouble while I was out." Wulfson glared at the Sauren.

The reptile spat out some blood in response. "This is hardly trouble."

"I still need to work on your definitions." The security officer sighed as he walked into his compound and surveyed the damage.

He looked at the students on the floor, grimacing at their condition, then turned to Kaiden. "Now, what the hell is this all about?"

CHAPTER SEVENTEEN

"Thanks, mate." Flynn sighed, taking the ice pack from Kaiden. "How are the others doing?"

Kaiden looked at their companions strewn around the central mat. Luke tried to sit up, but every time he managed to get a few inches off the mat, he would wince and then lie down again. Silas had a slightly easier time of it and now sat back-to-back with Raul to steady himself. Marlo was able to get back on his feet, but he'd worked his shoulders and neck nonstop since he recovered. Genos was looking over Jaxon's infuser, making sure it was installed properly and that nothing was damaged.

"On a scale of ten?" Kaiden considered the reality and shrugged. "Looking like a seven or eight?"

"They don't look that good to me," Flynn replied, placing the ice pack on his shoulder and holding it in place.

"I was talking level of pain," Kaiden admitted.

"Oh, then that's about what it looks like to me."

Kaiden looked over when he heard a door open.

Wulfson and the Sauren stepped out of the back office, the security chief holding a chest in his hand.

"You boys feeling any better?" he asked, placing the chest on the console table.

"It's only been twenty minutes, Wulfson. We're gonna need a bit." Kaiden glared, making his point.

Wulfson chuckled and pointed a thumb at the Sauren. "Heh, my friend is putting you to shame. He's already back to full health after that beating you gave him."

"I'm not sure if I would call it that," the Sauren muttered, running his repaired tongue along his teeth.

"You nearly bit that thing off, and it's already back together?" Kaiden exclaimed.

"The Sauren heal ridiculously fast," Wulfson explained as he opened the chest. "I've seen some torn to literal shreds and then watched as their skin and muscle repaired in real time, so they were back in the field in a little over an hour."

"As long as our hearts beat, we cannot be felled." The Sauren growled what might have been a challenge.

"Next time, go for removing the head or destroying the hearts. Otherwise, you're wasting your time and theirs." Wulfson snickered.

"You make them sound like they're zombies or something." Flynn moved his ice pack to his other shoulder.

"With the added accessories of retractable claws that can tear through steel, almost as many teeth as an alligator, and a hide that breaks most blades," Wulfson pointed out.

"While I find your little biology lesson nice and all, if you could tell me why he's here and why he wants me, I would appreciate it." Kaiden grunted with a meaningful nod at the Sauren.

"Ah, right getting to that." Wulfson walked over to Kaiden. "Have a hit of this first," he suggested and handed him a small vial.

Kaiden looked it over, a smile plastered on his face. "This is Dr. Soni's serum," he declared enthusiastically. "I thought she said she didn't have anymore."

Wulfson handed vials to the other soldiers. "I asked her to give me a few vials to have on standby after that time you ran into the dumbbell rack." Wulfson went back over to the desk, "Thought I might have accidentally killed ya with that one. Figured it was best to have a couple around in case you take enough damage that I need to treat ya with something right away."

"Why is it so small?" Kaiden inquired, looking at the tiny tube which contained maybe a third of the usual amount.

"I only had three vials and had to split them to give to your buddies." Wulfson leaned against the console and crossed his arms. "Plus, you need to start weaning yourself off the stuff. That's a diluted mix that can be drunk instead of injected, and it's enough to get you through the pain."

"You guys are really messing with my supply," Kaiden mumbled, downing the shot of serum.

"Nice to see where we land on your priority list," Silas retorted, swallowing his own portion.

"Right, now let's get started on the introductions," Wulfson began. "Wish I was here to do this from the beginning. It could have spared me the cleanup—or you guys a cleanup, seeing as no one is leaving till this place is tidy again."

The soldiers, with the exception of Jaxon, groaned at the news. "Shut yer traps. You're lucky I'm not adding punishment drills on top of that. But considering that all of you, with the exception of Kaiden, are first-timers, I'll let you off the hook."

"Keep offering them perks like that, and I'm sure they'll come running back," Kaiden jeered, sitting down next to Flynn. "All right, so who's your scaly friend here?"

"This here is War Chief Ran'ama Aboren Zin'til Arcquini. He lets me call him Raza for short," Wulfson announced, nodding at the Sauren. "He and I have been good friends for many years now."

"Where the hell did you two meet? At an underground gladiator tournament?" Flynn asked.

"I learned of your head officer when he was a sergeant in your planet's military," Raza related, his voice more collected and hushed than before. "When my people first made contact with your race, the various weapons and technology we discovered made us believe you were a worthy conquest."

"Wait, we were at war with you guys?" Marlo questioned.

"In the beginning, we had prepared for that," Raza answered.

"Raza was chosen to lead the initial hunting party and check us out. He and fifty of his best warriors raided Station Zappa. My company happened to be there as we were charged with transferring some supplies from Stockholm to the station." Wulfson leaned his head back as he reminisced. "My God, was *that* a thrilling battle. My company was comprised of one hundred and eleven men, and we had over three hundred guards in the station's security forces. We had the numbers advantage, but it didn't matter. It didn't seem like there was anything we could do to stop them until we got the clearance to use heavy weapons and explosives." He looked at Raza with a wry grin. "That finally got your attention."

Raza returned the officer's look for a moment before turning to address the others. "I had my warriors stand aside, and I challenged any one of the humans to face me in combat ritual."

"Combat ritual?" Kaiden asked. "Is something not translating correctly?"

"It's called the Mai'kolo, or something like that. It basically means a singular fight to decide the fate of a large battle," Wulfson explained.

"How did you even know what he was talking about?" Flynn asked, "Could you translate the Sauren language back then?"

"We had a Sauren dictionary that the Tsuna had given us. Had a couple of the techs use their EIs to help make sense of it all," Wulfson recounted. "It was pretty broken. We could only do so much in real time with a completely new language and everyone on edge. But I got the gist and stepped forward."

Raza brought out his claws, flexing them for a moment as he remembered the fight. "The battle was long and ferocious. I gained a new respect for your kind that day. There was at least one among you who could fight with the cunning and wrath of the Sauren."

"After three days, both of us were at our limit. These tenacious bastards got endurance like you wouldn't believe. But even they start feeling it after a while."

"Three days?" Silas stammered.

"Good God, man!" Flynn exclaimed, dropping his ice pack.

"How were you able to keep going for three days?" Kaiden asked.

Wulfson chuckled. "One of the crates in the shipment contained an experimental stimulant. After two days of chasing the bastards through the station, I was getting pretty soft. I took one to keep myself going, despite a few annoying techs and science idiots telling me it was dangerous." Wulfson whistled at the memory. "Let me tell you, those things made the blood in my veins damn near go nuclear. I was running around like my armor was on fire. It was a good thing these space dinosaurs can regenerate like they can because I swear, I would have been looking for other things to kill when they ran out. I probably accepted the match to keep my body moving just as much as I did to have a good fight."

"So you won?" Kaiden asked. "And you guys are friends now?"

Wulfson chuckled again, shaking his head. "Nah, I dropped. When that stuff finally got out of my system, I was worthless. Eight of my men had to carry my big ass to the station's med-bay. I detoxed for days and couldn't move a finger. It's why I try to stay away from experimental serums and the like as much as I can."

"So what happened to you?" Flynn inquired, looking at Raza. "Why did you let him go?"

Raza stood tall, placing his claws on either side of his chest, where his hearts would be. "My people are the greatest hunters and warriors in this universe, but we are not savages. Honor, respect, and tradition are always paramount to us. Wulfson proved to be a worthy challenge and an admirable fighter. I was at my limit, too. As a war chief, I represent the elite of the Sauren, and he still fought me to a standstill. It was enough for me to see that you humans were potentially more than merely game. We returned to our alpha ship and began to discuss our next move when one of the Tsuna delegates contacted us and told us that they had already made contact with you. We made a temporary agreement to halt our hunt and engage in discussion with your people."

"So you are our allies?" Silas huffed his lingering indignation. "Got a weird way of saying hello."

"Actually, the World Council has a bounty contract with them," Wulfson corrected. "There was a pretty strong desire to fight on both sides. Some members of the WC wanted to retaliate for the Sauren's attack and the Sauren... Well, we did kill some of their guys at the station, but they like a good war from time to time. So there was too much tension to really make a treaty, but the Tsuna found a loophole for us."

Kaiden gave Wulfson a confused look. "We contracted a planet? How does that work?"

Wulfson closed the chest next to him, and then shrugged his massive shoulders. "It's an exchange agreement. The Sauren are interested in our tech and weapons and the like, and we want to know as much about the universe as we can. So, in exchange for some of our tech and weapons, they bring back specimens and artifacts from the various planets they find."

"And they are less likely to kill people that are a boon to them," Jaxon surmised. "An impressive workaround indeed."

"We do not take many contracts. We are hunters, not mercenaries. But no honorable Sauren would kill a patron. It is against our code," Raza declared.

"And everyone abides by that?" Raul questioned. "You don't have rogues or traitors?"

"I'm sure every species does. We are no exception." Raza's voice deepened, a snarl escaping after every other word. "But those that turn away from our code are no longer considered Sauren. When they are caught, they are stripped of their armor and left to rot."

Flynn rubbed the back of his head. "What, you take off their leather bindings and throw them in a prison or something? I would think that breaking this code would make you do something a bit harsher than that."

"That's another translation error, kid," Wulfson stated. "Those leathers are decorative at best. Sometimes, they use them to help carry things or as whips, but that's not their armor."

"Then what is—" Flynn began before Kaiden nudged him sharply. Kaiden pulled down a jacket sleeve, exposing skin that he ran his finger across before pointing to the Sauren.

It took Flynn and the others a moment, but they all seemed to get it at once as their eyes widened. "So you skin them and leave them to bleed out and die..." Flynn croaked.

"If they survive the entire ordeal," Wulfson added. "And considering that their skin regenerates rather quickly, it's a pretty long and involved process."

Flynn reached up and rubbed his shoulder, his hand trembling slightly. "I see...yeah, that is suitably more terrifying."

"As much as this history lesson is so...engrossing, can we get back to why he said he was after me?" Kaiden asked.

"Wulfson requested me to," Raza stated.

"Do what now?" Kaiden yelped, jumping up. "What the hell did you do that for?"

"Training, as always," Wulfson replied nonchalantly. "I have to give you your due, boy. You're getting pretty damn good. I figured it was time to mix things up a bit."

"So you put out a hit on me?" Kaiden seethed.

"Of course not!" Wulfson sounded genuinely indignant. "You're my favorite pupil. I don't want you dead. Besides, if I did, I would do it, so don't feel like you constantly need to look over your shoulder."

"Yeah, because apparently, I got plenty in front of me to worry about," Kaiden sneered, rolling his eyes. "Also, I'm your only pupil."

"Not anymore, it seems," Wulfson said, placing his hands on his waist and looking at the others. "Seems I got myself a new crop of trainees now."

The others looked frantically at each other. "Well, you see this wasn't... This was more of a trial run and we..." Flynn stammered, trying to avoid Wulfson's expectant gaze. He looked at Kaiden. "Hey, mate, care to help us out here?" he whispered.

"Nah, y'all are conscripted now." Kaiden chuckled. "At

least you originally came here voluntarily. He dragged my ass here."

"Anyway, Raza was coming down here to deliver a few specimens to the Science Division here at Nexus. I figured since he was around, I would ask him to go a few rounds with you to see how you fared."

"Not great." Kaiden deadpanned.

Raza walked over to Kaiden, who tensed up as he retracted his claws and placed his hand on the ace's shoulder. "You might have lost the battle, but I will give you warrior's respect. You fought well."

"Um...thank you, war chief," Kaiden said with a small salute. Raza withdrew his hand. "Not sure if I would say we lost, though. I did have a full-powered rifle aimed at your head."

"This thing?" Wulfson asked, picking the rifle up from his desk. "Nah, this is an old bolt-model Artemis. It's great for picking off light-armored targets from a distance, but even at full power, it wouldn't have gotten through his skull. It's as thick as a ship's hull."

Kaiden's shoulders sagged. "Well, there goes my bravado." He sighed. "You sticking around, war chief?"

"You may call me Raza as Wulfson does," the Sauren stated. "I will be staying for a short while. The Academy has offered me lodging while I am on the planet." He brought his claws out again. "I hope to go on a hunt while I am here, perhaps stalk and dispatch some of the fearsome creatures you have here, such as the devil bird, avanyu serpent, giant squid, Loch Ness monster, and the Bigfoot."

Kaiden leaned over to Wulfson as Raza continued to

count the creatures he wished to hunt. "You might wanna tell him some of those aren't real."

"We don't know that for certain," Wulfson said with a smile. "And if anyone can actually find them, Raza can." Wulfson turned to address the group. "All right, you've had time to catch your breath. Everyone get up and clean this mess."

CHAPTER EIGHTEEN

It was almost ten o'clock at night when Kaiden and his group finally left the gym.

"Getting our asses kicked and then spending hours cleaning... Wulfson definitely has weird training methods," Marlo declared, his tone weary and dispirited.

"That's not how it typically goes," Kaiden muttered. "Except for the ass-kicking, that comes standard."

"We don't really have to come back, right?" Raul inquired fretfully. "I'm not sure if I want this to be a regular thing."

"Well, *I* won't force you," Kaiden said, glancing back with a sly look. "But do keep in mind that Head Officer Wulfson now knows who all of you are. If he wants you to come back, he can and will find you, and he can get away with a hell of a lot."

This caused some grumbling and sighs from the rest of the group, most debating on what they should do or whether to take the chance of skipping out of future training with Wulfson.

"I will be departing here." Genos spoke up, and the group stopped to look at him. He pointed to a building with orange trim. "That is the engineering dorm. I should return for the evening.

"You don't want to get some food before you head back?" Flynn asked. "I'm famished."

"Not required. I have a personal compartment containing a few meals I brought with me from Abisalo. I will have one of those tonight. I need to return to the dorm to continue my studies. This day of training lasted much longer than I anticipated."

Kaiden rubbed the back of his head sheepishly. "Yeah, sorry about that, Genos. I didn't exactly plan it that way."

"It is all right, friend Kaiden," Genos said, offering a hand. "It was most enjoyable after the bloodshed stopped. I can certainly admit you make things exciting."

"It's something of a guarantee when you're around me." Kaiden took the Tsuna's hand in a firm handshake. "I'll let you know the next time we have a little get together, see if you're interested."

"Certainly. Oh, before I forget…" Genos reached into a pouch on his suit, taking out the miniature Tesla generator from Kaiden's pistol and handing it to him. "Thank you for that. It will not work anymore due to the overload, but I believe you'll need it when you request a replacement."

"Thanks, Genos, that'll save me a headache." Kaiden withdrew his pistol and opened the chamber to slide the generator back into place "You have a good one."

"Which one, specifically?"

"Have a good night, Genos," Kaiden clarified with a grin.

"To you as well." The rest of the group said their farewells for the evening as he left, waving goodbye.

"Nice chap." Flynn stretched for a moment before crossing his arms behind his head. "So, do you guys wanna hit the cafeteria?"

They all agreed and had turned to head that way when Kaiden got a message on his display. He looked it over for a moment and saw it was from Chiyo.

Hello, Kaiden,

If you have the time, please meet me by the fountain. There is something I would like to discuss.

~Chiyo

"Well, that's rather cryptic," he mumbled. He removed his oculars and thought for a moment, wondering what to make of it.

"You coming, Kaiden?" Silas asked, noticing that he no longer followed them.

"Huh? Oh…sorry, guys, something came up. I'll have to skip this one."

"Where are you going? Some sort of errand for the professor?" Flynn asked.

"I'm not his whipping boy," Kaiden protested. "I'm going to meet up with someone before grabbing a bite."

"Don't be too long. Cafeteria closes soon," Luke warned.

"It closes at midnight. I'll be fine," Kaiden replied easily. "I'll see you guys around, and remember…" He looked back with a devious smile. "Y'alls' first real practice with Wulfson is next week."

He snickered when he heard more groans behind him

as he walked away. They were likely to say terrible things about him while he was gone.

Chiyo waited by the fountain, sitting on the edge. She saw on her network list that Kaiden was headed her way, so in the meantime, she took a moment to collect herself and run through what she wanted to say.

She didn't know why she'd requested that they meet there—the fountain from their first encounter. She supposed it was for the privacy or maybe a change of pace from their usual meetings at their table in the cafeteria. Whatever the reason, it made for a nice view, something pleasant to watch as she ran through her proposal in her mind.

"Chiyo? You still here?" Kaiden called.

"Other side," Chiyo replied, walking around to meet him.

"What's up? Your message was pretty vague. You got some problem you need help with?"

"In a sense, I suppose," she admitted. "Though it may be your problem as well, knowing your difficulty in keeping up with all the rules and events at the Academy."

"Oh, good, the confusing riddles are back," Kaiden lamented. "Can I simply pay the toll instead of having to guess what you're talking about?"

Chiyo sighed. "You know about the co-operative test coming up, correct?"

Kaiden nodded. "Yeah, the Co-op test…what about it?"

"Are you prepared for it?" she inquired.

"For the most part. I've been training like hell the last couple months. At this point, I can probably do the entire test myself, even if it's meant for two people," he declared confidently.

"Do you know what the test entails?" she asked, eyeing him skeptically.

"I'm guessing it's like the Division test, right? Just twice as hard and meant for two people," he replied, but she shook her head.

"This should have been explained to you during your ace workshop weeks ago. Were you paying attention?"

"Uh, when exactly?" Kaiden asked.

"More than six weeks ago. The ace instructor was filling in the rest of the class while you and I were talking about the pros and cons of different guns," Chief reminded him, popping into view.

Kaiden grimaced. "Oh, good, you're back. Do you still feel like you can take over the world?"

"Oh yeah, but I believe I shall show the peons mercy and let them continue with their miserable existences...for now," Chief said, trying his best to sound ominous.

"What a benevolent god you are," Kaiden sneered. "What would your title be? Chiefitus, the god of snark and sparkles?"

"Better than whatever you're in the running for. Kaiden, patron saint of disgrace and serum addiction."

"Serum addiction can't be a condition. That seems like a contradiction," Kaiden snapped, shaking his head. Remembering where he was, he looked at Chiyo. "Sorry about that, Chiyo. Got distracted by— You all right?" he asked, distracted by her stare. He followed her line of vision and looked over to what she seemed transfixed by—Chief. "Can you see Chief?" he asked, pointing in the general direction.

She nodded. "I assumed it was a projection or hologram, but I don't see a device. And if it was a projection, I wouldn't be able to hear it. How am I able to see your EI without connecting to your device or you displaying it?"

"It's a part of my swanky new upgrade," Chief explained. *"When I'm in visual mode, I can be seen by anyone close enough to Kaiden and wearing an ocular device. Impressive, right?"*

"What upgrade?" Chiyo inquired.

Kaiden sighed. "That Next-gen talent in the EI tree. I put one point in it, and Chief now thinks that he's EI Jesus."

"Fascinating." Chiyo took another look at Chief. "I've put a point in that talent for Kaitō, but it didn't allow for something like this."

"Not to stop you from getting into the zone or whatever is going on here, but did you call me over here for something particular or did you want someone to watch the fountain do that little water geyser show it does every hour with you?" Kaiden asked.

She shook herself out of her daze. "Of course. My apologies. What I intended to say is that the Co-op test is not like the Division test. It is done in teams of two, which can be any duo, no matter the division or class. The test gets its name because it requires each player to cooperate with the other, relying on each other's skills and strengths. It was actually created with each of the two individuals' specialty in mind. Each player has their own personal objective that they must complete before the duo can win.

If they fail to complete their objective or either player dies, the test is failed."

"Just once? No lives this time?" Kaiden questioned.

"Not in this one or any future tests. It's the real experience from now on," Chiyo stated.

Kaiden took a seat on the edge of the fountain. "I see. Well, I guess, if that's the case, when do we learn who our partners are?"

"You can choose your own partner as long as you both agree to team up for the test. As long as you do it before the deadline, that is."

Kaiden leaned back on his hands. "Oh, well that certainly works. When is the deadline?"

"Tomorrow night. After that, you will be assigned a random partner from those available," Chiyo responded.

Kaiden leaped up. "Wait, that soon? How long have we had to choose?"

"Since all of this was explained to you weeks ago."

"You really live for these little jabs, don't you?" Kaiden muttered. "None of the others mentioned anything about partnering up. Devious bastards, keeping me out of the loop."

"To be fair to them, they were probably under the assumption that you were aware of everything. Plus, I would think most of them would pair up with each other. They have known each other longer," Chiyo reasoned.

"That's true," Kaiden confessed. "I can't give them too much of a hard time." He looked at her. "So, what about you? Who'd you end up partnering up with?"

Chiyo took a deep breath, reaching down to her bag for

her tablet. "That's actually why I messaged you, to begin with."

Sasha heard a knock at his door. "Good evening, Mya." He spoke before the door even opened.

"How did you know it was me?" she asked as the door slid open.

"You are the only person I've been expecting," he stated as he typed on his holo-board. "Please have a seat. How can I help you?"

Mya slid a chair in front of Sasha's desk back and sat down. "It's about the League, actually."

Sasha nodded, continuing to type. "Ah yes, the League. Going well for you so far?"

"Pretty good for the most part...but I must admit, there have been a couple of bumps here and there."

"Oh? How so?" Sasha asked, true interest in his voice despite not looking away from his monitor.

"A couple of my picks did not end up partnering for the co-op test like I thought they would. They are good friends and had pretty good scores up till now, so I thought it might not matter. However, seeing as the test is coming up soon and one of my other choices hasn't even partnered with anyone, I might have some trouble in the future."

"You are referring to Chiyo Kana, correct?" Sasha inquired.

"I...yes, how did you know?" she asked, bewildered.

"I'm looking at your League profile." Sasha spun his monitor around to show her.

She smiled. "I was beginning to believe that you are omniscient."

"No need when you have a thorough database." He moved his hands from the board and rested them on his desk. "So, have you come to ask for advice or to talk options?"

Mya gave him a questioning look. "I wouldn't think you would want to help out the competition."

"The reason I stopped playing in the League was that it eventually grew boring for me. Too many people going for the obvious candidates and not preparing the right squad for the finals," Sasha admitted. "I gave other teachers and faculty pointers during the last few years. Even though I came back due to the potential of the students this year, it doesn't mean I'm not still willing to give a helpful tip to those who ask. It makes the challenge greater."

"You're not afraid to lose your streak?"

Sasha tapped his fingers on his desk. "I technically already have since I didn't continue. Plus, it's not like I would be helping out a novice. You got first place last year using an underdog team and an interesting lineup. I certainly respect that."

"Well, thank you," Mya said graciously, warmed by the genuine praise. "But it would seem my strategy is not panning out as well this year. Even with Chiyo giving me a boost, I'm six hundred and thirty points behind where I was last year."

"You also frequently swapped out students with wild-cards last year," Sasha noted. "Can't do that this year, can you?"

"Unfortunately not. I don't have the wiggle room I once did," she admitted. "However, I can still trade."

"That you can," Sasha agreed. "And I'm not much for playing coy, so I'm guessing you came to me for that very reason?

Mya pouted slightly. "You know, you can really be rather dry sometimes, Sasha."

"I spend most of my time surrounded by a lake. I'll be fine," he retorted.

Mya was silent for a moment before allowing herself a giggle. "Was that a pun, Commander?"

"I suppose so," he admitted with a slight smile. "But back to the topic. What are you looking to suggest?"

"I would like to trade for Jensen Lovett, your sapper," she stated. "He's partnered with my surveyor, so I was hoping that I could get him so that I could get the Co-op bonus for my score."

Sasha cocked his head. "You know, I am aware that you weren't looking for advice, but perhaps you shouldn't be so blunt with your intentions. You're giving me almost all the power in the negotiations."

"I like to lead with an honest impression," Mya countered. "But does that mean you're willing to trade?"

Sasha leaned back in his chair but continued to tap his fingers his on desk. "I am, but I don't think you're going to be excited about it."

"You want Chiyo?" she guessed.

He nodded. "She's the only one of any interest to me. I have no need for a surgeon as I already have Initiate Ziegler on my team. She's a battle medic."

Mya groaned. "I expected this, but it doesn't make the choice any easier."

"If it helps, do remember you get to keep the points you've gotten with Chiyo so far. Or, if you're unwilling to make that trade, you could ask Instructor Venture if he's willing to trade his enforcer, who's teamed up with your surgeon. That could be a strong pairing."

"Venture is more stubborn than you are when it comes to the League. I don't think he's ever traded or even swapped with wildcards. He likes to think he got it right on the first go."

"An odd deduction since he's never gotten higher than thirty-second place." Sasha chuckled.

Mya sighed, mulling over the pros and cons as she contemplated her options. "I feel kind of bad giving away my first pick—one that you helped me get."

"I have no idea what you mean." Sasha feigned ignorance with a sincerity only he could pull off.

"Of course not," she jested, then accepted the inevitable. "All right, I'll give you Chiyo. But considering that you also have Kaiden, aren't you worried both are going to give you trouble when it comes to cooperation?"

"I'm prepared to take that risk for the potential reward," Sasha assured her. He pressed Chiyo's icon on the screen, clicking the trade for option and selecting Jensen from his team. "Scan here to agree," he instructed.

Mya leaned forward and put her index finger on the screen. After a moment, a small *bing* sounded from the monitor, and the icons swapped teams. "Well, it's done now," she said as she stood. "Thank you, Sasha, and best of luck."

JOSHUA ANDERLE & MICHAEL ANDERLE

"To you as well, Mya. Have a good—" Sasha froze, his gaze fixed on his monitor, and raised an eyebrow in curiosity.

"What's wrong?" she asked.

He crossed his arms. "Nothing wrong, merely interesting." He nodded at the monitor for Mya to take a look. "It would seem I will be doubling down on my risk and reward."

Mya took a peek, her eyes widening when she saw the message onscreen.

Kaiden Jericho and Chiyo Kana partner for Co-op test. Bonus points earned if they pass.

"Wow…poor timing on my part." Mya sighed and fixed him with a mischievous look. "Wanna trade back?"

Sasha stared at her and shook his head, pointing toward the door.

CHAPTER NINETEEN

I t was a cool late-autumn evening as Chiyo made her way to the Animus center. She looked at the board to see which halls were available for use. Ten halls open for the first-years. Eight were at max capacity, while the other two were also nearly full.

"It would appear many of the students are preparing for the Co-op tests," Kaitō reasoned, appearing on the board.

"I would prefer a more secluded area," she stated, using the board to reserve a private room.

"Will Kaiden be able to access the private rooms?"

"He's a rank two, so it's one of his privileges. He shouldn't have any problems, but we'll have to send him a message and tell him."

"Tell me what?" Chiyo looked back to see Kaiden enter the hall. "We having a surprise party?"

"Good evening, Kaiden." She greeted him while continuing to work on the screen. "Good timing."

"I can be punctual on occasion, and I'm always down for a quickie when available."

Chiyo gave him a puzzled look, and he gave himself a quick knock on the side of his forehead. "I'm talking about missions, in this case." He looked at a board which now displayed a visual of an Animus pod. "Don't think that's even possible in one of those. I don't think they really have the space for it."

"Charming," she retorted dryly. "Have you used a private room recently?"

"A private room? For like a party or something?" he asked.

Chiyo sighed. "I usually find your obliviousness of the rules and regulations a refreshing change of pace, but the fact that it extends to things that can be helpful to you is a bit concerning."

"What's she talking about, Chief?" Kaiden asked aloud.

Chief appeared, floating in the air, *"She means an Animus private room. As a rank two, you can make a reservation once a week to use one."* Chief turned to address Chiyo. *"Sorry, Ms. Chiyo, he doesn't speak over one hundred I.Q."*

"Ms. Chiyo? Why are you so respectful to her and not to me? I never got a sir or captain...I'll even settle for a mister."

"The difference is I actually respect her," Chief stated bluntly. *"Funny how that works, isn't it?"*

"And I thought we were doing so well thus far," Kaiden whined.

"You gain and lose that respect every day. You used to be here." Chief hovered at around chest level, then lowered

slowly to hover near the ground. *"Currently, you are around here."*

Kaiden glowered at the EI for a moment. "Hey, Chiyo, you wanna trade EIs?" he asked flatly.

Chief turned an annoyed red, his eye furrowing. *"Your polls continue to drop, buddy."*

"As much as I find Chief to be an interesting…personality, and your EI implant a marvel, I am quite happy with Kaitō."

"I am fond of you as well, madame," the fox EI murmured appreciatively.

"You see? He's also a super smart EI, and he's nice," Kaiden grumbled.

Chief floated up to the board and looked at Kaitō. "He's also a fox. You can't trust foxes."

"Really? You gonna pick on him for that?" Kaiden huffed.

"Is there something wrong with my design?" Kaitō questioned, looking around his frame.

"Don't worry about it, Kaitō, Chief is simply petty." Kaiden crossed his arms and eyed Chief mockingly. "For someone who kept going on about how they transcend every EI out there, you sure still have a fragile ego."

Chiyo chuckled as Chief grumbled, "Even if I was interested in an exchange, it would not be possible between us."

"Why's that?"

"You said you had the Gemini factor, correct? It's what allowed you the ability to use the device in the first place."

"And do I ever feel so lucky." He deadpanned, though his eyes brimmed with laughter.

"I do not have the factor; therefore, the device would not work for me. It would be a waste," she concluded.

"Damn shame. You could probably get more use out of it than I do since you're a hacker."

"Perhaps, but just because I do not personally have the abilities does not mean I cannot use them," she hinted, a smile ghosting at the corners of her mouth.

"Is there something I should be picking up on?" Kaiden wondered aloud.

"The sense of foreboding?" Chief floated back to Kaiden.

"It'll be a little clearer once we've started." She pointed to the elevator hall. "Shall we go?"

"You got a room?" Kaiden asked as they departed.

"As a merit-based SC and a rank two myself, I also have the privilege, but you'll have to reserve it next week until mine resets."

"So there will be a next time?" he muttered under his breath. "I thought this was a trial run."

"We're partners now, Kaiden. I have no intention of switching. I can think of no better situation than the one we have now," she assured him as she pressed the up button for the elevator.

"Thanks for the vote of confidence…if I'm reading that right. So, what are we dealing with tonight?"

The doors to the elevator opened and they stepped inside. Chiyo pressed the key for the eighth floor. "A basic Co-op mission, a simplified version of what we'll be dealing with in the actual test."

Kaiden leaned back against the wall. "Got any ideas what we'll be doing?"

"There are a handful of possibilities, but the mission

objectives are not the most important aspect of these missions."

Kaiden held up a hand. "I know, it's cooperation—how the two students work with each other," he muttered haughtily.

She gave him a questioning look, and he shrugged in response. "Sorry, I've heard that from almost everyone any time it gets brought up, like people are afraid they're gonna get a sniper bullet to the dome if they don't repeat it incessantly."

"It's an important clarification to make. The mission objectives are simply the winning criteria. How you complete them together determines the true score."

"How does it work any different in a team mission?" he asked as the elevator doors opened.

They stepped out onto the eighth floor as Chiyo explained in a patient tone, "In a team mission, there are several members all working towards the same goal. In cooperative missions, there are several goals a duo or team must complete, and they must work together to complete them as efficiently as possible."

"So what does that mean, exactly?" he queried.

"I would say that there are things only I can do and things that you can do better than me."

"Was that a dig?" he asked, amused.

"Not at all. I can hack and you cannot, and I can fight but combat is not my forte, it is yours."

"I can hack," Kaiden challenged. "I learned some basic stuff from some of my gang's techs a few years back."

"I see...then I suppose I should change my view. There

are things you can do better than I can, and there are things I can do *much* better than you."

"That...honestly doesn't seem like much of a step up," he mumbled.

"We're here." They had reached the end of a long hallway and a single door on the wall in front of them. Chiyo placed her hand on a panel adjacent to the door. The panel flashed briefly and cleared for entry. The room was small, and in the muted lighting, three Animus pods were visible. They stood upright in the center with a small console behind them.

"Welcome, Initiate Chiyo Kana and Initiate Kaiden Jericho. This room has been reserved, and you will have four hours from when you enter the Animus. Please choose your parameters from the hub at the back of the room."

Kaiden looked around warily. "You know, a private room is usually nice and swanky...this feels like a reno-vated interrogation room."

"It's meant for Animus use only, no need for decora-tions or amenities," Chiyo stated briskly, walking over to the console.

"If you want, I can send in a request for some flowers and a cheese basket when you come back next week." Chief chuckled.

"See if we can get you an EI skin with a little bowtie. It would pull the whole posh atmosphere together," Kaiden gibed at the EI.

"Keep it up, and I'll be looking for an executioner's hood."

"Kaiden, would you come over here please?"

He walked around the console. "What's up?"

She nodded at the screen. "I want you to look over the mission and accept it before we begin."

"Pity, I was looking forward to going in blind. Makes it more excitin'."

"The test will be blind, so we must be as prepared as possible."

"I follow," he conceded, taking a look at the screen. "So what do we got?"

Mission: Co-op
  Map: Axiom Industries
  Players:
  Chiyo Kana (1ˢᵗ year)
  Kaiden Jericho (1ˢᵗ year)
  Mission Objectives:
  Both players will start outside the building and make their way in within ten minutes.

  Get access into the technology development department and retrieve the marked device.

  Take the device to the retrieval zone.
  Both players must survive.
  The device cannot be destroyed

"Seems simple enough," Kaiden said. "Have a look at the glossary."

Chiyo opened the tab. He studied the enemies they would face.

Human opponents:
  Security Force Soldier:

Description: Basic foot soldiers, dressed in white armor with blue uniforms.

Armor: Light

Weapon: Cobra heavy pistol or Spitfire light machine gun

Melee: Stun baton

Gadget: Flashbang

Special Abilities: None

Security Force Trooper:

Description: Elite soldiers with improved armor and stronger weapons.

Armor: Heavy

Weapon: Eviscerator Shotgun or Cyclone Machine Gun

Melee: Stun baton

Gadget: Stun Grenade

Special Ability: None.

"Well, they'll be a breeze," Kaiden said with a cocky smirk.

"Even the guards with heavy armor?" Chiyo asked.

"No worries. I've got ballistic rounds that'll crack those suckers open without a problem," he assured her. "Might have to do a gadget swap when we get in, now I think about it… What else they got?"

"There are a couple of different robotic enemies we'll have to deal with." Chiyo switched to the next page.

Robotic Opponents:

Defense Model-Guardian:

Description: Mass produced, mid-range defense droid. Travels on treads and has a short body and rounded head with 180-degree vision.

Armor: Medium

Weapon: Single burst laser on right arm.

Melee: Four-pronged claw on left arm with electrical nodes for tazing on contact.

Gadget: None

Special Abilities: Alarm function.

"Those might be a pain in the ass." Kaiden sighed. "I'd have to be sure to take them out quick so they can't sound the alarm."

"I'll worry about that. I can deactivate their remote access to the alarms and blind their vision. Just be sure not to deal with too many at once," Chiyo warned him.

"I'll do my best, but I got to say that I'm not exactly the greatest at stealth—"

"He once leaped onto a group of guards in another test actually screaming 'Ssssteeeallllltthhh!' like it gave him power or something," Chief related with perverse humor.

Chiyo looked quizzically at Kaiden. "I was making a point to Flynn, our marksman...can't really remember what I was trying to get across, but by God, did I do it." Kaiden grinned.

"Please try to keep that to a minimum here," she requested. "There are a couple more units we have to worry about, so please continue."

Defense Model-Scarab:

Description: Small, quick moving, spider-like drones that move in packs to overwhelm and capture targets.

Armor: Light

Weapon: Laser blasters on the top of the body.

Melee: Will use their long, sharp legs to stab or entrap their target if they get close.

Gadget: None

Special Ability: None

"Oh good, those little bastards," Kaiden growled with something close to sadistic pleasure.

"You deal with them a lot?" she inquired, her expression openly curious.

"A few times, but the worst was during the Division test. Remember that big-ass war machine I told you about?"

"I do. I couldn't find anything relating to it afterward."

"I told you I blew it up from the inside, but I skipped past the part where I had to deal with literally hundreds of these damn things while I did it." He shook his head in annoyance at the memory. "I think I was more relieved to be rid of those things than that big walker."

Chiyo looked at the visual of the drone. "I'll be sure to keep a lookout. They're pretty basic and therefore easy to get into. I'll see what I can do once we begin."

Prowler Model-Hellcat:

Description: A four-legged automaton that can reach speeds of thirty-five miles an hour to chase down targets.

Weapon: Small stun laser on head.

Melee: Claws and fangs meant to trap or maul targets depending on orders.

Gadget: Knockout gas deployed from mouth.

Special ability: Thermal and Night Vision.

Kaiden let out a quick, surprised whistle. "Those are new."

"I've had to deal with them in a couple of my previous scenarios. Never a problem as I was usually not near them..." She looked up. "You, however—"

"Will be playing the mouse in a very violent game of cat and mouse, I figure." He sighed.

"While it will be important to be mindful of the robotic opponents, this is where the cooperation comes in." Chiyo reminded him. "In this situation, I will be able to get us into the building, and I can deal with the drones remotely. You'll have to be the one doing most of the footwork and dealing with the security soldiers."

"That's something that is certainly my speed." Kaiden nodded approval. "Do we have a map?"

"Not available, at least in the mission set up. I can get us one when I'm inside their system."

"So then it's a smash and grab?" Kaiden asked. "We'll get in there, and I'll run through and do my thing. If you can get the map and keep the drones off me, then we'll have this done in no time."

"Not exactly." She drew a breath and fixed him with a

focused look. "They'll probably activate a lockdown if you're not careful. In that case, I'll have to spend time and concentrate on keeping doors unlocked or even more time unlocking them if they do close before I can get to them. There might also be turrets and barricades along the routes."

"And a pit of acid, wall spikes that close in on you, and sharks with lasers attached to their heads," Kaiden scoffed. "I'll be sure to bring explosives."

"What I'm saying is that you should allow me to properly set up before we begin," Chiyo stated firmly.

"How long will that take?"

"Around thirty minutes to an hour, depending on the variables and if I do it properly."

"Good Lord! Do you redecorate the office while you're there?" Kaiden let his mockery creep though. "I thought you guys were masters of getting in and out of networks unseen in seconds."

"I very much am, but I'll be hacking into the entire system, not one specific piece or area. That takes time," she corrected him, again with an air of extreme patience.

"Doesn't the actual test have a time limit? You won't be able to set up like that when we have to do the real thing," Kaiden argued.

"True, but this is simply one kind of mission. I'll need to do it like this so that I can see how to best assist you during following missions—identify which areas are the most important and which are frivolous. That will make things go much smoother in the future."

Kaiden paused, surprised by her explanation. "You're doing this to help me?"

"Technicians, as a division, are not for frontline assault.

We help from the backline or the shadows—or through the system in the case of a hacker like myself. We need to work together, Kaiden. I know that you'll take on the dangerous activities, so I'll need to know how I can help you best for the test and any other situation we may have to face together in the future."

"I...I see." Kaiden felt a little humbled. He had mocked Chiyo's suggestions, thinking she was being too methodical or even paranoid. She did have that special insignia for a reason, he reminded himself, so maybe he should defer to her for now. "Thanks...I'll give you the time you need."

"Thank you. I promise to work as fast as I can," she said, her smile one of obvious relief.

Kaiden rubbed the back of his head. "Don't worry about it. I'll find something to do."

Chiyo stood up. "Unless you want to look at anything else, we can begin."

Kaiden looked at the screen for a moment, pressing a tab giving it a cursory study.

Synchronicity: 5

Tangibility: 5

Equilibrium: 5

"Nah, I'm good." He moved toward the pod opposite Chiyo. "You got any games or anything loaded up, Chief? Maybe I can freshen up on my poker while are waiting."

CHAPTER TWENTY

"Mission *beginning in ten minutes*," announced a synthetic voice as Kaiden appeared in the Animus. *"Please make final preparations."*

He looked around and appeared to be in the middle of a forest. Focused now, he peered through the foliage to see the lights of a large building in the distance with a ten-foot metal wall surrounding it. "Chiyo? You make it in yet?"

He felt a couple of quick taps on his shoulder. "Behind you, Kaiden." Chiyo stood in her gear, a dark-blue set of light armor. She had no helmet, but instead, a holo-visor completely covered her eyes in shimmering light.

"You look like you're headed to a rave." He chuckled.

"This visor allows me to run three times the number of programs and applications that I can normally with my basic optics," she explained, bringing up her loadout window. "Along with allowing me to issue commands and actions mentally."

"That certainly sounds nifty," he said appreciatively as he opened his own loadout. "Can you cast with it?"

"Not like you can. I need to either hack into a system and make a path for Kaitō to access remotely or be granted permission." She pressed an option to alter her armor, changing to a black bodysuit with a dark-grey chest piece, knee pads, and gauntlets.

"You gonna be all right in so little armor?" Kaiden asked with concern. "I would guess you can maybe take a couple of good shots before you're down."

"That's why I have you here. You're the one who will deal with most of the gunfire. Will *you* be okay?"

"I can dance around the fire just fine," he declared. "Besides, if I kill them first, I won't have to worry too much about lasers and bullets coming my way."

Chiyo closed her loadout screen "I would recommend you change to a mostly non-lethal loadout."

"Why's that?" His tone sounded both curious and hesitant. "I'm game to take your advice this round, but non-lethal isn't really my style."

"Think of it as a chance to expand your repertoire," she advised. "I told you that I'll deal with most of the robotic enemies along with the security system. That leaves you with the security force. They are equipped with vita tethers that will alert other guards to your location if their heart stops beating. Stunning them or knocking them out will give you more respite before others come. In addition, most electric stun guns can overload simple locks and machines, giving you a quicker way to get through doors and shut down defenses."

Kaiden peered back at his loadout, sighing. "Chief, you wanna lend a hand here?"

The bulbous EI appeared on the screen. *You know, while I'm going to agree with pretty princess logic, I have to admit I wasn't prepared to ever have to look for a mostly 'considerate' loadout... give me a moment,* he requested, disappearing as the various weapon tabs opened and were quickly scanned through.

"Pretty princess logic?" Chiyo muttered as she walked up beside Kaiden.

The ace sighed. "His nicknames don't usually stick the first couple of times. Don't worry about it. At least he complimented you. I'm usually partner or dumbass if he wants to show he cares."

"You two have an odd dynamic."

"It works for the most part. At least currently...I think I'm going to hold off on giving him another Next-Gen upgrade, though."

"Usually, I would tell you that should be a priority. However, your EI seemed rather advanced even in his previous state. I can only imagine what he can do now with an upgrade."

"So far it's only given him a glow-up and sparkles. I'm not quite sure what else he's got in him," he admitted.

"Done," Chief shouted, and a number of option appeared onscreen. *"Take your pick. All options have the Chief seal of approval."*

Kaiden looked through the choices.

Main Weapons:

Medusa Stun Rifle:

Description: A Nexus Tech designed stun rifle that, after a brief charge, fires a bolt of static energy that will knock out the target and lock up their muscles for up to an hour. The blast bypasses physical armor.

Amnesia Tranquilizer Rifle:

Description: A long range rifle that fires darts filled with a potent tranquilizer called the Amnesiac Sedative. The sedative works quickly, and each cartridge contains ten rounds. There is a brief moment of delay between thirty seconds and one and a half minutes before the target is fully knocked unconscious. However, they begin feeling drowsy and disoriented almost immediately after they have been struck.

Important Note: Remember to aim for exposed portions in the armor. The needles can burrow into bodysuits and other thin material but are not thick enough to bypass even light armor.

Kaiden cocked his head to the side. "Just two options?"

"*It's all you got at the moment that would work for this scenario. The other options are experimental stuff the Nexus techs are trying to test.*"

"I'll probably be going through corridors and hallways for the most part, right?" Kaiden asked Chiyo.

She looked at the building. "There might be some wider spaces in there, but if our priority is to retrieve the device and leave as quickly as possible, I would say that most of your time will be running through confined spaces."

Kaiden reached out to press the tranquilizer rifle. "I

guess I'll go with this. Better to have something I can repeatedly shoot than something that needs to charge up each time to fire."

"An understandable choice, but you'll be sacrificing the possible boons of an electric weapon in this scenario," Chiyo pointed out.

"Ah, but not so, madame," Chief stated. *"Wait until you see the sidearms."*

The rifle was accepted, and the screen changed to a new set of weapons.

Sidearms:

Jupiter Pistol:

Description: A compact pistol that fires blasts of electricity with one hundred milliamps, enough to cause pain and seizure in an armored target and fry most electrical devices.

Raijū Arc Pistol:

Description: This pistol ionizes the air, allowing one shot to travel through the air and hit multiple targets. Best used against synthetic targets but can still knock out the first target hit and cause pain to any other targets struck by the jumping electricity.

The Sandman:

Description: A small grenade launcher that fires explosive canisters that emit a cloud of anesthetic gas that causes disorientation and then unconsciousness after a few seconds of exposure.

Warning: Gas masks can lessen or nullify the effects.

"That last one sounds pretty cool...but considering I already have the tranq rifle, best to grab one of the other ones."

"I recommend the arc pistol. I use them myself from time to time, and they will prove the most useful against any robots or drones that I cannot get too," Chiyo suggested.

"I'm playing it your way this time around, so I'll take your word for it," Kaiden said as he selected the arc pistol. "What's next?"

"Melee. I'll speed this up since y'all don't have a lot of time left." Chief changed the screens quickly. *"You can either keep your blade, or if you want to go whole-hog on this pacifist run-through, you can choose either a stun baton or a shock gauntlet."*

Kaiden's interest piqued for a moment. "What's a shock gauntlet?"

"What you probably think it is. It's attached to one of your hands, and you can either tell me to turn it on or pump your fist three times to manually activate it. It delivers an electric smack that is enough to stun an opponent or overload any systems they may have in their helmet, so you have an opportunity to finish them off."

"Does it work against bots?" he asked as he opened the description box and looked at the 3D visual.

"Not great against the hellcats and little scarab bastards, but it'll probably be enough to knock them away if they get too close."

Kaiden smiled. "I'm feeling experimental. Give me the gauntlet."

"Coming right up." Chief activated the selection. *"Finally,*

there's your gadgets. You've still got the shock grenades and barrier from before. They seemed good to me unless you wanna look at some alternatives."

"The shock grenades might be a bit much in this scenario. Those little bastards are loud."

"They're grenades, so most of them are," Chief noted dryly. *"If you want, you can go with some smokes or knockout gas canisters, but those might be picked up in the sensors. Other options are a heart-rate radar to locate targets in a wide radius, thermal goggles, or you can try a security drone."*

"What does that do?"

"It has an electric blaster and has three functions, defense, attack, and patrol. Defense means it hovers behind you and keeps your flank protected. Attack means it assists you in battle and attacks any target you command it to, and patrol means you can control it remotely and use it to look around corners and the like. The downside is that it requires both gadget slots to use—one for it and the other for its chip that you gotta slide into your mask to control it."

"Can't I just cast you into it?" Kaiden queried.

"My guess is you can, but the loadout screen won't let you choose only the drone. I keep running the command but no dice. It looks like Laurie hasn't gotten to that little hotfix."

"Of course not. Little details like that would get in the way of him creating a robot that shines your shoes while cleansing your colon." Kaiden sighed. "Guess it's fine. Sounds like too much of a pain, plus it doesn't look that sturdy. One good shot and I'm out of a drone."

"You want to stick with the current stuff?"

"Is there an EMP or something?"

"Oh, yeah, that wouldn't be a problem," Chief snarked.

"I would think that you were protected against one," he argued.

"I am, but the rest of your gear isn't. An EMP would be a last resort option. You would be hobbling yourself for a kill switch. Not to mention if you use it in the wrong place, you could knock Chiyo's device out too."

"Okay, good point. What are you thinking, Chiyo?"

"I believe what you currently have will suffice." She nodded, and Kaiden and Chief looked at one another and finished the loadout. "We should prepare to depart. Should everything go as planned, then you will hopefully be dealing with minimal combat anyway."

"As much as that makes for an easy time, it's not really my style." He accepted his loadout with a grin. "I mean, gotta have a love for your work, right?" His new gear flashed into existence on his back, hip, and arm as he spoke.

"I find joy in a successful mission, not during one," Chiyo responded, walking to the edge of the forest. "Kaitō, scan the area."

Kaiden leaned up against a tree. "I'll get ya to cut loose when we do things my way. I mean, if you think about it, you're kinda like a cybernetic puppet master, and that's kinda like playing one of those strategy games."

"With the exception that if I fail, it could lead to my death—or my team's," she retorted.

"Games can be played with high stakes," Kaiden countered. "I know what it means to feel like you're responsible for the lives of others. It's one of the sad facts in life that you can't control everything. So you gotta have a bit of fun with the things you can."

Her scan completed, she looked back at Kaiden. "You can say this while we're in the relative safety of the Animus, but what about in the field? In reality?"

"That's when you really need it," he argued. "If you're in a bad place, panic and desperation are more likely to get to you when you shoulder too much and things don't go your way. Gotta roll with it. I told you that before, remember?"

"I do, but every situation cannot be handled the same way. It's an admirable outlook you have, but what if something should happen in which you have absolutely no say in what happens—where you have to follow orders?"

Kaiden took out his pistol and inspected it morosely. "I can play ball now and then like I am now."

"What if you need to do so all the time?"

"Like where exactly?" he challenged.

"After we graduate, what if you're sent to work in the military? Or perhaps in the security forces of a large company? You won't be in command or even autonomous." She looked back at the building, her gaze searching for an entrance. "Will you be able to cope?"

"Ah, right, almost forgot about that contract thing..." He gave it a few seconds of thought. "I'll find a way to make it work."

"Someone with your skills will probably have their pick of many potential contracts, so you might find one that suits you," she stated thoughtfully. "But you're still under contract either way unless you have the means to buy out your own contract."

"That's an option?" he asked.

"Mission begins in two minutes. Please prepare to depart starting zone."

"Come over here, Kaiden," Chiyo requested. Kaiden walked up to the edge of the forest and stopped beside her. She pointed to one part of the wall. "There's a personnel door in that wall. Let's start there. I'll hack the door and any cameras nearby, but I'll need you to take care of any guards in the vicinity."

"Where do we need to get to for you to set up?" he asked as he withdrew his tranq rifle, checking the weight and balance quickly.

"A quiet area away from most of the traffic and the guards will suffice, but the best location would be in their security room or an area that would allow me access to as much of their system as possible—possibly the CEO's office or a room with a central hub."

"The CEO's office would certainly be nice and posh, but they like to keep to themselves at the top of the building." Kaiden looked up at the top of the tower. "Looks like that's around twenty stories up—a bit of a climb with time being a factor. But a place like that probably has maintenance hatches and personnel shortcuts we can exploit. If you can find a map once we get in there, we can use that to reach the security room or central hub or whatever and find you a nice, comfy spot to do your thing."

"Are you sure?" she asked. "We'll have to keep as quiet as possible to get there without catching the attention of the guards. If we're caught or the alarm is sounded, I won't be able to do much about it without setup."

"Just got to be subtle about it," Kaiden advised.

"I thought you said that's not your style," she said with a curious tone.

"Oh, it's not," he confirmed. "But that's why I've got you,

infiltrator. Do your thing while we make our way through, and I'll keep as quiet as I can in over a hundred pounds of armor and equipment."

Chiyo glanced at him for a moment before showing a small smile and nodding. "Understood. Follow my lead for now, then when I've opened their system, I'll follow yours."

"Sounds like a deal," Kaiden agreed, raised his rifle, and looked down its sights. "Give us the go sign, announcer."

"Mission begins in five...four...three...two...one...begin!"

With that, Chiyo and Kaiden made their way toward the gate and the first test of their new partnership.

CHAPTER TWENTY-ONE

K aiden grabbed the lever, grunting as he forced it up, and heard the hiss of released air as the hatch opened. He ushered Chiyo into the crawl space and followed after her, reaching back quickly to grab a handle on the inside of the hatch and close it behind them.

"The ladder is straight ahead," she said, as they scurried rapidly through the vent. "So far, no one seems suspicious, assuming they don't find the guards you knocked out."

"We'll be fine," he assured her. "I threw them all in the garbage bin. Unless they regularly check for their buddies taking naps among the trash, I think we'll be in the clear for as long as we're here."

"You certainly seem positive about that," Chiyo noted, pulling herself out of the shaft and into a small circular area with another ladder going up four floors.

"Are you suggesting I don't know how to get rid of a body?" Kaiden asked, feigning annoyance. "I'll have you know that was the very first merit badge I ever earned."

"I don't think that is an approved skill for the scouts," she countered, pressing herself against the wall to give Kaiden enough room to climb out of the vent.

"Wait, the scouts have merit badges too?" Kaiden joked as he pulled himself up and held onto the ladder.

Chiyo brought the map up on her tablet, turning off her visor momentarily. "Up to the top of the ladder...that'll bring us to the tenth floor and seventy yards from the security room. You go first and scout for guards."

"Gotcha." Kaiden nodded, hoisted himself up, and ascended quickly, Chiyo following closely behind. "How should we get into the security room?"

"We can use a guard's access badge when you knock one out. If none are available, then I'll try to open it quickly or we may have to create a distraction to lure one out of the room, allowing me to sneak in."

"By yourself? I would guess there are at least a few guards in there. You don't want me to head in first?" Kaiden reached the top and a small ledge providing access to another shaft to crawl through. He leaned forward and began to move toward their destination.

"I'll be fine against a small number of guards. I'm equipped with a heavy pistol, enough to put down a few guards in quick succession."

"You have a heavy pistol? And you had me go full zap on this mission," Kaiden grumbled as he scurried along the vents. Chiyo reached the top of the ladder and followed him inside.

"I will only need to deal with a small number of guards. Hopefully, you won't have to deal with too many, but you will certainly have to deal with more than I will. It would be best to not have to deal with a whole building's worth of guards at once."

"I could make a game out of it. See how many I can take down every minute or so. Speaking of that, I wonder if I'll get enough SXP to level again. Got a couple of talents I've been eyeing."

Chiyo lowered herself down, slowing her crawl to reduce the potential bumps and clangs that could alert the guards to their presence. "I didn't mention it before, but I'm glad you've finally started activating your talents. I told you they would be quite useful," she whispered.

"They are definitely helpful in the right situations—like facing down a Sauren war chief," Kaiden admitted.

"Wait, what was that?" Chiyo asked curiously.

"I'll tell you later," he promised. "We're almost at the end. Let's go silent for a moment." They crept up to the vent opening, a simple grate instead of an emergency hatch. He reached back, and Chiyo handed him a small curved prong. After he'd peered through to make sure no one was coming, he slid the prong through the openings of the grate and unlatched the locks. He checked the hall one more time, looking left and right as he opened the barrier slowly and climbed out, unfolding his rifle quickly to have it at the ready. Satisfied that the coast was still clear, he kneeled and helped pull Chiyo out of the vent, closed the grate, and put the latches back in place.

She handed Kaiden her tablet. "I now have access to personnel trackers," she stated in a hushed tone as she turned her visor back on. "Down the hall and to the left, you'll find a high-ranking guard. Take him out and get his access card. It will either be on his armor or around his neck. I'll head over to the security room door and take out any patrolling guards."

"They wouldn't have access to the room?" Kaiden asked as he looked his gauntlet over.

"According to my readings, they would only have low-level clearance and would need a voice or identification check," she explained as she drew a stun baton. "The other guard's card will open the door automatically."

"I follow. I'm on it. See you in a bit," he acknowledged and handed her tablet back.

She reattached the small device to her gauntlet. "Return to this spot when you're done. The security room is at the end of this hall and to the right. Don't forget to hide the body." Chiyo snuck off while Kaiden went to find the other guard. He followed her directions and peeked around the corner to see the guard looking out a large window in the lobby with his helmet off while he talked on a phone.

Kaiden sighed as he looked down at the shock gauntlet again. "Guess I'll have to use you later," he mumbled, "This guy is damn near gift wrapping this for me." He raised his rifle and aimed at the guard's neck, waiting for him to finish his conversation.

"I'll see you then...all right, later." He finished, and Kaiden fired as soon the phone moved from his ear. The dart landed in the back of his neck. The man didn't seem to feel anything as he placed the phone in his pants pocket and reached for his helmet on the ground. As he picked it up, he stumbled slightly. He shook his head in confusion as he pulled the helmet on. His movements slow, he picked up his rifle that leaned against the wall and took a few steps before collapsing.

Kaiden folded his rifle and placed it on his back, moved quickly to the guard, and searched for the card. He noticed a pistol holstered on the man's waist. Swiftly, he checked for any DNA locks before opening the holster.

"What are you doing?" Chief asked, appearing over Kaiden's shoulder.

"Seeing if this pistol is locked in any way," Kaiden said, giving it another once-over before opening a compartment on his thigh and sliding the pistol into it.

"So much for stealth," the EI snorted.

"I feel better knowing I got something with a little punch if things get hot," Kaiden said defensively. "Besides, if she gets a heavy pistol, then I get one too."

"Oh, that is the most childish playground bullshit that I've ever heard. What, is a pistol your teddy bear that you can't have sweet dreams unless you're tucked into bed with it?"

"I'm being thorough," he protested. "I don't plan on using it. And besides—"

"Frank? Is that you? You done with that call yet?" another guard asked, close enough to round the corner in a second or two.

"Dammit," Kaiden grunted. "Chief, activate the gauntlet."

"It's on," Chief confirmed. Kaiden saw small pins rise on the top of the glove and heard a low hum. The knuckles and back of his hand grew a little hot. *"Knock his ass out."*

He dashed forward. The guard turned casually into the lobby, and Kaiden slammed his fist into the front of the man's helmet. He grabbed him as he tumbled to the ground. It sounded like he tried to yell, but his words were mumbled from the shock, and the helmet's mic no longer functioned. Kaiden punched him two more times and felt the guard go limp.

"Man, this thing is nice." Kaiden admired the gauntlet for a moment as electricity sparked between the pins. "Gotta remember to use this more often." He clenched his fist three times and the gauntlet shut off.

Carefully, taking care to make as little sound as possible, he placed the guard on the floor. After a moment's thought, he used his rifle to put a dart into his exposed neck.

"Nice double tap," Chief chirped.

"A beatdown like that would only keep him cold for a few minutes. Best to make sure he stays down," Kaiden reasoned. He went back to the other guard and saw a lanyard falling halfway out of a pouch on his belt. Quickly, he opened it and fished out the card he needed. "Got it," he said triumphantly as he stood and looked at the two unconscious guards.

"Need to hide them," Chief warned. *"Where's a good spot?"*

Kaiden looked around, noticing bathrooms behind him. "That'll probably work. Put them in the stalls."

"You really don't think other guards will come by for a whiz and not notice them? Or that they've been indisposed for an hour or more?"

"Wasn't going to stick them in the men's bathroom," Kaiden retorted.

"Ah... Well, I haven't seen too many female guards around, so there's certainly less foot traffic. Go for it, man."

After hiding the guards, Kaiden doubled back to the vent and headed toward the security room, his rifle in hand. He made sure to check each hall he passed in case Chiyo had missed anyone but saw no one along the way. He certainly remembered seeing at least a few in this direction when he'd looked at the map.

"Probably dumped them all in different rooms," he reasoned. "She works quick, and she is certainly efficient with that baton."

"No doubt, infiltrators work best as hackers, but they are also field agents. She's definitely got a few tricks up her sleeve."

"You said she got here as a merit-based special case, right?" Kaiden whispered as he continued to creep through the hall.

"Yeah, that's what that golden triangle on her jacket means," Chief confirmed.

"So that means she was already going to be an infiltrator the minute she set foot in the Academy?"

"That's usually how it goes. She could have probably chosen from a couple of different classes, but when the board admits you like that, they have a certain class in mind."

"I wonder what she was doing before she got in here." Kaiden peeked around the final corner at the door to the security room. "Wonder what kind of life she was living that she was ready out of the box like this."

"You came to the academy nice and trigger-happy. There are a handful of cases like that," Chief reminded him.

"Yeah, but I spent most of my childhood and teenage years in a gang. That merely makes me good at shooting and staying alive, and better at one than the other." Kaiden folded his rifle and hooked it to his back. "The whole hacker-and-spy combo is a bit different." He walked down the hall, pressing up against the wall on the side of the door and near the panel. "Chief, open comms."

"Comm open."

"Chiyo, I'm here. Where'd you go?"

"Opening the door twenty feet down the hall. Don't shoot," she responded.

Kaiden saw the door open and Chiyo roll out. "Was that for flourish?" He chuckled under his breath.

"It was a supply closet. I was waiting in there with an unconscious guard. It was rather cramped." She moved over to them. "You have the card?" she asked, her hand outstretched.

Kaiden nodded, took it from his belt, and handed it to her. She pointed at the opposite side of the wall, motioning for him to move to that side. He complied as she took his previous position.

"When I open the door, you take out the guards inside."

"Not a problem. This gun should make that pretty easy." Kaiden held up the arc pistol.

"That could potentially strike the equipment. If the computers get fried, we would have to find another place to access the systems, and we would probably trigger an alert," Chiyo warned.

"I thought the point of this thing was to fry devices." Kaiden huffed as he put the pistol away.

"Feel free to use it in any other area, but for now, please stick with the rifle."

He removed the cartridge. "I got three shots left in this. Works out perfect."

"Shouldn't you reload?" she asked.

"I got three shots, and there are three guards. No worries."

"Are you sure you can hit all three of them quickly? You don't have much room for error as their armor doesn't have many exposed points," she pressed, clearly uncomfortable with his decision.

"Is that a challenge?" he asked, stroking his chin as he raised his rifle.

"I only wanted to confirm that you can do what you're saying," she responded, her tone clipped and defensive.

"How about this..." He took the cartridge out and slotted in a fresh one. "If I hit all three guards with only three darts, we do the rest of the mission loud. My way."

"How does that..." Chiyo began, only for Kaiden to place a finger against his mask where his mouth was.

"We've done what is essentially half this mission your way. Once we get inside and you get all up in their systems and have yourself a little hacking party, we're pretty golden, right? I've seen your way and it works pretty well, but if you want the real Kaiden Jericho experience, it involves blood, bullets, and explosions."

Chiyo was silent for a moment. She pressed her hand against the side of her visor. Something popped up onscreen, but Kaiden couldn't make it out. "There are one hundred and five security guards in this facility, along with thirty Guardian drones, six dozen Scarabs, and twenty prowlers. They would all be coming for you."

"There are technically one hundred guards. I've knocked out five so far."

"You knocked out three on the way in and the one with

the card," she said, holding up a finger for each guard she counted.

"Another guard came around the corner while I was searching for the card." He held up the gauntlet. "By the way, this thing is fantastic."

Chiyo looked at the gauntlet for a moment and then back at Kaiden. "You don't have your usual weapons."

"I'll consider it a handicap." He shrugged.

"And if we fail because of this?" she asked.

"Then I'll follow your lead the next time we practice, and for the test, it'll be done however you want it and I'll oblige," he promised, placing his free hand against his heart.

Chiyo raised the card in the air. "You have three shots."

He smirked and lowered his rifle, holding it in both hands, and moved from the wall to the door. "Plenty."

Chiyo ran the card down the scanner, opening the doors to the security room. Kaiden stood and looked down his sights. He identified one guard standing in the corner, not even paying attention, and put a shot in his neck. He shot the second guard sitting at a desk in the top of the arm in an unarmored section between the shoulder and forearm. Another guard sat at the controls and did not look over. Kaiden snapped the rifle over to him quickly, aimed, and fired. As the guard stood in surprise, the dart lodged into his neck.

He smiled. That was enough to win the bet. Time to do what he planned to do. He activated his gauntlet and rushed the guard at the controls, getting one good hit across the face. In a swift, smooth movement, he leaped over the desk behind him and kicked the second guard to the floor before driving the pins in the gauntlet into his neck and shocking him. As he scrambled up to attack the final guard, the man was already staggering due to the effects of the tranquilizer. Kaiden walked up to him, grabbed the front of his helmet, and shoved him into the wall. The guard sagged, and he released him. There was a soft thump as the man slid into an ignominious heap on the floor.

Kaiden looked back to see Chiyo in the doorway, surprise evident on her face. "You know, I did hit each of them with a dart, but either way..." He took a seat and placed his legs on the desk the second guard had sat at previously, linking his hands behind his head. "I did only take three shots."

CHAPTER TWENTY-TWO

K aiden looked at the two weapons he'd found on the guards. The third one in the corner only had a pistol on him. He ran his hands over each gun, inspecting them while Chiyo hacked into the building's systems. "Chief, scan these things and give me the low-down, would you?"

"Let's see what we got." A white line ran back and forth along the weapons. *"Descriptions onscreen."*

Tera Sovereign Packleader Shotgun:
Description: A weighty but powerful plasma shotgun. Medium range and slow fire rate, but it can tear through even heavy armor in one hit at the right distance. Modern upgrades increase the natural distribution in energies so that the user can fire up to twelve shots before venting.

Havoc Munitions Dust Devil Machine Gun:

Description: The favored machine gun of the Gallows Dancers Mercenary company. Fires in a three-round burst. This laser machine gun can deal multiple enemies or a single, heavily armored target with ease. Requires venting after every forty-five shots.

"Man, they sure got chirpy interns to make those descriptions," Chief muttered.

"Neither of them is a bad choice, really. Maybe I should duel-wield?" Kaiden pondered the pros and cons, unable to make his mind up.

"You're going to want your second arm for that shotgun. One blast will knock your shoulder out of joint if you're not careful," Chief warned.

"Guess I'll go with the machine gun." Kaiden pulled his tranquilizer rifle off his back and laid it on the table. He gave it an affectionate pat, then picked up the Dust Devil and put it on his back. "It was fun putting people to sleep, but now it's time to make sure they are wide-awake. You know, before I kill them."

"That sound more badass in your head?"

"Actually quite a bit, yeah." Kaiden sighed.

"Are you sure you want to do this?" Chiyo asked as she continued typing into the console and activating commands in her visor. "We can still finish this relatively easily."

Kaiden walked over to her, turned around, and leaned against the console top. "Hey, no going back on the deal now. I won the bet, even if I was going to totally bullshit my way into winning otherwise."

"I just wanted to be sure. I'll keep my word." She opened the door to the security room. "Once you leave, I'll lock the door behind you. I'm sure they'll realize something is wrong once they activate the alarm and the lockdown doesn't begin."

"I'll keep them busy...and you know what? I am going to take this with me," Kaiden declared as he scooped the shotgun up. "Variety is the spice of death, after all. Oof... Man, this bastard is heavy."

"Variety is the spice of life, is how the saying goes," Chiyo corrected.

"Not in my hands." Kaiden smiled. "Now, before I set off, where exactly am I setting off to?"

Chiyo brought the building map up on the big screen of the console. "The room with the device is in the center of floor fifteen. Once you have it, you'll need to make your way to where we started. That's the extraction point."

"We going to meet up before jetting off?" he inquired.

"I'll make my own way back as I need to stay in the system as long as I can. Once I leave this console, my power will be much more limited. But my commands should remain unless someone shuts them down or takes control back, but even if they try to after I leave, it should give us enough time to escape."

"When will you get out?" he asked as he primed the shotgun.

She looked at him, her visor constantly showing different commands and code running across the screen, appearing and disappearing. "I'll try to stay as long as I can, but between the lockdown override and me taking control of their robotic units, they'll know something is up soon enough. Most likely, they'll try to kick me out from another console or send a team to eliminate me. Hopefully, by the time you retrieve the device and exit the fifteenth floor, I will have departed."

"Well, don't wait around for my sake. This was my idea," Kaiden stated, a ripple of concern stirring.

"Of course, but this is also your command now. You helped me to the best of your abilities during my command, and now I shall do the same."

"Keeping those bots off me and the doors wide open is more than enough. I'll see you soon." With that, he marched out the door, pausing for a moment as he looked down the hall. "Which way to the elevator?" he called back as the doors shut.

"Go to the lobby. They are down the left hall," she answered over the comms.

"Appreciate it. Keep your eyes glued to me. You're gonna see what having a little joy in your work looks like."

Two guards walked up to the elevators on the fifteenth floor, preparing to finish their shift. As they waited for the elevator to arrive, they busied themselves with inspecting their guns or looking around at the décor—or lack thereof —around them.

They made terrible small talk.

The elevator dinged, announcing its arrival. One of the guards had focused on a piece of art on the wall when he heard a loud bang from somewhere in front of him. He hit the floor as he saw his partner fly back to land a few feet away with a hard thud. He struggled to get up and grab his rifle, but a heavy weight slammed into his back and kept him down. His expression a mixture of pain and consternation, he craned his neck to look up at an armored person in a mask and wide-brimmed hat holding a shotgun. The figure stood literally on top of him.

The stranger looked down. "Hey there, buddy. I'm looking for some knick-knack currently held by your tech department on this floor. You mind helping a nice guy out and pointing me in the right direction?"

The guard reached up to his helmet, activating his comms. "We got an intruder! Fifteenth floor," he shouted.

Kaiden shook his head, drew his pistol, and fired down at the guard. "Terrible service. I even asked nicely," he grumbled.

The alarm sounded. He heard other guards storming down the halls and heading his way. A quick glance above the elevators revealed glow strips lining the ceilings with messages announcing an intruder alert and that defense units had been activated and were on their way.

"Well, that won't be too helpful." Kaiden chuckled, removed a shock grenade from his belt, and pressed the trigger, holding it down. "For them, at least."

Several guards entered the lobby, raising their guns at Kaiden. "Ah, good evening, gentleman—and lady, I see you over there." Kaiden pointed in the direction of the female guard. "I need directions to your tech division on this floor. Now, who will oblige?"

"Get down, *now*," one of them commanded, and a few more guards joined the line-up.

"Guess I'll have to find it myself," Kaiden lamented. "I know you're all technically AI, but you could have had a heart and helped a poor fellow out. But since you're going to be so rude, I won't be needing your services." He flung the shock grenade at the group, leaping back as soon as it left his grip. The guards were torn between trying to shoot him and trying to dodge the grenade. A few tried getting out of the way, but due to Kaiden priming it, it exploded only a couple seconds after he let go, shocking all the guards and stunning a couple of the heavies in the back of the group that Kaiden took out with a couple of rounds.

Chiyo stopped the lockdown activation quickly. She rewrote the commands for the defensive droid units, causing them to see the guards as hostile and ignore any other target. She leaned back as she watched Kaiden move rapidly through the floor, taking out several guards with ease on his way to the room.

"To your left, Kaiden. Take the hall to the left and then go right four doors down," she advised over the comms.

"Thanks, Chiyo, What do you think so far?"

"Are you curious or looking for a compliment?"

"I'm honestly curious, I swear it." She saw him lean around the corner as two guards rushed up the hall. He whipped around the wall and fired two shots. Almost simultaneously, the guards were knocked back as their armor split apart.

"I think that all this commotion is causing all the red flags in my mind to wave furiously, and that this is quite different to what I had planned when we first got in here." She used her visor to issue commands to close off the stairway door and prevent a group of guards from entering.

"Well, that's par for the course, obviously. But this has got to be thrilling, right?" Kaiden asked. He stopped as he saw a guardian robot roll past him. He watched it go by and turn, then begin to fire at a guard in the hallway behind him. "Got the robots already. Nice work."

Chiyo switched screens to see a trio of hellcats running after a group of guards. "Thank you, but as for whether or not this is thrilling...I am alone in the room at the moment, so the action is quite comfortably far away from me."

"But it's fun as a spectator, right?" Kaiden pressed.

"You *are* fishing for compliments."

"I'm only trying to prove that our future lives of explosive missions across the stars don't have to be all numbers and monotony," he explained. "And, I have to say, it absolutely boggles my mind that I have to debate that. Which way do I go now?" Kaiden looked around the hall as he popped the vent on his shotgun open.

"Take another right, second hall on the left, and straight down to the central room," she directed. "I understand what you are trying to say, Kaiden. But you have to know that not everything you do will be like this. Sacrifices have to be made at some time, and during other times, it's simply a matter of putting the mission before yourself."

"Trust me, I'm well aware of those cases. Why do you think I'm cutting loose right now? My last mission was all about teamwork and working towards a common cause and all that junk. Still had fun, though. Until I was blown up."

"You were blown up?"

"Yeah, that's something else I'll tell you about later. All I'm trying to say is—" Kaiden turned to see a guard hobble into view, looking like he'd been mauled by a hellcat. "You have to live a little…unlike this guy." He fired a shot while holding the shotgun with one hand. The weapon spun out of his hand and into the air, hit the ceiling, and crashed to the floor as the shot hit the guard and knocked his helmet off in a spray of blood.

"Ow," Kaiden whimpered as he rubbed his arm.

Chiyo saw this moment of buffoonery and responded with a slight chuckle. She looked at another monitor and saw a team of four guards headed her way. "Please hurry and finish the mission. It looks like I won't be staying much longer." She rerouted a couple of guardian droids to come her way.

"Yeah, right, I'll get on that in a minute." He winced as he made his way into the central room and looked around for the device. "Hey, Chief, what's this thing look like again?"

"*Onscreen,*" Chief said, bringing up a display of the device. It was some sort of power core kept in a white briefcase. "*What the hell are you doing? Showing off?*"

"I'm having a laugh." Kaiden rolled his shoulder as he searched for the container. "Most of my missions are these serious team exercises or solo rescue ops or something. It's been a while since I've done anything how I like doing things—dancing around gunfire, taking your enemies head-on, that sort of deal."

"Just don't try to strike a pose and then get shot in the head or something. Your moments of idiocy kill me a little bit each time," Chief muttered.

"You lose data bits or memory space instead of brain cells?" Kaiden chuckled, finally seeing the briefcase on a table next to a few other devices.

"Pity I can't— Hey, I feel something." Chief cautioned.

"What's up? You sound rather serious," Kaiden noted as he opened the briefcase to make sure the device was inside. Confirming that it was, he closed it, took the machine gun off his back, and used the magnetic strap to keep the case in place on his back.

"Give me a sec... Ah, dammit, I knew it." Chief growled his frustration.

"Knew what? Fill me in here," Kaiden demanded, opening his machine gun and heading back to the lobby.

"Axiom Industries was a real place. A company owned by the Asiton corporation."

"Asiton? You mean like the guys who created that big ass robot from the loadout training map?"

"The Reaver, yeah. I'm picking something up. It's coming this way from outside the building."

"It wasn't in the glossary," Kaiden pointed out.

"Neither was the Reaver if you recall. That didn't stop it from showing up."

"You think another one is here?" Kaiden increased his gait, running through the halls now.

"Something like it is. You need to get out there but send a warning to Chiyo first," Chief advised.

"Chiyo, are you outside yet?" Kaiden asked, trying to retrace his steps as quickly as possible without drawing attention to himself.

"I am. Just made it out and heading to the retrieval point," she responded.

"Get back inside. Chief says there's something on the way," he warned, his tone urgent.

"I didn't see anything on the radar, and I blocked any requests for outside reinforcements. We should be— Wait, there is something coming. It's in the sky and coming straight down towards the building."

Kaiden finally found himself back in the elevator lobby. He looked down the hall and saw a row of windows. He ran over, activating the machine gun as he moved, and shot out one of the panes. Without further thought, he leaped from the building and fell the fifteen stories to the ground. The shocks and dampeners in his boots and leg armor absorbed most of the impact, but he still felt a thudding pain shaft through his legs. He ignored it and ran into the field, looking for Chiyo.

He saw her a couple of hundred yards ahead and raced over to her while looking up in the sky to see what was coming. What he saw caused him to stop in his tracks, his eyes wide. He yanked the case off his back and ran over to Chiyo, handing it to her.

"We won't make it to the spot before it gets here. Get back inside and keep the device safe."

"What about you?" she asked, a slight hitch in her voice as she processed everything.

"I'm going to keep whatever the hell that is busy, but I need you to see if you can figure out what it is and what we can do about it," he explained in a rush as he watched the thing draw closer and closer. "I don't think my rifle is gonna cut it."

CHAPTER TWENTY-THREE

C hiyo sprinted across the lot, heading back to the building from which she had just escaped. Her head raced with thoughts and ideas of how to deal with this incoming threat. Questions about where it came from and why it wasn't in the description intruded, distracting her from the more immediate need to find a way to destroy it.

She would find out later; she always did. For now, she had to get the device to safety and find a way to help Kaiden.

He watched as the thing in the sky came spiraling down, but as he began to raise his machine gun, a thought stopped him.

One that Chief also decided to voice.

"You need to get the hell out of the way," Chief commanded. *"That thing will crash into the ground, so it's your ass if you stay here."*

"That just dawned on me," Kaiden admitted, holding

the machine gun to his chest and sprinting away across the lot.

"*Get close to the building,*" Chief ordered. "*It can still change direction and hit you.*"

"Then why can't it hit the building?" Kaiden yelled.

"*Of course it can. But if this is part of the scenario, then that thing won't attack the building itself. The Asiton droids were programmed to not attack anyone affiliated with Asiton Corporations.*"

"I thought the Asiton wars began because the robots broke their programming and attacked humanity as a whole?" Kaiden replied frantically. This was so not the time for a history lesson.

"*Let's hope it hasn't gotten that far. Move it!*" Chief hollered.

Kaiden turned and ran toward the building, moving as fast as he could on his stiff legs.

"*Impact in ten,*" Chief announced.

Kaiden slid under a carrier just outside a loading dock, peering from beneath it at the object about to smash into the earth. He closed his eyes and braced for the impact. Instead, he felt a large rush of wind and heard a loud whirring, but no cracking of the ground or cars and trees sent whirling in the air.

He opened his eyes to see a large white machine. It looked like a stealth bomber with large wings on a triangular body, two massive, spinning blades on either wing keeping it afloat. The sharp triangular head held a single red-eye which currently focused on examining the lot as the robotic creature hovered a few feet from the ground.

"Oh, good, it's only a robotic pterodactyl," Kaiden joked.

"That's an Asiton Lancer, one of the fastest robots capable of flight in its time," Chief revealed without humor.

"Great. Now that I know what it is, how do I kill it?" he asked.

"Not with that dinky machine gun, that's for sure."

"Helpful," Kaiden sneered. "Got something a bit more morale-boosting?"

"You still got that arc pistol, don't ya?" Chief asked.

He reached to his hip and brought out the arc pistol. "Yeah, what about it? This thing is smaller than my machine gun."

"Good things come in small packages." His body began to shift, taking the form of the Lancer in a tiny wire-framed display. Chief's eye appeared in the body of the display.

"Wow, that's new," Kaiden said in shock.

"Like it? Just one of a number of new tricks I picked up with my upgrade." Chief chirped happily for a minute before narrowing his eye. *"But we can admire me later. Right now, we gotta worry about taking out that Lancer."*

"What are ya thinking?"

"As long as that thing can fly, we ain't going to be able to do much good. But if you can short out those propellers, it'll have to land," Chief explained, highlighting the propellers in the visual.

"It's that easy? It doesn't have any backup generators or nothing?" Kaiden wondered at the apparent stupidity of the design.

"Nah, part of the design was that the blades helped stabilize the Lancer in flight and acted as a perpetual generator so it could remain in the air for long periods of time. Take them out, and it will have to conserve as much power as it can and make a land-

ing," the EI explained. *"It ain't gonna be easy, either. You gotta hit those blades dead on. Otherwise, there won't be enough power to short them out, or it'll simply get absorbed by those dispersers in its wings."* He pointed out the two rods on either wing.

Kaiden nodded. "All right, sounds good. When it lands, can we wait it out until it powers down?"

"Nah. When on land, its internal power can still last something like twenty-four hours. But the real problem will be its surge laser."

"What's a surge laser?"

The carrier above them exploded. Kaiden covered his head as he heard another explosion behind him. He rolled out from underneath the carrier and looked at the Lancer, the arc pistol at the ready.

Chief transformed back into his normal form. *"That! That is a surge laser,"* he yelled. *"It fires from the eye and takes a few moments to charge. Keep moving and keep out of the way."*

"How close do I have to be for this arc pistol to work?" Kaiden asked as he held down the trigger and began to charge the shot.

"It should work within fifty yards," Chief answered.

"That's getting damn close." Kaiden huffed, then saw the Lancer's eye begin to glow. "Aw, hell!"

"Move! Once it fires the beam, it only travels down a line. If you can leap out of the way, it won't follow."

Kaiden continued to watch as the Lancer targeted him. When he saw the eye reach a bright red glow, he heard Chief shout, *"Jump now!"*

He dove ahead, hearing the blast cut into the cars and concrete behind him as he rolled across the pavement. He checked his legs to see if he had been hit, but he wasn't so much as singed. "That wasn't so bad," he said with a cocky smirk.

"It's charging up again," Chief warned. Kaiden looked up to see the Lancer hovering just above him. He yelped and took off, leaping over the hoods of cars and toward the gate. He heard the beam fire, this time rolling under a van as the beam disintegrated numerous vehicles in a straight line. Kaiden crawled out quickly and turned to see the Lancer rise up in the air and glide toward him.

He took the opportunity to attack, aiming down the arc pistol's sights just in front of the Lancer's path and to the right, aiming for one of its propellers. He fired as it drew close, watching as a stream of electricity surged through the air. The Lancer banked away. The electricity followed and hit the tip of the wing but not the blades.

"Dammit!" Kaiden swore, turning to run as he saw the Lancer begin to charge another blast.

Chiyo made it back to the security room, scrambling over the bodies of the guards that she had the guardian droids attack. She sat at the console and placed the briefcase on the ground beside her, then focused on the monitors for the outside cameras. The design of the creature was immediately recognizable, and she gasped. It was an Asiton model droid, but what was it doing in this scenario? She looked up to the corner of the monitor at the Axiom Industries logo, recalling a history lesson where she learned about Axiom's involvement in the creation of some of the Asiton designs.

Was that why it was there? Was this some sort of secret objective for the map? She forced the questions to the back of her mind and looked quickly through the system for anything that would allow her to deactivate or take control of the robot. Nothing seemed even a remote possibility. Whatever was issuing commands to that thing, it wasn't coming from there.

She looked back and saw Kaiden with the large machine in pursuit. He dodged blasts from its powerful laser and tried to return fire. He aimed at the sides of the machine rather than the head or chest but seemed to be missing whatever he was trying to hit. Then she saw the propellers. He must have been going for those. She scanned the shape of the attacker through the monitor and brought up a description. An Asiton Lancer, it had rods on the tips of each wing to absorb electrical energy.

Chiyo cursed under her breath. Unless Kaiden could get a direct shot, he wouldn't be able to hit the propellers. The shot would simply be absorbed by the rods on the wings. She looked at the various monitors, trying to find something that would give her a clue or an idea she could use. Her gaze homed in on the central room where Kaiden had found the device and noticed a few other things around the room. She opened a file containing all the current projects, one of which caught her eye.

"Kaitō, listen. I'm going to open a path to the guardian closest to the Tech development wing. I need you to take control of it and grab this device and take it outside," she commanded quickly.

"Certainly, madame. What will you be doing in the meantime?" Kaitō asked.

"Giving Kaiden a chance to do whatever he's trying to do. Also, Kaitō, just in case whatever I'm planning doesn't work out, prepare to use the Hacker Suite."

Kaiden threw a shock grenade in the air close to the Lancer and blasted it with the arc pistol. The grenade exploded and filled the sky with electricity. Some of it coated and coursed around the body of the Lancer before disappearing into the dispersers.

"Damn," Kaiden growled, running back down the lot and towards the building again.

"What was that?" Chief asked.

"Something I picked up with the strategist's talent. You can overload a shock grenade with more electrical power and create a surge of electricity. Thought it would be enough to cover that flying metallic bastard and shut him down. Those rods are annoyingly effective."

"Unfortunately so," Chief agreed. *"You heading back to the building?"*

Kaiden picked up the pace as the Lancer turned and began to follow him. "I'm going to have to rely on your theory that it won't attack it, though it doesn't seem to have a problem attacking the lot and all the vehicles. Still, it hasn't shot at the building yet."

"To be fair, you weren't in it," Chief reminded him.

"My point exactly, but I'm running out of cover here, and I need to regroup and figure out a way to deal with this. See if Chiyo's found anything."

"It's charging again," Chief cried. Kaiden looked back to see the now familiar infernal glow of the Lancer's eye.

He braced to jump, now only less than a hundred yards away from the building. As he tensed in preparation, he saw laser fire and electricity pass overhead. The lancer banked out, firing the laser into the night sky as it was driven away by a volley from overhead.

Kaiden looked over to see all the defense robots now in the parking lot, firing at the Lancer. As he watched, he heard a ringing in his head and saw a flash on his display. *"Hey, Kaiden, that Kaitō guy is hailing you,"* Chief stated.

"Chiyo's EI? Put him on," Kaiden ordered.

"Sir Kaiden, Miss Chiyo apologizes for not calling you over comms. She's left the security console again and is headed this way and is controlling the robots you see before you using her visor and tablet. That means she's had to stop non-essential programs and keep as much focus as possible, you understand?"

"Yes, Kaitō, it's fine. What do you need?" he demanded.

"To inform you that the madame has come up with a plan to take out that flying menace," Kaitō exclaimed.

"I'm happy for any ideas at this point," Kaiden said, putting the arc pistol away.

"My idea is just fine. You are just not trying hard enough," Chief nagged, looking away.

"She found a laser cannon in the tech development files and had me fetch it. I've been charging it using a guardian droid's power core, and it's nearly complete. She's controlling the other droids remotely and will create a distraction while you take the shot and destroy that Asiton robot," Kaitō explained

"Sounds like a plan to me." Kaiden looked around the

group of defenders for a droid with a laser cannon. He saw Kaitō's avatar fading in and out. "Kaitō? What's wrong?"

"I am split among several area...it is hard to retain the connection...." Kaitō said, his voice flickering in and out. *"Please hurry and find me. I must disconnect and focus on my other duties."*

"Of course, but where are you? Kaiden looked frantically at the group of robots again.

"I'm in the loading bay... I couldn't risk getting myself...and the laser cannon destroyed. Come and find me... I'll be waiting near the edge...of the dock." The fox EI disappeared from the display.

Kaiden continued his sprint past the flaming carrier he had previously hidden under and leaped up to grab the edge of the dock. He pulled himself up and heard the Lancer fire from above. It had changed its target to the dozens of droids, buying him a brief respite.

"Kaitō! Are you here?" Kaiden called, looking among the cargo crates and forklifts for the droid the EI was in.

"Over here...Mister Kaiden..." a droning, muffled voice said. Kaiden turned as a guardian droid rolled into view. It held a large silver blaster with a wide, round barrel in its arms. "Here...is the cannon...it is nearly filled."

"What is wrong with your voice?" Kaiden asked as he looked up at the face of the droid.

"Speaking...using Guardian droid's...voice box...meant for function...not form...basic and garbled...speech...not helped by...power drain."

"Well, thanks for getting this to me," Kaiden said appreciatively. Another blast was heard outside, and he placed his hand against the cannon. "How long until it is complete?"

"*It is...fiiiinnnnisshhed.*" The last word faded into silence as the lights in the droid went dark.

"Kaitō? You all right?" Kaiden asked, waving a hand in front of the droid.

"Kaiden, are you there?" Chiyo called over the comms.

"I'm here Chiyo. Is Kaitō all right? The droid he was in just turned off."

Kaiden could hear Chiyo breathing heavily as if she was running. "He's fine, but I can't say the same about most of the other droids I had control of. That laser is exceptionally powerful."

"No kidding. I reached the same conclusion when I was shot at," he said sarcastically as he grabbed the cannon in both arms and hoisted it on his shoulder. "I've got the cannon. What's the plan?"

"I'll distract the Lancer with the remaining droids under my command, while you take out the monster with that cannon."

"Does it have enough power to do that?" Kaiden looked the cannon over, doubt clamoring in his mind.

"It's stronger than the laser the Lancer itself is using," she replied. "But you'll only have one shot, so you need to — Oh, no."

Kaiden heard a lot of loud clangs from outside before they were followed quickly by many loud explosions.

"What the hell was that?" he yelled, seeing dust and scrap metal flung through the air outside the loading bay.

"The lancer carpet-bombed the remaining droids," Chiyo said solemnly.

"It has a compartment in its chest with about a dozen frag bombs. Good news is they're probably spent now."

Kaiden ran up to the open bay doors and set the cannon down. He peeked out to see the Lancer circling the lot. "Well, now we have no more droids, I'll have to pray I can sneak up on the bastard or something. How long does it take for this thing to fire?"

"Approximately seven seconds." Chiyo sounded certain, so he accepted the assumption.

He sighed, picked the cannon up, and aimed at the Lancer. "Hate to have to bet this on a prayer, but if we don't have anything else—"

"Kaiden, wait!" Chiyo yelled, catching Kaiden off-guard. He almost dropped the cannon.

"What's wrong?" he demanded belligerently, checking to make sure the Lancer hadn't seen him.

"The plan will continue. I'll get the Lancer to hold still."

"How? All your bots are gone," Kaiden pointed out with hesitation and disbelief.

"I have a way, but I'll need you to trust me. And we have to do this very, very quickly for it to work."

CHAPTER TWENTY-FOUR

"Chiyo, I'm in position. Whatever you're planning, please do it quickly. I'm exposed down here," Kaiden muttered over the comms.

Chiyo crouched down, looking at the Lancer through shattered windows as she waited for Kaitō to open the path.

She only needed one.

Grimly, she hoped that once the Lancer focused on Kaiden again, that would cause enough of a distraction for Kaitō to create a small opening. Then they could be rid of this monstrosity.

"Kaiden, you need to get its attention," she requested.

"Oh, joy, because we had such a laugh a few minutes ago," he complained.

"I know it's asking a lot, but the Lancer can only run so many internal tasks at once. If it spots you and begins to prepare an attack, that will mean it's focusing less on internal security, and Kaitō can create an opening for us."

"You do know that if I die we fail? I love a good practical joke, but to get this far and lose doesn't seem worth it."

"I am not joking, Kaiden," Chiyo asserted, her tone tense and a little breathy.

"Not to mention that I can't really move quickly or dodge while carrying this big bastard cannon. If I get blasted, I gotta imagine the pain of getting fricasseed by a laser has got to suck, even if it is reduced in the Animus," he lamented.

"Please, Kaiden, we will get out of this," she promised, allowing herself a small smile. "Besides, didn't you say that you prefer explosions?"

Kaiden snorted over the mic. "Using my own words against me? You are learning pretty quick." A few moments of silence stretched before she heard him sigh. "All right, get ready."

Chiyo saw an eruption of electrical energy. Kaiden had thrown a shock grenade into the air. The Lancer noticed it too, looking first at the blast and then down at Kaiden. It descended, its eye immediately beginning to glow.

"Madame, I've created an opening. Activate the suite when you're ready," Kaitō advised calmly.

"Aim the cannon, Kaiden, and get ready to fire. We only have one shot," Chiyo ordered. She activated her visor and looked directly at the Lancer. "Activate Hacker Suite."

For a moment, the world swirled together as Chiyo's vision blurred and morphed. When it cleared, she was looking at Kaiden from above and could hear the command to kill repeating over and over. She mentally silenced the command and held herself aloft. She heard a loud hum and felt a powerful heat above her which she cooled. The heat dissipated and the humming silenced.

"Go on, Kaiden, finish this…" she muttered to herself as she watched the cannon lock onto the target. He aimed directly at the Lancer's head. She had to remain within as long as she could. If she let go too early, the Lancer could act quickly enough to escape the blast. But if she was too late… It definitely would not be a pleasant experience.

She saw the cannon reach an apex. Kaiden released the trigger, and all the energy gathering fell into the chamber and exploded out of the cannon.

"Release!" she commanded, her vision distorting again but quickly reforming. She was back in the building and watched as the laser evaporated the Lancer's head and melted the top of its chest for good measure. It fell from the sky, crashing into the lot and smashing anything beneath it.

"You all right, Kaiden?" Chiyo asked.

"Yeah… Yeah, I'm good. That cannon has got a hell of a kick." He chuckled. He was silent for a moment, and his tone held a mixture of surprise and curiosity when he finally asked, "What did you do? It just hovered there, stopped charging the laser, and looked at me. Like it was begging me to kill it."

Chiyo smiled. "I'll tell you later. For now, let me go and get the device and let's finish this run. We're probably almost out of time now."

"Ah, kin Jaxon," Genos greeted the Tsuna ace as he walked

JOSHUA ANDERLE & MICHAEL ANDERLE

up to the engineer's pod. "How may I be of assistance? Did you want me to look over one of your weapons? Or perhaps give some pointers on how best to battle a synthetic opponent?"

"No, thank you, Genos. I am not here for any of that." Jaxon waved a hand dismissively.

"Perhaps a game of Xakchet, then? I have all the pieces here in this bag in my pod compartment." Genos turned to open the compartment when Jaxon laid a hand on his shoulder.

"As much as that sounds enjoyable, I have come on a more serious matter."

Genos stood. "What is wrong? Have you heard some bad news from Abisalo?"

"No." Jaxon shook his head. "It's not about our people. It's specifically about you, Genos."

"What have I done?" he asked, placing a webbed hand in the center of his chest.

"This issue is something you haven't done—or have yet to do, perhaps." Jaxon handed the engineer a tablet showing Genos' profile. "I am one of the five overseers among the group of Tsuna here and am responsible for ensuring that all the Tsuna under my care are advancing their studies and following the rules of the Academy. That includes you as well."

"Am I not?" Genos asked, scrolling down to his scores and showing them to Jaxon. "I have compared my scores with many others. I am not only the top Tsuna engineer but one of the top engineers in the entire first year."

"And that deserves recognition and congratulations," Jaxon remarked. "I should probably be clear—I'm not here to reprimand you. Rather, I am here looking for an answer."

"To what question?"

"You know about the cooperative test coming up?"

"Yes, of course. I have taken an extra hour to study every night in preparation for the last few weeks."

"Certainly a positive step, but I bring it up because I noticed you have not partnered with anyone to take it." Jaxon blinked a few times in rapid succession, a quirk that indicated that the Tsuna wanted an explanation.

Genos placed the tips of all of his fingers together, separating and connecting them over and over in a rhythmic way. "Ah, of course. It is not a problem. I will be assigned a partner tomorrow evening. I am confident in my skills and will be happy to support and advise whomever I am partnered with."

"Do the skills you are confident in include your social and interactive skills?" Jaxon asked.

"I know many human customs and traditions, and I can interact with many devices of dozens of origins," Genos responded, continuing to tap his fingers together.

Jaxon reached up with one hand and held the fingers immobile, staring Genos down. "We may have only seen each other during celebrations and clan revelries, but I am quite aware of your nervous habit, kin Genos."

He let go and Genos separated his hands, holding them behind his back. "You always did seem to have the sharpest senses among our kin."

"Why are you so nervous to answer this question?"

Genos took a long drag from his infuser, shutting his eyes for a moment. "I thought that I was past my insecuri-

JOSHUA ANDERLE & MICHAEL ANDERLE

ties and confusion," he began, his voice low and tentative. "When I was one of the chosen to come here, I was excited. To explore a new planet and meet a new culture—so much to learn and discover about both them and myself. But once I got here, all I could think of was our planet and our people."

"You grew homesick, as the humans define it," Jaxon surmised.

Genos nodded. "It would come in bouts, sometimes long, sometimes brief, but the more I could feel myself developing and my mind expanding, the more I leaned on the teachings and traditions of the Tsuna."

"You are a truly studied Tsuna of both heart and mind, kin." Jaxon laid a hand on Genos' shoulder. "There is no shame in that, certainly."

"You do not understand, kin Jaxon. I wanted, for so many of my years, to break away from all of the bindings of our people. I may not have been a sinner, but I did things the way I felt best served me and what I wished to accomplish with the life I had. I wanted to immerse myself in something new, be open and more than merely what I was instructed to be." He gave his companion a wary look. "Be more like you, I suppose."

"Like me? How so?" Jaxon's expression remained unchanged.

"I thought my assignment here would allow me to act on every impulse I had. But once I did...I was a bit of an outcast. I suppose we all were. But I gained new friends, both in our group and among the humans, like Chiyo and Kaiden."

"You seem to get along well with those two particularly."

Genos nodded. "He is an honorable human. Quick to violence and has odd words and odder thoughts, but a good companion and friend. He and Chiyo both helped me through my crisis of class."

"I feel I might be missing something, Genos. You said that you have been in a state of conflict since you got here, but besides the homesickness, I do not hear anything negative about your time here. What am I missing?" Jaxon asked.

"I am…jumping around, as Chiyo calls it. I'll focus," Genos promised, placing a hand on his chest again and lifting two fingers in the air. "I have been riddled with doubts about my place. Back home, I did not want to be trapped by my designation. I love our people and Abisalo, but I do not want my life directed for me according to hierarchy and traditions."

"I understand." Jaxon nodded. "I had a similar bout of uncertainty. It was probably what led me to volunteer to come here as well."

"But that's the other thing that bothers me. I feel that I cannot truly appreciate what being here means. On the one hand, I consider every choice and decision and how it would affect what the clan will think back home. As for the people here… There are many good people, but some of the looks and whispers… Surely you must have also noticed that they do not understand that we have vastly better hearing than they believe we do."

This caused Jaxon to release a quick but honest chuckle. "Indeed, it's quite humorous at times how openly they talk about things under the guise of secrecy. They have no idea that nothing is very secret to a group of people accustomed to talking and hearing on a planet covered by water."

Genos also cracked a small smile. "It's part of the reason I don't let it affect me too much. They simply do not know much about us. We are fascinating to some and terrifying to others. Until the novelty wears off...I suppose we can't be seen simply as ourselves."

Jaxon was silent for a moment, giving Genos some time to collect himself. "Forgive me once more, Genos, but why does this stop you from finding a partner for the Co-op test?"

"I suppose that I don't really know where I really belong, so I don't know who to ask to partner with me for the future. If I cannot ground myself, how will I help my partner through their problems and journeys?"

Jaxon stared at the engineer for a moment before his shoulders hitched and his chest expanded. Genos saw bubbles form and spin quickly around his infuser. He was laughing.

"I am happy that you seem to find some amusement in the situation." Genos sighed. "I am at a loss."

Jaxon continued to laugh for a few more seconds but stopped and collected himself after a moment, then cleared his throat. "Genos, your worries and fears are valid to me and true to you. I do not dismiss them. However, you seem to believe that the partnership you enter into for the cooperative test is for a long period of time."

"Is it not?" Genos asked, repeating the same rapid blinking quirk that Jaxon had earlier.

"No, it is not, my kin. It is temporary and only lasts

until the end of the test. If you happen to get along with your partner, that's great, but it is not a binding partnership."

"I... Ah...I...well, it would appear I may have let this put me into a bit of an emotional spiral as it were." Genos looked fretful, his fingers returning to their habitual nervous gesture of joining and separating like they had a life of their own.

"It is reassuring to see you think about the wellness of others even as you contemplate your own issues. Your sensitivity and earnestness were always welcome traits in you," Jaxon assured him.

"Thank you, kin Jaxon," Genos replied with a slight bow of his head.

Jaxon reached over and grabbed the tablet from him. He pressed a few keys and showed it to him. "Since you do not have one, I would like to offer myself as a partner for the coming test."

"You do not already have one?" Genos questioned. "You seem to be well respected among both the humans and the Tsuna. I would have imagined you would have been partnered long ago."

"I too fell a bit behind while contemplating several options and my place here in the Academy," Jaxon admitted. "Consider this an offering and a promise that we will both help one another find their place here."

Genos looked at the tablet and then back at Jaxon. "Of course, my kin," he promised, accepting the Co-op invite on the tablet.

"That was your suite?" Kaiden asked incredulously as he and Chiyo walked out the gate of the facility with the briefcase now on his back. "You can possess robots?"

"That's one way of putting it." Chiyo sounded nonchalant, which gave him pause.

"My suite simply slows down the perception of time and gives me what is essentially super-vision." He shrugged. "What are the specifics of your suite?"

"It can be any piece of technology, and it's more like interfacing with them. Kaitō creates an opening in the system of whichever device or droid I am looking at within the vicinity. Then, once that is created, my brain waves are enhanced by the suite and I meld with the device, allowing me to control it as if it were my body for a short period." She felt a spike of dizziness and leaned against him for a moment until she found her footing. "Even that small amount of time was enough to make me nauseous."

Kaiden tapped a finger against his chin. "What would have happened if I shot the Lancer down while you were in it?"

"It causes a mental dissonance. My body would shut down, and I would go into a coma until Kaitō was able to create a new link and essentially re-activate me."

"How long does that take?"

"In the Animus, not long—anywhere from five to ten minutes. But in the real world, it's much more dire. Some who were lost never came back, or their bodies expired before a new connection could be made."

"That's actually pretty damn frightening," Kaiden admitted. "The worst I get is migraines and delirium."

"I need to rest," she muttered. "How much further to the extraction zone?"

"We're here, actually," Kaiden revealed, leaning Chiyo against a tree as they waited for the dropship to arrive. "So what did you think, all in all?"

"I might be able to give a better opinion if my head was not swirling." She grimaced before looking up at him with a smile. "But we work pretty well together. It was an enjoyable first mission."

"Even doing it my way?" he asked. The trees shook, and the grass flattened into a path when the dropship swooped in and hovered over them.

"That was enjoyable as well. And rather exciting." Kaiden held a hand up to his ear to show that he couldn't hear her over the noise from the dropship. She simply nodded as he helped her up and they scrambled on board. The world began to fade away as a "Mission Accomplished!" banner appeared.

CHAPTER TWENTY-FIVE

It was Wednesday night, two nights before the beginning of the Co-op tests, and Sasha was busy at his computer, sending the final reports to the board before the actual tests began.

"*Commander Sasha?*" Isaac appeared on a small tree on Sasha's desk.

"Yes?" Sasha asked, paying only partial attention as he sent off a message to Head Monitor Zhang and began writing another to board member Fargo.

"*It is the professor. He's here to see you.*"

Sasha nodded. "Send him up."

"*He's already—*"

"Good evening, Commander." Laurie greeted him loudly as he walked into the office.

"Your continual lack of patience and the inability to wait for permission is a constant irritation in my life, Laurie," Sasha grumbled, continuing to type furiously as the professor walked over to his desk and took a seat.

"I like to believe that I'm on your list of friends who can come in whenever they please." Laurie smiled as he placed an EI pad on the commander's desk.

"I don't have one of those," Sasha retorted.

The visitor frowned, tapping a finger against his chin. "Open-door policy, perhaps?"

"I don't have one of those either."

"Well then, I'll make it a personal privilege," Laurie countered with a smile.

"I have no control over your fantasies, so I suppose I'll simply have to agree with you there." The commander sighed and stopped typing to glance at him. "Either way, I'm assuming you've come to inform me of new developments concerning our findings?"

"Indeed." Laurie nodded, activating the pad. Aurora appeared, awaiting instructions. "Aurora, would you please show the commander the video of Kaiden's run-in with the Lancer?"

The EI nodded before disappearing. A video screen took her place, displaying footage of Kaiden running through a parking lot while chased by a winged machine. Sasha watched it for a few moments, analyzing the battle. "An Asiton Lancer?"

"Correct. The second time Kaiden has had to deal with one," he confirmed.

"When was this taken?"

Laurie paused the video. "A few weeks back."

"And you're only now informing me of this?" Sasha inquired, his tone slightly agitated.

"I was slightly busy with the various experiments and projects the board has been boring me with, not to mention our own little project. I'll get back to that in a moment, but when Aurora completed that task, I had her do a sweep through the Animus Center archives. That's when she found this."

"What's the background?" Sasha asked as he reached up to the video screen and began to scan through it slowly. "Was this another map that Kaiden was provided?"

"No, I took those away from his available options and locked them out for the time being," Laurie informed him. "This was actually a Co-op scenario that he was running with his test partner Chiyo Kana. She was the one who set up the scenario for them."

"The last time Kaiden faced an Asiton robot was during the loadout training. He didn't create that scenario either, obviously," Sasha muttered, more to himself than out loud.

"I looked through the coding again. Another set of new code was in place, but this one was more subtle and less structured."

"How so?" Sasha asked, moving back from the screen and looking at him expectantly.

"It was a simple trigger. When a certain event took place on this map, the Animus would load in an Asiton Lancer to appear and attack the initiate who was participating in the mission."

Sasha glanced at the video screen again, taking a long look at the Lancer. "The initiate? A specific initiate and not merely any student?"

"That event was triggered when a particular ID matched with the system and was the one in the map."

"Kaiden," Sasha said. He balled his fists and rested his chin on them, releasing an exasperated sigh. "They're still going after him? They have to figure someone is catching on, even if it's not specifically us."

"I believe they are trying to get as much data as they can before they have to lay low. My guess is that they are keeping the technician and Animus support channels tapped to see how much ruckus is being raised. Since Kaiden is coming to me personally each time one of these events happen, I've been able to keep that to a minimum and see how this develops."

"Have you checked that channel for taps?"

Laurie nodded. "It's standard protocol for my team to check it every six hours, with constant detection and fire-wall plugging. We are not simpletons."

"And the Animus support?" Sasha pressed, considering all the implications and searching for answers.

"I'm going to need you to be the one who checks that," Laurie stated. "It's not my usual practice or even a standard request for me, so my doing it would probably raise a few eyebrows. However, you could have it checked more thoroughly as a board member and raise little suspicion if you simply played it off as maintenance or something like that."

"I'll have it done tomorrow morning," Sasha promised. "But since you've brought it up, have you checked other less technological means of spying?"

Laurie leaned back, a small, knowing smile forming on his lips at the commander's words. "You believe that we may have a spy amongst us?"

"It would not shock me, though we've only gathered a little information on this Arbiter Organization. They are obviously interested in Kaiden for whatever reason and seem to want to use the Animus and the ark academies for their own ends. Having a few moles—or, at the very least, agents working for Nexus—would further their agenda, however vague it might be for us currently."

Laurie held up his wrist, showing his companion a circular device he wore. He pressed a couple of buttons on it and the video screen disappeared, replaced by several lists and logs which appeared in the air. "I would agree, which is why I am personally going over the backgrounds and recommendations of all transfers to the tech department. Aurora is also checking their logs for anything that looks like it could point in our new friends' direction."

"It's a good start," Sasha said, studying the different screens as if searching for anything immediately suspicious that he could find with a cursory glance.

"What about your friends? Were they able to find anything from the letter you gave to them?" Laurie asked.

"I'll be meeting with another after the tests, but one of them was able to get back to me last night."

Laurie scoffed. "And you were all ruffled about me keeping things from you."

"It's not a lot. Otherwise, I would have summoned you right away," Sasha responded, "I'm gracious enough to figure that you may have other, more important things to do."

"That all depends on what you found, Commander. I might think it was plenty important," Laurie countered.

Sasha flipped the screen of his computer around, showing Laurie a letter.

We will be prepared. Should these aliens prove to be hostile... assume the worst. Even if they are truly...the same cannot be said for whatever else lies beyond. We are no longer alone. I find that...frightening than when we believed that we were.

~AO

"What is this? It seems unfinished." Laurie frowned his annoyance.

"I believe that it is as well." Sasha turned the screen around to face him. "It appears to be another message to the organization, but this one was created more than fifty years ago."

"That was around the time of the first contact with the Tsuna, correct?" Laurie pondered this, considering its significance.

"It was. My informant was able to gather this message from declassified documents from around that period, using the same system you did with the World Council newsletters and messages. Since this message is missing a number of lines and words, he felt that they were either in documents still classified or possibly other messages or files from the time that he could not find or get access to."

"It appears I'll have to widen Aurora's search parameters."

"Were you able to find anything new in what you did sort through?"

Laurie reached into his coat pocket. "I did. About two dozen other messages were hidden in over ten years' worth of pamphlets, news articles, and the like. Nothing that said anything any different from what we found from the first message" Laurie retrieved a small drive and handed it to Sasha, "but feel free to look them over. You might find something I didn't."

Sasha took the device and placed it in a small drawer.

He closed the drawer and pressed his thumb to a small scanner on the front, locking it.

"This one is quite interesting, however," Laurie continued. "The other letters always said 'we' or 'us' like the messages were for the group as a whole. This is the first one I've seen with someone referring to themselves with 'I,' a curious development."

"I would suspect that at one time, this was overseen by a single individual, or at least an organization with a head official," Sasha commented.

"So that 'AO' at the end may not mean the Arbiter Organization but someone's initials?"

"I believe so," he confirmed.

Laurie grimaced, thinking about the implications for a moment. "Considering how long ago this was...it could be possible that whoever this was is still very much alive. Perhaps they are the leader of this new organization or offshoot?"

"Potentially, but we'll have to dig deeper. I would argue that whoever this AO may have passed some time ago, and the Arbiter Organization are carrying his ideals forward."

"And they are apparently theatrical enough to name their organization to incorporate this fellow's initials." The professor chuckled. "Should make for a fun challenge should we ever meet them face to face."

Sasha looked at the open messages, reached over and closed them, and opened the video screen again. "What did Kaiden have to say about the fight?"

"I couldn't tell you. He hasn't bothered to drop by since the last time I saw you," Laurie confessed.

The commander raised an eyebrow in confusion.

"Really? You would think he would find this to be something that warrants concern."

Laurie coughed slightly and rubbed the back of his head. "Well, there are a couple things that may have caused him not to think so."

"Which are?" Sasha inquired, leaning forward.

Quickly, the professor brought up the mission details window for the video. "One is the map, which is based upon a raid of the Axiom Industries towards the tail end of the Asiton War. My guess is that either Kaiden or Chiyo probably chalked it up to that. Surprise enemies aren't abnormal in certain scenarios."

The commander looked it over briefly before looking back at Laurie. "Perhaps, but considering his previous fight with the Reaver, I would assume he would put two and two together."

"That would be the other reason...which is to say me." Laurie shrugged. "I've told you that I've tried to dissuade Kaiden from thinking too deeply about these anomalies, chalking them up to glitches and the like. I would say that this has worked out quite well. Alarmingly so, as he seems to not even bat an eyelid in this encounter, although that may be due to the fact that he's running around so much."

"If this escalates, that could prove to be a fatal thought process," Sasha pointed out.

"Oh, don't be so melodramatic. It's obvious that who or whatever is doing this is not out to kill our dear boy Kaiden but seemingly trying to test him to some degree," Laurie refuted.

"The fact that you of all people are telling me not to be melodramatic is an irony that I'm well aware of," the commander muttered. "We already discussed the fact that it was the implant that was tampered with and not anything concerning Kaiden himself, so what exactly are they looking to test in your theory, Laurie?"

"The integration and uses of the implant, for one. Also, the advancement and improved sentience of the EI would be the other." Laurie shrugged again, raising his hands in apparent impotence, then lowering them back into his lap where he clasped them firmly.

"Improved sentience? What are you talking about?" Sasha's voice hiked up a slight pitch in annoyance and surprise.

"I'm guessing you haven't interacted with Kaiden's EI that much?" the professor inquired. The commander shook his head. "He calls it 'Chief.' Quite a handful that one, but when you get another chance to talk with Kaiden, see if you can get a little time with the EI. It has one of the most vibrant personalities that I've ever seen, almost—"

Sasha cut him off. "If you're going to say human, I would stop. An EI reaching that level of advancement..." He shook his head as if trying to dislodge the idea. "You know how that ended with the Asitons."

"Fine then, I won't, but it still stands that Kaiden's EI is far more advanced than almost any other. Certainly more so than any other Nexus EI, or even Aurora here." Laurie pointed to the EI pad.

"You're saying that one of our students—an initiate at that—has an EI on par or surpassing even yours?" Sasha asked, hesitation and incredulity evident in his voice.

Laurie shook his head. "Not more advanced in terms of

power or ability. Aurora is certainly at the top when it comes to personal EIs, but advanced in development."

"Kaiden's EI chip is no different from any other EI chip. I gave it to him myself. I passed it along from a potential student the day before Kaiden joined," Sasha reminded him.

"Good thing you did too. I don't think that Hargrove boy would have been nearly as much fun as Kaiden has turned out to be. But it's not the chip that's the factor here. It's the implant. That makes the connection between the EI and its host stronger than ever before. It allows the host to gain SXP at an accelerated rate and allows for easier access to the Animus along with other fun little abilities, but the EI gets something in return."

"This is starting to sound troubling, Laurie, I don't recall you ever mentioning that the EI would gain sentience." Sasha's tone was clipped and precise, an indication of his disapproval. "You know how dangerous experiments like that are."

"The Asitons…yes, you just mentioned that." Laurie scoffed with a wave of his hand. "I merely said that the EI gains improved sentience. All EIs have some level of sentience. It's how they can formulate personal strategies and assist their hosts in combat. This one is simply capable of learning more at a faster rate and developing a unique pattern."

"What kind of pattern?"

"The kind that allows it to bond more with its host and excel to a level beyond the rudimentary skills of the traditional EI."

Sasha took a deep breath and exhaled slowly, his forehead creased in concentration. "So this is the next evolution of the EI?"

The professor smiled. "I suppose advancement would be the correct term considering it's a piece of software, but evolution works in this context too. It is more...organic." He stood quickly. "I'll personally scan through every map available and look for changes, delete them, and send you the details. For now, let's put on a happy face and keep these events close to our chests."

There were any number of questions to ask the professor regarding specifics about the implant, but Sasha knew he had to get his work done and that where Laurie was concerned, he was more likely to play coy than give him straight answers. "Fine. We'll continue this some other night."

"I promise that nothing bad will happen. I made a promise to Kaiden to watch over him. He is my experiment, after all." Laurie turned the EI pad off and placed it in his pocket. "Plus, I've grown fond of the boy, so I'll be sure to keep a close watch." He snickered as he walked to the door. "I do have to say, the irony of you using the Asitons as the model of the disasters that could happen when technology gets out of hand... It is ironic, considering where the EI come from."

With that, the professor left, leaving Sasha alone in his office, silent for a moment as he looked out the window and began to contemplate his next move.

CHAPTER TWENTY-SIX

"Get the hell out of the way! He's got a bench," Luke shouted as Raza roared and threw said bench at the group.

Izzy and Silas dove toward the wall. Kaiden rolled beneath the bench's trajectory while Marlo braced himself, catching the wooden missile as it plowed right into him. He staggered back a few steps but found his balance and hurled the bench to one side.

"Nice catch, big guy," Izzy yelled, helping Silas up. Luke, Marlo, Silas, Izzy, and Kaiden were in another bout of training with Raza. It was the day before the test, and the group had scheduled one last session before they made their test preparations that night. They wanted a bit more conditioning and asked Raza to give them a light workout.

That did not happen.

"He's charging," Silas called as the Sauren took a stance on all fours before leaping at Marlo. Luke got to his friend's side quickly, and the two large soldiers braced themselves to catch Raza as he landed. They struggled against him, Raza growling as he pushed back. The two strongest soldiers in the room were almost lifted off the ground as they tried to keep the vicious alien in place.

Kaiden ran up to the beast, his gun in hand. He raised it to the reptilian's eye and fired. Though the gun would do little good if he shot the Sauren in the body, the eye was a weak point he could exploit. It worked rather well as Raza roared in pain, allowing Marlo and Luke to get a better grip as Silas and Izzy came rushing forward with several weighted ropes. Izzy tossed one to Kaiden, and they bound Raza quickly. Silas threw a pair to Marlo and Luke once they had the Sauren wrangled so they could all pull him down.

They had him bound in place, but as the five of them pulled against the ropes with full strength, Raza roared in anger and began to twist and turn within the bindings. He created sufficient slack to snatch Izzy's rope and pulled hard. She collapsed to the ground, loosening her team's hold.

Raza twisted against the ropes, this time grabbing Kaiden's and Silas's ropes in each hand. He whipped the two off with a sudden yank. Now with enough room, he snaked his claws into the bindings across his chest and severed them. Marlo and Luke let go before the sudden release caused them to fall.

As Kaiden, Silas, and Izzy scrambled to their feet and the five prepared to attack once again, loud claps resounded through the room.

"Good teamwork there. Not easy to catch a Sauren,

even for a few seconds," Wulfson bellowed, walking out to the mat.

"Man...you always stop things...just when...it's getting good," Silas grumbled between loud pants and heaving breaths.

"I don't think...that was a...good spot," Izzy countered, wiping her brow.

"Would you consider...your first time better?" Kaiden jeered as he rubbed his bruised ribs.

"Fair enough...this was good compared to that," Izzy admitted. She rubbed her shoulder and scowled at the memory of the last time she joined the group for some training and got slammed down on the mat by Raza.

"Out of the seven times I've gone against this guy, this probably ranks top three," Marlo declared, resetting his neck with a cracking sound. He winced.

"Where would you put our first fight?" Luke asked.

"Oh, that's at the bottom. I got knocked out cold that time." Marlo chuckled.

"You guys need to remember that you aren't trying to win but survive," Wulfson argued. "It's an important distinction to make."

"A little hard to keep that in mind when this guy can dig out our guts on a whim if he wanted to," Silas pointed out.

"Hey, Raza, I wanted to ask—are humans a delicacy on your planet or merely sport?" Kaiden asked, his hand still on his knees as he looked up at the Sauren.

"Humans are our patrons for now, but I have heard that some of our men have dined on mercs and terrorists while here... They did not find the taste satisfying." Raza snorted as he rubbed his eye. "A good use of your ticklish weapon,

Kaiden. I'll have to remember to bring my battle cowl for the next match."

"That hide of yours doesn't leave me a lot of options," he muttered as he looked at his pistol. "I wanted this thing so badly, but it's really not coming through for me. I wonder what it takes to get a real gun around here."

"Being a member of the staff," Wulfson stated, folding his arms. "Or on the security patrol, but you don't take up vocations until your master year, so cool your jets."

"Damn," Kaiden grumbled as he straightened up and stretched. "When this place gets invaded, you're going to wish I had a real gun."

"Ha! There hasn't been an attack on the Academy since its inception. Besides, even if there was one, they would have a hell of a lot harder time getting through that barrier than dealing with one fool with a pistol," the security officer snarked.

"You haven't seen how good I am with a pistol, obviously."

"Enough to get turned into a laser-blasted pin cushion."

"You are my big ass Scandinavian cheerleader, Wulfson." Kaiden chuckled. "What's next?"

"It's two o'clock. Silas and I have a couple more hours to kill before our workshops," Izzy stated.

"Marlo and I wanted to get one more round in the Animus before we went to bed," Luke said, walking over to the group.

"You and Marlo are a Co-op team? What's your team name, 'Two tons of fun?'" Kaiden chirped.

"The Twin Titans would work if Marlo ever changed classes," Izzy pointed out.

"We need a name?" Marlo asked.

"Nah, we're just messing with ya," Kaiden admitted. "I guess it never crossed my mind, but who's partnered with who? We got Marlo and Luke, and I know you and Silas are a team, but what about Flynn?"

"He's with Amber." Marlo stretched his neck from side to side, easing out the remaining kinks.

"Raul is with Cameron," Luke added.

"That sounds like it could be disastrous." Silas grinned.

"They bicker constantly but work pretty well together," Luke said with an affirmative nod.

"Speaking of Cameron, he's been able to weasel his way out of training with us for the last couple of weeks. I'll need to hunt him down next time." Kaiden spoke with a little menace in his voice.

"Hunting down the bounty hunter...that should be fun." Izzy laughed.

"What about you, Kaiden? You get stuck with a wild-card?" Silas inquired.

"I've got a partner, no thanks to any of you," he sneered.

"I would have partnered with you—you know, if you weren't so trigger happy," Marlo admitted while looking away sheepishly.

"I thought you lived for carnage. Besides, with all that armor you got, what's the worst that would happen?" Kaiden retorted.

"I'm not really in a hurry to find out. I mean, the last time we worked together in a mission was the Division test, and I got launched by a devil bird," Marlo recalled.

"I'm pretty sure that wasn't specifically my fault."

"I thought you would partner with Jaxon. You two seem to get along pretty well," Silas said with a slight shrug.

"I thought they wouldn't let two people of the same class partner together. Although I wasn't thinking much about the test at the time," Kaiden admitted.

"Usually, they don't, but there's a workaround if you partner with a Tsuna of the same class. It's one of the ways they are trying to build relations," Izzy explained.

"I wonder if there are any human and Tsuna mixed teams?" Luke spoke it as a question and looked around at his companions as if hoping for an answer.

"I can think of a couple. Adrian Lanni the Goliath is working with a Tsuna Hacker named Mera. And there is a Tsuna Surveyor named Lok working with Mary Tulio, a Marksman." Izzy counted off the numbers on her fingers.

"Well, nice to hear bridges are being built," Kaiden commented.

"What about you? You didn't say who you partnered with," Marlo reminded him.

"I've teamed up with Chiyo."

"Chiyo Kana? The Infiltrator?" Luke inquired.

"Yeah, we work pretty well together, all things considered. She's a bit pedantic, but that's to be expected, considering her class. But we've run a few missions, and they've all been successful."

"I've heard a few interesting things about her," Silas interjected. "She got in for her skills—a merit-based SC and apparently, a really damn good infiltrator."

"Yep, seen the golden triangle and her skills first hand." Kaiden nodded.

"She's apparently the daughter of the head of a Zaibatsu

in Japan. Rumor is that she actually got her skills doing some shady work for her parents before coming here," Silas added.

"A lot of students were or still are suspicious of her. They think her parents sent her here as a scout or spy or something." Izzy seemed intrigued by the possibility.

Kaiden flashed back to the first night he met Chiyo and the students who accosted her. "I guess that's why she had to deal with all those dickbags before," he muttered.

"I try not to judge anyone by rumors and hearsay, and I've never met her myself. But if she's as good as you've confirmed her to be, better to have her on our side, yeah?" Silas said reasonably.

Kaiden nodded and cracked a wry smile. "Oh, definitely, she'll get the job done. I'm actually looking forward to the test now. See what kinda stuff they throw our way."

"Guess that only leaves Jaxon. He never told me who he was pairing with," Luke said.

"He's actually with Genos." Kaiden looked back at the titan.

"Who's Genos?" Izzy asked.

"Ah, that's right, you never met him," Kaiden recalled with a tap against his forehead. "Genos is a Tsuna mechanist. I actually met him at the carrier stop before coming here. Real nice guy. Apparently, he's Jaxon's clanmate, like a cousin or something in their culture."

"I see, and he's Jaxon's partner?" Izzy questioned, curiosity evident in her expression.

"Genos apparently had some trouble finding a partner, and he offered to be his teammate."

"Aw, that's nice of him." Izzy smiled. "Guess the frosty Tsuna ace has a little warmth, after all."

"Looks like it. Hopefully, he can help Genos to be a little more grounded. I'm actually worried he might be a bit soft to be in the field. Mechanists apparently see a lot of action," Kaiden admitted.

"Seems you are just as sappy when it comes right down to it." Luke chuckled.

"Can't be an asshole twenty-four seven. It can get a little exhausting."

"Could've fooled me," Chief snarked.

"Quiet, you," Kaiden commanded.

"Getting back to the matter at hand...what else do we gotta do?" Silas asked, looking at Wulfson.

"Well, you're actually off the hook for the rest of the day. I've gotta meeting with a couple of board members to talk about an upcoming shipment and then I'm taking Raza to look at the Animus center."

"Raza wants to use the Animus? I thought only humans and the Tsuna could actually use the Animus without, you know, having their heads explode or something."

Raza stepped forward. "I do not desire to make use of the device. I would like to look it over and observe it in use to see if it would offer anything to my people."

"The World Council and the Sauren delegates are taking baby-steps to perhaps allow the Sauren to one day make use of the Animus as well. It'll probably take a decade or two of testing, but they could start making headway sooner or later," Wulfson explained.

"Animus trained Sauren... Considering how deadly

they are without it, that's actually a frightening proposition," Luke muttered.

"We may not use it at all. If it is not up to the standards and desires of our current training, then there would be no point," Raza observed in a disinterested tone. "I don't see how virtual simulations could have the same impact as actual fights."

Kaiden laughed. "Oh, trust me, there's impact."

"And yet you train with Wulfson and me outside the Animus," Raza challenged.

"It's the best of both worlds, right? I can't go on a mission every day or take down a mercenary group on a whim."

Raza laughed, a deep, rough echo booming through the room. "You should join a Sauren hunting party. You would have your fill of battle on a daily basis."

"Might have to take you up on that one day," Kaiden agreed.

"If you do, I hope you don't get warp sick, lad. The Sauren travel through gates constantly," Wulfson interjected.

"Wouldn't know. I've never been off Earth," Kaiden confessed.

"Well, that'll be something you can look forward to next year." Wulfson smirked. "In the meantime, keep training in the gym or wherever you choose, and good luck to the lot of you on your tests."

The group said their goodbyes as Wulfson and Raza left the training room. They headed to different corners to gather their things. "So, anyone wanna place bets on who gets the top score among us?"

Silas laughed. "Says the guy who broke the high score of the Division test and has a top-level Infiltrator on his team? You trying to run some kind of racket?"

"I mean...we don't truly know what we'll face during the tests," Kaiden pointed out. "Maybe I'll have to deal with another of those giant war machines and I won't have all of you around to take the blasts for me."

"I think I'll pass," Silas concluded after a brief moment's thought.

"Luke and I will probably get a ton of points," Marlo boasted.

"I'll ignore the pun." Kaiden snickered as he put his pistol in its holster and one strap of his backpack over his shoulder.

"I'm serious. I'm a demolition soldier, and Luke is a titan. We'll probably be dealing with waves of enemies."

"We'll most likely take down more foes and get more points in our first five minutes than you will in your entire test," Luke challenged, slamming his fist against his chest.

"The test doesn't only score kills. You also have to factor how quickly you complete your objective, how much damage you take, doing bonus objectives, and all that stuff," Izzy reminded the large duo.

"You have to remember that not every team has a soldier or field-action class. What would, say, a mechanic and a medic have to do?" Silas asked.

"Whatever it is, can't be that fun." Kaiden shrugged without real interest.

"See? Trigger happy," Marlo exclaimed, heading towards the door.

"Says the guy who carries around a giant cannon," Kaiden shot back.

"Oh, come off it. Let's get a bite to eat before we head out to workshops," Izzy suggested from where she leaned against the wall next to the door.

"I am feeling a bit peckish," Kaiden admitted.

"You going to go for more training tonight?" Silas asked him as he shouldered his own bag and walked up to the door with the rest of the group.

"I've got a few points from the last few missions. I'll go over them tonight while Chiyo looks over records of other Ace-Infiltrator tests to get an idea what we're in for."

"At least one of you is putting in real work." Luke chuckled.

"I heard that, tin man," Kaiden sneered.

The group walked out of the room and then the gym, laughing and cracking jokes as they prepared for their latest challenge.

CHAPTER TWENTY-SEVEN

J axon rolled through the closing doors and Genos dove in behind him. "How much time do we have?"

"A few minutes at most, kin Jaxon," Genos replied, venting his machine gun. "I was only able to sabotage a dozen of the guardian droids. They will buy us some time from the scarabs and swarmers, but the numbers are too great for us to deal with them in the long term."

"It will be enough," Jaxon said with determination, venting his rifle and retrieving his hand cannon with his free hand. He turned around and shot a power box linked to a doorway. The doors opened, and Jaxon ushered Genos along. "Go. When they get here, I will take them."

"I'm not sure if I can rewire the core in time. And if they are too great in number and defeat you..."

Jaxon put his hand cannon away and placed a hand on Genos' shoulder. "You can finish the objective. You are beyond skilled enough to do it quickly. And I am more than prepared for them."

Genos looked at his Tsuna clansman for a moment before nodding and handing him his machine gun. "This will aid you more than me." Jaxon looked at the gun for a moment, then nodded and holstered his pistol and took the proffered weapon.

Genos turned to leave. "I will keep up with you over the comms. We must be sure to get out of this together."

"Have no doubt about that. Now go!" Jaxon demanded, slamming the vent of his gun shut and taking aim at the closed door, awaiting the horde of bots.

Kaiden looked over his talent options with a sigh. He had four points to burn and was considering his options.

Beast Master: Increases knowledge of wildlife and their weaknesses in combat.
    Status: 0/5

"I haven't run across many guard dogs or attack muskrats in the simulations," Kaiden said dryly and continued to scroll down the screen.

Scent Trail: Enhances the ability of smell, allowing the user to better identify and track targets using the target's scent.
    Status: 0/3

"That's...certainly different," he muttered, looking the talent over with a wary eye. "I wonder if there's some overlap with tracker and bounty hunter. I'd bet Raul already has this."

Deadshot: Increases natural aiming ability.
    Status: 0/2

"How did I miss that the first time around?" Kaiden wondered as he removed his oculars and looked around the room. A desk stood in the corner near the door, and he got up from his bed, retrieved two empty canisters from a shelf, and placed them on the desk before walking back to his bed. He reached over to his nightstand for the static gun safely stowed in its holster.

He aimed at one of the canisters, took a deep breath, and centered his sight on the small top of the canister. Carefully, he fired and saw the charge hit just below the top of the bottle, flipping it in the air before it crashed to the ground. He placed his oculars back on and looked at the talent once more.

"Accept talent," he ordered, looking at the Deadshot icon. He waited for a moment to feel the same rush he had when choosing his talents back with Laurie. A small vibration followed as he closed his eyes but nothing close to the level of the first time around. He frowned as he looked back to the other empty canister. Taking less time to center himself, he raised his gun again and fired. This time, the charge hit the top of the canister, which flipped in the air and then landed back on the desk, wobbling for a moment before standing still.

"Huh. Well, it appears I *can* be an even greater shot than I already am." He chuckled and placed the gun on the nightstand.

"Your little bout of target practice is going to get that gun taken away from you," Chief stated.

"I'll tell them the bottles attacked me and it was in self-defense," he joked.

Chief rolled his eye. *"Of course, the bottles were planning a revolt for centuries. You snuffed out their leaders before it was too late."*

Kaiden chuckled before leaning back on the bed. "The upgrade wasn't as intense this time around. Was that because of the talent I chose or simply because I've gotten used to it now?"

"The talents can't be fully integrated until you are actually in the Animus. A fact you would remember if you actually took the Animus workshops instead of constantly running off to do training scenarios."

"That's what I have you for, to fill me in on all the boring stuff," he retorted as he slid the gun back into its holster and opened the nightstand drawer to store it once more.

"Oh, good, I'm a glorified secretary," Chief lamented.

"More along the lines of a floating library, but that could work too." Kaiden continued to scan through the other talent options.

"How are you trying to build?" Chief asked, appearing in the lenses.

"What do you mean?" Kaiden asked, momentarily distracted by the question.

"Your build. It's a term that means you choose your talents in such a way that you are trying to reach a certain end goal. To be a better fighter, to sustain yourself in the field, that sort of thing."

Kaiden mulled it over for a moment before giving a nonchalant shrug. "I guess I'm just trying to be more of a badass than I already am."

"You say that so much you make it sound like it's a profession or title to acquire," Chief mocked. *"Ladies and gentlemen, your entertainment tonight is Kain the bloody face versus Kaiden the southern badass."*

"You make it sound like that's a bad thing to aspire to," he sneered. "I'm a soldier. Every soldier has got to have a little badass in them."

"Fine, we'll go with that. But what, specifically, do you want to be a badass in?"

"I don't know. I'm kinda winging this at the moment," Kaiden admitted. "Maybe work on being a punisher, someone who can really take it to my enemies. Or maybe something like a walking killing machine, nailing hostiles in a swarm of gunfire."

"Ladies and gentlemen, Kaiden has decided to take on a new title: Kaiden, the destroyer of worlds."

"Yeah, yeah, I get it," he chided. "Do you have a problem with that? I'm playing to my strengths."

"You're gonna be good at that stuff anyway. Expand your mind a little. That strategic mind talent worked out pretty good, didn't it?" Chief reminded him.

Kaiden thought about it. "I guess it did, all things considered. Made fighting Raza and Wulfson more bearable, at least. It's worked all right during the training missions with Chiyo too."

"*Then you should focus on that,*" Chief declared. "*It lets you still work on your fantasy of being Kaiden the doom lord while giving you a different trick up your sleeve. Diversify your skill portfolio and all that.*"

"I guess it'll make the Ace tests a lot easier." Kaiden pondered the options. "But maybe that's something I should leave for later. I should focus on my own skills for the test tomorrow."

"*Has Chiyo told you her talents?*"

"A couple days ago. You were there, obviously. You didn't hear?"

"*I was too busy trying to get into that stupid fox's systems,*" the EI answered.

"To do what?" Kaiden questioned, looking up at the EI's avatar.

"*So that we could share information and perhaps get to know each other better,*" Chief said sarcastically. "*At least that's what I told him. I wanted to see if I could outsmart that smug vulpine bastard.*"

Kaiden laughed. "What is your deal with him? You've only interacted with Kaitō a few times, and you act like you two have a blood feud. Ironic, considering the intangibility and all."

"*You can't see it, but that is a devious sonofabitch...I'll get him, you wait and see,*" Chief threatened as he turned a deep shade of hateful red.

Kaiden continued to chuckle. "Your irrational hatred of him is just damn funny to me." Kaiden released a couple of quick laughs before turning stone-faced. "But seriously, stop trying to tamper with my partner's EI. You know how much trouble that would cause?"

"I wasn't going to do anything too bad. Maybe delete some memory files or upload a couple terabytes of porn, maybe change his color to pink so that he could be Kaitō the fox princess of the cyber forest. You know, some good-humored pranks."

"You know, this is saying a lot about your maturity level." Kaiden sighed. "I can't even believe you're able to try to do that on your own. I guess I'll have to be more specific in my orders."

"I am here to serve, good sir," Chief bellowed, spinning around in the lens. *"And since I am here, and while we're on the subject, might I make another suggestion for your talents?"*

"Why not?" Chief changed the tab and scrolled down the screen,

Next-Gen: Increases EI processing, scanning, and hacking capabilities.

Status: 1/3 (Requires two points to upgrade)

Kaiden narrowed his eyes. "Hell no."

Genos ran down the hall, his pistol in hand in case he should run into any droids along his path. He found the door to the core room. It was thick and durable, so he wouldn't be able to get through with his pistol. He would have to double back and find the power source and deactivate it. If only he had some sort of large explosive.

"Intruder at the door to the core room. Intruder! Intruder!"

Genos looked back to see a havoc-model droid. It stood seven feet tall and was encased in heavy armor. Solid black with a red visor, it sported a chain gun for a left arm and four claws on its right, shimmering with electricity.

It would do.

Genos retrieved his hover-board. There wasn't much room to maneuver, but the havoc-model droids were built for heavy attack and not maneuverability. He merely had to get around it, and he would be in the clear. He raced down the hall toward the droid, put his pistol away, and activated his mechanist gauntlet, a metallic device that wrapped around his arm and held numerous tools for his use.

The droid's chain gun began to spin, firing a multitude of bullets at the Tsuna. Genos was able to stay out of the reach of the slugs, sliding slightly to the left as the droid fanned its gun across the hallway. He jumped off his board, and it slammed into the wall and then to the floor. Genos landed and dashed towards the droid, which turned slowly to aim back at him. He slid under the attacker and leaped onto its back. Holding fast with one hand, he placed four of his fingers together. Four panels slid over them on his gauntlet to create a crowbar that he used to pull the back of the havoc droid's head off.

"Danger! Hostile tampering with unit," the droid bellowed, reaching back with its electrified claw to try to grab at Genos. This was exactly what he wanted. He ducked out of the way of the strike, holding on to the droids opposite

shoulder as he formed a "C" with the gauntleted hand. The gauntlet created a clamp that he used to catch the droid's electrified prongs. He whipped it back, then plunged it into the machine's head.

The droid thrashed around for a moment as Genos leaped off. The lights behind its visor disappeared, and it fell to the ground. He had to hurry since it would reboot soon. Quickly, he recovered his board and used it to move the droid near the door. He opened the mechanical chest and found its power unit. A small prong appeared when he raised his pointer finger. He used it to move some of the wiring around and then flicked the finger in the air. The prong disappeared, and a power drill took its pace. Genos used it to open a panel connected to the power unit. He flicked the finger again, and this time it changed to another prong with a four-point claw that he used to remove two small nodes in the panel.

The core began to emit immense heat, and Genos stood up and ran to the end of the hall. He took cover behind the wall and peeked around the corner to see the droid beginning to reactivate.

"Warning! Power overload. Explosion in—" The droid exploded before finishing its warning. Genos placed his hands over his ears and dropped to his knees as the force of the explosion threatened to knock him off his feet. When it died down, he looked back to see both the droid and the door in pieces. He could have done something a little more subtle, but now wasn't the moment.

Conscious of the time, he ran through the doors and identified pieces of several other droids that were apparently also caught in the blast. Maybe this had been the correct option, after all. He saw a large window at the end of the hall. Inside was an orb with bright lights illuminating the space and several large tubes attached to it. This was the core, and the mission was to shut it down before it went critical.

He ran over to the control panel and saw a warning reading that there were only two minutes until detonation.

Genos breathed a sigh of relief. Plenty of time.

He activated the emergency venting and powered down several machines and devices throughout the facility, including the swarmers and scarabs, something he was sure kin Jaxon would approve of. Then he used his gauntlet to pry open the console, extending his finger again and summoning a pair of snippers.

With extra care, he cut through several wires, causing a slow shut down of the core. Too much at once could cause a power dump and they would be dealing with a different but equally problematic explosion.

"Intruder in the core room. All guardians requested for defense," a synthetic voice announced through the speakers above the console.

Genos frowned. He should have taken precautions. With a shrug, he snipped the wire that allowed the voice to talk. It would still send out a warning, but at least it would be silent.

He finished his work and watched as the core began to cool. A quick glance at the panel showed the energy draining quickly. It would take a few more minutes, but they were in the clear.

"Intruder! Intruder! Must eliminate intruder," a cacophony of several synthetic voices declared. Genos turned to see a

small team of six guardian droids coming down the hall. He yanked his pistol out and hid behind an adjacent console. Now, all he had to do was survive.

As he prepared to turn and battle the incoming droids, he heard laser fire erupt down the hall. Metal hit the floor, followed by the electrical zaps of fried wires. He peeked around his defense to see Jaxon walking towards him, his rifle in one hand and Genos' machine gun in the other. The guardian droids lay in a heap on the floor.

"Excellent display of violence, kin. I trust everything went well?" Genos asked as he stood and walked over to meet Jaxon.

"It certainly went better once the nuisance droids deactivated. Your doing?" Jaxon inquired as he tossed Genos' machine gun back to him.

"Indeed. This console also had access to control the droids throughout this building. I had to shut down a few of the functions to cool the core down and figured that would be quite helpful," he explained as he inspected his machine gun.

"A sound decision. Although I'm guessing that didn't include all of the droids considering…" Jaxon motioned at the guardians he had just eliminated.

"Only some. I couldn't risk shutting everything down at once."

"Understood. It'll give us something to do as we make our way out of here, assuming the core is deactivated?"

Genos looked over to the console now pried apart with severed wires strewn about. "Quite deactivated. It'll take a couple more minutes to power down completely. Would you like to destroy it to be sure?"

"I'll trust your judgment. The objective was simply to deactivate it before meltdown, and you accomplished that. We can head out," Jaxon ordered.

"Following right behind you," Genos acknowledged, raising his gun.

"And Genos? Well done." Jaxon walked out through the destroyed doors and into the hall.

"Thank you, and to you as well, kin Jaxon. I am now looking forward to my future missions," he whispered and followed Jaxon quickly as they began their retreat.

CHAPTER TWENTY-EIGHT

Kaiden sat at his usual table, finishing off his pancakes as he looked around at the couple of hundred students around the plaza. Some sat in groups, talking excitedly, while others scarfed down their breakfast, in a hurry to head to the Animus Center. It was barely past six in the morning, and the Co-op tests had already begun.

Kaiden tapped his plastic fork against his cup of juice, looking around for Chiyo. It was kind of odd for her to be this late.

"*You ready, partner?*" Chief asked, appearing over his shoulder.

Kaiden gulped down the last bit of pancake. "More than I was for the Division test. But can't say for sure. I don't really know what we're going to be dealing with."

"*You and Chiyo have run seven missions leading up to this. I'd have figured you're pretty well prepared.*"

He drank the last of his juice. "Just as long as we don't

329

have to deal with a flock of devil birds or a mechanical Kraken or some other weird crap, I think we'll do fine."

"Think about the points that would be worth, though," Chief pointed out.

"You think I'll get another rank-up by the end of this?" Kaiden asked, wiping a napkin across his lips before crumpling it up and tossing it on the tray.

"According to the rules, it is a possibility if you and Chiyo are among the top ten."

"Top ten? That's all it takes now? You had to be top three in the last test," Kaiden grumbled. "Guess they'll let anyone rank up nowadays."

"You've been rank two for four months, wiseass," Chief sneered. *"Besides, it's top ten overall. This isn't done in groups, remember? You've gotta get top ten among all other duos."*

"Oh...well, that's much more interesting." Kaiden took another look around at the massive group of initiates. "Still, we've probably got this in the bag."

"Good morning, Kaiden." Chiyo took the bench across from Kaiden, setting down her tray and tablet. "I trust you are prepared for the tests?"

"Mornin', Chiyo. I'm as good as can be. Though I could be a little more if you were able to...you know..."

"I researched a number of previous Co-op tests that involved soldiers and infiltrators as I said I would. There were a number of different variables but nothing that I would think we'd have issues with."

"That's gre— Wait, *soldiers* and infiltrators? Why soldiers in general? What about aces and infiltrators?" Kaiden asked.

"There weren't any that I could find, even going back to

when aces were originally called leaders. It would appear that we are coming into this test as a completely new type of Co-op team. I'm excited to see what will unfold," she said nonchalantly as she added some fruit to her oatmeal.

"Nothing at all? Isn't this academy like twenty-five years old or something? That seems highly unlikely."

"Not really. Aces are the leaders of the soldiers, right? Most of them probably partnered up with another soldier or field class over the years. Infiltrators do their best work in the shadows, even better when they can get things done from far away. So it probably didn't mix all that well for the greenhorns," Chief interjected.

"An astute observation, Chief, and a good morning to you as well." Chiyo waved a spoon in greeting.

"Howdy, Chiyo, it's good to see—"

"Salutations, Kaiden and Chief. I wish you both the best of luck in the coming test." Kaitō appeared in Chiyo's tablet screen.

"Kaitō...yay," Chief murmured, earning him an annoyed glance from Kaiden.

"I guess we'll have to go in somewhat blind. But no big deal. Considering the scenarios we've run, I feel pretty good that we'll have no problems with the test," he stated firmly.

"I wouldn't be so sure," Chiyo warned. "These tests always have unique parameters, and they often use enemies and maps that we are unfamiliar with. The test is to see how well students are able to handle these unknown situations along with their cooperative abilities."

"Well, we've got that down, for the most part, right? I'll follow you all sneaky like until we get to the mainframe or whatever, then I'll go off and have myself some fun and get the item we need to retrieve or the merc leader we need to kill off. We'll be golden."

"As much as I appreciate your optimism and the fact that this particular strategy has worked so well for us thus far, we should wait on these decisions until we are actually in the test," she advised.

"Speaking of actually getting in the test..." Kaiden fished out his oculars. "Chief told me that some of my talent choices won't really kick in until I get in the Animus, so if I start shakin' like I'm caught in a paint mixer, that's only me playing mental catch-up."

"What talents did you select?" she asked.

Kaiden nodded to her tablet. Chiyo looked down to see the screen change to Kaiden's talent tree, the new talents glowing with a dim light.

Deadshot: Increases natural aiming ability.

Status: ½

Increased Casting: Increases the range (15m) that the EI can cast and the distance between the user and EI can be before losing connection.

Status: 1/3

Strategic Mind: Learn dozens of strategies per upgrade and how to apply them in the field. Increasing your ability as a leader.

Status: 2/10

"You upgraded your Strategic Mind talent again," she observed. "A wise choice. That will certainly prove helpful for the coming trial."

"I chose that and the Increased Casting because of Chief. He wanted me to upgrade the Next-Gen talent, but considering what one point in that talent did to him... Well, I wasn't in a rush. I choose those two as a compromise."

"You simply can't handle what I've become. It is understandable for a plebe," Chief accused balefully.

"And the Deadshot?" Chiyo asked.

Kaiden whipped out his pistol and twirled it in the air. "It's my primary skill. Always good to keep that nice and shiny."

She nodded, looking at a group of students who went to toss their trash and head towards the Animus Center. "I have a request, Kaiden."

Kaiden stopped twirling his pistol and slid it back in its holster. "Go ahead."

"It will take a few more minutes for me to finish up. Since you seem to be done eating, would you head to the Center and sign us in? You will be given a colored chip that will let us know which group we will be in and when we will start."

He picked up his tray. "I gotcha. See you in a bit." He merged quickly into the crowd.

"You know, I don't think that Chief likes me very much," Kaitō commented.

"What makes you say that?" Chiyo asked as she spread some jam on her toast.

"I believe you would call it a vibe?"

She shrugged "Let's play nice for now. We have enough to worry about with the test."

"Are you truly that concerned, madame?"

Chiyo looked in the direction of the Animus Center. "It is always wise to be cautious... But considering who I'm with and how everything has gone, maybe not as much as I once was."

Kaiden pushed his way through the crowd outside the Center. They were less of a line than a huddled mass, so he assumed it was a first come, first served thing. He made his way to a staff member who was surrounded by a couple of dozen other initiates, all clamoring for one of those chips.

"Hey! Watch yourself." A blond-haired student scowled at him. He tried to elbow him out of the way, only for Kaiden to snatch the back of his jacket and fling him behind him. The hapless student was almost trampled by the other students behind them.

"What? You're not gonna take his lunch money too?" Chief chuckled.

"Hey, that dude could end up facing down a merc company someday. That's much worse than a little shove."

"Not likely, a green circle means he's in the Logistics division. Probably going to be in munitions, survey, or supplies. Might end up being in charge of a company that hands out bounties and missions. You know, someone you might be working for someday."

Kaiden paused for a moment. "Maybe I should help him up..."

"Hey, Ace, you're next," the official called. Kaiden turned to see him looking right at him. He walked up to the staff member as the man looked back down at his tablet. "State your name and Co-op partner."

"Kaiden Jericho. My partner is Chiyo Kana."

The man nodded and punched the information into his tablet. He removed a small disk from a tube on his belt and slid it into the tablet. There was a small pause before the disk was ejected and he handed it to Kaiden. "That chip contains your profiles and is your entrance into the test, so don't lose it. You're in the silver group, and you'll be called after the blue group."

Kaiden nodded as he took the chip. "Appreciate it."

The man smiled. "Good luck. You—Battle Medic—get over here."

Kaiden walked away and headed into the Animus Center. He placed the disk in the pocket on the inside of his jacket and went to find a chair and wait for Chiyo. As he settled in, he opened his friend network and activated the tracker so Chiyo could find him easier. He leaned back to relax for a while before they were called. Considering the volume and the fact that he would have to wait until all members of the previous group had finished, it might be a while.

"Ah, friend Kaiden. Good morning to you." He looked up to see Genos and Jaxon walking his way.

"Is the hallway in the Animus our special meeting place or were you hunting me down?" Kaiden quipped as he stood up and shook the Tsuna's hand.

"I wanted to wish you well before the tests. Kin Jaxon

and I are in the blue group and will be going in shortly," Genos explained.

"Blue group, eh?" Kaiden mulled over this as he looked at the two cerulean-colored aliens. "That's a bit ironic."

"I noted this as well," Jaxon stated dryly.

Kaiden chuckled softly. "You guys know where the others are?"

"Luke and Marlo, along with Silas and Izzy, are in the red group which is currently undergoing their tests. They should be out shortly. Flynn and Amber are in the silver group, according to the board." Jaxon pointed to a large monitor behind Kaiden. He grunted in annoyance that he hadn't seen it previously. "As for Raul and Cameron, I don't believe they have arrived yet, so I assume they will take their test sometime in the afternoon if they don't hurry."

"They might have slept in. Not the most organized, those two." Kaiden grinned.

"The tests span two days, so they can still take the test tomorrow if they do miss it. Though I believe they will be docked points if they don't sign-in within the next two hours." Jaxon frowned as he considered this.

"Maybe we should start looking for their replacements?" Kaiden suggested sarcastically.

Jaxon shook his head. "Do remember that they are two of the top soldiers in their classes. They may currently lack discipline, but they are not to be counted out."

"Just wishful thinking, Jax. Besides, I don't really want Cameron to fail. I wouldn't have such a convenient punching bag, otherwise."

"That would be tragic. Sparring partners are difficult to

come by." Genos made a sound that might have been a chortle.

Kaiden simply smiled and nodded.

"What about you, Kaiden? What group do you have?" Jaxon asked.

Kaiden patted his chest where he'd stored his chip. "I got silver like Flynn and Amber, so I'll be on after the two of you."

"Luke told me you are partnered with Chiyo Kana, the Infiltrator." Jaxon sounded curious.

"Yeah, we're actually a pretty good team. We've won every scenario we've run over the last few weeks."

"Good. It would be troubling to see you fail here. The Co-op tests are less forgiving than the Division tests should you fail."

"That was never an option for me in the first place," Kaiden stated proudly.

"To all members in the blue group, please head to halls four through eight to begin your Co-op tests." The voice of Head Monitor Zhang rang out over the speakers and monitors through the building.

"Looks like you guys are up," Kaiden said. "You will do great."

"Will you watch from the observatory?" Genos asked.

Kaiden thought about it. "Sure, Genos. Better to watch y'all beat the test than sit here twiddling my thumbs. I'll be cheering for ya."

"You have our thanks." Genos bowed slightly. "We will watch you in turn once you begin your test."

"Always like playing to a crowd. I'll head over there

now." He placed a hand across his chest and pointed two fingers into the air. "Good luck, you two."

Jaxon and Genos stared at him in silence, making Kaiden lower his fingers slowly. "Am I not doing it right?"

"No, you're fine. It's merely...odd seeing a human do one of our salutes," Jaxon said.

"The form could be better, and the fingers come out slightly after the hand is laid upon the chest. It might just be how your body moves," Genos observed, tapping a finger against his infuser in thought.

"You try to do something nice for the aliens, and you get judged for your posture," Kaiden grumbled as he lowered his arms and sighed.

"I'm sorry, I mean no disrespect. I greatly enjoyed your lame attempt at one of our sacred signs," Genos fretted.

"I think I liked it better when you weren't sure what words meant." Kaiden sighed before cracking a small smile and knocking the back of his hand against Genos' shoulder. "I'll be watching. Y'all go out there and kick ass."

"We will probably shoot most things, but I shall keep that in mind." Genos made another bow and performed a more fluid version of Kaiden's salute. "Farewell, friend."

Kaiden chuckled as he watched Jaxon as Genos walked away. "See, much more endearing."

"We shall see you once we finish," Jaxon promised over his shoulder. Kaiden gave him a swift nod, and the aliens left the building to head toward their test hall.

Chiyo was just about to enter as Kaiden was leaving. He tapped her shoulder and beckoned her to follow.

"Where are we going?" she asked.

"Headin' to the observatory. Gonna watch Jaxon and Genos take their tests," Kaiden answered.

"I see he got around to telling you about that," Chiyo noted.

Kaiden scratched the back of his head sheepishly. "Yeah, said that 'Geno' was a dirty word or something. Surprised that didn't get back to him sooner. He didn't tell me what it meant, but if people were calling me 'shithead' or 'dog tits' all the time, I would probably have piped up."

She sighed, then chuckled. "It was a technical error, and it's nothing as bad as that."

"What *does* it mean?" he asked.

"I'm sure he'll tell you later, or you could brush up on your Abisa."

"Doubt that." Kaiden huffed. "The only other language I know besides English and 'smartass' is Spanish, and that's because I lived in Texas. You want the best food, alcohol, and repairs, you only get them by going to the source."

"Well, just be sure not to mix it up from now on," she advised. "You got our chip?"

Kaiden took the disk out of his jacket pocket and handed it to her. "Silver. We're up after them, so I figured this would be more fun than sitting in the hallway."

Chiyo placed the chip in her tablet. "Nothing but our information. I was hoping we would be able to glean something about our test from this."

"There might be something. A good hacker could find out," Kaiden taunted.

"Then I should look into it when we have the time," Chiyo retorted.

His smile widened as he looked back at his partner. "It appears that I'm more of a bad influence on you than I thought."

Chiyo put the tablet away with a small grin of her own. "Trust me, looking into things that I shouldn't is quite natural to me without your prodding."

Kaiden laughed as they made their way to the observatory and their first look at what they might encounter.

CHAPTER TWENTY-NINE

Jaxon and Genos leaped out of the dropship and observed their surroundings. It was nighttime, and they stood in the sand of an arid desert surrounded by large dunes.

As Jaxon took a look around, trying to determine the best direction in which to move, Genos came up and tapped on something on his armor.

"Kin Jaxon, you are wearing your infuser," he noted as he continued to tap against the glass of the tubing.

Jaxon ran a glove across the device and looked at him. "So are you."

Genos stepped back and gripped his infuser. "Odd, I have never had the infuser load in with me before."

"Neither have I," Jaxon concurred. He opened the mission details in his helmet and looked them over.

"It must be a part of the test. An extra difficulty, perhaps."

"Considering the area, this is a map that is designed to

be one of the most difficult for us. As Tsuna, the Earth's sun and climate are already difficult for our biology. Without our infusers, an area like this will cause a rapid rise in temperature and asphyxiation, both leading to heat death," Jaxon surmised as he continued to read through the mission details.

"I don't recall seeing them while we were constructing our loadouts." Genos ran his hands over the device around the neck of his armor, noting the notches and protective wall. "At least they're armored."

"I would guess that they do not have Tsuna off-world armor with interior infusers loaded into the Animus yet. But I can't find anything here to say that they took away our interior cooling or emergency supply of immerse-gel." Jaxon opened a compartment on his belt to reveal three small tubes. He took one and examined it. A thick purple gel slid around the tube, and he nodded as he put it away. "Small blessings."

"Still, we should be patient and cautious. In this environment, even a small breach in our armor could prove fatal," Genos advised.

"I agree." Jaxon closed the mission details screen. "We are to make our way to a stronghold fifteen miles from our current location. There, we must retrieve an experimental cannon and destroy the base before heading to an extraction point."

"Understood," Genos acknowledged as he took his machine gun off his back. "Which direction?"

His partner pointed up the hill. They hurried up and lay down atop the crest. Jaxon retrieved his rifle and looked through its scope. "It's to the north, but I see a camp in the distance." He zoomed in on a small group of mercs in an encampment several hundred yards away. "Do you think we should go around? Or would there be an advantage to taking it?"

"Might I see your rifle?" he asked. Jaxon nodded and handed the gun over. Genos took a quick look through the scope before handing it back. "There is a hovercraft at the camp. I can activate it, and we can use it to approach the stronghold."

"With the accelerators in our suits, we run at a baseline of twenty miles an hour. It would be a quick trip around this and any other camps along the route," Jaxon pointed out.

"True, but the sand that we would kick up as we ran would make our movements obvious. Along with that, our armor generates a large enough amount of heat for thermal scanners to detect us, even in this climate," the mechanist explained. "Using the hovercraft would be more advantageous in not raising suspicion, and if they require a code or signal to enter the main camp, there is a possibility that I can find and activate it with the hovercraft."

"A well-thought-out plan, Genos, good deduction."

"You were thinking the same thing?" Genos asked.

"It is part of my responsibilities to know my environment and the best way to accomplish a mission with a number of variables. But I feel it is important for any field class to consider these issues and how best to surmount them."

Genos giggled for a moment, and Jaxon looked over with a quizzical look. "That is funny to you?"

The Tsuna continued to giggle as he explained, "I was

thinking about friend Kaiden. You two are in the same class, but you seem to have very different ways of approaching situations. You are strategic and calm, and he is... Well, I have only seen his Division test recording and that battle against the Sauren, but he does not seem to be...that."

"Kaiden has his own way of applying his skills and his own way of leading. It is...certainly different, but he will come into his own." Jaxon looked back into his scope. "You should also keep in mind that if he is watching us in the observatory, he can hear you."

Genos snapped a quick glance at Jaxon and then up at the sky as if looking for a camera. "That, um, that was not a negative observation, friend Kaiden."

"Cheeky bastard," Kaiden sneered, leaning back in his chair and crossing his arms. Chiyo chuckled beside him. They sat in observation room thirty-eight, which was designed like all other observation rooms—a small square space with ten seats. A tablet on a small table between Kaiden and Chiyo allowed them to control the different viewpoints and gave them a bigger view of the map. A large monitor on the wall in front of them provided a bird's eye view of the two Tsuna as they made their plans.

"Hey, Kaiden, Marlo said he, Silas, Izzy, Flynn, Amber, and Luke are looking for ya and wanted to know if you wanted to watch Jaxon's test," Chief notified him.

"Well, we're already here, obviously. Give them the room number and tell them to get their asses over here asap. It looks like the good stuff is going to start soon." Chief disappeared from view.

"Genos has a good mind for field work," Chiyo noted. "I wonder what will happen when they reach the main base."

"I wouldn't be too worried. We got in a brawl with a Sauren a few weeks back that we thought wanted to kill us, and he was practically Zen through it all."

"You got into a fight with a Sauren? Was it the same one you told me you were training with?"

"Raza, yeah. It was a hell of an introduction," Kaiden recounted. "But Genos was able to take down a barrier that protected Wulfson's guns and charge one up to full power while Raza was rampaging around the place. I think he's more of a warrior than even he realizes. It's probably because he isn't used to fighting that much, but being good in a battle doesn't always indicate who's the better killer."

"A surprisingly astute observation, coming from you."

"Does everyone see me as a blood-lust-filled jackal?" Kaiden sneered.

"Kaiden, the destroyer of worlds, remember?" Chief jeered in his head, causing Kaiden to scowl.

"I can have more tact than that when I want to," he said defensively.

"The numerous guards, mercs, and droids you've slaughtered through our missions alone would beg to differ," she countered.

"Hey, it's to our benefit that we take out as many as possible. For SXP and so they don't come after us later in the mission."

"During our third mission, I was able to block the alarm, and you still made a point to go into every room and take out any merc you came across, including the group playing poker in the basement," Chiyo recalled dryly.

"As I just said—points," he retorted.

"We would have gotten more points if we finished the mission within thirty minutes. Due to your...methodical style, we were in that mission for more than four hours."

"Methodical. I think that's how I'll refer to it now."

Chiyo sighed as she looked back at the screen. "It appears they are about to begin."

"Are you ready, Genos?" Jaxon asked as he put his rifle away.

"Indeed." The engineer nodded, drawing his pistol. It was a device that fired a remote access antenna, allowing the user to take control of most basic hardware.

"You take care of the two guards next to the hovercraft and create a distraction." Jaxon held his knife, a long, eight-inch straight blade. "And I'll take care of the trio around the tent."

"I believe this will allow me to do both at once," Genos declared.

His partner gave one final nod, and they both crouched and began moving towards the camp.

Genos made his way behind a stack of boxed supplies. He peered around the corner to see both guards looking away, one at a tablet and another at the sky, a perfect moment. He aimed at the one on the tablet and launched a round to his back, then quickly fired another shot at the second guard. With a calm movement, he opened a screen on his gauntlet and pressed a separate command for each soldier.

The guard on the right dropped his tablet, reached around his helmet, and tried to tear it off. No oxygen reached his lungs as Genos had activated his gas mask but not the oxygen tank, causing no air to enter and locking the helmet in place. The other guard seized up and fell to the ground as Genos locked the mechanical joints in the suit.

With futile scrabbling, the first man continued to try to remove his helmet. He ran around the hovercraft, flailing to catch the other guards' attention. They stood and one rushed over to help, and Jaxon used that moment to sneak behind one of them and sink his blade into his neck. He leaped over the man and drove the knife through the visor of the second guard. As the asphyxiated defender fell, Jaxon flung the knife at the remaining man, piercing his shoulder. The Tsuna ran up and pulled the knife out and dragged it across his guard's neck. The man shuddered for a moment before grasping at his throat and falling to the sand.

"Well done, kin. Not a single shot fired." Genos unlocked the door to the hovercraft.

"Can you activate this?" Jaxon asked as he stowed his knife.

"Of course, but if you wouldn't mind checking the guards for an access card or...actually, one moment." He walked over to each of the downed mercs and removed their helmets, then studied them quickly.

"What are you looking for?"

"A signal chip. I could manufacture one if there is a record of them in the hovercraft, but that would take some time. It would be much easier if we simply had one already in…ah, here we are." Genos pulled a small chip from one the helmets and inserted it into his own. "This should prove useful. Now, if we can get a little cooperation from the last one." He looked over to the guard who was trapped in his armor.

The two walked over to him, hearing muffled yelling from behind the mask. "I turned off audio," he explained. "One moment." He pressed a command on the screen of his gauntlet that unlocked the helmet. With a deft movement he pulled it off, and they heard the guard yelling an alert.

"*Intruders at Outpost Blue. All* other men dead. Send reinforcements and alert the main base."

"Outpost Blue? This seems to be a running theme for us." Genos chuckled.

"You blocked his radio, correct?" Jaxon asked.

"Of course. It is a basic rule."

The guard continued to yell, apparently oblivious to their words. Jaxon sighed as he shoved a boot in the merc's face and pushed him into the sand. "What do we need from him? I would like him to stop talking."

"It's a simple precaution. I wanted to create a couple of messages for any guards at the gate just in case." Genos studied the helmet. "I blocked his radio, but his words might be stored on a recorder or internal hard drive. I could fashion a few dialogues using those."

Jaxon continued to push the merc down with his boot. "I have my own ways of getting what we need."

"That would be helpful," Genos responded. "I think it

would be most interesting to see whose methods are quicker. Use the recorder in your helmet and try to get some basic affirmations and a reason why we are return-ing." He turned away and plugged a wire from his gauntlet into the helmet. "Oh, and please, do try not to wear him down too much. We need it to sound convincing."

Kaiden whistled. "Wow, those guys are hardcore when they wanna be."

"It is surprising how…good they are at this. I was under the impression that the Tsuna were more into the sciences and exploration than war," Chiyo admitted.

"Hey, the Sauren are technically explorers too. Doesn't stop them being really good at shedding blood," Kaiden explained with feeling. "Besides, they have warrior clans. It figures they got to know a few things about it after all this time."

The door to the room opened. They looked back to see the rest of the invitees walk in.

"How's it going, mate?" Flynn asked with a wave.

"Y'all just missed Jaxon and Genos take down a camp of mercs," Kaiden said with a nod at the screen. "Now they are…uh…" Kaiden watched as Jaxon took his knife and leaned down over the merc. "Well, Jaxon is having a polite discussion at the moment."

"Is that sarcasm or is this another cultural thing that I'm not aware of?" Silas asked as he frowned at the view onscreen. "Because I'll have to politely decline to partici-pate if he ever asks me to."

"Nah, that's just Jaxon's way of interrogating. He plays up the whole invading alien angle. Works pretty well," Luke stated.

"How'd you guys do?" Kaiden inquired.

"We passed with a final score of seventy-six thousand." Silas looked at Izzy. "Could have had a time bonus if someone didn't have to look in every nook and cranny for bonuses."

"Hey! Those bonuses were worth more than the time bonus," Izzy argued. "Besides, it's a matter of scout pride to look into crannies."

"You're supposed to establish footholds and excel at hit-and-run tactics and objective retrieval," Silas retorted. "You're not a surveyor with a better gun."

"I have many talents," Izzy declared with a flourish. "Besides, you can't deny that I saved your ass in that trench."

"The trench you pushed me into?" Silas inquired.

"That was to save you from a rocket blast!"

"The one I warned you about?" Silas chuckled. "Followed by you pushing me into a trench."

"You're hopeless." Izzy sighed.

"While they continue to bicker, what about you and Marlo, Luke?" Kaiden asked.

"We did…all right," Luke muttered as Marlo sighed.

"Turns out that they did have waves of enemies…lots of waves." Marlo grunted, the sound despondent.

"But you got lots of points, right?" Flynn asked as he took a seat next to Kaiden.

Marlo shrugged. "Oh, sure, but remember what Izzy said about taking hits being deducted from your score?"

"We scraped by with a final score of thirty-seven thousand," Luke grumbled.

"That doesn't sound too bad," Kaiden remarked cheerfully.

"You need a minimum of thirty thousand to pass," Chiyo explained. "Unlike the Division test, you only receive fifteen thousand for completing the objective. The rest of the points come from eliminations, class bonuses, time bonuses, and secondary objectives."

"Ah... Well, at least you passed." Kaiden tried to sound reassuring.

"Yeah, barely, but Mr. Kitzinger, my workshop teacher, is probably gonna make me do extra training," Luke whined.

"Not to mention what Wulfson is gonna do to us," Marlo added. Both giant soldiers shivered.

"At least I'm not the only one worried about that now," Kaiden whispered to himself.

"It looks like Genos and Jaxon are getting ready to head to the main base," Chiyo reported. The rest of the group took their seats and watched the screen as the two Tsuna climbed into the hovercraft and sped out of the camp.

"Now the real show starts," Kaiden exclaimed.

CHAPTER THIRTY

J axon and Genos raced through the desert. The sand slapped against the windshield of the craft. Genos hunched low, scanning through the screen on his gauntlet.

"What are you looking for, Genos?" Jaxon asked, his gaze alternating between the map on the visor of his helmet and looking out at the terrain for other camps and possible ambushes.

"Trying to figure out the best way to destroy the facility. We were not given much information, but if they have a core I can overload or a munitions bunker, it should not be difficult. However, I am not seeing anything specific in the details."

His partner chuckled. "That would be giving us an advantage. This test is to prove our skills in a situation where we have nothing but our commands and the resources we have available. Our weapons, our armor, our minds..." He looked at his kin. "And each other."

Genos looked up with a polite nod as he turned off the screen. "How do you believe we should approach this?"

Jaxon thought for a moment. "We have two goals, the destruction of the facility and the retrieval of the cannon."

"According to the mission details, the cannon is a secondary objective, it is not required to win."

"Genos, I do not say this to belittle you, but you should take some inspiration from the wisdom of the old warriors. It is a command to retrieve the cannon. Just because we do not need it in this scenario does not mean we should make a habit of not obeying the commands given to us, no matter how small."

"I see…" He looked down at his gauntlet for a moment, clenching his fist. "Then we will have to focus on getting the cannon before we destroy the base. Doing one before the other could prove to be an issue when we need to escape."

"Agreed, but we don't need to do them exclusively," Jaxon suggested. "Once we are inside and have a better understanding of what we need to do, we will make a proper plan. For now, we will simply work to take the fort together. They are sure to have many troops and droids at their disposal, so I need you to sabotage or convert as many droids as you are able to. Then, if you see any vehicles or mechs that you can tamper with or override, use them to create a distraction while I find the cannon."

"Are you sure that you will be fine alone?" Genos asked worriedly.

"Your concern should be directed at yourself. For this to go smoothly, what I am asking is for you to be the focus of their aggression. Can you handle that?"

Genos nodded, taking out two small grenades from his belt. "I have shock grenades to deactivate the droids and stun or possibly take out the human opponents. And these..." Genos picked up one of the grenades, a clear receptacle filled with small round devices. "These are seeker drone grenades. When detonated, the drones attach themselves to any droid or machine that can be physically rerouted. Droids and turrets will attack their owners and machines with no action functions will be deactivated. I will merely need to be in an area where I can make the most use of them."

"Then we will find an area with as many droids as possible. That is where we will begin our strike," Jaxon decided.

Genos put the grenades away and activated a console between them. "The hovercraft has two small cannons mounted on top. I will use this to begin our assault while you enter the building. If you find a core room or munitions bunker or anything that will allow us to destroy the base, let me know."

"Of course. I don't believe I have the skill or enough explosives to do it on my own." He pressed a button on the side of his visor, deactivating the map and wiping it clean. "Be prepared, Genos. We are here."

The guardsman at the gate looked over the dunes to see one of their hovercrafts moving toward them. He checked the schedule and saw nothing to indicate that they were expecting a rendezvous with one of the outside camps.

Cautious now, he activated the signal check and received a positive reading from the hovercraft.

"Outpost Blue, why are you here?" the guardsman asked into a comm mic.

"Need supplies."

"According to my reading, you were supplied nine days ago with enough rations for two weeks. Why are you here early?"

"Supplies were lost to blight scarabs," the hovercraft driver reported swiftly.

The guardsman sighed. "Goddamn scarabs. None of you are infected, right?"

"No."

"Either way, you should check with that medic droid we captured, just to be safe. You're allowed in for two hours to restock and get a check-up, but your asses better be gone before midnight," he commanded and entered the code for the gates as the hovercraft approached slowly. After a few seconds, the gate was completely open, and the vehicle moved through. The man closed the gate behind them.

He looked through the small window to see the sand kicking up and heard a hollow wind in the distance. His face grim, he spat out the window of his station before closing it. A sandstorm was rolling in.

"Quite providential." Genos hummed as he tossed the outpost guard's helmet behind him. "It would appear we will have some cover as we undertake the mission."

"A sandstorm?" Jaxon asked, getting a nod from Genos. "Looks like we have gotten a bit of fortune on our side. Make sure to activate your helmet's ventilation and seal your infuser. Don't want that to get clogged."

"Already on it," his partner assured him but checked his infuser anyway.

The base was a lone rectangular building, gray and sand-covered with few windows. Jaxon glanced around quickly. A few droids walked around with a dozen or two mercs lounging in a disinterested huddle close to the main structure. Perhaps Genos would have an easier time than he'd thought. Which immediately made him believe that inside would potentially be filled with guards.

Then, as they drove around the corner of the building, Jaxon's eyes widened as he saw a large tank hovering above the sands. The triangular-shaped vehicle carried one large cannon on the roof and two laser guns on the front.

Jaxon turned to Genos. "Will you be able to keep yourself safe from that?"

His partner looked at the tank and nodded enthusiastically. "Actually, I believe this could be fortuitous."

"How so?" the ace Tsuna asked.

The engineer fished out his grenades and offered them to Jaxon. "Please, take these. I have a plan."

"And what would that be?" Jaxon inquired, looking curiously between the tank and machinist as he took the grenades.

"I will explain, but first, may I borrow your knife?"

"We'll be ready to patrol in five," the tank operator called back to the two mercs in the carriage with him.

"Then I gotta take a leak. Can't stand using the little porthole," one of them grumbled, opening the top entrance and climbing out.

"We can just leave without him," the other offered after the hatch closed.

"He'll whine to the captain about us leaving him. Between you and me, the only reason they tossed him in here with us was so that he wasn't walking around here bitchin'," the operator growled.

"Next outpost they set up, they need to dump his ass over there." The merc snickered.

"Maybe put him over by the sand drift line. Let him get hammered by the rebel mortars," the operator agreed.

The hatch opened again, and the operator primed the tank. "You get it all out of ya?" he sneered.

He got no response. "So now you shut up," he muttered to himself. "You ready to go, you whiny bas—" A knife dug into his skull, stopping him midsentence.

Genos tore the knife out of the operator's head and thrust it into the other merc's throat. He dragged the body behind him and took over the controls. "Jaxon, I'm ready."

"I'm getting the hovercraft in position. Are we good to go?" Jaxon replied over the comms.

"Yes. Please check that the turrets are on auto-fire."

"They are and will begin to fire once I leave the vehicle. You are sure that they will not fire at us?"

"Of course. I set them to attack anything that is not a Tsuna," Genos answered.

Jaxon chuckled. "Clever use of our biology. I did not think that would be an advantage here."

"I like to think rather uniquely," Genos responded, taking the controls and moving the tank forward.

He already knew how to drive and use the tank, having spent over a month learning about the ground-based vehicles of Earth. He drove it to the right side of the building, aiming the cannon at the wall. "Viola, activate."

"How can I be of service, Genos?" his EI asked, taking the form of a purple jellyfish on his visor.

"I will man the main cannon if you would please take control of the mounted lasers and deal with any hostiles that try to attack us." Genos took the EI chip out of his helmet and placed it into a slot on the console.

Viola appeared on a screen at the top left. *"Of course, Genos. Any other requests?"*

"Get access to the venting and power core. I'll need them in case this turns out to be a mistake." He looked at the hovercraft as it glided behind the tank. "Are we set to begin?"

"On my mark." Jaxon began counting down. Genos hovered his thumb over the cannon's firing trigger. "Begin."

He fired the cannon. It sounded like thunder, and a brief flash of light appeared as the wall shattered from the blast. Jaxon raced towards the newly formed entrance as the mounted lasers fired at the mercenaries, who were in disorder from the blast.

Genos could hear the guns on the hovercraft firing behind him. The defenders would be in shock for only a few moments before retaliating. But hopefully, more would rush out of the building and give Jaxon the space he would need to recover the cannon.

A green flash indicated the cannon was ready to use again. He aimed it at the front of the building. While his partner focused on one objective, he would begin the other.

Jaxon fired twice with his rifle, hitting a merc in the chest with both shots. He quickly fired a third round, catching another man in the side of the head. Cautious but swift, he made his way deeper into the base, feeling the foundation shake as Genos fired another shot from the tank's cannon. He had to hand it to his kin, he was rather good with the large weapons.

As he continued down the hall, sand poured in from the storm behind him. He stopped at an intersection and looked around the corner when he heard the clanking of metal skittering along the floor. A group of guardian droids approached at a steady pace.

He mentally ticked off the models that Genos had told him the seeker grenades worked on: scarabs, swarmers, raiders, hellcats, and guardians. Swiftly, he took one of the grenades and activated it, then tossed it at the droids and heard it burst apart. He looked around the corner again to see the mechanicals had stopped in their tracks.

A trio of guards came around the corner down the hall. They stopped when they saw the droids standing idle, yelling at them to move. The droids turned and fired on the mercs. Jaxon nodded in approval as he continued to run through the building.

"Kin Jaxon, did you use one of my seekers?" Genos asked over the comms.

"I did. It worked quite well." Jaxon reached a crossway and tried to make a fast decision.

"It granted me access to their database. I have a map of the building."

"Send it to me."

"Right away."

The map appeared in the corner of his visor. He spied a room labeled "holding" and decided that was where he would start his search.

He ran right down the crossway, taking out another group of guards along his path. As he turned into the corridor leading to the holding room, he was stopped by a duo of havoc droids.

"Eliminate intruder," one shouted as they turned to face the Tsuna. Jaxon grabbed a shock grenade, activated it, and threw it at the feet of the droids. Their guns began to spin. The grenade went off, and a surge of electricity enveloped them before their guns wound down. He raised his rifle and fired two shots through each of their heads, which immediately exploded. The bodies toppled to the floor.

He moved past their remains and opened the door to the room. A guard appeared from behind the door. Jaxon flipped his gun around quickly and smashed it into the man's face. He recoiled in pain as the Tsuna took out his pistol and pumped several shots into his chest.

Jaxon stepped over the guard and raised his pistol when he saw a white droid with a green visor and a health sign walking towards him. *"Good evening, sir. I am a Vita model health droid; do you require a medical exam or patch up?"*

Jaxon lowered his pistol. "I am looking for a cannon." Jaxon pressed his finger against the side of his visor. A light emanated from it, and a holographic image of the cannon appeared in the air. "Have you seen it?"

"Why, yes, it is right over there." The droid pointed to a grey case in the corner. Jaxon walked over and opened it, revealing a slim white tube with a handle and trigger, a contorted orb sticking out of the end.

Jaxon was puzzled. It didn't appear that powerful. He felt another tremor as a blast hit the opposite side of the building. Pushing his curiosity aside, he grabbed the weapon and strung it on his back. "Genos, I have the cannon. Are we clear to depart?"

***

"A moment, Kin Jaxon. I am dealing with…some trouble," Genos stated as he strafed the defenders from out of the line of sight of two tanks that had appeared from the bay of the building.

"Where are you? I will help."

"I will be fine. You get out of the building and rendezvous at the gate," Genos instructed. "Viola, it is time."

He turned the cannon toward the gate, firing one last shot and destroying it. He could feel the inside of the tank grow hotter, and a loud hum sounded from the core. With a measured motion, he removed the EI chip out from the console and slid it back into his helmet. He sent the tank charging forward and locked the command before running to the back of the vehicle and using the escape hatch to bail out.

The tank took a shot from one of the opposing tanks' cannon, but it continued its charge, slamming into the two before exploding. Both crashed to their sides and erupted in flames.

Genos stood and grabbed his rifle. The sandstorm now raged at its full velocity, but his Tsuna eyes could see in a spectrum larger than a human's, and he had no trouble eliminating a few guards on his way to the gate.

"Genos, are you at the gate yet?" Jaxon asked.

"Right here, kin Jaxon," he shouted, waving at the ace as he ran up to him. "Did you get the cannon?"

"I did, but looking at it now, it does not seem to be much of a cannon." Jaxon removed the weapon from his back and handed it to Genos.

He looked it over while Jaxon stepped forward, taking a look at the base. "The main base still stands, albeit barely. Let us see if we can find another tank or some explosives to—" Jaxon stopped as he saw Genos aiming the cannon at the building. "What are you doing?"

"Please step back for a moment, Jaxon," he requested. The Tsuna obliged and stood behind his partner as he held the trigger down and continued to point at the building. After a few moments, Genos lowered the weapon and placed it on his back next to his machine gun.

"Did it not work?" Jaxon asked.

"It will work soon," Genos replied, walking past him.

"What are you—" Jaxon looked back as he saw a brilliant light coming down onto the building, bright even through the sand.

"I suggest we run now—very fast," Genos advised calmly. Jaxon nodded, and they took off, racing as fast as they could away from the building.

They reached the dune just outside the gate, and a loud explosion erupted behind them as the two dove to the ground. Jaxon looked back to see a laser coming down from the sky and crashing into the building, completely decimating it.

Jaxon looked over to Genos. "That cannon…it was…"

"A guidance system for the actual cannon." Genos pointed up at the sky.

"A satellite cannon—" Jaxon looked up in surprise.

Genos nodded. "You were right that we should always listen to all objectives, kin. It would seem some prove quite useful."

Jaxon smiled under his helmet as he stood. "You did well. Never question your place here," he commanded, offering Genos a hand.

The engineer accepted the ace's assistance. "I will be sure to never have those doubts again," he promised as his partner pulled him up.

Jaxon saluted him before they made their way to the rendezvous point and victory.

CHAPTER THIRTY-ONE

The Tsuna stood in front of the screen in their Animus hall, awaiting their final score.

"How do you think we fared, kin?" Genos asked.

Jaxon stood with his arms crossed, considering their mission. "We were in and out in just under an hour with little damage to ourselves and much destruction to our foes, and we completed the bonus objective. I think that all of that combined will grant us a rather favorable score."

"Hey, Genos, Jaxon!" a voice called. They looked back to see Kaiden and their friends at the doorway of the hall, kept out by a pair of guards. "Y'all did a damn fine job. What's the total?"

"We are awaiting our final score," Genos called back. Kaiden nodded as he turned to the guards who kept shoving him back.

"Those who are not participating in the test cannot enter the halls," Jaxon noted. "Doesn't seem to have stopped Kaiden and the others from trying."

"They seem quite enthusiastic," Genos replied with a bubbly inflection. "That also bodes well for our judgment."

"Agreed. Though it could be problematic for them if they have points deducted for breaking the rules. I'll tell them to wait for us in the lobby." As Jaxon began walking over to the group, he heard a loud ding and his partner grabbed his shoulder.

"Kin, our scores are being shown."

He looked back to see the scoreboard on the monitor. It showed the twenty-five duos in the blue group and began at the bottom. The pair watched as different duos appeared and had their final score tallied, the bottom names barely securing a passing grade of thirty-four thousand.

The board continued to climb, reaching the top five positions, Genos and Jaxon had yet to appear.

Fifth Place: Andrew Crane and Olivia Green (Raider / Machinist): 103,400 points.

Jaxon saw a blond-haired man and a woman with long silver hair give each other a high five.

"Good for Olivia," Genos said cheerfully.

"You know her?"

"We share a workshop together—Battle Engineering. She and I often vie for the top score in the class."

"Then it appears you will surpass her for the time being." Jaxon looked back at the screen as it changed to the fourth place bracket.

Fourth Place: Silva Zabka and Jade Valsina (Scout / Biologist): 107,600 points

"Valsina? That's the human translation of one of our avian creatures back home, is it not?" Genos inquired.

"Unsurprising, considering that she is from Abisalo."

Jaxon pointed to a female Tsuna in the distance who was hugging a human girl.

"It appears we are not the only Tsuna doing well here," Genos said with a proud smile.

"Hopefully, the Conclave will take note."

Third Place: Roger MacClintock and Honor Harrington (Pilot / Navigator): 108,200 points.

"A wise combination," Jaxon said.

"A bit boring though, wouldn't you say?"

He looked at his partner with surprise. "I would have thought you would approve such a symbiotic pairing."

"Well, it is certainly a smart combination, as you say…" Genos looked at his partner and smiled despite his mask blocking most of his mouth. "But an obvious pairing doesn't mean one automatically gains the best results, as we have proven."

"It appears so," Jaxon agreed, tapping his fist against his chest before looking at the screen once more.

Second Place: Jaxon Cage and Genos Aronnax (Ace / Mechanist): 111,400 points

"Well done, kin!" Genos placed a hand on Jaxon's shoulder.

"We did well, Genos," he acknowledged. "Perhaps well enough to end up in the top ten groups overall?"

"Perhaps." Genos nodded. "Even if we did not, this is much better than I would have dared to hope only a few weeks ago. I am exuberant."

"As I am, though I may not show it," the ace admitted. "Come, let us go and meet our friends before they set off for their own tests."

"Do you not wish to see who took first?" Genos asked.

"That is their victory, whoever it is," Jaxon stated as he turned from the screen. "We have our own to celebrate."

The group now stood in the lobby of the Animus Center, crowding around the two Tsuna.

"Awesome job, Jax," Luke bellowed, grasping the Tsuna's hand in a firm shake. "Always gotta be showing off, huh?"

"You did very well, Genos," Chiyo said sincerely. "You showed great strategic thinking throughout the test. I am most impressed."

"Also a knack for explosions," Kaiden added. "I really liked those."

"Thank you, everyone." Jaxon expressed his pleasure with a slight bow. "Thank you for watching us during our mission."

"You guys were amazing," Marlo professed. "Might need to take a few more cues from you next time around."

"I'd be happy to assist." Jaxon held a hand out to Genos. "I'm sure Genos would also have a few tips he'd be willing to share."

"Um, well, perhaps. I still think my abilities in battle could use some work. My expertise is in mechanics and modification," Genos blustered, fidgeting his fingers as he clasped and unclasped them.

"Also explosions," Kaiden reiterated.

"That works for me. I'm a demolitionist," Marlo pointed out.

"Oh, then I probably do have a few things I can assist you with," Genos chirped.

The group continued to talk excitedly amongst themselves as the screens around the center changed to reveal the Head Monitor. "Congratulations to the blue group. All twenty-five teams passed their tests."

A small number of cheers erupted from the crowd. "It is now time for the silver group to begin their tests. If you are in this group, please make your way to halls four through eight to begin your test."

"That's us, then," Flynn stated, looking at Amber.

"Pocket healer. That's neat," Kaiden commented cheekily.

Amber stared at him in annoyance. "I'm a battle-medic, remember? I do more than just spray people down with healing beams."

"You look good while doing it?" Izzy asked.

Amber smiled as she cracked her knuckles. "That too, but it's the battle part I was referring to."

"You probably won't have to do much healing since I'll be sniping our targets from a plenty safe distance," Flynn said cockily, making a shooting motion with his fingers.

"You still have the disk, right?" Amber asked.

"Oh, yeah, I sure do..." Flynn began rummaging through his different pockets. "Uh...somewhere, anyway."

Amber sighed as she pointed down at his feet. "You put it into your boot so you wouldn't lose it."

"Right!" He laughed, bending down to fish the silver disk out of his left boot. "Good job remembering that."

"I knew one of us had to be responsible." She gave him a playful jab to the ribs.

"You still got ours, Chiyo?" Kaiden asked.

She nodded and held up her tablet. "We are to head to hall five for our test."

Flynn slid his disk into his wrist-mounted tablet. "We are…in hall seven."

"Looks like I won't be able to hold your hand to calm your nerves," Kaiden jeered.

Flynn gave him a wry look. "I'll be fine. Besides, I got a pocket healer, remember?"

"I thought you weren't gonna get shot?" Amber muttered.

"I mean, that's the plan. But I wanna make sure you've got something to do too." Flynn chuckled.

Amber rolled her eyes and began to walk away. "Just be sure that you take down the targets I call out. Keep yourself useful, and I'll get you something pretty when this is all done."

"Hey, I'm more than my rifle," Flynn yelled back, jogging after his partner.

"Think they're gonna be all right?" Silas asked as the marksman and battle-medic ran off.

"They'll be fine," Marlo assured him. "Amber told me they've been like that since they were kids. They bicker like that all the time before we run missions and stuff. This is actually quite tame for such a big thing. Before the Division test, they were jabbering at each other for the entire week leading up to it."

"You guys gonna watch us?" Kaiden asked.

"For sure. Might have to flip a coin and see which one we're gonna be watchin', but I'm sure you'll fill us in with your boasts and usual braggadocio," Silas said with a smirk.

"Just know that we'll be going to Chiyo for fact-checking," Izzy added.

"Your cheerleading could use some work." Kaiden pretended indignation. "Can't you do a little jig or something?"

"There are a few clan dances and ceremonies we have for sending off those going into battle, but I do not believe we have the time," Genos offered.

"Not what he meant, Genos." Jaxon chuckled.

"You can always use the console in the observation room to switch between test channels. You can watch both teams," Chiyo reminded them.

"You'll probably just wanna stick to our test, though," Kaiden said with cheerful bravado. "You know I like to keep things interesting and play to the crowds."

"I recommend we hold off on that until we begin," Chiyo said with a dramatic roll of her eyes.

Kaiden looked back at her over his shoulder. "Don't worry, you can lead until you're all cozy in your little infiltrator's nest, then I can have my fun."

"Again, we don't know if that will work this time around," she reminded him. "Just be prepared for anything."

Kaiden nodded. "Don't worry about it, Chi, we've got this."

"The remaining members of the silver group must go to their designated halls at this time. The cooperative test will begin shortly."

"That's your cue, showstopper." Izzy pointed to the elevators.

"Hey, guys." The group looked over to see Cameron and Raul walking up to them. "What did we miss?"

"A hell of a lot," Luke told them slyly.

"Where have you been?" Silas asked.

"Slept in, then the pampered idiot over here took forever in the shower." Cameron sneered, pointing a thumb at Raul.

"I want to be refreshed on a test day, put my best foot forward," he retorted, running his fingers through his hair. "Nothing a grimy lout like you would understand."

The two began to bicker, and the rest of the group sighed or shook their heads. "You guys can fill them in on the way. Chiyo and I gotta head out," Kaiden said.

"Best of luck to you," Jaxon said.

Genos nodded. "I know that you will do well, friends."

The rest said their goodbyes as Chiyo and Kaiden left for the elevators. They waited in silence, Kaiden humming to himself as Chiyo removed the disk from her tablet and put it away in her bag. Once the elevator opened they stepped inside, and Kaiden leaned against the back and Chiyo to the side. No one else entered as the doors closed and the elevator ascended.

"You ready?" Kaiden asked.

"Of course. I would have insisted on more training otherwise," Chiyo answered, looking his way.

"Just wanted to say before we get in there, thanks for the offer to team up. Hate to think what scrub I would have been saddled with otherwise."

"It was my pleasure. This has proven to be quite a fruitful partnership."

"Time to see how the fruit bears, eh?" he jested.

Chiyo stared at him. "Kaiden, have you ever considered you have Witzelsucht syndrome?"

"What's that?" he asked as the elevator stopped on their floor.

"I'll… You can look it up later." Chiyo stated in a slightly strangled tone. The doors opened, and they left to find their hall.

———

Kaiden stopped in the middle of the room to look around at the other duos. There were ten initiates, including himself and Chiyo—five teams to a hall. He looked over to the hub to see Chiyo handing an advisor their chip. He looked at her a moment before waving. "Advisor Faraji, how's it going?" he called as he walked over.

"Hello, Kaiden, good to see you again." She offered him her hand.

He shook it. "How have you been?"

The pressure around his hand tightened, and he winced slightly. "You would know if you actually showed up to my workshops once in a while," she pointed out, a now unnerving smile on her face.

"I show up. I just don't stick around that much," Kaiden sputtered, trying to pry his hand from her grasp. "I'm using the Animus like you taught us. That's gotta count for something."

"Oh, it does, but you could learn so much more than the basics." She released him. Kaiden yanked his hand back and rubbed it as Akello looked at her tablet. "Well, considering you're partnered with Chiyo, maybe she can start getting you to shape up a bit."

"You're in her Animus workshop too?" Kaiden asked.

The infiltrator nodded. "I find the teachings and inner workings of the Animus fascinating. Advisor Faraji is a very engaging teacher."

"Why, thank you, Chiyo." Akello beamed.

"Kiss ass," Kaiden muttered.

Akello narrowed her gaze. "Chiyo happens to be one of my top students if you must know."

"Yeah, kiss ass," Kaiden repeated.

Chiyo looked glumly at him as Akello shook her head. "What have you gotten yourself into, girl?"

"I can attest to Kaiden's abilities, though there are some things we may not see eye to eye on."

"Well, I can agree with that, at least." Akello tapped on her tablet and pointed to a pair of Animus pods down the line. "Pods nineteen and twenty are yours for the test. Once the preparations are complete, you will be synced and have five minutes to learn your mission and assemble your loadout." The pods opened, awaiting the pair. "Good luck to you, Chiyo."

"What about me?" Kaiden asked.

Akello frowned. "Don't fuck this up for her."

He scowled, flexing his hand as he stared the advisor down. "Is one of the trials of the test to see if I can pass with lowered self-esteem?" he jeered.

Akello snorted. "I'm not sure anyone can actually put a dent in your massive ego."

"It is one of a large number of things that make me so great," Kaiden murmured as he inspected his hand with mock nonchalance. "Though Chief does try his damnedest."

Akello laughed, ushering them off with a wave of her tablet. "Get in there and good luck. To both of you."

They nodded and headed over to their pods. Kaiden hopped into one, leaning forward as Chiyo climbed into the other.

"Got any last bits of wisdom before we head down the virtual rabbit hole?"

Chiyo sat back and glanced at him. "We will plan accordingly when we get the mission details. Until then, simply relax and make sure that you keep yourself in check throughout the test."

Kaiden flicked a thumb to the advisor. "So, what she said then?"

"I'm not sure if I would put it like that…" She smiled, her expression almost conciliatory. "But it is a solid piece of advice."

"Duly noted," Kaiden said with a smirk.

"The test is about to begin. Everyone get into your pods and prepare for sync," Akello ordered.

Kaiden leaned back, looking up at the ceiling as the door to the pod closed. The glow strips illuminated, and the scanner traced along his body. He heard the familiar hum as the Animus booted up, closed his eyes, and clenched his fists.

"Let's kick this pig," he declared as he drifted off to begin their test.

CHAPTER THIRTY-TWO

When Kaiden opened his eyes and looked around him, he noticed he was in some sort of carrier. There was a row of seats along either wall, but he saw no driver or driving mechanism in the front of the room. It was eerily silent.

He focused on getting his bearings but began to feel slightly woozy. Some of his muscles twitched, and a massive influx of information began swirling around his head. He knelt on the floor to steady himself until the feeling passed and the new data began to settle.

"Are you all right, Kaiden?"

Kaiden looked up to see Chiyo seated in one of the seats near the back of the row. "Yeah, I'll be all right. It's the new talents loading in," he said groggily. "Did you know you can take out a battalion of enemy troops with a bundle of mangoes?"

"Yes, although they were all poisoned and not quite a battalion. You are referring to the sabotage of a Black Lake merc group's food supplies by Captain Jean Lafayette, correct?"

"That sounds about right." Kaiden nodded, standing up once again. "Where are we?"

"Inside a burrowing carrier. I recommend you take a seat and buckle in. We will be leaving soon."

"When is soon?" he asked, then heard the roar of an engine and saw orange glow strips line the floor and ceiling of the carrier. He was thrown to the floor as the vehicle sprang to life and sped forward.

"It would appear I was a little late with the warning." Chiyo activated the computer on her gauntlet as Kaiden pushed up and dragged himself down the line until he was across from her.

"Just a tad." He grunted as he grabbed the back of a chair and hoisted himself onto it, buckling himself in. "We'll work on the proper amount of time it takes to warn someone later. You got our mission details?"

She took a few more moments to read the description on her screen, sighing when she looked away. "I do. It would appear that I was right to think that our normal strategy would not work here."

"What do we got?" Kaiden asked, bringing up his loadout screen. "And should I get a bigger gun?"

"Honestly, it would appear that we have not done enough training for this sort of scenario."

"That bad?"

She shrugged. "Maybe not bad, per se, but it will require much more work than we have typically done thus far. This is a data point retrieval mission."

"You make that sound so ominous," Kaiden muttered,

looking through his various guns and gadget options. "How is that so different? We find out where the data is stored, get you in there to do your thing, get the data, and blast our way out, no biggie."

"True, a regular data retrieval mission would be no problem for us, but this is a data *point* mission," she clarified.

"And that one word turns this into a clusterfuck?" Kaiden inquired, mulling over explosive options.

"We will be looking for three specific servers throughout the facility…" Chiyo pressed a button on her gauntlet, and a projection of a large four-story building appeared as a hologram. "I will need to manually hack into these servers and retrieve specific files. I am already trying to find their locations."

Kaiden saw a multitude of red dots blinking around the building. A few would disappear at one time, and the number grew smaller and smaller. "The glossary states that there are no robotic hostiles that we have to face, only mercs of various specialties."

Kaiden opened the glossary in his visor, taking a peek at the enemies they would face.

Red Sun Grunt:
   Armor: Medium
   Weapon: Light Assault Rifle
   Gadget: Fragmentation Grenades
   Description: Basic mercenary infantry, plentiful but easy targets for skilled soldiers. Laser and plasma rifles will blast right through their armor.

Total: 150

Red Sun Heavy:
    Armor: Heavy
    Weapon: Shotgun or Heavy Assault Rifle
    Gadget: None
    Description: Heavily armored mercenary soldier, usually one or two in a squad. Their weapons can shoot through most medium armor within a few blasts. Requires explosives, heavy arms, or several successful hits to blast through their armor.
    Total: 75

Red Sun Pyro:
    Armor: Medium
    Weapon: Flame Caster
    Gadget: Oil Grenades
    Description: Frontal assault unit that wields a fire-emitting weapon. While most armor sets have interior cooling mechanisms, the chemical fire that the Pyro's weapon casts out will overwhelm the target and cook them alive in their armor. However, their weapon is attached to a tank of fuel on their back that can be exploited.
    Total: 50

Red Sun Shocker:
    Armor: Light
    Weapon: Arc Blaster
    Gadget: Shock Grenades

Description: A fast and dangerous specialist that uses their arc blaster to zap their target with large discharges of electricity, disrupting equipment and stunning them. After several shocks, the cumulative effect could lead to heart disruption and death.
Total: 30

Red Sun Goliath:
  Armor: Mech Suit
  Weapon: Nova Cannons or Plasma Lasers
  Gadget: Self-Destruction Core
  Description: *Red Sun mercs piloting stolen or repurposed mechs. Frontal assault with basic weapons is foolish, but there are usually weak points that can be exploited or some mechs can be hacked.*
  Total: 5

"It's not a total loss, you can hack the mechs," Kaiden pointed out.

"That, and there are a few turrets I might be able to use to our advantage. We'll have to plan accordingly." The last bunch of lights around the hologram finally dissipated, leaving three blinking lights at each level and a large glowing blue one at the top. "I found them."

"So, one on each floor. Looks like all that climbing around in vent shafts will have a use, after all." Kaiden smiled. He looked at the larger blue dot and pointed to it. "What's with baby blue up here?"

"That would be our bonus objective. While we are recovering the data from the other three servers, there is an optional code we can download as well. Each server has a piece of the code, and once we collect all three, we can use it at this main server at the top of the building."

"To do what?"

"Doesn't say," Chiyo admitted. "I would guess that it gives us overall control of the base. It would make escaping much easier."

"I was going to bet it just makes the whole thing explode… I've still got twenty Nexus credits left over. Wanna gamble?"

Chiyo stared at him for a moment before shaking her head and looking back at the hologram. "Once we're inside, we will simply have to make our way to the first server on the ground floor. Each server room has a main-tenance ladder that leads up one floor to the server above. If we do this quietly, we should face little resistance as we complete the main objective."

"And the bonus objective?" Kaiden enquired.

She studied the map, chewing on her bottom lip. "There doesn't appear to be a ladder to the main server room, but we can exit on the third floor and go into the main hall. It has a staircase to the top floor, or we can take the elevator. There are also the ventilation shafts as you said, but I can't get a good layout of them with the map provided. There might be a more detailed map on one of the servers."

Kaiden examined his loadout screen for a moment before sighing. "Hey, Chief, see if you can find some silenced weapons or something. Looks like it's going to be another one of those missions."

"On it. Let's see if we can get us something with a sneaky

look without sacrificing a bit of the ultra-violence," Chief chirped, scanning quickly through the loadout.

"Thank you, Kaiden," Chiyo said as she opened her loadout screen and began to make a couple of changes.

"For what?"

"I didn't even have to ask you to change your weapons this time around. It shows that you are learning how best to tackle a mission."

"I'll have a chance to do it my way later," he said with an indifferent shrug. "Besides, this is the real deal. I'll be happy to do it your way if it gets us a smooth victory."

She looked back at the hologram of the building. "I'm not sure about smooth, but this is the best way to approach the mission with as few problems as possible. It'll take some time for me to break into each server without the proper codes or an access key. I'll also have to make sure I don't trip any alarms unless you want three hundred and ten armed mercenaries to come knocking at our door."

Kaiden crossed his legs and leaned back, resting his head in his linked hands. "Wouldn't bother me none."

Chiyo closed out her screen, an arc pistol and sub-machine gun taking the place of her old guns and her infiltrator armor replaced by a dark-blue light armor set. "I admire your confidence. Although I must say that every declaration you make does make me wonder if you truly believe yourself to be that good or are merely in denial about the overwhelming odds."

"I find it to be a combination of actual skill and reckless abandon," Chief reported. *"Found you a couple of guns to look over. Got a rifle and a machine gun. Both fire marbles using electromagnetic lining in the guns, making them near silent."*

"Marbles? Won't they simply shatter?" Kaiden asked

"They are made out of the same stuff that Flynn's spikes are. They are small and more compact, so you get way more rounds per clip. It'll take a few shots to get through armor with the machine gun, but a good shot with the rifle can crack medium armor and pierce right through the visor of any helmet. If you got the skills."

"Trying to bait me?" Kaiden sneered.

"Always gotta make sure you're not getting too big for your armor-plated britches, especially now," Chief retorted.

"Don't worry your bulbous self about that. I'll be good," Kaiden asserted. He made a quick selection to trade out his frag grenades for shocks, then decided to ditch his stealth generator as well—a recommendation that Flynn made before his last training mission, warning that the armor he wore made too much noise for it to be any use. Quickly, he traded this for a portable barrier. "Give me the rifle and leave me Debonair. Chiyo's got herself an ark pistol so I'll use hers if need be."

"And what if I need it?" she asked, giving him a questioning look.

"If we get into a firefight and you wanna use it instead of me, that's certainly your prerogative," he responded. "But I'm basically your bodyguard for this mission, so keep that in mind. Besides, you have the sub-machine gun."

Chiyo took out the sub-machine gun and looked it over. It was a Nexus typhoon model that fired plasma shots in a whirling cone pattern, allowing for both focused fire and a wider spray for large groups. "You don't want this instead?"

"We may not fire a shot if everything goes well. Besides,

I'm not much for machine guns if I can help it. I don't pray all that often, so spraying and praying won't make it much easier."

Chiyo clipped the sub-machine gun back on her waist. She unclipped the ark pistol and handed it over to Kaiden. "Go ahead and take it."

Kaiden looked down at the pistol before glancing up at her. "I wasn't trying to guilt you into giving it to me."

"You are my bodyguard, as you said. In light of what's best for the mission, it would be wise for you to have as many options as possible."

He reached over and took the ark pistol from her hand, clipping it to the opposite end of his waist from Debonair. "More toys for me, then. You spoil me."

"Just don't look for reasons to use it unnecessarily," she warned.

"I promise to try not to," he smirked, holding two fingers up in a scout's honor gesture.

As she grimaced, the glow strips began to flash, and the hologram of the building disappeared, replaced by a screen with options. "What's going on?"

"We are nearly at the building. We have three options for where we can depart."

Kaiden leaned forward, trying to look at the screen. "What are they?"

Chiyo read through the options. "The carrier can drop us off a full mile from the building, allowing us a safer exit but leaving us in the woods to make our own way to the target. The second option is to leave us just outside of the back of the building. We should be undetected, but we'd still have to make our way inside ourselves. The third option is right beneath the building."

"Underground? How would we even get out?" he asked.

"There's a cave underneath the building. My guess is that it was for testing purposes or to smuggle wares and chemicals discreetly. We would be dropped off in the middle of the cave. From there, we can make our way through the system until we find an entrance into the basement and make our way up. However, the risks are that we have no map of the cave system and that we could run into guards. If a firefight broke out, we would not only give away our position but could trigger a collapse and fail the mission before truly beginning."

Kaiden frowned over the dilemma, sketching directions into his palm with a finger. "Not having a map shouldn't be a problem. They probably have a light trail or directions for their flunkies in the cave itself. As for the guards… Well, that will be a problem no matter where we get dropped off. At least we can use the walls and tunnels of the cave to our advantage rather than running out in the open."

"So we should choose the cave, then?" Chiyo asked.

"That has my vote."

She looked back down at the options. "We only have thirty-two seconds to choose… I'll follow your lead for this one," she agreed and pressed the third option. The screen disappeared, and Kaiden saw a countdown appear in the front of the carrier, starting from sixty seconds.

Handles descended from the ceiling. He unbuckled himself and grabbed one of them. "You ready, Chiyo?" he asked as his rifle and gadgets appeared on his armor.

She stood and latched on to another handle. "Of course."

He gave her a reassuring nod before looking back at the timer. He could feel the carrier rumble around him as they began to ascend and breach into the cave.

"How fast do you think we can get this done?" he asked, yelling as the rumble grew louder.

"We get a time bonus if we finish within an hour and a half," she replied.

Kaiden drew his rifle with his free hand. "They are either really generous with that bonus, or they are seriously underestimating us."

The carrier pushed through the last bit of earth. Kaiden raised himself as the vehicle shuddered to a halt, and for a moment, everything was still. The glow strips dimmed and a door at the front opened. Kaiden peeked around the entrance to see if they had alerted any guards. Confirming that they were in the clear, he leaped out the door and into the cave. "Come on," he ordered, raising his rifle to his shoulder. "Let's do this fast and make it look good."

CHAPTER THIRTY-THREE

K aiden and Chiyo moved cautiously through the tunnels leading from the cave, following a line of glow strips they found embedded into the wall.

"You're sure we are going the right way?" she asked.

"Well, following these lights means there are only two ways to go. Worst case scenario is that we went in the opposite direction and will probably end up at the entrance to the cave and will have to double back. But for now, let's have ourselves a nice leisurely walk through the tunnels that are possibly crawling with enemy mercs who would like to riddle our bodies with laser fire."

They continued in relative silence, the wind occasionally howling as it funneled through the narrow space. Small droplets of water fell from the stalactites. As they rounded a corner, they could see a light emitting from further ahead. Kaiden held Chiyo back as he raised his rifle and looked down the scope.

"There are two guards that I can see. They're at the

base of a ramp." He lowered his rifle. "Looks like we found our entrance into the building...or the entrance to something. As long as it doesn't lead us into a room with a pit of spikes, I'd say it's better than sticking around here."

Chiyo brought the hologram of the building out, now much smaller than it was in the carrier. "Once we're inside, I'll be able to map our position. Then we'll simply have to make our way to the first server room, and we can begin."

"How do you want to play this?"

She shut off the hologram. "Take them out."

Kaiden was taken aback for a moment. "Just like that?"

"We haven't seen too many hostiles down here, but I don't want to risk them finding our carrier and alerting the others to intruders. Once you dispose of them, I can set up a signal loop in case anyone checks in. It's the easiest solution."

"I'm starting to like the way you think." Kaiden aimed his rifle. "I mean, I guess I always have, but now there's an edge I find... Oh, hell."

"What's wrong?"

"Two more guards are coming down the ramp. I can't tell if it's a shift change or if they are joining the other two... I guess I can take them all out without a fuss if I make my shots right."

"Hold for a moment."

He looked back at her. "Problems?"

"If it is a change, then the other two will probably report to someone for a new post or before they retire. That could complicate things."

Kaiden sighed and looked back at the mercs for a

moment. They chatted amongst themselves. "Maybe Chief can lend a hand?"

"Doing what, exactly?" the EI inquired. *"There aren't a lot of options around here. You want me to take over a glow strip and change the colors? Maybe distract them with a dance party?"*

"You've been talking all that good shit for the last few weeks...can't you get into their helmets so we can hear what's going on? I increased your casting range for a reason."

"Not without an open link, dumbass. They are closed off. If one of them opens a link I can sneak in, but unless one of you can—"

"Miss Chiyo, might I make a recommendation?" Kaitō requested.

Though he didn't say anything, Kaiden could hear Chief babbling angrily to himself.

"Yes, Kaitō?"

"Though we cannot fashion a false signal to get them to open their comms, if you could perhaps create a malfunction or distraction they would report it, and then Chief could enter the link that way?"

"And how pray tell, dear fox, would you recommend we do—"

"On it," Kaiden said cheerfully, aiming at a small generator and firing a single shot into the bottom of the machine. The generator popped and powered down, causing a few of the lights to go out. The mercs jumped at the noise and looked at the machine. One walked over to it and examined it for a moment before pointing to one of the other mercs and motioning him to make a call.

"When he opens his comms, get in there, Chief," he ordered.

"I just want it on record that this was somehow my idea," Chief grumbled. Kaiden saw one of the guards tap the side of his helmet and Chief's avatar disappeared from his visor.

"How did you know that would work?" Chiyo asked.

"That's a basic Ironhead portable generator. They have the problem of short-circuiting and popping a gasket after too much use. We used them on a few gigs back when I was with the Dead-Eyes. Damn things were useless half the time, but they were cheap and plentiful," Kaiden explained. "Figured they would call in for repairs or to make a report if one blew but had to make sure it didn't look too obvious. That's why I popped the bottom—to make it look like a blowout."

"What's the problem, twenty-seven?" a nasal voice sneered over the comms. Kaiden held a hand up to Chiyo as he listened in.

"Another one of the damn generators blew. Can we get some real equipment down here? Or at least a generator that doesn't pop on us every week?"

"I'll make a note to send another down there. Is everything still working?"

"We've got a backup generator here, but it's going to be the same damn problem in another week. Get us a real generator."

"You're just bitchin' because you have nothing else to do. Start the backup generator and I'll put in a request to the boss, but good luck getting him to care. Why bother giving you jokers in the cave the good stuff when all you do is stand around with your dick in your hands all day?"

"Whatever. When is the shift change? I wanna get out of this dump."

"You still got two hours. Find some tunnel worms to shoot or something to keep yourself looking busy."

The guard grunted and signed out, cursing the operator after he finished.

"We're good. Change isn't for two more hours," Kaiden confirmed.

"All right, then we're in the clear. Take them out, and we'll head in," Chiyo acknowledged.

He nodded, placed the rifle on his back, and took out the arc pistol. "Chief, while you're in there, could you create a distraction?"

"Causing grief does seem to be my forte," Chief chirped. "Just tell me when."

Kaiden crouched down and began to move forward, keeping low to stay out of sight as the guards reconvened back on the ramp. He held the trigger of the arc pistol down, beginning its charge. "Make sure the channel is closed and then do it."

The guard Chief had infiltrated cried out as the EI let loose a blast of high-pitched noise in his helmet. The others looked at him in confusion as Kaiden ran up and pointed the pistol at the one at the back of the group. He released the trigger and a blast of electricity jumped at the guard, causing him to sputter and jolt before the electricity jumped to the guard beside him.

Kaiden used the confusion to holster the arc pistol and draw Debonair. He took out the remaining guard with a shot in the head before blasting the two stunned guards. As they fell, he leaped over the railing of the ramp and pumped his fist, activating the shock gauntlet, and pummeled the last man into the ground.

He stood over the fallen defenders for a moment, checking them for movement. When he was satisfied that they wouldn't get back up, he put his pistol away, deactivated the gauntlet, and motioned for Chiyo to join him. "Good work, Chief."

"That's the only kind I do," the EI bragged, his avatar reappearing in Kaiden's visor.

Kaiden walked up the ramp and to the door. He pressed a button on top of the latch and popped it open as Chiyo came up behind him. "After you," he directed, sweeping a hand forward.

"Well done," she complimented as she walked by him. He followed quickly and shut the door behind them.

"Weren't you going to do that signal thing?" he asked

"Signal loop, and Kaitō already did it for me." She showed him her console and a line that read, *"Signal loop uploaded and activated."*

"That little weasel thinks he's so great...I did all the real work." Chief growled his annoyance.

"Settle down, your majesty. Not becoming of a god to get all spiteful."

"Depends on the god...I can be quite wrathful," Chief retorted.

Kaiden chuckled as he glanced back at Chiyo, who was looking at her console. "You got a better idea of where we are and where we need to go?"

"I do. We are in the basement, and we need to go there." She pointed over to the far wall and a stack of boxes.

"Is there something in the boxes we need? Did they stick the servers in there?" he snarked.

Chiyo walked over and moved a couple of boxes from

the top of the pile, revealing a large grate behind them. "We'll climb the vents. I don't know where they will take us exactly, but it's safer than walking up the stairs and through the hallways."

Kaiden sighed as he moved over to help her move some of the boxes. "I just wanna take this moment to say I'm not exactly partial to vents. I merely happen to use them often. I don't want 'vent climber' to be on my list of things I'm known for."

"I've found them to be quite helpful in my work. Some corporations and companies are smart enough to add defenses in the vents, but they are easily shut down, and they make convenient routes," she asserted as she took out a small device and pressed a switch, causing a drill to pop out.

"You have an omnitool?" Kaiden asked.

"It takes the place of my melee weapon. It's much more useful with my skill set," she explained as she worked at the screws holding the grate in place.

"Not as fun as mine." He admired his shock gauntlet with a satisfied smile.

"Perhaps in your view. I find it far more satisfying to complete a mission without the enemy or target ever knowing I was there. Truth be told, I've probably seen more violence in my time working with you than I have in all my other training combined."

"Well, that's the Kaiden Jericho guarantee. One I proudly endorse." He cracked his knuckles for emphasis. "Although you only mentioned training. Does that indicate you're used to a bit of violence yourself?"

Chiyo pried the grate off the wall. "I am familiar with it,

unfortunately." She placed the grate carefully to the side and climbed into the narrow space. "Let's go. I'll take the lead until we get to the server."

Kaiden decided to let her words lie and climbed in after her. Inch by inch, they crawled their way slowly through the building.

"We're clear," Chiyo stated, opening the small vent and dropping to the floor of the windowless room. She moved aside and waited for Kaiden to climb down. "Are you coming?" she asked after she heard him jostle around for a bit.

"Give me a minute... Hold this, would ya?" He dropped his rifle from the vent. She caught it and stepped back a little further as his legs lowered from the ceiling before he fell completely through the aperture, landing a little less gracefully than she had.

She handed him his rifle as he staggered to his feet and rolled his shoulders. "Before you judge me, you should note I'm wearing way more guns and armor than you and I'm not exactly built for shimmying," he lamented as he took his rifle back from her.

"I'll make a note of it." She looked back at her console. "Give me a moment to establish our position, then we can find the server."

Kaiden nodded and crept towards the door. He reached for the handle and turned it slowly, peering through the crack to check for mercs, then frowned as he looked outside. The place was built more like a warehouse than a conventional building. The hall was massive, and he noticed various mercs loitering all around. He couldn't see how they could sneak around with this many adversaries present.

"I've found it. The server room is about one hundred yards to our left. How does it look out there?"

"Not great," he grumbled. "It's a large open space. Can't speak for whatever is above, but we don't exactly have a lot of hiding options out there."

"We could always go back into the vents. A server has to be kept cool, so there is probably a passage directly to the room."

Kaiden shut the door softly and turned to face her. "I don't have a grappling hook, so I'm gonna have to climb my heavy ass back into that vent. I don't think I'll be the quietest little mouse while scrabbling to get back in there. I'd rather not have the mercs charging in here and shooting me in the ass while I do it."

"Then what do you suggest?"

Kaiden paused for a moment, then held his rifle up and looked at the door. "Do you have a stealth generator, by chance?"

"I saw you change yours out for a barrier. If you're thinking we can shadow our way there, you should have kept it."

"I didn't want it for me. I'm asking, do you have one?" he repeated.

"I do not, but considering I do have the Red Sun's colors in my database..." She pressed an item on her console and then tapped the Nexus symbol on her armor.

The colors of her armor changed to make her appear as a Red Sun merc.

Kaiden looked her over for a moment, a small chuckle escaping his lips. "You might be the most waifish grunt here, but that'll have to do."

"What are you planning?"

"A little distraction. I know I said I would be your bodyguard but think about it like this. If there is no one to attack you, then I won't have to be there to guard you, follow?"

"I do, and that's insane. You can't take on the entire base, Kaiden," Chiyo argued.

"Technically, I've already taken out four of them, so it's not all of them at once," he countered sarcastically.

She sighed, shaking her head. "If even one of us dies, the mission is a failure. It's too much to risk."

"Look, even I'm not stupid enough to take on three hundred odd mercs at once with a rifle and some shock grenades. But I can get the ones out there to pay attention to me while you go and take care of the servers."

"At least you admit that your level of stupidity does have an upper limit. I was beginning to think it was endless," Chief jeered.

"That will still kick up the hornet's nest. It will make everything that much harder," she insisted.

"Since you won't have to bother with disabling alarms and all that, being able to get the info from the servers should be much quicker, right? When you get it all, I'll meet up with you on the fourth floor, and we can activate the main computer and get the bonus objective. Plus, think of all the sweet, sweet points we'll get."

"Kaiden, I really..." Chiyo sighed, crossed her arms, and looked back up to stare at him. "How do you propose to accomplish this?"

"Well, I'm going to—" They heard several loud metal clangs and the loud hissing of air. He leaned against the wall and opened the door again, taking a look outside. He saw a large mechanical suit with two cannons on each arm. A merc leaped out of it and made his way over to a trio of others in the distance.

Kaiden smiled under his mask, looking back at Chiyo. "You were right Chiyo, it was probably a stupid plan...but this new one is muuuch better."

CHAPTER THIRTY-FOUR

C hiyo moved quickly and quietly through the ducts, her mind conflicted as she tried to focus on her priority of getting to the server and trying to keep herself calm in the face of Kaiden's ludicrous plan.

"Chiyo, you there yet?" he whispered over the comms. She made her way to a vent along the route. The room below held several servers with three guards loitering around.

"I'm here," she responded, continuing to study the room. "There are three guards here, blocking my path."

"They won't be there for long, I imagine." She could hear him rustling around over the mic. "You're hot-micing, Kaiden."

"Oh, my bad...just getting in position. The mech jock went to take a piss or something. I have a straight shot to it."

Chiyo sighed. "I'm going to ask this one more time, fruitless or not. You are sure that you want to do this?"

"It would be a waste not to at this point. You know how hard it was to sneak my way over here around all these grunts?"

"Just…please don't mess this up."

"Oh, I'm going to mess a whole lotta things up, but not this," Kaiden promised.

Though Chiyo could feel the trepidation and anger boiling up in her, she couldn't help but smile a little. She was worried about the outcome, but if this did work out, it would make for a very good story.

"Tell me when you're about to begin."

"In a bit…just waiting for someone to get the damn hatch open," Kaiden muttered, sneaking a look over the crate he was hiding behind.

"Don't bitch at me. The systems in this thing are all messed up. Must have been cracked by some dimwit who forgot to pay attention during the class on operator resets," Chief retorted. *"I'm cleaning up the place and getting it prepped for ya."*

"I just need it to work. I don't need it to have video streaming and automatic cup holders. Air conditioning might be a plus, though."

"I'm talking about making it move and fire right. If you want it to walk forward instead of dancing to the left when you push the movement joystick forward or fire the cannons instead of activating the self-destruct function, you need to give me time to fix this thing."

"Good Lord, how badly did they mess that thing up?"

"They're a bunch of intergalactic thieves and murderers. No

pride in their mechanical and technological work." The EI scoffed. *"And...that should do it."*

"Timing could have been a little better. The jock is coming back," Kaiden said, taking aim at the pilot as he walked back over to the mech.

"Can't rush a proper recalibration. I'll get it ready for ya."

"All right, let's get this going. Chiyo, get ready. It's going to get hot real damn quick."

"Understood, good luck," she acknowledged.

"Chief, open the mech's hatch."

The EI complied, and the entrance opened. The jock paused in confusion and the two grunts next to him looked at the mech, giving Kaiden a perfect sight of all their visors.

He shot the three mercs, lining up three straight shots through the weak point in their helmets and dropping them instantly. Without hesitation, he slung the rifle onto his back and ran for the mech, leaping onto the leg and pushing himself into the pilot's chair.

"Close the hatch and start her up," Kaiden commanded. The opening shut with a loud metallic clang and Kaiden grabbed the two joysticks on the dash. The console lit up with various toggles and switches, and a screen in the middle showed the fuel level, cannon and boost charge, and general integrity.

"You know, we did this so quickly that I never had the chance to ask when the last time you rode a mech was."

"I've tooled around in a couple powerlifters before," Kaiden said as he looked around at all the various options available.

"Those aren't battle mechs. What the hell do you think you're doing?"

"I figured you'd make a good co-pilot. A large screen in front of him activated, giving him a view of what was going on outside. He saw a few guards looking his way, and one pointed over to the bodies lying next to him, seemingly shouting to get the others' attention.

"I don't exactly have the time to give you a full introductory course," Chief exclaimed.

"Well then, we can just go over the basics." Kaiden moved one of the controls to point at the group of mercs, hovering his finger over the trigger on the front. "I think we'll begin with a little target practice."

There were two loud blasts from outside the room. The guards scattered quickly and ran out the door, leaving it empty and allowing her to leave her hiding place in the vents. She dropped down and quickly located the proper server. Wasting no time, she slid a drive into an open port, and Kaitō appeared in her display.

"What do you require of me, madame?"

"I need you to locate the files we need from this server and the first part of the code for the main server above. I'm going to see if I can access the turrets and any other safety features on this floor from the console over there," she explained and headed across the room.

"Should I make sure to block any alerts sent out?"

Another round of blasts rocked the room, dust and debris falling from the walls and ceiling. "Do what you can, but we are prioritizing speed over caution this time around," she stated, hoping in the back of her mind that

Kaiden didn't get too out of control and accidentally level the room.

"Then it should only take me a couple of minutes to locate and download the files. I'll be back shortly." With that, Kaitō disappeared, and Chiyo looked through the various commands on the console. She soon found the main security functions and the turret commands.

"Kaiden, you there?" she asked.

"A little busy. Got a couple of those little zappy bastards running around me and— Oh, just stepped on one," he replied, demented mirth in his tone.

"I need your mech's registration number and your ID. That way, I can command the turrets to fire at everything but you and your mech."

"What was that? Sorry, too busy smiting," Kaiden called.

"Sorry, Chiyo, he's one great big ball of id at the moment. I'll get you the numbers. Kaiden's ID is SC-A111, and the mech's registration is...D10-D3UX."

"Understood, thank you, Chief. Inputting now."

"Wouldn't putting in Kaiden's ID be a bit dicey in this situation? Like they would know who to look for after we got out of here?"

"Normally, it would be. I would hide the tag while we were here and wipe it from the system afterward, but I don't think we have to worry about Animus creations coming to life and attacking us in reality."

"Fingers crossed." Chief chuckled.

"Miss Chiyo, I have finished my objective. Ready to disengage from the server," Kaitō announced.

"Good work, Kaitō. I have just finished changing the security protocols." Chiyo shut off the cameras and alarms

—more out of habit than from a real need, considering the circumstances—along with changing the turrets attack parameters. "We won't have to worry about those, at least. Activating the maintenance ladder." She pressed a button on the console. A hatch opened in the back of the room and a ladder descended.

She walked over to the server and removed the drive, placed it back into her console, and made her way over to the ladder. "Kaiden, I have retrieved the first batch of data files. I'm heading to the next floor now. How are you faring?"

Kaiden let loose another blast from the cannon. A group of five mercs were either blown to bits or knocked away to slam into the walls around them. "Chiyo, I think this mech may be the greatest piece of technology ever developed."

"I'm still here, jackass." Chief grunted loudly in displeasure. *"Besides, this is only a cracked Enforcer model. You should see the Titan models Tera Sovereign have developed. Those are... Are you crying?"*

Kaiden coughed and sputtered, shaking his head. "Nah, of course, I'm not. It's just... The universe can truly be a wonderful place sometimes, you know?"

"I don't need to be programmed with the basic understanding of human emotions to know that you being choked up over this is a little warped."

"Not as warped as the bodies of the jokers who keep coming after me. It's like shooting fish in a barrel. Only I'm shooting a big ass—" The mech was knocked back. Red lights began flashing in the cockpit, and he saw from the information screen that they had taken damage on the left shoulder. "Laser? What the hell was that?"

"You forgot this wasn't the only mech in this place for a moment, didn't ya?" Chief reminded him.

Kaiden looked out through the screen to see two other mechs coming down the hall side by side, one with cannons like his and the other with a large laser ray on the left arm and a claw on the right.

"Bastards are ruining my fun," he grumbled, shifting to the left to dodge an incoming blast from one of the attackers. "Got any advice, co-pilot?"

"How could a lowly piece of advanced human and hardware-integrating technology like myself be of use?" Chief asked facetiously as another beam nicked the side of the mech's left leg.

"Now is not the time to get spiteful," Kaiden declared, firing one blast at the mech with lasers. It staggered back, and he released the second blast at the cannon mech as it began to fire. One shot narrowly missed him and the other hit the ground, knocking the attacker to the side and crashing it into the other.

"Hell yeah! Bring it. Oh, hell, they're getting back up. Seriously, Chief, options?" Kaiden yelled.

"You got that barrier projector, right?"

"Yeah, but I don't think—"

"Shut up and put it into the compartment I'm opening. There are two wires that connect to two ports on the gadget...connect them."

Kaiden hauled out the projector as a slot opened on the panel. He grabbed the wires and found the ports on the projector, connected them quickly, and set the projector down before he manned the controls again. "What am I doing, Chief?"

"Give it a second." Kaiden saw a shimmering light envelop his viewing screen as a barrier was projected around his mech. *"That'll give you some breathing room. It enhances the strength of the shield, so you should get some better use out of it. Now, do your best not to die while I go into phase two of my master plan."*

"What plan is that?" he asked, firing another round at the mechs. They leaped out of the way using the boost jets on their backs. "Oh…that's handy. I should use that."

"Just stay alive for a couple more minutes. Focus on the one with the cannons. I'll be right back." With that, Chief disappeared.

"Chief? What the hell did you—*laser!*" Kaiden yelled as he jerked the sticks to the left to dodge the beam. His mech toppled to the floor. He tried aiming the cannons at the approaching mechs, but one of the cannons was caught under the weight, allowing him only one.

He aimed for the cannon mech, as Chief had instructed, hoping that his EI had a damn good plan. He shot the left leg of the attacker, blowing it apart, and it crashed into the floor.

"Ha! Gotcha, you bastard," Kaiden bellowed with glee before noticing the other mech beginning to fire. "Oh, shit."

He activated the boost and the mech skidded across the floor, trailed by the laser beam from the hostile. They slammed into a wall, shoving the mech upright but knocking Kaiden's head into the side of the cockpit. His vision blurred and his head pounded, but he gripped the controls and tried to aim for the laser mech. Whatever Chief was doing was taking too damn long.

The view screen lit up as the barrier was blasted, and they were knocked back into the wall. Kaiden recovered and saw the cannon mech had turned his way. "You bastards are real killjoys, you know that?" He tried to back the mech up.

The laser mech marched forward, its laser charging. Kaiden began to wonder if he should bail and then looked around and realized he didn't know where the ejection button was.

"Chief! Where the hell are you?"

The laser mech aimed at Kaiden's cockpit, then stood there unmoving for a moment before the body turned around and shot clean through the other attacker. An explosion of mechanical parts and debris erupted.

He was stunned, and could only watch as the hatch of the mech opened and it used its claw to grab the jock inside. It threw him to the floor and stomped on him, then turned back to Kaiden. It closed the hatch and walked over, using its claw to help the mech back to its feet.

"Override successful," Chief declared, appearing in the viewing monitor. *"Let's see that shifty bastard Kaitō do that!"*

Kaiden laughed as he realized what had happened. "I guess I'm not the only one who likes to put on a show."

"I've got my own kind of flair, but I thought you'd appreciate it," the EI chirped.

"Hey, Chiyo, we now got two mechs running around and causing a ruckus," Kaiden advised her.

"How's that?" she asked.

"I procured one for myself after deposing the jock from his duties just before he blew Kaiden's mech to pieces."

"I was baiting him," Kaiden argued unsuccessfully.

"Baiting him into killing you? Well, it's an unorthodox method, one that would have led to immediate loss, but it would have been successful, so congrats?" Chief joked.

Kaiden sighed and decided to take his loss without further debate. "How are you doing Chiyo?"

"Almost done with the second server. I'll head to the third one right away, so you should begin making your way to the fourth floor."

"On our way," he acknowledged, walking the mech to a service elevator at the end of the bay.

"I've hacked into their cameras, and there is a large group of mercenaries heading your way from all points in the building. Considering the damage you've caused, I would say it is whatever is left of their forces."

"A hundred and seventy-seven units remaining, by my count."

"You didn't happen to see the other two mechs in that bunch, did you?" Kaiden asked

"Oh, good, now you remember," Chief muttered.

"I did not. They may be guarding the main server room," Chiyo responded

"Then I guess we should hightail it." Kaiden continued toward the elevator.

"Hey, Kaiden, wanna make a bet?"

Kaiden turned his mech towards Chief's. "What kind?"

"See who gets the most kills from the remaining batch of mercs."

"Yeah, I'll take you on. What are we betting on?"

"If I win, I want another Next-Gen upgrade, and no pussy-footing around it either. It will be your top priority."

Kaiden grimaced for a moment before a devilish smile crossed his face. "All right, but if I win, you have to apologize to Kaitō and try your best to be buddies with him."

"What? But I hate him."

"I know, and I'm going to have a grand old time watching you squirm through it all."

Chief's mech scratched its hull with its claw as if it were thinking. Then it raised its laser and pointed it straight up. "Fine, I'll take that bet." Chief fired a laser and a beam seared through the ceiling. Several bodies fell from the floors above, charred and partially disintegrated. "That makes seven for me."

CHAPTER THIRTY-FIVE

Chiyo quickly climbed the ladder to the third floor and the final server of their main objective. With their victory in the first part of the test all but assured, she began to wonder how they should approach the bonus objective.

When she reached the top, she glanced over the exit, just to be safe. There were no guards lingering, and the room was empty. The loud blasts of cannons and static hiss of laser fire from below indicated that the mercs were throwing as much of their might at the two rampant mechs below as possible.

She walked over to the correct server and inserted the drive. Kaitō, knowing his part by now, began his hunt quickly while Chiyo checked the console and overrode the security for the third level.

That done, she took a seat and looked over the mission details once more.

Obtain data from servers (2/3)
  Escape enemy building
  Bonus Objective:
  Access main terminal on top floor using codes from the three
servers

She frowned at the screen. What were they supposed to do once they accessed the terminal? Also, how would they escape? She supposed if Kaiden and Chief were successful in their hunt, they could simply walk right out of the base with no worries. If they had to, could they double back to the carrier in the cave and use that to escape? She didn't recall seeing an option to drive or operate it.

She put her questions to the side, deciding they would figure it out once they got there. The thought brought a quick grimace. She was beginning to think like Kaiden.

"Kaiden, I've almost finished downloading the final batch of data. I'll be heading up to the fourth floor using the stairs since you have been kind enough to distract all the guards. How are you progressing?"

Kaiden slammed the arm of the mech into a group of four mercs, and they crashed onto the floor. As one of the heavies moved to pick up his gun, Kaiden fired a round from the cannon and blew him up. The blast created a hole in the floor that two of the other mercs fell into.

"Winning, currently. I'm at sixty-three, and Chief is at fifty-nine."

"Sixty-four now, dumbass," Chief corrected as his laser powered down. *"You're trailing, and there's only fifty left!"*

"You're up by one," Kaiden sneered. "That's not trailing."

"It's a precedent for how this bet is going to end."

"That in your best hopes and dreams you going to win by the skin of your teeth? At least your expectations are realistic." Kaiden fired down toward the end of the hall as a trio of heavies rounded the corner, blowing them away. "But still wrong."

"I looked through the cameras again." Chiyo interrupted their debate. "I still don't see the other two mechs. It would appear that I was correct in guessing that they will be guarding the way to the bonus objective."

"We'll meet you there, promise," Kaiden vowed. "Just let us finish up here." With that, he charged down the corridor. He looked at the scanner on his screen and saw over a dozen blinking blue lights. Usually, that would indicate friendlies, but since he wasn't a Red Sun merc, that indicated targets.

He strafed around the corner and was greeted by two blasts of fire from the Red Sun pyros, frying his shield. He plowed through them, punting one down the hall and firing at him. The pyro and the canister on his back blew up, showering the other mercs in flames.

"We don't have to leave the building itself intact, right?" Kaiden asked as he saw the flames beginning to creep up the walls.

"I don't see anything in the mission details that indicates we do, but your timing for these questions is horrible," Chief remarked snidely.

"Oh, blast yourself," Kaiden retorted, taking out a

couple of mercs trying to make a run for it. "And that makes my total seventy-eight."

"I just took out the last of the heavies and shockers. I'm at seventy-nine," Chief informed him gleefully.

"You're one ahead again? You pulling my leg?"

"You can check the count on my screen once I win. But for now, there's three pyros and fifteen grunts left along with the two goliaths."

Kaiden sat back for a moment. He didn't see any more mercs running around. Quickly, he tapped a finger along the side of his helmet. "Hey, Chiyo...mind looking around for the last batch of mercs for me?" he whispered quietly into his comms.

"Hey! That's cheating," Chief bellowed.

"You can hear me? That was a direct line to Chiyo," Kaiden exclaimed.

"I might be piloting this mech, but I'm still partially in you, idiot. I can still hear what you're doing."

"Then in fairness to your game and trying to speed this along, the rest of the grunts are above you," Chiyo stated. "From what I see, the pyros are using their oil grenades to soak the floor. It looks like they plan on dropping their chemical fire on top of you in hopes of melting your mechs."

"Is that right? Like directly above us?" Kaiden asked.

"Yes, some on top of you and some on top of Chief."

"Are you directly above us?"

"No, I am a little over two hundred yards away. I've retrieved the drive and will be heading to the stairs in—"

"That's all good. See you then," Kaiden said, looking at Chief a long way down the hall. They both raised their weapons and fired, blowing through the ceiling. Those mercs not annihilated in the blasts fell down to land beside them.

"Round them up," Kaiden shouted, stomping and crashing into all the mercs around him. He looked on his screen of confirmed kills, reset when they began the bet. He was at eighty-seven.

"Chief, what are you at?" he demanded.

"Eighty-six."

"Ha! I win, I'm at eighty-seven." Kaiden cheered, stopping for a moment as he counted the numbers. "Wait, that ain't right...that's one hundred and seventy-three... Without the other two mechs. That should mean there's one hundred and seventy-five of the other mercs. Where are the last two?" Kaiden scanned around until he finally saw two mercs hobbling down the hall. "Gotcha!"

As he aimed his cannon, both mercs disappeared in red light. When it faded, bits and pieces of scorched armor lay in a heap. Kaiden looked up to see Chief coming over, his laser pointed outward. *"Nah, I think I got them."*

Kaiden slammed his fists into the mech's console. "You shifty son of a bitch. Those were my kills."

"Could've been, but your little bout of showboating cost ya. I believe that makes me the winner."

"Hell no, we still got the mechs upstairs. If I get both of them, then I win."

"Ha! You couldn't handle two mechs about fifteen minutes ago. What makes you think that you can handle them now?"

"I've got more practice now. Plus, my cannons got more firepower than your laser."

"Maybe, but you gotta remember who's in control of this

baby," Chief chirped, aiming the laser at the ceiling. "*I can reroute the power to funnel into the laser, maximizing its output and damage. I'll fricassee those two bots before you get a chance to line up a shot.*"

"Not if I get there first," Kaiden challenged. "I'll boost my way up to the fourth floor and—"

"Kaiden, *don't,*" Chiyo ordered. "All this destruction has already made the building unstable. If it collapses, even your mechs will be crushed. Use the service elevator and join me at the top."

"I can't let this glow stick dungball win, Chiyo."

"*And I can't let him have the chance to win. Pride is at stake and all that.*"

Chiyo, uncharacteristically, growled over the mic. "Chief, you're an EI. You're supposed to work with your host and not against him."

"Right. You should listen to her, jackass," Kaiden jeered

"Kaiden, you're an ace. You are supposed to lead by example and do what's best for the unit," she scolded

"I...um...oh, right," Kaiden mumbled.

After a few moments of silence, Kaiden heard Chiyo sigh and her voice return to her usual calm tone. "You've done well. You have defeated almost every hostile in the building, and we have completed our main objective. We have fifteen minutes to spare to get our time bonus. In truth, we can leave now and still probably come out close to the top if not at the top. But I've gotten to know you better over these last few weeks, Kaiden, and while some of your ways exasperate me, I do know that you would never intentionally botch a mission, nor would you do a haphazard job. I am assuming you do want to clear the mission completely, correct?"

"I do," Kaiden asserted.

"Then please, just do this one thing for me, and we can finish the rest of the mission your way. Besides, I would think both of you would be forfeit if you died."

"I mean...that wasn't a rule. But I guess that would violate the spirit of the competition."

Kaiden nodded to himself. "Give us a minute, Chiyo. We'll be right up."

"I'll meet you there," she said before signing off.

Kaiden and Chief walked over to the service elevator, Chief casting himself into the panel and calling it down before returning to the mech.

"Hothead," the EI muttered.

"So am I taking after you or are you taking after me?" Kaiden jibed.

"I'm more of a snarky bastard...but all the same, I guess."

"Look, if it means that much to ya, I'll get the upgrade when I get two more synapse points. Win or lose."

"Mighty kind of ya," Chief said. The elevator descended, and the massive fenced doors opened. Kaiden and Chief walked the mechs inside.

"Just promise to not be such a dick to Kaitō, all right?" he requested.

Chief's mech tilted slightly to look at Kaiden's. *"You're gonna have to win to make that happen."*

Kaiden frowned, gripping his control stick. "Snarky bastard."

Kaiden and Chief stepped out of the elevator, and Chiyo waved them down.

"Hey, Chiyo, know which way to go?"

She pointed away down the long hall. "It's at the end on the left—one of the only rooms up here."

"This is a big top floor; those ceilings are about thirty feet up," Chief observed.

"Gives us plenty of room to maneuver," Kaiden noted. "Hey Chief, open up and let Chiyo in. She wouldn't be able to keep up with our mech's gait."

"Fine, fine, but I still got control till we get in there," Chief said. The mech knelt, and the front hatch opened. *"Come on into Chief mech walker's finest, miss Chiyo."*

She climbed in and sat back as the hatch closed and the mech stood. "Thank you, Chief. We have a little over eleven minutes before we run out on the time bonus. Let us finish this."

The mechs charged down the hall. Kaiden saw Chief's laser begin to glow brightly. "You charging your laser when we're not even around the corner yet?"

"I told you before, by shifting most of the mech's power into the laser cannon, I can take them both out in one shot. Then we're free to wrap this up with no fuss."

"Just be careful," Kaiden ordered as they neared the corner. "I'm going to say that they are expecting—"

As Chief's mech turned the corner, it was blasted back by cannon fire and crashed into the wall. *"Chiyo!"* Kaiden shouted, moving his mech in front of the other as a laser shot beamed right for them.

The laser collided with Kaiden's shield. He looked down at the specs and saw that the shield was at low power. Hastily, he looked up to see cracks forming, and the barrier became more translucent. It shattered as the beam dissipated.

"We're all right," Chief called. *"Took a little hull damage. I'll get the mech up and—"*

Kaiden raced down the hall. The two mechs stood on either side of the large door to the room. He activated his boost jets and leaped in the air and landed between them. He flipped a switch on the mech's console, granting him the ability to control each arm individually using his control sticks. Calmly, he aimed to his right and left, flipped another switch to enable his view screen to give him visibility to either side and saw both mechs turn to face him. As he'd hoped, he now had a point-blank shot at the pilot's seats.

He fired both cannons, and the blasts ruptured the metal hulls almost instantaneously. Both defenders collapsed, and he could see the smoldering interiors with no remaining jocks, though he saw a single hand still gripping one of the control sticks in the laser mech on his left.

"Well...shit." Chief sighed. *"Good work, partner."*

Kaiden flipped the two switches back in place and turned the mech to see the other walk up behind him. "You all right, Chiyo?"

"I'm fine. Chief was nice enough to deploy the security foam to keep the impact to a minimum."

"How did you know how to get manual control of the cannons? I thought you said you never used a mech before."

"Like I said, practice. Also, I was messing with the different knobs and such on the way up the elevator."

"Oh, that's what you were doing? I thought you were trying to find the radio."

"That was the last of the mercs," Chiyo stated. "We have seven minutes. If you could please get us inside, Kaiden?"

"Certainly." He turned the mech around and blasted the door open. They walked inside to see a number of computers along the walls. A large device with a circular top stood at the back with a six-foot-wide console at its base.

"That must be it. If you would please let me down, Chief," Chiyo requested. The mech knelt and opened its hatch. Kaiden leaped out of his own as well and followed her to the terminal.

"So, still don't wanna take a bet on what this thing will do?" Kaiden asked as he leaned against the console while Chiyo typed away.

"You have not had your fill with Chief?" she questioned.

"It's a double bet. I get to win two."

She looked at him. "I suggest you find satisfaction in winning one bet and passing the test."

Kaiden shifted his head from side to side and mulled it over. "I guess that'll do."

A screen popped open and requested the code to activate. Chiyo inserted her drive into a port on the console. They waited a moment as the code was uploaded and then saw the device behind the console light up.

"What's going on? Is it exploding?" Kaiden fretted.

"No… It's a beacon of some sort," Chiyo said, looking between the information appearing onscreen and the console.

"To call down a Red Sun ship to destroy us?"

"No. It's opening a warp gate." She looked at another screen. "Look."

Kaiden watched and saw a large circular building retract its roof and a massive silver ring rocket into the sky. It sailed into space after a few moments, and a multitude of lights emitted from the boundaries of the ring, converging into the center and then expanding into a large blue pool.

They saw a huge capital ship appear from within the ring, followed by several smaller vessels, both human and Tsuna.

"When did this happen?" Kaiden asked.

Chiyo looked at him. "What do you mean?"

"I'm guessing this was based on an event or something? Seems kinda random for a mission."

"Nothing in my files matches this," Chief stated.

"Nor mine," Kaitō added.

Chief's eye furrowed. *"Didn't need your input there, pal."*

"What were the rules of the bet, Chief?" Kaiden reminded him.

"I'll get around to it," Chief grumbled.

A "Mission Accomplished" banner appeared on the screen and floated above them. "Huh, didn't even have to leave the building." Kaiden scratched his head in bewilderment.

"I believe the idea is that this fleet will be converting this into a base of operations…if it is still salvageable."

"So how do you think we did?" he asked.

"We will know once we leave and the final scores are tallied."

"I know, but I want your opinion. Feel like partnering again in the future?"

The room around them began to disappear, replaced by a pure white backdrop. Chiyo looked around. "Our ways of doing things may never truly match, but I always appreciate a different point of view."

"So is that a yes?" Kaiden asked.

She looked back at him. "Considering all that we have accomplished despite our differences, this has worked out better than I could have hoped."

"I have a way of knocking people dead, literally and metaphorically," he bragged.

She turned to him. "I don't know when the next time we work with each other will be. But I will be happy to work alongside you if you are willing." She smiled as their forms began to fade.

He nodded and smirked. "Be happy to." They drifted away from the Animus and back into reality.

CHAPTER THIRTY-SIX

K aiden sat up as his Animus pod opened, leaned against the side, and looked at Chiyo as she awoke from the sync. "How are you feeling?"

She sat up straight and stretched her arms. "Quite well, considering I never had to fire a shot through the whole mission."

"It's one of the many bonuses for using the Kaiden Jericho gold package for all your merc handling needs," he joked, climbing out of his pod and offering a hand to help her out of hers.

She accepted, and he pulled her up. Chiyo grabbed her bag on the side of the pod, and they walked over to the front of the hall where a few other duos were already waiting. They turned and clapped as the two arrived, congratulating them. Advisor Faraji walked up and shook their hands. "Great job, you two."

"All of you were watching?" Kaiden asked.

Akello pointed to the monitor. "Technically, we're

watching all of the matches, but yours certainly seemed to get the most attention."

Kaiden elbowed Chiyo playfully in the side. "Told ya I could put on a hell of a performance."

Akello coughed to get their attention. "Actually, there were bets going on among the early finishers to see how long you would last or how many kills you would get. All but one thought you would bite it before finishing off the last of the enemies, though a couple did think you would make it to the top before getting blown to bits by the other mechs."

Kaiden crossed his arms and looked at Chiyo. "See, I'm not the only one who gambles. It's a perfectly normal and fun activity."

"I'm not sure I would describe it as normal. As far as fun goes, you do realize they were expecting you to fail?" she asked.

"Hey, not everyone is good at it," he said with a shrug. He eyed the other initiates before looking back at Akello. "So, who won?"

The advisor pointed to herself. "I did, actually, and now I've got a group of students to help me with clean up and inventory this weekend."

This caused the others to groan or sigh in disappointment before Akello hushed them. "Final scores won't be tallied until the last three teams get done, but I think I have a good feeling on how you did."

"Don't need any sixth sense to know that we killed it in there. Along with many a merc," Kaiden declared.

"The other teams should finish momentarily. Unless one of them wipes out at the very end, we should have a full group of successful completions." Akello looked pleased.

"Hey, Miss Faraji. You might wanna check out Harrison and Jones. Looks like they are about to fly through an asteroid belt," one of the initiates called.

"Oh, that sounds like it could be potentially devastating. I gotta watch this...you can relax until the others are finished, but don't leave the hall." Akello turned and skipped back over to the monitors.

"Hey, let's watch that too. I always like to see the ships burst apart in space. With no sound, you just see them turn into a big ball of fiery plasma. It looks like a shooting star that explodes," Chief said with glee.

"As much as that sounds fun and all, I believe there's another matter we need to get to first, Chief," Kaiden stated.

The EI appeared in the air, narrowing his eye in confusion. *"What are you on about?"*

"Chiyo, you mind taking that tablet out and bringing Kaitō up?" he requested.

She looked questioningly at him for a moment before shrugging and retrieving her tablet from her bag. She activated it, and Kaitō appeared on the screen. *"How may I be of assistance, Mister Kaiden?"* he asked.

"All I need from you, Kaitō, is to simply be here. It's Chief who has to do something," Kaiden glanced at the floating orb, "considering he lost the bet."

Chief's eye widened, and he changed from a disgusted green to an angry red, then to an unhappy blue. *"Now? Really? Don't you want me to stew on it for a bit? Really think long and hard about my past misdeeds and personal issues and come back after a few eternities?"*

"As much as that would amuse me, I'm also liable to forget about this with how crazy shit gets around here," Kaiden admitted.

"I know. I was banking on that."

Kaiden frowned and motioned towards Kaitō. "Do it, Chief."

Chief sighed as he turned slowly towards the synthetic fox. He rotated his eye over towards Kaiden once more, almost begging for mercy, but Kaiden simply shook his head and waved the EI away.

"Right... Kaitō...you are a nos... You seem to be... Look, I know we've never really got along since we first met," Chief began.

"We haven't? I always found you a fascinating individual," Kaitō responded, clearly perplexed.

"You see? Trying to turn this all on me. It's things like that which gave us such a rough start." Chief growled with real indignation.

"You are really sucking at this, Chief."

"I told you I needed time to prepare." Kaiden glared at him.

Chief shook himself from side to side in frustration before turning back to Kaitō. *"Here...just...give me a moment to gather my thoughts..."*

As Sasha rewatched the final moments of Kaiden and Chiyo's test, he continued to wonder about the ending. It was oddly robust for the close of a test mission. Typically, the students had to make their way to an extraction point or they were simply pulled out once their objectives were complete. He zoomed the camera into the screen over their shoulders, seeing the warp gate launch out of its confinement building. It looked like a proper launch sequence, and he wondered if this was based on something real or created simply to add flavor. He'd have to get together with Laurie.

The door to his office opened, and Mya stepped in. He greeted her with a smile as he minimized the viewing screen on his computer. "Hello and good afternoon, Mya. How may I help you?"

"Just coming by to see you and ask how Kaiden and Chiyo did," she said as she took a seat.

"You weren't watching?" he asked.

"My duo were doing their mission at the same time, and I was finishing up a report and answering messages. I can only do so much multitasking," she explained with a weary sigh.

Sasha folded his hands and leaned forward. "And how did they do?"

"Pretty well. They passed, but they had to pull out before getting their bonus objective. Their score is probably a little over average as Jensen was able to take out almost fifty percent of their hostiles with a mortar he was able to repair."

"You don't have the final scores yet?" he asked.

"They were in hall five and are waiting on the final teams to finish."

"Hall Five?" Sasha took a look at his screen. "A happy

coincidence. Kaiden and Chiyo were in that hall as well. We will learn their scores in a moment."

"How do you think they did?" she asked again.

"Chiyo performed admirably. Quick, efficient and no mistakes. She is a gift to her class."

"Yeah, go ahead, rub it in," Mya grumbled. "Glad she's working out so well for you, but considering you didn't mention Kaiden, I'm guessing he's not so much of a gift?"

Sasha paused for a moment, looking back at the screen. "Maybe not to his class, but he is a gift to his enemies. In the same way as leaving a wooden horse was a gift to the Trojans."

"He took out a bunch of enemies too?" she asked.

"He actually took out every last one," Sasha confessed, and Mya's eyes opened wide in shock. "Scorched earth is either Kaiden's favorite tactic or simply his default setting. It makes for a very engaging watch if you are not in the field with him."

"And to think I once pointed a turret in his face... You don't think he holds grudges, do you?"

"Not ones that aren't childish, perhaps. But he's never mentioned that incident to me, so I don't think you have reason to worry." Sasha placed his chin into the palm of his hand. "Though I must say, it doesn't seem the best first impression to aim a large gun at a new initiate. Quite unlike you, Mya."

"It was a joke. I wasn't actually going to fire it...I mean, not unless he really was a trespasser. Though if someone was able to sneak their way into Nexus Academy, they would potentially make a good recruit."

"That raises a few questions..." A ding sounded from

Sasha's computer, and he looked at the monitor. "I'll leave the questions for later. It would appear the final team has finished. We are about to get the scores."

"Oh! Let me see."

Sasha turned the monitor sideways so they could both look. "Keep in mind this is only for these ten duos. We won't know the final overall scores until the last group has finished."

"Still, we get to know the points that will contribute to our League score," Mya reminded him.

"Where are you currently?"

"Bottom ten, but with all the changes with the test currently going on, I can't say for sure. Yvon did pretty good and got sixty-three thousand points, but if Sandra and Jensen got at least seventy thousand points, the bonus will jump me back toward the top."

"Then I offer my best wishes to you."

"Wish I had a wishbone to break."

"If you find one, you might want to use it to get Chiyo back."

She sneered playfully at him. "You know, you should get me a drink sometime for giving her to you."

Sasha chuckled. "I believe we made a fair trade. But once I win, I'll be sure to invite you to dinner for your contribution."

"That works too." She beamed.

The scores continued to appear. Mya leaned in once she recognized the names of her duo.

Sixth Place: Jensen Lovett and Sandra Galileo (Sapper / Surveyor): 72,100 Points

She pumped her fist. "All right, with that score and the bonus I get from the team-up, I'm back in the top five."

"Congratulations. Now let's see where Kaiden and Chiyo landed."

"Oh, like that'll be a surprise," Mya said with a pout.

Third Place: Roland Zoller and Mack Derringer (Vanguard / Decker): 103,600 Points.

Kaiden whistled. "Getting into the big stuff now." He looked over to see two large men shaking each other's hand before they switched positions and began arm wrestling in the air. "In more ways than one, I guess."

"And just because I tried to sabotage you on multiple occasions, it doesn't mean that I necessarily wanted you to burn out or deactivate. It was...a measure to keep you at arm's length or however we EIs try to keep one another at a distance. It was because I wasn't maybe so accepting of myself..."

"Is he still going on?" Kaiden asked, bewildered.

"At this point, I believe Kaitō is acting more as a psychologist than someone who is being apologized to." Chiyo chuckled as she switched the tablet to her other arm, flexing the free arm and wincing. "My arms are beginning to tire."

"Hey, Chief, wrap it up!" Kaiden ordered.

"I'm doing this properly. Don't rush me."

Kaiden rolled his eyes as he looked back at the board.

Second Place: Farah Grey and Monica Jest (Diplomat / Administrator): 109,800 points.

"They must have negotiated the hell out of something." Kaiden chuckled.

"Kaiden, this means we are in first," Chiyo pointed out.

"That was in doubt?" he asked, truly curious.

"So, to summarize all this...I guess I'm sorry for being a dick, Kaitō," Chief finished.

"That was...quite a lot to hear. You have truly come up with some interesting ways to describe me," Kaitō responded.

"I pride myself on my insults game. But from now on, I'll be sure to only use it to come up with interesting nicknames and the occasional creative curse," Chief declared.

"Well, I suppose at this point, I should say thank you for the apology I didn't know I needed. And I accept," Kaitō said with a nod. Chiyo placed the tablet back into her bag.

"Looking forward to the future, you sharp-nosed...nice guy." Chief corrected himself hastily at a quick glare from Kaiden.

"That's about the best way this can turn out, I guess." Kaiden snickered.

First Place: Kaiden Jericho and Chiyo Kana (Ace / Infiltrator): 200,000 Points.

"Holy hell!" Kaiden exclaimed. "Someone tell me that's a new record."

"It's actually the highest amount of points a team can score during the Co-op test," Akello informed him. "Though it actually hasn't happened in over a decade, so congratulations are still in order."

"Great job, partner," Kaiden said, clasping a hand on Chiyo's shoulder.

"You did excellent work, Kaiden. It was fun. Not something I thought I would be saying at the end of a test."

"It's the inviting and sunny atmosphere I bring with me everywhere I go."

"Along with clouds of doom, rains of destruction, and the occasional grapefruit-sized hail of stupidity," Chief added.

Kaiden frowned at him. "I see your new attitude doesn't extend to me."

"It's the kind of snarky and joyful atmosphere I bring," the EI chirped, *"And since I have your attention, you should know that after all that destruction and data mining, you have a couple synapse points to spare, and as I recall, you made a promise just before we finished."*

"I'll load it up the next chance I get, probably later tonight," Kaiden promised. "For now, let's go see the others. They're probably down in the lobby."

"Bloody hell, are you serious? Two hundred thousand points!" Flynn exclaimed.

"Overkill just isn't a thing to you, is it?" Luke asked. The group crowded around Kaiden and Chiyo in the lobby.

"There was plenty of killing. But Chiyo was the one who actually got the data and the bonus objective," Kaiden said, pointing a thumb her way.

"We both fulfilled our roles. Although you have an interesting way of leading as an ace," Chiyo commented.

"I made the same observation while watching you two. It is very hands-on, as you might say," Genos noted.

"I'm more of a delegator. Besides, I figured if there was no one going after her, I fulfilled my role just as well as if I'd gone the sneaky way." Kaiden grinned.

"Still, a full two hundred thousand. You've got first place, for sure," Amber stated.

"How about we go and celebrate?" Kaiden asked.

"What about us? We're up next," Cameron huffed.

"Oh right... Well, fair is fair. We'll watch you guys eat it and then go party," Kaiden jeered.

"Acting all cocky now. We'll put on just as good a show," Raul challenged.

"Looking forward to seeing what you got," Kaiden retorted.

"After the tests, we get a break for the holidays. What are everyone's plans?" Marlo asked.

"I'm hoping to head up to the mountains and do some skiing. Silas will probably be bundled up in about a dozen covers if he goes," Izzy joked.

"Surprisingly, living in the Caribbean doesn't really prepare you for snowy weather." He deadpanned.

"Helping my mom make and study new serums and medical devices, a merry medic Christmas," Amber said sarcastically.

"I'll probably stay at the Academy; my folks are going up to the Ziggy Station till the middle of January," Flynn said.

"Same, though I might make a trip to Seattle to see a friend. But I figured I might as well keep up with my talents." Kaiden whipped out his pistol and twirled it. "It might shock you, but you can't stay this good without practice."

"Humility must also dampen your skills," Cameron quipped under his breath.

"I will shock you with this," Kaiden taunted as Cameron

raised his hands in mock surrender.

"A few other Tsuna and I will be reporting back to the delegates. Once we return, I will begin further training in preparation for the deathmatch," Jaxon said.

Kaiden almost dropped his pistol and snapped his neck turning to Jaxon. "Your conclave is going to make you guys fight to the death?"

"No, Kaiden, he's talking about the Academy's deathmatch," Amber said, sounding reassuring despite what she was talking about.

"We're going to fight each other to the death?" Kaiden paused for a moment before looking back at Cameron and raising his pistol. "Can I start now with him?"

"Kaiden, it's another test. The final test for the initiates," Chiyo explained. "It will take place within the Animus. Please, put the shock pistol down."

Kaiden lowered and then holstered his gun. "Deathmatch… Well, that certainly sounds like something I would participate in, usually for money."

"Technically, it's the much more plain 'squad match,' but most students and faculty have picked up the nickname," Silas interjected.

"Group Red, would you please report to your designated halls for the final group of Co-op tests," a voice announced over the speakers of the center.

"That's us," Raul said. "We'll see you guys afterward, then we'll have that party."

"Best of luck to you," Genos exclaimed.

"Go and kick ass!" Luke bellowed.

The rest wished them luck, and they turned to go back to the observatory one last time.

As they walked across the pavilion, Kaiden took a moment to really look around the Academy and at the group beside him, thinking about what he came there with and what he had now.

For a moment, he recalled everything he had been through before making it there. And as he observed the comrades he had made and the partnerships he had forged, he took a moment to wonder.

"What's up with you?" Chief asked. *"You're falling behind the others."*

"Yeah, I'll catch up," Kaiden acknowledged. "Hey, Chief, you know how you felt when you got that first upgrade?"

"Oh, I'm still all aflutter, but what about it?"

"That moment when I first activated it, and you went dark…what did you feel?"

"Uh, I don't really know. Things were a little wonky at first, and then I simply felt like a completely new me. Even better than my already majestic peak."

"I think I feel ya there." Kaiden pulled out his oculars and put them on, bringing up the talents screen.

"What are you doing?"

"I've got some time to burn, and I did promise you that I would give you your next upgrade. Figured I'd go ahead and do it now." He opened the EI tree and looked through the options. "Might as well get it out of your system before you keep me up again tonight."

"I think all that time in the Animus has started to make you weird, even a little sappy. But I ain't complaining if it gets me my fix," Chief declared.

Kaiden hovered over the 'Next-Gen' talent icon. "You ready?"

"Hell yeah, let's bring on the new me."

Kaiden smiled as he accepted the talent. "I agree."

Thank you for not only reading this story, but also these author notes here at the back.

A little about Animus: Initiate (Book 01)

It has only been about 12 days since the first book in this series was published. Unlike many of my other collaborations, I didn't immediately put it out to my fans upon release day because the focus wasn't to go *to* the fans of The Kurtherian Gambit.

When I worked with Joshua to build this new Universe, I wanted to head towards another type of story.

One that was straight up Sci-Fi yet leaned into the crowd that loved stories set in a virtual world, yet touched the 'real' world.

Characters

Joshua and I went round and round on the characters.

Having worked a lot of collaborations, I believe I have a pretty good feel for when a collaborator is feeling the characters and enjoying the story we are creating.

I would come up with a character, and he would give me something like 'Well, ok, you are driving this and I can make that work' which I started to understand was 'wow, don't like that, but I don't want to push dad too much.'

I chose to pull out of him characters *HE* liked. After listening to his thoughts, I would say something like, 'Wow, ok, well, I guess if you are writing this, I can try to make this work...'

Both of us are willing to give a little, but still have a point we can't cross. It took some back and forth for us to find our main character Kaiden Jericho that worked for both of us. The fact I'm a born Texan (like Joshua) had nothing to do with Kaiden's location. He came in from the beginning of Initiate and it has *everything* to do with it being the state Joshua is both from and presently living in.

I was surprised to read the first part of the book (since it was set in Seattle, I hadn't considered Kaiden to be from anywhere farther away than the West Coast.)

HA! *Joke was on me.*

I thought we had one book per year of school...

In one of the reviews for Initiate, there was a comment from a reader who thought Book 01 was going to be the whole first year of the Nexus Academy.

So did I.

I think I mentioned last book that I wrote the main beats for book one, then Joshua and I reviewed and reworked the beats to the first book. Joshua kept extending the book with new scenes.

What was supposed to be one book, became *three*.

Mentally, I'm exhausted when a story hits 70,000 words. I just want the end to occur. I don't know how many times writing The Kurtherian Gambit series I would eye the word count, wondering if I could just cut out some of the story, and finish at 64,000. I don't think I ever did, but I know one time I finished at about 68,000 and threw in the towel (so to speak.) Only to have my production editor Stephen Russell ask me about the missing battle scene.

I stared at the computer, re-reading his question over and over when I realized I had to bang out another 5,000 words minimum (I think it ended up 8,000 words) to finish the book.

I still shiver thinking about that moment.

So, anyone that can write stories beyond 75,000 words I tip my hat. I just don't have the desire to keep going. I need a break.

I hope you liked this book.

If you like this, or *any* book on Amazon, consider leaving a review as they help all of us Authors as we produce books, and see whether you, our fans, like them or not!

Ad Aeternitatem,

Michael Anderle / Joshua Anderle

CONNECT WITH THE AUTHORS

Michael Anderle Social
   Website:
   http://kurtherianbooks.com/

Email List:
   http://kurtherianbooks.com/email-list/

Facebook Here:
   https://www.facebook.com/OriceranUniverse/
   https://www.facebook.com/TheKurtherianGambitBoo
ks/

Made in the USA
Columbia, SC
18 November 2020

24767619R10271